The Fuehrer's Blood

Shreyans Zaveri

The Fuehrer's Blood

Cover page design – Bismark Fernandes
Cover page R&D – Mazyar Sharifian

Production acknowledgments
SZPixelpro
ZE
Mitokondria Films

ISBN-13: 978-1533680204

ISBN-10: 1533680205

Preface

Although a distant memory already, the World War II remains one of the greatest wars witnessed by mankind.

No amount of words can describe or heal the pain which it inflicted upon millions of individuals; and through it all, the one name that intimidatingly stands out in context is Adolf Hitler. Eons ago, a group of Germans went into hiding and formed the most successful anti – Nazi group, "Blood Moon". This group remains the most elusive secret group of that era. They were an exceptionally rare breed; and through this story I attempt to shed some light on their valor, one which has gone rather unnoticed till date.

As an author of fiction, I am happy to have had the privilege of listening to World War II brave hearts. Thanks to my family and their close business relations with Germany, I have been privy to a treasure trove of first-hand information on this topic. Furthermore, I am absolutely intrigued by the history and social fabric of that era. These curiosities coupled with an endless imagination made me delve deeper into this subject and hence "The Fuehrer's Blood" was born.

"The Fuehrer's Blood" will take you on a journey seldom traversed. It is a vivid eye opener to one of the most potent controversies that brewed during the war. With Hitler's henchman Han mysteriously landing behind enemy lines and Blood Moon converging with him to find Hitler's personal diary, it is a tale few have heard of before.

The novel has been in active production for five years and has undergone endless refinements to present a well-crafted narrative to you. The following pages will take you behind many forgotten lives; I sincerely hope that you will enjoy reading it as much as I enjoyed putting it together.

Shreyans Zaveri

Acknowledgements

This book wouldn't have been possible without the countless inputs, help and hard work of an astounding number of people. It is practically impossible to name each one of them here as it will run into a number of pages. However, the very fact that this book is complete and out in the world is because of the trust which people have shown in me. Naming a few who have been indispensible to the creation of this book

Venkatesh Chari – for showing tremendous trust in my abilities, **Pooja Kulkarni** – for putting up with my endless whims & braving the storms with me, **Priyanka Dave** – for believing in this project from the word go, **Jheel A Shah** – for believing in me, **Shailesh & Rajul Zaveri** – for being the ultimate parents, **Shrenik & Rujuta Zaveri** – for the rock solid support, **Aarthi Kannan** – for helping me strengthen my sensitive gut, **Ms. Komala Devarajan** – for being the best teacher ever, **Mrs. Sai Sudha** – for the figures of speech, I still have the book, **Mrs. Radha Mani Sharma** – for being a teacher reminiscent of a mother, **Amrita Shetty** – for being the first one to see the author in me, **Aarti Soni** – for listening to the first story I ever wrote, **Aditi Shah** – for those fantastic conversations and stealth mode travels, **Rushab Shah** – for that silent admiration & rock solid protection from killer weeds, **Prithvi Shah** – for looking up codes at the age of seven just to see me, **Jharna Shah** – for being an awesome alligator, **Archana Kannan** – for the sanest advice, **Dr. Mr. & Mrs. Kannan** – for showering exceptional love and affection, **Parul Sarin** – for excellent & honest critiques, **Sonal Shah** – for always being there, **Kiran Kumar Zaveri** – for being the torch bearer of a great family, **Mr & Mrs. J. Zaveri** – for watching over me, **Sagar Pagar** – for the dreams that we have forged, **Sidhant Kapoor** – for endless enthusiasm, brilliant music & coffee, **Adwait Rajeshirke** – for being a great friend and emergency contact in life threatening situations, **Harsh Sampat** – for being my wingman through thick & thin, **Mr. & Mrs. P. Kulkarni** – for never ending patience and encouragement, **Mr. & Mrs. Dr. Chari** – for being my second set of parents, **Maithili Gupte** – for being the first persons to read this novel, **Abhishrey Zaveri** – for being the little sword wielder, **Keshav Ji** – for the warmest smile, **Mithul & Nikita Shah** – for the timely calls to check on me, **Priyanka Kulkarni** – for the infectious enthusiasm, **Pallavi Gupta** – for the mighty pen, **Jinang Kothari** – for the timely critique, **Mr. M. B.Shah** – for being the first person to prophesize my choice of profession.

There are many others who wish to be anonymous but each one of you has contributed greatly to this work of art. For this, I couldn't be more grateful!

JSZ

Contents

"Where will you be driving to now?"
"To freedom" he replied.

Oblivion

Han was perched precariously on the topmost branch of a tall swaying tree. Like an outgrowth from the tree, he sat still and steady. One hand held out his sniper rifle while the supporting arm revealed a sturdy watch. The time was ticking rather loudly in his ears, as if his watch knew what was about to take place. He patted his hand warmly. It was time.

Loud thunder claps in distant mountains sent aftershocks across the angry skies. As he momentarily observed lightning streaks pulse through the clouds, Han's gaze shifted from his timepiece to the skies. They lit up the trees and dark eerie forests at intervals. The light breeze that touched his face was damp with rain as thunder rumbled far above. Yet again he glanced at his timepiece. The glint in his eye was the only give away that something important was about to take place; otherwise he didn't even move an inch; not even a flinch of his muscle. Looking through the eyepiece on his rifle, Han took aim. It was an exquisitely crafted rifle, with small intricate engravings of ancient runes running around it. There was a clap of thunder, louder and crisper this time.

It was accompanied by a slight drizzle. 'This is it' he thought. 'The storm was moving closer.' His calculations were correct and now he had to be quick. If the rain picked up, his position would become vulnerable. He drew a deep breath and composed himself; bringing his breathing to a near halt. With mechanical precision and a practiced sniper's eye, Han pressed the trigger; synchronizing it with the ticking of his timepiece and the thunderous clap of the clouds . It was just perfect timing. Nobody noticed that there'd been a gunshot; or the consequent thud as a guard of the Red army fell within the watch tower. The gunshot was perfectly timed and camouflaged with the thunder clap.

Two massive towers of the Red army camp stood, well-hidden by forests around them. While one of the towers rose straight up from the ground, the other branched out from the mountain surface. From a few hundred feet away, no one, no matter how keen the eyesight, would have been able to spot the surprisingly huge Russian camp hidden in these forests. The tower posts and guards were strategically placed to notice intruders approaching from miles away. One watchtower was closer to where Han was perched, and the other was diagonally opposite to it. The camp was protected by a mountain range from the other sides, so these two were the only watch towers that had to be cleared.

Han could see another centrally placed light tower but it was impossible to know if there were guards inside. The light tower would be an excellent vantage point to spot intruders. He had to make his move before the other guard noticed an empty post at the opposite end. As the timepiece ticked, Han fired a second shot; again, it was easily muffled by the boom of thunder clap.

But a stray leaf had been caught in the line of fire as the bullet seared through it. The leaf appeared fresh green, with smoked edges as Han held it in his hands, lost in thought. Life was throbbing in the leaf- Han could feel it, as well as the tense air all around him.

Han's mind was no longer loyal to his task, instead, it began to stray back in time, and like a heavy burden, his thoughts weighted down on him. It was difficult to come to terms with all that had transpired. An owl screeched in the nearby mountains, startling him back to his senses. He quickly gathered himself and scanned the area; his green eyes glinting with precision. Through the tree cover, he tried looking for disturbances and spotted a lone Red army soldier manning the gate far below.

Stealthily, he climbed down the tree and positioned himself behind a massive boulder, waiting for the soldier to finish his round. 'This does not call for a gunshot' he thought.

By now, the rain had progressed from a slight drizzle to a turbulent noisy downpour; with the skies becoming more and more involved, rumbling in anger. With the soldier's back turned to Han as he took rounds of the periphery, Han swiftly and deftly pulled out his hunting knife. He covered much ground as he effortlessly sprinted towards the soldier.

The soldier turned around & panicked at the sound of sudden footsteps. Han called out mockingly; "hand to hand combat soldier?" and plunged his knife deep into the soldier's heart. With no time to react, the soldier fell, his mouth still agape. Warm blood gushed onto Han's hands.

He laid the soldier to rest and swiftly took his coat. He pulled over the heavy Russian coat as it covered his torso, hiding a rugged and worn out oval dog tag. With his agile, six feet tall figure, Han easily dragged the soldier's body into a bush where it couldn't be spotted. He opened the gate leading into camp and slid inside. There were no other soldiers; the watchtowers were empty and the gate now unmanned. Pulling out bundles of dynamite from his backpack, he started plugging in the fuse wires. Han secured one pack at the gate and the other a little away at a tunnel opening.

There were huge underground tunnels running in & around the camp which the Russian forces used for storage and other emergencies arising out of severe weather conditions. It was a brilliant design and had proved its worth under extreme war time crisis. These tunnels housed their lighting rigs, power supply and radio equipment. Any attacks on the ground level and they could still function at full force from within these tunnels.

The story of the forest lands was a wistful one. Originally, it had been habited by a peaceful population. In the recent war, it had however fallen under Nazi rule and then to Russians by tactical infiltration. Han had once studied a map of these tunnel systems procured by the 'Abwehr', which was a primary Nazi intelligence agency. These tunnels were his only chance of getting inside the heart of the camp. To ensure the dynamite was secure, Han stealthily concealed it under foliage. He checked his surroundings once again for soldiers before blending into the dark tunnels and vanishing into them. So far, his plans had worked out brilliantly.

The Russian camp was a maze of bunkers, air raid shelters, soldier tents and officer cabins. A massive three storied building christened 'Beast Bunker' stood in the exact center of the camp. The structure, made with reinforced steel was practically impossible to infiltrate. This entire undercover camp ran across the huge length of ancient woodlands of Bialowieska. They were deep dark forests; certainly, they could hold onto secrets, not revealing them till the time summoned.

In pitch blackness, Han kept moving along. Occasionally, he would break into a jog to cover more ground. At regular intervals he secured dynamite at tunnel openings or turnings. He had a small bobbin that rolled out trigger wire as he ran. The tunnels followed a honeycomb pattern, more or less opening into each other at every alternate turn. Anyone without a keen sense of direction could be lost inside these for days at end. Certainly, this was not Han's case. He juggled through the maze like a practiced runner. Han was laying wired dynamite that was connected to a core trigger in his backpack. The core trigger could be fired with a secondary one that functioned over a short wave radio signal. As he kept moving, he would connect the dynamite even further. Han suddenly hit a straight long passage and a narrow endless tunnel was now visible with no openings except a sharp turn at the very end. He could see a faint light at the end of this narrow tunnel and he sensed that he was on track. He scanned the long tunnel, checking for disturbances. One side stretched straight into darkness while the other had a faint light at the far end. Drawing a heavy breath, Han sprinted towards the light source.

He covered the long dark patch as fast as his feet took him and stealthily approached the turning. Han gripped his handgun as he took a sharp right at the end. A sudden bright light hit his eyes and he saw massive rigs towering in front of him. As he lay down his guard, cold sweat globes dropped down his skin. The rigs in

4

front of him were an array of fuse boxes maintaining power supply to upper cabins. The absence of guards in this area struck him by surprise. He'd have expected soldiers to be stationed around these rigs; that made sense, didn't it?

Han carefully walked around and noticed a straight narrow ladder over him, going at least twenty feet above. It went as high as the tunnel and then stretched further into a dark narrow cavity. There was a circuit diagram showing him exact sections connected to the light rig. Studying the light rigs, he figured out the best possible switches to disconnect.

Before he could deal with the lights, he removed the remaining dynamite from his pack and placed it in the center of the chamber. He knew, a dynamite here would take out electric supply and radios throughout the camp. Also, dynamites placed at regular intervals of the connecting honeycomb pathways would cause massive damage and chaos in the camp, rendering the tunnel system useless.

Han hoped he wouldn't have to use the dynamite; he simply wanted to accomplish his mission. He rummaged through his back pack; it was empty now except for a battered diary with deep crimson stains on its cover. He tucked it away safely within his jacket and discarded the backpack. Han looked around the room and up the ladder once again.

'It's time,' he muttered to himself. Out came his hunting knife, faithful and blood stained. As it sliced through wires, a few fuse clips were undone effortlessly.

Commotion erupted in the completely dark cabin above. Two Russian soldiers were frantically running around trying to figure out the reason for darkness and shouting away check lists to each other. General Igor appeared calm throughout. He got up, lit an oil lamp, set it on his table and went on with his work. They never usually faced these black outs here and victory was at hand. He didn't want a senseless power cut to dampen his spirit on the war front. The light from the lamp was faint and flickering, casting dark shadows over areas around his writing desk.

Igor gave a pathetic look to the fumbling soldiers and went about reading from the files strewn around him. The page read 'First of May, 1945' and an endless list of names followed it. One of the soldiers opened the cabin door and went out to check the cause of electric failure. A draft of cold air gushed in; yet Igor was so caught up in his work that he didn't notice a gun barrel slipping towards him in the dark.

In the dancing shadows, the barrel crept forward to where he was seated. Igor looked up, alarmed. Han's face appeared, shadows playing on his stern features. The angry glint in his green eyes however remained constant with rage. "Konstantin?" he asked in a hushed voice, barely moving his mouth. The general looked up at Han but remained silent because the gun was a few inches from his face. "Konstantin?" Han asked again, his voice a bit more urgent and angry.

Before he could question Igor any further, Han heard footsteps behind him. He swiftly moved into the shadows. Igor got up and made no sound for he knew the gun was still pointing at him from darkness. Igor was contemplating escape; his gun was loaded with poison laced bullets from his personal cabinet. In that instance, a soldier barged in and rammed into Han who was hidden in darkness. That was all the time Igor needed. He flung the oil lamp from his table into the dark corner where Han was and shot with his gun. Muffled gun shots rang through the darkness and Igor fell to the floor, dead from Han's swift bullet. The soldier screamed in alarm. The damage was done; the oil lamp had connected well, lighting up Han's right arm in flames. Igor's bullet however only managed to scrape Han's thigh. He turned around punching the soldier in the face and his hand connected with the trigger in his pocket as he activated it.

Dynamite exploded somewhere in the distance. It was a small blast, just one of the dynamites that he had planted at the gate from where he entered. Soldiers outside rushed to the explosion site in alarm. Nobody noticed a small fire raging in the cabin through the frost glass windows.

Inside the cabin, Han was trying to douse the flame on his right arm; while the soldier lay dead with a gaping wound on his neck. Thoughts were racing through Han's head; he still had to find Konstantin and move on to hunt Himmler. Han's hand was singed and bloody as he threw himself out of the door and ran towards the center cabin. The rain felt cold and sharp on his burnt hand, icy stinging pain shot up through his arm and the bullet scrape on his thigh. He had no time to waste.

'This is where Konstantin should be' he thought and ran towards a centrally placed cabin. The map of the underground layout was fixed in his head but the camp was differently setup on ground level. Han kicked open the door of the center cabin. Another soldier sat inside and before the man could react, Han shot straight through the unwary soldier's head.

He could not afford to be quiet and stealthy; it did not matter anymore. The cabin was empty otherwise, the only sign of life prior was the now fallen soldier. Han looked around frantically; it did seem to be a General's cabin. It was well furnished and equipped from inside. He noticed a door with strange multiple locks on it as he scanned the area. He had to act fast, the dynamite was doing its job but that diversion wouldn't last long. The Russian camp was in a state of alarm with soldier's running back and forth from the explosion site. Han looked out from the window of the cabin and his expression contorted in rage. At last he saw his victim, Konstantin.

The menacing Russian warlord flanked by his guards was marching towards his cabin shouting orders and looking mad as hell. He stood nearly seven feet tall. He had cropped black hair and wore a long black overcoat. His physique was reminiscent of a bull, bulky but muscular. He commanded an air of supreme discipline and fear. Konstantin stopped short of the cabin as a soldier came running to him, reporting the blasts.

Finally, Han had come face-to-face with his enemy, after nearly three years of tracking him. The surge of adrenaline through his system wasn't unexpected. Here stood Konstantin, the notorious Russian warlord. And this, was Han's chance to take him down. The German sniper aimed from within the half open cabin window as his anger ebbed. "No waiting for thunder claps now" he whispered to himself. His breathing wasn't composed to his usual aiming stance. His heart was palpitating and his body twitched as he aimed and applied pressure on the trigger. The door of the cabin crashed open and a soldier stumbled inside. Han instantly pulled out his Walther hand gun and two shots echoed simultaneously through the air.

The soldier collapsed on the spot as the bullet made contact with him. Konstantin roared in agony and instantly turned around clutching his arm and panting, Han had missed. For the first time ever, his bullet did not find the heart. "Nazi cowards" howled Konstantin. He was now protected by soldiers all around as they formed a human wall and frantically searched for the source of firing. Han dared not shoot now, the soldiers around were too many to take at one go. Instead, he made a dash for the back door. Jumping over the bodies of fallen soldiers, he ran out into the open. The rain was coming down harder than before. Han ran through the back side of the cabins, not daring to look behind him. He removed the detonator; 'it was time to rip apart the entire tunnel systems' he thought and pressed the trigger. The radio wave activated the core trigger that was resting near the light rigs. After a few seconds the signal was relayed and a deep rumbling explosion resonated. Han could feel the blow beneath his feet. The reverberations rippled through the grounds and into the forest. The lamps went out; only faint blue early morning light remained and the entire Russian camp was doused in instant darkness. Fires erupted from hatches in the grounds as dynamite exploded throughout the tunnel systems. The soldiers cowered in fear as the iron hatches flew high into the air. Konstantin however maintained his poise as he glanced through the commotion. A stray hatchet flew towards him and without as much as a flinch, he punched away the heavy metal. This explosion was another diversion and Han hoped to escape under its guise. But Konstantin was thinking along the same lines. Far away, he saw Han running towards the forest boundary. "There he is. Get him" he roared, dousing the sound of rains. He ordered his soldiers to fan out in teams and ignore the explosions. In response to Konstantin's orders, the soldiers fetched their flashlights and dispersed to hunt down the intruder. Han had to cover little more ground to reach the forests and he ran with all his might. The forest was getting closer; the thick and dense trees would hide him from the Red army. "Nazi!" Konstantin roared in the distance. Han never once looked back and dashed into the forest. 'He would have to hunt from the forests now. Wait until the commotions settled and attack again' he thought, as he ran blindly into the trees, constantly changing paths to throw his pursuers off his trail.

The sound of the wind grew shrill and strong within the trees. He had to get a headway and hide in the forest. He heard distant barks; the Red army had unleashed their hunting dogs. Han's heart was hammering against his ribs and in spite of the cold rain; steady sweat trickled down his forehead and neck. He felt a little uneasy as he exerted his body to the hilt. Han covered ground quickly keeping up his pace, he looked back as the surroundings passed by in a blur. Good for him, the soldiers hadn't caught up yet. He ducked and jumped the unusually thick forest growth, distancing himself from his pursuers. As he turned around to look behind, his boots caught a wire on the forest floor. Han stumbled, yet he kept up his pace. Suddenly the noise of wind grew extremely shrill and intense. It grew heavier and before he noticed, a huge bark flew towards him and slammed into his face with bone crushing force. The wind was knocked out of him and his face twisted in a painful bloody mess. He was thrown back by a few feet, his jacket ripped apart and the black diary flew out onto the grounds along with his rifle. The Russians knew these forests well and kept them protected with wire traps. He groaned in pain, but he knew that wasting even a fraction of a minute could be the end of him. Han tried to gather himself and get up. But he felt another collision; his head throbbed in severe pain. 'The Russians had caught up with him, already?' he thought. Han looked up dazed and unfocused. One of the soldiers had connected a baton with his head. His eyes now watering searched for a route while his mind contemplated escape. Powerful hands suddenly lifted him off the ground. The world around him was spinning and his body ached in severe pain. He was exhaling blood from his nose and mouth. The bullet scrap on his thigh was suddenly itching and he heard angry snarls all around him. A powerful flashlight met his face as he tried to squint his eyes. He tried to loosen the grasp of the soldiers but they held on with an iron clasp.

Leather boots met gravel in a thick, slow and sickening sound. Konstantin came to a halt in front of Han. He stood tall and looming as he seethed in anger and pain, all at once. Two soldiers held Han captive while others kept their guns pointed at him, ready to take him down at his slightest attempt to move. Konstantin's left arm was bloodied with a crude band tied across it. Fresh crimson blood dripped from under the band. "So, you are the dreaded Nazi sniper?" Konstantin asked him, letting his words linger for a moment. One of the guards handed Konstantin Han's fallen rifle. Konstantin looked at it with awe. "You are indeed the dreaded Nazi sniper, the one they call Adolf Hitler's shadow. And here you stand cowering like an insect in front of me, at my mercy."

Konstantin was barely an inch away from Han's face as he spoke. Han was hanging a few feet above the ground. The soldiers pulled him up so he could face Konstantin at eye level. "You come into in my camp, blow it apart and think you can run, you Nazi bastard. You puncture a bullet through me and you think you can run?" Konstantin growled in rage. Han looked up.

This indeed, was his face-to-face meeting with Konstantin. It wasn't quite the way he'd planned it, but not even that could stop him from spitting on Konstantin, and replying "Yes; I can."

For the huge figure that Konstantin was, he was very quick and agile. Enraged by Han's action, he pulled out his blade and plunged it deep into Han's side. Han screamed in agony, so deep was his scream that it echoed with great reverberation disturbingly throughout the forest range. A few birds took flight into the darkness. Han felt blood gushing from his side and heard Konstantin laugh loudly. His world slowly blacked out; and there was extreme pain as Han faded into oblivion.

Berlin Bleeds

Thick black smoke emanated from the devastation; nothing was left nothing untouched. The smoke settled over the once magnificent city, in its wake was a disabling sense of despair and a horrid stench of death. Savage fires took over the city; turning buildings into rubble and blending roads until they became dust. In the places where tall buildings once stood, now there was debris and shards of glass.

The Russians had tactfully targeted major government buildings first, by this act, they'd wisely crippled the enemy's decision making system. Soldiers of the Red army could be seen running in and out of ruins, shouting orders and gunning down opposition. Few Red army soldiers were seen celebrating in glee and the relentless firing of battle tanks at intervals shook the very heart of Berlin.

This was the Red army soldiers' last street fight with what was left of the German army. Now, the soldiers fighting from Berlin were merely protecting what remained of their homes. Red army soldiers mercilessly gunned down opposition as they swept street after street and house after house. It seemed like a lazy chore to them; as most of Berlin had fallen into their hands.

With no end in sight to their suffering, civilians and soldiers alike, willingly walked into their own deaths as they saw no definite end to this suffering. One after the other, they pressed the hard cold metal to their skins and pulled the fatal trigger. It was glaring: the German army, divided, weak and uncoordinated, was no match for the massive Russian forces. In small pockets within the city, a few generals of the German army tried leading their paltry squadrons and task-forces to attack, but without much success.

General Helmuth Wielding, the last commander and defender of Berlin, maintained a calm stance although his heart was bleeding. He was thinking with the logic only a General could possess in such times; and here was his rationale: if he could buy more time for the fleeing people, he would have achieved something from this unending feud.

He had, against his wish, been given the task of defending Berlin. His plea to the Fuehrer to let the people break out had fallen on deaf ears. The Fuehrer, Adolf Hitler was in a state of despair and panic as the enemy forces closed in on him. All he seemed to be able to say, in his broken state, was that the men should keep on fighting. If one didn't know Hitler, you would think he had gone out of his senses!

Finally, General Helmuth Weidling gave in to his fate and took charge of defending the city. He was putting to use the meager resources he had and divided the soldiers into eight fighting squadrons named A through H. They had no impressive names and no lengthy protocols. The squadrons consisted of army men from the Wehrmacht Heer and Waffen SS divisions. General Helmuth also included young members of Hitler youth, Berlin police force and older members of the Volksstrum. Their orders were straightforward and clear. "Go out and save the people."

As the Red Army marched in, Berlin's fate was sealed with immediate effect. No victory would be achieved; but they could make the loss more tolerable, maybe?

Russian ground forces had sworn that they would unfurl Red flags over Berlin on the first day of May. They were living up to their word and with only a few hours away from their complete victory, buildings in the heart of Berlin already had Russian flags fluttering over them.

It was official. Berlin lay defeated and dead. The streets were piled with bodies of soldiers and civilians alike. Men of different races and nationalities, who fought in opposing armies, lay united in death as they were heaped over each other. Horrific cries of pain were etched on some barely open mouths and contorted faces as they embraced death; willingly or otherwise. It was an odd assortment of people who now came together to defend their homes and the falling city.

The snipers hid inside ruined buildings and took out Red army soldiers manning heavy artillery, while some of the younger members took to the streets and laid mines to blow up tanks. The older and more experienced members tried to take command and lead these teams. Random instances of such small battles were seen breaking out through the city. A mere forty five thousand men fought the onslaught of more than two hundred thousand Russian soldiers.

The communication systems of Berlin were dead and not many messages were relayed through the city. Groups of civilians took refuge in underground shelters and hospitals. They were lost and dejected at the horrific events that unfolded over the past few days. The Nazis collapsed instantly after their leader had disappeared. Now, there was no government or military left to protect them. All they could do was to hide and find way to somehow survive. Slowly but surely, Berliners were inching towards an austere defeat.

A line of buses snaked through the outer city routes. Most of the transport system had fallen prey to the ongoing war and public transport across Germany had suffered a massive setback. What had evolved as the 'Kriegsbauart' or the war time class useful for supplying wartime amenities was now completely destroyed. Hitler's strategy of 'Blitz Krieg' had been modified and used upon his own lands.

The plan devised by the opposing forces was aptly named "the transportation strategy". This bombing strategy had rendered transport systems completely useless throughout Germany. It destroyed the main supply links and hence dealt a massive blow to the wartime supply system. Drivers and guards had chosen to keep a few of the buses running on their own accord. These were men who had united under the banner of peace, working in the underbelly of Berlin as they strove to protect the remaining people of Germany.

As the bus moved slowly through rubble covered roads, two guards stood up front, clearing away debris and keeping a look out for anything strange. From a distance the driver saw a small boy strewn on the road. His eyes were open, steel gray in silence, yet wanting to scream out in pain. The eyes of the occupants of the bus followed the surreal image of this boy, and many more bodies strewn across the roads, and as they did, their minds steeled.

The passengers were an assortment of people who pledged peace and sat huddled in the bus. There were wounded people sleeping on the floor. Many of them were bleeding and blotches of blood was visible throughout the bus. Few mothers held on to their kids, unable to believe that they held no beating hearts. Lifeless and unmoving they remained wrapped in a protective embrace.

This bus had no destination. Most people only remained in it because it provided shelter and a few hoped that the closer they got to Berlin, the greater their chances of re-connecting with their loved ones.

The clouds in the azure blue sky dazzled with a brilliant mixture of colors, radically pink in some places, with shades of violet and glimpses of gold. They cast a heavenly glow over the entire field. A fair young woman stood in the farms. She looked away into the endless horizon with her hazel eyes, watching a flock of cranes fly into the sunset. Theodor's heart began to race as he looked at her. Her skin was bathed in an unnatural glow; in his mind's eye, she looked like an apparition bathing in the heavenly light of the gods. A light breeze caressed her delicate features.

Who was this goddess? He wanted to reach out to her, to touch her and be with her. He felt the warmth of her presence so close to him and yet, when he opened his eyes, she was standing so far away. Theodor began sprinting across the field, running towards her. He called out her name but she did not turn around. 'Was she able to hear him?'

Maybe she couldn't hear him clearly enough. He thought, as he quickened his pace. He ran faster with all his might, trying to get close to her. Wind picked up speed from the opposite end as if trying to resist Theodor catching up with Adelheid. An unusual tension built up within him and there was a sudden blinding flash of light. Theodor covered his eyes as he kept running towards her. Somewhere in the distance he heard a scream. It was none other but Adelheid's. Her loud, shrill scream pierced through his thoughts like a sharp ray of lightning. He only stood there, helpless.

Theodor woke up with a start. With his heart beating against the innards of his ribs, he was sweating profusely. He sat inside the bus, his eyes half open, head resting on the window. He was trying so hard to calm down.

The war had taken its toll on him, just as it had on countless others. Otherwise a dashing German in a weary uniform, the trio of fatigue, hunger and the devastation of war took a sad toll on his overall outlook. Theodor was completely covered in blood and dirt. Nonetheless, his bright brown eyes and his sharp features stood him out.

He had never wished to fight in the war; the burden to be a warrior had been thrust on him, as it had been upon millions of other citizens. His family had been wiped out by the air bombings from enemy wrath.

His love had survived though. This was the only comforting thought he had, that Adelheid lived. At least, that much he believed, it was the only reason he still had a shred of hope in an otherwise fallen system; and he clung to the thought with every bit of mental strength he possessed.

Theodor smiled as he remembered the only letter he'd gotten, written in Adelheid's writing. That piece of paper, although weary from being read over and again, was neatly folded in his breast pocket. It had given him the will to live through all the harrowing moments on the field.

And then, one day, when he couldn't bear it anymore, Theodor had abandoned his posting and being on the run ever since. He had removed visible effects from his uniform that would hint at his posting and military history. Since he received the letter from Adelheid, his only aim was to reach her. More than anything else, he wanted to find out where she was and to be with her. Berlin was where she would be if all had gone as planned but now the news pouring in was grim. The Fuehrer had fallen and along with him, the Third Reich had collapsed. If the news was anything to go by, then Berlin was wiped out. Theodor felt numb with agony. His head exploded with thoughts of disastrous consequences. The Fuehrer, Adolf Hitler, the man responsible for all of this lay dead and Berlin was left defenseless.

The bus came to an abrupt halt and shrill far away whistles bore through the silence of dusk. Theodor got up and looked around. There was confusion as everyone looked out trying to guess the reason for their sudden halt. He could see fear in everyone's eyes as they remained silent. They looked out, expecting to see bomber aircrafts or enemy soldiers.

Theodor scanned the faces around him, in the process, locking eyes with a handful of fellow soldiers. None dared to speak. Cold silence filled the air. He had come here with the only aim of finding Adelheid and he knew what he had to do next. Taking a deep breath he got up from his seat, moved through the crowd and stepped off the bus.

His world swooned. Right before his eyes, Theodor was faced with the most painful sight he had ever witnessed. He held on to the bus for support, as he took in what was left of the ruined city. The city lay in ruins, completely devastated, burned and razed to the ground. He saw fire being hurled at Berlin from ruthless Red army launchers. Tears swelled up inside him as he tried to control his emotions. Even the little hope he had of finding Adelheid seemed to be vanishing along with the rays of the dying sun but if he were to ever find her, it would be here.

With his deepest fears re-surfacing, Theodor took painful steps towards the city. He knew not if he would find his love here or meet his own end. He was prepared for the worst and held on to the letter as his last dreg of hope. Somehow, the touch of the letter gave him courage and pushed him forward into the bleeding walls of Berlin. If at least, to find out if she lay among the ruins, or if she had, by some shred of divine luck, survived the unbelievable raid.

Blood Moon

Deep within the bleeding walls of Berlin was a small forgotten house. Like others around it, this house was also covered in dust and bathed by debris. Outside, the streets were strewn with countless dead bodies and rubble. Stepping one's foot inside the house revealed a dusty sight; the house smelled of must. Had anyone lived in it over the last 10 years? Windows were covered in brownish black paper and paint. The paper was peeling at places and paint strokes across the windows were shabby.

The house was cluttered with fallen objects, paintings, cutlery and cracked wooden panes. Few intact photo frames surprisingly were still hanging on the walls. It was hard to believe that this house was once a place inhabited by peace loving families. Deep within the house where the kitchen and a small dining table lay, was a trap door that led to an underground cellar.

The kitchen was a complete mess and the dining table had broken into half. A large wooden beam had fallen right onto it, splitting it into two. The trap door on the kitchen floor opened to steep wooden steps going underground. It led to a small strange space where an odd army of men sat. This cramped space had a door on one side and a thick bunch of wires that ran through the other. There was a radio rig in one corner and weapons stacked on the other. A huge pile of files was stowed away on a small rack and the space beyond it extended into a dark cellar like area.

"None of our informers made it back from the Fuehrer bunker and we still have no communication from Han." A huge soldier by the name of Ralf spoke to the small group of people. Ralf was muscular and tall. He wore a military uniform with both sleeves of his shirt deliberately torn off, showing his massive chiseled arms. He had messy short black hair and tiny black eyes that jutted out of his otherwise white form. He smoked a cigar as he conversed. "In any case, we need to get to Han somehow. We need confirmation on Hitler's death. The Russians are at our doorstep and if we don't confirm this, we will not be able to do much for the protection of Germania."

The next person to speak up had a sense of authority around him. He looked like the most senior person in the gathering, one whose opinion mattered.

"Gentlemen", he said, his voice echoing. Everyone looked at General Felix as he spoke. General Felix, probably in his late sixties was an Ex – Nazi officer. He had innumerable scars all over his face and his silver white hair gave testimony to his age and wisdom. Felix was dismissed from duty by Heinrich Himmler on account of treason to the Fuehrer and in turn to the Reich. Himmler was Hitler's trusted man, but since there was not enough proof against Felix, he lived. And since Hitler had trusted Felix's judgment in past war matters, he was given a fair hearing in court. Felix understood the Fuehrer's mind and didn't risk his life further. He went into hiding as soon as he was dismissed. He was sure that Hitler or Himmler would've put people behind him and the court hearing was just a disguise.

"Right from time, we'd known that this little group that we have formed" he gesticulated with his right hand at everyone in the room; "was destined to perform terrible tasks. That in turn constantly puts us on the throes of extinction but we have survived. Many other groups had the courage to stand up and rebel but we have been most successful and are now close to achieving what we set out for. With the gift of birth, our death is promised. We might as well go roaring into battle than sitting and warming these chairs."

It was no different than any of his previous comments. General Felix always charged up the atmosphere with his talks. "If this be the mission that wipes us out then so be it. We will at least make the change that we are meant to make" Felix concluded and looked at the others.

"I have a small concern, General" Albert interjected. "Yes please" Felix replied gesturing Albert to talk. Albert was relatively smaller and wore round rimmed spectacles. His hair was long, messy and unkempt and he always spoke very softly. He opened up a huge map in front of him. "If we are looking at getting to Han, the last coordinates that we have of Konstantin are around this area." Albert plunged into explaining the location. "Considering the possibility that he has gone after Konstantin and that he is not yet dead."

"Both possibilities considered Albert" General Felix interrupted. "I am sure Han has gone after Konstantin. That is why he broke protocol and went behind him before time. As for his death, either he or Konstantin is dead. There is no uproar from our Russian messengers meaning Konstantin is alive and I know Han. He won't die before killing Konstantin." A slight smirk crossed General Felix's face as he spoke with utmost conviction and trust in Han. Albert nodded and continued talking. "So this area belongs to the Russians" he said and drew out a small circle on the map. "It's within their territory now and Konstantin or the 'Minotaur' as they call him is housed deep in this fortress of a camp that he runs. How do you propose to get to him? And even if we do get in, how and where do we communicate with Han? He could be anywhere." Albert circled the remaining areas on the map and presented his dilemma as he sat back, looking at the people around for some response.

"He does have a point General. Have we no communication from the other sources?" asked Falko. Falko, lean and agile, spoke about these matters as leisurely as if they'd been planning a visit to the movies.

"No, there is no news from other sources. We need confirmation on Himmler's death. As a matter of necessity, we must kill Konstantin because he has enough information about us. Also, confirming Hitler's death is of utmost importance as already mentioned. I have been undercover for nearly seven years now. I wish to spend the remaining years of my life in freedom and not exile. And for that we need these three people dead" General Felix spoke, holding up three fingers indicating the priority of killing them.

"We cannot trust any outside sources as of now. All of us here are all that we have left" Felix said, scanning the room with his eyes. "Our very success depends on discretion; we have survived so far because of that single factor, he signified by raising up one finger. We can attempt to get to Han and discover if he has more answers. I understand the validity of your arguments, gentlemen; but I have no other choice. If any of you have more feasible options, I would like to hear them" he concluded. An uncomfortable silence fell over the small room, so much that one could easily hear the breathing patterns of everyone around. Far away explosions were causing the ceiling to reverberate as loose dust kept falling on them. Suddenly, with a disturbing crack and hiss; the radio came to life.

Albert got up on his feet and picked up the receiver. "Please identify yourself" he spoke over the crackle. "General Felix?" A raspy voice urgently inquired. Everyone turned around to face the radio. General Felix snatched the receiver from Albert's hands. "Yes, this is he." he replied.

"The shadow has been captured by the Minotaur. He lives but not for long. The road has been paved for you. All is ready as discussed earlier. Relay coordinates if mission is being undertaken. I will contact again" the voice concluded over the radio. Albert turned down the dial to lower the disturbing hiss.

"You all heard that, Han is alive. We must get him out of there. Fabian is well placed within the territory of Konstantin's camp. His information is true to the last word" General Felix spoke as he settled back into his chair. "Han holds the answers. Himmler, Hitler and Konstantin" General Felix continued talking as he looked at others who sat there with grave faces. "If Hitler or Himmler resurfaces, we will have to go undercover for life." General Felix's face mirrored that of his team, a grave look settling over his weary face. "What if Hitler, Himmler and Konstantin live? What help or use is Han to us anyways?" Ralf interjected. "Han went rogue on protocol, he shouldn't have! If he is acting on his own accord or worse still, on Hitler's orders, we are all marching into a death trap, don't you think?" Ralf pushed his argument further.

Everyone fell silent at his statement. General Felix let out a sigh and moved closer to the group. "Han has known Hitler from the inside. If Hitler is up to any plan, chances are, only Han knows of it. Last time I met Han, he was sure about something which Hitler promised him" Felix explained to the group of people.

"Since when do we believe in Hitler and his promises?" It was Ralf, firing questions with his head cocked to one side, directed at Felix. Albert tried to hide behind the open map. He was afraid Felix would get angry with these constant interjections. Felix continued pacing the room, his hands firmly placed behind his back and a strong air of authority encompassing him. "I understand your concern. Han is important to us and we must get him out of there. Even if Hitler lives, Han can go after him and take him out. He is the only one who can and who will go after him no matter what. He is the best sniper this country has seen; he has protected Hitler for all these years. I personally think Han is our best chance" replied Felix.

Ralf appeared a little frustrated at Felix's response. This mission was dangerous enough, as it was and still, there seemed to be no definite answers. "Traugott on the other hand is trying his best to figure Himmler's whereabouts" continued Felix. "Himmler, we can still tackle. I will personally hunt him down if need be, but Hitler is out of my league" Felix abruptly stopped talking. They heard sudden footsteps above them and all of them fell silent as a muffled humming sound emanated. "That old fool" said Ralf. "Can't he keep it low?"

Above them, on the ground floor, an old man moved about. He had a long grey beard and as he moved about, his robe-like tunic flapped all over the place. He was fixing himself a smoke as he filled tobacco into an exquisitely crafted ivory pipe. He hummed a song that eerily resonated through the broken house. It was extremely quiet and death-like but for the steady hum that escaped his lips. As he hummed and moved about the kitchen area, a huge explosion suddenly sliced through the dead silence.

The old man looked out to see a massive fire raze the streets outside. A picture frame fell with a disturbingly loud crash as the entire house rattled from the explosion. A huge ball of fire, dust and spent life erupted from the explosion. The old man smiled as he filled his pipe. Through the painted windows, the explosion looked like a huge moon covered in blood. "I can see a Blood moon from my window. What better place to situate the headquarters of Blood Moon" he amusingly muttered to himself as he prepared to light his pipe.

Light Flickers

The man walking in the shadows, shoulders slightly hunched, subtly checking his corners with sharp eyes for danger, was none but Theodor. The sun was down, leaving the city looming under dark obscurities. It was with extreme caution that he took every step, so as to avoid drawing attention from enemy soldiers.

Tired and battered from the endless journey he'd been on, he dragged himself, with his only driving force being the hope to find Adelheid somewhere in this mess. He had entered from the western zone where the battle was less intense as compared to the head on attack from other sides. The south, south-east and northern frontiers were directly under attack from opposing forces. From the area where Theodor entered, there were large gaps in military ranks, facilitating the escape of people. Civilians and armed personnel alike were trying to get out of Berlin and onto safer grounds. It was only a matter of time though, till the Red army closed borders and completely captured Berlin. The city roads were a chaos, with half of them ripped apart with gaping holes in the earth, while the other half was covered with debris and dead bodies.

Any dead or deformed body that came in Theodor's way made his heart scream in fear. His heart thumped almost loud enough for anyone nearby to hear, as he considered the possibility of one of those bodies bearing Adelheid's face and shape! What if she was one of those dead people strewn mercilessly on the floor? He kept moving and dodging through shadows, all in a bid to avoid confrontations.

His most recent line of thought involved getting to a city hospital or an air-raid shelter where civilians might be hiding or recovering. His best hope were the hospitals, as it was one place any enemy, no matter how inhumane, would shy away from inflicting any direct harm.

And then, he saw them. Out of the corner of his left eye, Theodor saw Red army soldiers marching towards him from the opposite street. He quickly ducked into a nearby alley and strode away in the opposite direction, getting as far away from them as possible. He couldn't really decipher any streets or addresses.

He had been to Berlin only once before; what lay in front of him now was beyond recognition, and he was usually good with roads and paths. There were obviously no street signs left, with all major landmarks he remembered already razed to the ground. The darkness was enveloping as night approached rapidly and the city no longer had any standing light poles or electric supply to light it up.

The Red army soldiers in the alley behind Theodor fired a few rounds into the night air; they were not on guard, instead, they were merely making a mockery of the fallen city. With most of Berlin conquered, they had little opposition to worry about. The streets were otherwise deserted for miles together and void of life. Theodor continued his walk, dodging in and out of shadows.

Slowly but surely, his eyes accommodated the darkness. So far, so good. He thought. He had travelled deeper into the city with no substantial encounter as yet. He did try to move closer to the escaping people to strike a conversation. But he couldn't make any abrupt movements to reach them and at every few steps into the city, he would see Red army soldiers fanning out. It was a task not to be seen by any of them. No doubt, the darkness had helped matters. But as much as it'd been of help, the darkness also made it challenging for him to traverse, as random bullets were flying through the air making it difficult for him to move freely.

Theodor now hit a straight narrow ally as he continued forward. Far away at the end of the street, he noticed a strange halo emanating from a corner window. He couldn't tell if it was a shop or a house but the light was striking in this darkness. 'Was it a reflection? Or a trick played by some half dying fire?' he thought. Theodor strained his eyes to see better, yet straining didn't help him comprehend what the strange light was all about. The light seemed to flicker like a small fire would. Theodor hesitated for a while, thinking of whether to change his direction or go towards the source of light. Chances were, the Red army soldiers had set it up. 'Who else would openly light a fire in such a situation?' his mind was racing with thoughts. He had to take his chance for he didn't know if he would reach anyone else. Carefully, Theodor inched closer towards the light. Keeping to the shadows, he moved slowly, trying not to make any noise. His heart was beating faster than usual, and his mind was racing with several thoughts. It finally settled on one thought: if he found a fellow German, he could hope to find other civilians.

Theodor sneaked around the place trying to look in through a crack or an opening. Quietly he moved around the periphery, there was no sign of life around and it seemed quite deserted from the inside. There was however a dim light flickering in the house, yet he saw no other movement. He nudged the door a little, but it remained stuck. Out of fear, he looked around the street to see if someone was approaching. It was dead and empty, so he took his chances by trying hard to push the door open. It didn't budge. He glanced below his feet, there was debris piled up along the edge of the door. As silently as he could work, Theodor swiftly pushed away the rubble and tried thrusting his weight onto the door; yet it remained as immovable as ever.

Theodor took a few steps behind, his heart beat picked up and fear crept into his mind. Once again, he glanced along the street, 'no sign of life' he thought. He moved into a short sprint and rammed into the door, it budged slightly and a chain rattled on the inside. A grunt escaped Theodor as he rubbed his arm. He waited for someone to answer from within or make some movement. A few uneventful seconds passed. The flickering light went out suddenly.

There was definitely someone inside; Theodor thought to himself. If it was the Red army soldiers, they would surely have barged out to kill him by now. Theodor knocked on the door and waited; still there was no answer. He confidently stepped back and ran towards the door. 'They have to be civilians' he thought, as he launched himself onto the door hoping to break it open. He was waiting for contact and nearly hit the door but the impact never came. Instead, the door flew open and Theodor couldn't stop himself in time, given his momentum.

Massive hands grabbed Theodor and thrust him towards the corner of the room. The intensity of his sprint coupled with the thrust from unknown hands sent him flying across and he crashed into a kitchen rack. He let out a short scream as he fell flat on his face and the cabinet along with a number of vessels collapsed on him, making a colossal racket.

The footsteps and voices he heard were as disordered as the loud thumping of Theodor's heart. His brain was working in overdrive. He heard the door slam shut again. "I told you to put out the light." He heard someone order in anger. Theodor tried to shun the throbbing pain that had begun on the side of his head, trying to get up he pushed the mountain of broken kitchen ware off him.

He had to gather himself and tell the inmates that he was here in peace. He opened his mouth in an attempt to form a sentence, but before any word could come out, a massive blow struck his head. More voices, an insane throbbing of his head, and then, Theodor's world began to spin. He should get up, he knew that much. He attempted to, but as he did so, he knew he didn't have the strength to hold his weight.

That was the last thing he remembered, before he blacked out; with blobs of flickering light in the background.

Bane

A few hours had passed since Han pulled his triggers on the Russian camp. Soldiers were running around, trying to get the camp back to its optimal working condition. Light poles and alternate power sources were a few of the things being set up. Since more men had to be deployed to keep the camp running, security at the periphery of the camp was a bit loose.

Coupled with that, more and more soldiers were also being called upon and diverted towards the final battle in Germany. On the ground level, the camp didn't seem affected apart from a few places where the earth had cracked open. Deeper below, the scene was different. The tunnels were ravaged by the blasts. The radio and light rigs were blown and their water supply was cut off as the underground thermal pumps were rendered useless. This campsite was a very crucial marker on the illegal activity map for Russian warlords. The blasts caused by Han affected operational activities within the camp and restoring it back to full working potential was the Minotaur's primary concern.

Konstantin sat in the dimly lit cabin as a doctor attended to his wound. Not a flinch from Konstantin, as the medic dabbed some cotton-wool soaked in Eusol over his nasty bullet injury. The radio in front of him crackled to life. "Konstantin?" a voice hurriedly spoke over it. Konstantin did not bother to budge and continued smoking his cigar. A soldier ran into the room and stood opposite Konstantin.

He eyed him and nodded, releasing a puff of smoke into the small room. The soldier relaxed and took a seat opposite Konstantin. He picked up the radio and responded "This is Viktor. Konstantin is out." "Where is he?" The voice cut through. "General Igor too is unavailable over radio" the voice sounded frustrated and angry. "There is a power failure in the camp and they are both outside inspecting it" spoke Viktor.

"Generals inspecting a power failure?" the person on the opposite end swore into the radio. "I will contact you again in fifteen minutes. Go fetch them, I have news to discuss. Berlin will be ours soon but their leader is not in our clenches yet. Konstantin must get to work immediately." "Yes sir, I shall" Viktor's speech drowned over the radio as Konstantin turned a dial to build up crackle. He pulled out a plug, and now the radio was dead.

Viktor looked at Konstantin with surprise filled eyes. The doctor had finished tending to Konstantin's wound and quietly took his leave. A fresh bandage was tied around the wound, but that didn't stop the wound from oozing out blood, leaving a crimson spot on the white bandage. Konstantin looked at it as anger built up in his eyes. "We have a lot of explaining to do back at the high command" Konstantin said, in a deep menacing voice. He settled back in the chair as he looked at Viktor, his cigar clenched between his teeth.

"We will tell them that someone within the camp conspired and killed General Igor. I leave it to you to fetch one of our soldiers and do the rest" Konstantin ordered; exhaling slowly as he looked at his wound again. Viktor bowed and began to reach for the exit. Konstantin slowly raised his hand and motioned him to settle down. "I have a consignment that will be arriving shortly." Konstantin bore into Viktor's eyes as he spoke. He pulled out the cigar and sniffed it. "I have authorized lift off for two aircrafts from Berlin. They must be leaving now as we speak. They carry materials of immense value. I want those aircrafts emptied and the material brought into camp. Take as many soldiers as you need. If anything happens to the material, I will have your neck"

Konstantin swore and broke the cigar into two. Viktor was intently listening to his master, not daring to flinch or look away.

Konstantin looked at the cigar and smiled mildly. "I must control my anger lest I waste a lot of cigars"; and then he burst into laughter, his voice echoing throughout the room. . He roared like a maniac and banged his massive fists on the table. The table creaked under strain and a few things kept over it rattled. "I will look into it personally my lord" Viktor finally replied. "I will take escort groups and get the material safely into camp. Any particular handling measures for the said consignment?"

Viktor asked, trying to get more information about this strange material that was to arrive. "Nothing in particular" said Konstantin. "And once inside the camp, transport it straight to the Beast bunker." "Yes my lord, it will be done" replied Viktor. The conversation drifted into an uncomfortable silence; with both Konstantin and Viktor looking around, while seated. The mighty winds carried far away dog barks into the silent cabin. Viktor was getting restless and wished that Konstantin would dismiss him.

"Did he speak yet?" Konstantin clenched his jaw and abruptly questioned. Viktor looked scared. All along, he'd been expecting this question from Konstantin. "Nothing yet" Viktor curtly replied. Konstantin flexed his arms and leaned forward on the table, his features contorting in anger. "That bastard sniper, I will see him shortly. I know what can make him talk" he swore. Larger globs of blood oozed out beneath the band tied around Konstantin's arm as he clenched his fists in anger. Viktor noticed this and got up from the chair. "I will go fetch the doctor" he said. "No" shouted Konstantin. He strained his muscle and flexed further as more blood oozed from the wound. "It will heal. What use is the blood in our bodies if it won't heal?"

Konstantin settled back into his chair. "What about the forests? Did you fan them?" asked Konstantin. "Yes my lord" replied Viktor. "Nothing substantial was found. No traces, no weapons and no other forces. We are sure Han was alone" he said. Konstantin was obviously not convinced, and the smirk on his face showed that. "Keep the search on, and do not ignore any signs. Once the camp is restored back to its full working potential, divert our guards back; so as to strengthen our security" he ordered. Viktor nodded in understanding. "I hope our prisoner has been secured in the chamber?" Konstantin questioned further. "Yes. As directed, all entrances have been dismantled and the only one leading to his cell is guarded by the best of our soldiers." Viktor replied as Konstantin stared at the ceiling.

"When is my marksman arriving?" Konstantin threw question after question at Viktor who by now, had a look of uncertainty clearly printed on his face. Yet, he spoke on. "Last we communicated, he was on his way. Exact location remains undisclosed but he was confident of reaching before nightfall today" replied Viktor. "Brilliant" Konstantin barked. "Once he is here, I have other matters to look into and while we are on that subject, any correspondence from my German friend yet?" Konstantin yet again bore into Viktor's eyes as he questioned him. "None as yet my lord, we tried contacting him via the means you asked. He seems to be absconding." Viktor answered slowly as he was scared to come open about the truth. A hint of worry flickered over Konstantin's face. "It will put us in a very difficult situation if he doesn't respond soon" he said.

The door flung open with a massive thud and the sound of ravaging winds was suddenly audible inside the quiet cabin. Viktor instantly turned around and pulled out his gun. He stood on guard covering his master. Konstantin however didn't even flinch. "Ah, the 'Bane' I called for is here" he said easing back into his chair. "There are serious security issues that need to be addressed in this camp. I walked in, right up to your cabin without being spotted even once." A crisp voice spoke from the corridor. The door slammed shut again as a powerfully built figure walked in. He was drenched from head to toe but his posture was rock solid and unwavering. He pulled out his rifle and placed it on the table.

Konstantin got up and smiled. "You were spotted by my faithful hounds; as each of your footsteps was monitored for nothing misses my eyes or ears, Fedor. Now come, there is work to be done" Konstantin happily roared. "I am yours to command my lord" Fedor curtly replied. A mad laugh escaped Konstantin as he cackled loudly like a maniac- drowning out every other sound in the room.

Darkness

From what seemed like a mile away, words were flung all over the place. They didn't make any sense, and Theodor, straining his eyes as far as it'd agree to be strained, saw his much beloved Adelheid's face in the distance.

The voices, her face; was any of this real? It was a strange feeling, he couldn't tell the difference between what was real and what seemed to spring out of his thoughts. Crazy little blobs of lights were fading in and out of sight as the fazed surroundings became clear. As he attempted to move, a torrent of pain surged through his body. His head and side where he collided with the rack was hurting terribly.

Finally, as he tried to blank out the pain, Theodor opened his eyes and looked around. He instantly realized what had just happened and began to panic. Had he been captured by the Russians? a thought struck his mind. From out of nowhere a deep voice spoke "You are not dead." Theodor panicked further at the unknown voice and sat straight on the make shift bed. "It was only a blow to your head. You have been moaning as if you are dying for the past ten minutes" said the voice.

Theodor inhaled deeply and coughed as he took in a waft of foul smelling smoke. A man with a huge unkempt beard and long hair sat in front of him. He had deep wrinkled skin and sagging eye bags through which his blue eyes stood out glinting sharply. Theodor was still in pain and was thinking about how wise it'd be for him to ask questions about where he was. The old man sat on a pile of boxes like a king would sit on a throne and smoked his exquisitely crafted pipe. "My name is Traugott" the old man said in-between long puffs. Theodor gave him a blank look as Traugott continued to observe him. He spoke again. "Don't worry I am not going to kill you. I am with peace" he said and raised his hand as if volunteering for a peace march.

"Where am I?" Theodor mustered courage and asked the old man. "You are in my palace of course" the old man replied mockingly as he lifted his hands, showing off the small dingy place. He shifted a bit, settling deeper into his makeshift chair to get comfortable. Theodor looked around the place. It looked like an underground shelter. The room was filled with boxes and piles of papers. Wires ran around the entire room in a thick bunch and only one light source hung in the center. The smoke played around it, casting unnatural shadows around them.

Theodor turned over and placed his feet on the floor. He still felt dazed and confused. How could it be that an old, frail man had hit him hard enough for him to have blacked out completely? It surely didn't make sense. "Are you running away from the war or are you here looking for someone?" Traugott asked casually as he smoked. The question caught him off-guard. Theodor didn't know if to tell the truth. He hesitated for a moment.

"I am trying to reach a civilian shelter or a hospital" Theodor softly replied. "Looking for someone then, I see." Traugott instantly shot back. "I thought as much. Only a fool would otherwise walk around Berlin at such an hour. Are you from around? Which infantry did you serve?" Traugott kept the questions coming from in-between long puffs of smoke.

Theodor rubbed his head as he thought. He still wasn't sure if it was safe to spill out his entire truth. "Still hurts does it?" Traugott shot back as he watched him rubbing his head. "Ralf has a mighty arm I must say. If I were you, my head would have rolled away by now. I was up there lighting my pipe and I heard you banging on my door. I quickly called Ralf. To tell you the truth, even I panicked. Ralf came up and grabbed you with his bare hands and..." He didn't finish the sentence. Instead, Traugott punched his fist against the palm of his hand, motioning an impact. "We might have opened the door but you decided to break it down so I had to call Ralf." Traugott continued talking as if discussing the weather.

"Is there a place around where the civilians are holding out?" Theodor abruptly changed the topic of conversation. Traugott was caught off guard and he slouched back into the boxes. They bent a little under his shifting weight. "Well, there are a lot of such shelters, to tell you the truth soldier. Every other house will have people hiding in them and there are a few hospitals surviving in the epicenter of battle too. Are you looking for your family?" he asked.

"Yes" replied Theodor. "I am looking for someone." "Just one, you say?" Traugott was sharp and kept pressing on with his questions. Theodor felt frustration build up within him. He didn't feel the need to justify every bit of information to this old man. "There are people hiding here too." Traugott motioned towards a door as he spoke. There was just one door in the room and it was closed shut. On the opposite side there was a ladder that led straight up to a trap door. From beyond the door, Theodor could hear faint voices and he walked towards it. "Not so fast." Traugott let out a wisp of smoke as he spoke "They are civilians; they are hiding in fear but have pledged peace. They have no allegiance to the Nazis or those Communist bastards out there. You need to remove your coat and leave all your weapons before entering."

Traugott motioned for him to remove his effects. "Pledge that you come in peace or leave" he concluded. "Why should I trust you?" Theodor asked him. The old man smiled and showed him a bunch of keys. "You will need these to open the door, soldier" he said. "What if you kill me?" Theodor asked, gauging the old man for anything that'd make him distrust him, he wasn't too sure about giving up his gun to a complete stranger. Traugott swiftly got to his feet. He was pretty agile given his age and he stood way taller than Theodor. "Now, either leave all your weapons here and enter in peace or prepare to be shot." Traugott removed a gun from his shabby robes. "I don't have all day to waste behind you. And you are right, if you annoy me too much. I might just kill you." Traugott stood with his gun pointing at Theodor as he finished his ultimatum.

He continued smoking his pipe casually as if they had been simply discussing daily news. Theodor had tested his luck too far; now he knew what he had to do. Theodor threw his over coat and a hand gun which he'd hidden beneath it. "For a soldier, you have a pathetic choice of weapons" Traugott spoke as he studied the hand gun that Theodor laid down. "Is that all?" Traugott asked him in between puffs. Theodor tersely held up both his hands challenging the old man to check his clothes. Traugott gave him a suspicious look and began unlocking the door. After a few key turns in various locks, the door opened and Theodor walked in with Traugott.

It was a small dark basement room filled with civilians. They looked at Theodor as he entered their sanctuary. Traugott closed the door behind them and led the way. "I would suggest you shed that uniform. People in this room are done with the war. They want an end to this" Traugott spoke as he walked around. Theodor followed the old man as he made way through the crowd of people. "We won't last here forever" Traugott continued talking "We are just trying to hold out until a complete surrender is declared. The Red army is bound to barge in and find us anyways."

All the while, Theodor was looking around trying to find Adelheid. His eyes moved from one face to another in the room. His heart sank as he looked around and found nothing. There were kids, women, soldiers and injured people. Small hammocks were suspended throughout the room. Babies were made to sleep in those while the others just stood by. Only the wounded were given place to sleep. "Didn't find what you were looking for?" Traugott asked him in his deep voice. Theodor nodded in despair and asked "Can I look through the other door?" as he studied the room. "You will find nothing there that will help, but you can stay if you want" said Traugott. "I can't promise anything but it might buy you time. Wait it out till the war ends and then go looking. Or you can leave right now, the choice is yours."

He patted Theodor softly on the back and walked away from him. "Also, you may find some leftover food and water over there." Traugott pointed towards a corner as he walked around.

Theodor mumbled a few words of appreciation. His was a world filled with chaos, and he was lost in it. He could easily step out and continue his journey. But deep down inside he was afraid. He feared that a stray bullet would find its way into his body and snuff the life out of him as he wandered around in Berlin. A civilian came up and handed him two pieces of moldy stale bread. Theodor slowly shifted his gaze to them man's face, and then to the fungus covered bread. He lunged at the food and stuffed it into his mouth. He didn't realize how hungry he'd been till he consumed a good part of the small piece of bread. The man who had offered it to him simply smiled and turned away. Theodor looked longingly at the other piece as he slouched beside the locked door.

He looked around the place as he ate the remaining bread. Nostalgic memories of a different place and time filled his thoughts. When he'd been younger, his family had moved to the underground shelter during the Great War. It was much like this place. There was a radio in the center of the room and limited rations were stored. This room too had a radio inside. A small one kept in the center, over which the inmates would hear important announcements. Theodor closed his eyes and tried to rest, grateful for the food that travelled down his throat and into his stomach.

Still, his head hurt terribly. He cursed this Ralf, whoever he was, for giving him a headache. He rubbed his head and tilted back towards the wall as he watched the ceiling. He felt fear surging through his mind at the thought of the dangers that could befall him as soon as he stepped out of the door. The old man was right; if he stayed here he might live a little longer. The sight of this shelter terribly reminded him of home. In quick succession, diverse images from his past flashed in his mind. One which refused to leave, was an image of when he was a teenager, a young chap who'd barely formed opinions about the world. His father had returned from war duties and was staying home for a few days. "This wretched war is going to wipe us out." Theodor would hear his father yell in frustration as the bombs fell from the skies. They made way into the underground shelter to protect themselves from the bombings.

Theodor, his parents and little sister Sarah were waiting in fear as the merciless bombs ripped apart their town. With just basic amenities to survive on, they didn't have a great life but the Bachmeier's managed to pull through. The bombs that fell from enemy aircrafts were massive and the underground shelter resonated with deep sound of explosions. Theodor shifted uncomfortably in the underground shelter at Berlin.

His eyes had shut in exhaustion and now, he'd slipped into the peaceful world of dreams. He was constantly on the move and any little sleep that he got, caught up with him instantly. Theodor's mind flashed the dream forcefully as he slept. The overhead beam creaked and groaned as it moved under strain of the mighty blasts. "Come here, move" Theodor's father yelled as he got to his feet and moved from under the beam. His mother too followed suit as they huddled under a cave like cavity. Theodor was scared; he sat there frozen in fear. He somehow couldn't move. Sarah tugged at his hand and ran to her waiting parents. Theodor's father lifted Sarah and held her close. "Come Theodor. Come son, take my hand, you have to move away from the center. It might collapse" his father shouted. Another loud explosion went up on the farm lands and without warning the ceiling cracked as Theodor screamed in alarm.

The door against which Theodor was resting thrust open; jolting him out of his dream. His heart was pounding against his ribs as his anxiety peaked. A gun was pointing at Theodor's face. He froze and held his hands up in surrender. A huge figure in military uniform stood towering in front of him. He held out a finger indicating for him to keep quite. Another soldier crept out from the room and fanned across. Everyone in the room was silent and still. The mothers quickly went to their children and covered their mouths to stop them from crying or making any noise. The small light went out from the room, plunging them into complete darkness.

The huge soldier moved towards the wall and held his gun ready. A subdued flash shone through the cloth and glass cover of the basement window. Theodor could hear voices outside. Surely, Red army soldiers were hunting for people. All life in the room was extremely still as the seconds passed slowly and everyone held their breaths. Even the smoke in the room hung there, still and lifeless. After what seemed like ages, the huge soldier finally moved. Everyone relaxed a bit and shifted from their places. Traugott lit a small oil lamp and placed it on the table.

A few people huddled close to the radio to check if there were any new announcements. A faint crackle built up on the radio as they tried to tune it. The soldiers were heading back into the room from where they'd emerged. Theodor caught a glimpse inside. It was a cramped room with the weirdest assortment of equipment. There were radio rigs, racks of weapons, stacks of papers and a riot of wires running around. Theodor inched closer to the door to get a better look, when suddenly the huge soldier blocked him.

"Stay out" he ordered and stood in his way, towering above everything else in the room. Theodor noticed a few more people inside the room. A tiny bespectacled man was busy trying to listen to something over the radio. Traugott came and stood beside Theodor. "Looks interesting doesn't it soldier? Our very own operating base, right here in Berlin. I named it the Blood Moon headquarters" Traugott boasted. "Traugott?" the soldier held out his hand stopping him mid-sentence. "Ah, come on Ralf. What do we have to lose now? It's all over. Old man Felix still wants to keep it low ehh? He still got a secret plan up his sleeve?" Traugott looked at Theodor and pointed to the huge, intimidating soldier. "This here is Ralf. He is the one who saved you, took you in and gave you that headache" he said. "He didn't save me" Theodor shot back instantly. Traugott pushed Theodor in and shut the door behind them. The room was a complete mess but it did look like an operating base.

Theodor noticed the soldiers working hurriedly in the cramped room. "Ralf you need to work out details of an escape route and report back instantly" another soldier spoke, as he walked up to them. He fixed his gaze on the newcomer and sized him up. "Who is this?" he asked pointing at Theodor. "He is harmless" Traugott replied with a smile. "That is not my concern Traugott" he retorted.

"Yes Lieutenant Falko. He is a soldier, he walked into Berlin and we took him in" Traugott answered in a mocking tone. Falko's eyes bore into Theodor's and he asked "Took him in? Who put you in charge of recruitment?" "NO" Theodor yelled in shock. "I am just taking shelter here" he hastily replied. "Well then keep him out with the civilians; he has no business being in this room!" Falko made it clear as he continued going through details in a file that he held. "I am a better soldier than you think. But I choose not to fight anymore. I am done with this war"

Theodor retorted without thinking. His anger didn't show signs of ebbing because of the way he was being spoken to. Falko shut his file and slowly moved closer to Theodor speaking in a mere whisper "This war will end when it has to, soldier. You do not get to choose that. All you can choose is the type of end you want to see to it. Throw him out Traugott, we have much to do" Falko concluded.

By now, the others were listening to the conversation that Theodor and Falko were having. Theodor was fuming as he stood there looking at Falko. Ralf and Traugott stood aside watching in silence. "Ralf ?" a commanding voice emanated from within the room. "Are the details of our route ready?" Ralf was shocked. He sprang to his feet and moved deeper into the room. From the shadows emerged General Felix. Everyone including Traugott instantly moved away from the center and stood in attention. "Time is of the essence gentlemen. We need to evacuate soon. Albert, has the information been decrypted?" General Felix asked, holding out his hand. The spectacled radio operator handed out a paper to the General. "Few more messages are on the way. We should be getting them soon. It's difficult given the breakdown of radio equipment throughout Berlin. I am trying to leech off various enemy radio frequencies" Albert replied as he copied more codes on paper. General Felix was studying the paper as he spoke "Traugott please lead him out" pointing at Theodor. "Gentlemen settle down. I have mission briefings ready for us" he continued talking as Traugott held Theodor by the arm and pulled him out. Theodor tugged his arm free and walked out feeling extremely frustrated and angry. He had to overcome his fear and move out. There was no point waiting in this shelter. These bunch of soldiers looked like nothing but trouble. 'Mission briefings at the losing end of war. Bunch of maniacs' thought Theodor. He walked out of the room and started gathering his stuff. He put on his coat and secured his hand gun. He had to keep looking and searching for shelters. He was bound to find Adelheid somewhere. He couldn't let fear becloud his search. Traugott stepped out of the room, looked at him and said "Here take this." He held out his gun for Theodor to take. Traugott had somehow known that Theodor wouldn't stay for long. "I don't need that" Theodor shot back without bothering to look at Traugott. "Take it soldier. You will have a few more rounds of fire power with you. And just to set things straight, you can come back to take shelter. Germany will need a new beginning once this war ends. Fine and able men like you can help rebuild our nation." Traugott walked around the room as he spoke and settled into his pile of boxes. He pulled out his half spent pipe and began smoking again. Theodor gave him one last look and climbed up the ladder. "Close all doors shut as you go out, and watch your back" Traugott spoke as Theodor climbed up the trap door and closed it shut.

He surfaced on the top and scanned the place from outside; it must have been a fine looking house once upon a time. The trapdoor opened into the living room. Theodor moved around slowly and looked out from the painted window; he was now faced with pitch blackness. He tried looking through cracks in the panels. No sight of light. It was absolutely black outside. With all of the courage he could muster, Theodor pulled open the door. A draft of pungent air hit his nostrils as Theodor stepped into the dead night of Berlin. Slowly, he closed the door behind him and walked ahead. He had come out from the other entrance and this door opened onto the main street. His eyes began adjusting to the darkness as he walked onto the streets of Berlin.

A few random gun shots were heard far away in the distance but nothing near where he was walking. Theodor quietly walked through the ruined streets and turned to hit the parallel alley. Another body was strewn on the road. His heart began beating against his rib cage. It was a little girl, probably in her early teens. Her foot was sticking out at an abnormal angle and her face was smeared with blood. He gathered himself and walked on.

A pang of guilt built up within him, had he become so selfish that the death of others didn't matter to him anymore? Whenever he checked a lifeless body, he thought of Adelheid and when he was convinced it was not her, it no longer mattered to him. With these thoughts heavy upon his mind he continued walking into endless darkness.

Hurricane Fire

Theodor could barely see as he cautiously navigated through the stifling darkness. He kept to the shadows as he skirted around edges of houses and broken walls. Suddenly, out of nowhere, a powerful punch landed on his face and threw him off his feet. Massive hands grabbed him before he could react and thrust him against a wall. "I found a soldier" A man spoke through the darkness. His accent was different and heavy. Fear crept into Theodor's mind and his heart froze in fear.

A flash light met his eyes as he squinted and two more soldiers arrived on the scene. His heart sank slowly; he'd been captured. Left with no time to react, a cold gun barrel touched his throat. Theodor tried to lose his mind of the fear that had wrapped itself firmly around it, as he attempted to plot an escape. There were two of them; one was holding his hands back while the other held a gun to his throat. They pulled him out onto the streets and prepared to march him. Theodor struggled to break free but they easily overpowered him.

"Where were you walking to you Nazi filth?" One of the soldiers asked. Theodor thought it was best not to reply and silently cursed himself for not shedding his uniform before now. Up ahead, Theodor could see a faint flickering light. Was he being taken to their commander? Thoughts began racing through his head. He tried looking around to spot alleys in which he might be able to run and hide. While these thoughts clouded his mind, he heard a sudden whistling sound and in rapid succession, a bullet hit one of the Red army soldiers in the chest. Instantly he fell to the ground while the other soldier shouted in alarm. Theodor ducked and fell flat to the ground, face first. He crawled and took shelter behind a ruined wall. The Russian soldier came after him and another shot rang through the air hitting the Russian. These were sniper bullets! Theodor instantly realized as the Russian collapsed right next to him with a lifeless thud. Theodor frantically scanned the environment to see the source of firing as he heard alarmed cries of Russian soldiers ahead.

One of the soldiers who held him captive suddenly dashed from behind the darkness and ran towards the light source. Theodor mustered enough courage to jump out of his hiding place. He had to tackle the soldier before he alerted the others. The Russian soldier was running and shouting desperately. Theodor caught up with him and landed a punch on his back.

The soldier yelped and fell to the ground. Before Theodor could reach him, the soldier swiftly turned around and kicked him in the stomach. Theodor was caught unawares and received the full blow as he fell backwards. The Russian soldier swiftly got to his feet and dashed ahead. As the Russian covered a few steps, yet another bullet whistled through the air and struck him in the head. He screamed and crashed to the ground, a thick pool of blood accumulating around his head. Theodor looked around, troubled and scared.

The snipers seemed to be friendly as they didn't attack him yet but he was still in the line of fire. Theodor quickly dragged himself behind a broken down jeep as he noticed a parked Russian jeep ahead, he strained to spot the snipers through the darkness but couldn't locate any. Another crisp whistling sound emanated from close by and smashed the glass of the Russian jeep.

Theodor ducked in reflex as he tried to protect himself from the resilient snipers. Another gunshot; and yet another. The mechanical firing came from two different directions now. Theodor suddenly heard a small cry and the door of the Russian car crashed open as one of the bullets made contact. A body fell out and in the next instance, gun fire rang from the car. A soldier dashed out and ran away, firing blindly towards the car behind which Theodor hid.

Theodor ducked and held still as the bullets ricocheted off the body of the car that he was hiding behind. He heard a crackling sound around him and suddenly felt a light flicker somewhere close. A glass pane in the overhead building shattered and a sniper landed on his feet.

He was quick and agile as he recovered swiftly from the fall and ran towards the Russian vehicle. Theodor mustered courage and looked up to see what was happening. Yet another crash resonated through the air and another sniper landed next to Theodor. This sniper was bulkier than the previous one, he seemed slower but composed. Theodor panicked as he looked at the sniper. "We're friendly" replied the sniper as he bent low to take aim through the looming darkness. Up ahead by the end of the street, a Russian soldier had struck a flare signal.

The sniper wasted no time and shot the Russian soldier. Theodor heard a distinct moan followed by a thud. The other sniper inspected the vehicle to see if any other soldiers remained. Theodor climbed out from behind the car and saw the sniper running back towards them. "We need to get underground" he shouted. "This bastard has sent up a signal to the armies waiting outside. They will send heavy fire our way any minute now. You need to get into a shelter" the sniper standing next to Theodor spoke. Theodor looked troubled and confused as the other sniper joined them. "Let's get out of here, quick" he said panting a little. The three of them looked at each other and without another word ran into the streets.

Far away, the wail of the attack was audible. "We won't make it" Theodor shouted through the frenzy. "I have seen these missiles work. They are the BM-13 launchers; the blast radius is too big and they won't stop at one" he concluded. The snipers didn't seem affected. "Keep running soldier. We need to get into a nearby underground shelter" one of them shot back as they ran. Theodor turned at the junction and followed the snipers closely. Up ahead, they could see a half broken house that could provide some shelter. Suddenly they heard wails of the launchers from far away and a distinct swish through the skies. The hurricane fire had begun.

Heavy Water

Fedor walked around the camp, inspecting it as Konstantin and Viktor tailed behind him. Konstantin was engrossed in a book that he held open before his eyes. Fedor had spent an hour inspecting the camp and the mess made by Han. "Any valuable insights?" Konstantin mockingly questioned. Fedor left his inspection half way and walked up to them looking frustrated.

"The security measures are weak right now, they are too easy to break into and we need to dispense our resources efficiently. Right now, pull out all men and assemble a team to transport the materials that you talk about" Fedor explained as he whistled and called a guard. The guard responded and came running towards them. "Get us chairs and a table" ordered Fedor. "We can shift inside" offered Konstantin. "No" Fedor replied "we will waste time." The guard rushed back with three chairs and another guard followed closely, carrying a small table. Fedor rolled open a map of the camp and placed it on the table. Konstantin looked mightily impressed with Fedor while Viktor eyed him suspiciously. Fedor had the air of someone who didn't divulge much about himself; someone you could never be too sure of.

They settled on the chairs and Fedor instantly jumped to explaining what he had learnt. "Our priority now is the Beast Bunker, we are housing an important prisoner and we also need to consider the new material headed our way."

"He is just a sniper and now our prisoner, nothing much to worry about" Konstantin snapped back as he slammed his book shut on the table. "He is not 'just' a sniper; he is a trained 'beast' and an important prisoner as I rightly called him" retorted Fedor.

"There was a reason why Hitler chose him. He alone is worth much more than a hundred clumsy soldiers of our camp." Fedor spoke with mild anger and frustration in his voice. "If he could break into our camp, my lord" Fedor instantly changed his tone as he explained further "he might very well be able to break out of it."

Fedor never liked to be questioned or held up for justification. "Last I knew you were here on my orders, Fedor and not the other way round" Konstantin commented with a final authority in his voice. "He is housed in the suspended chamber, I have personally designed that. No one has ever dared break into it. He is secure enough" he concluded.

Konstantin nodded and pointed towards the map "Continue" he said. Fedor went back to the map and started drawing lines as he explained. "This here is a mistake. We need immediate water supply to run the camp" he said pointing at the water supply source on the map. "The lights can wait, everything else can wait. Restore the water supply first and other activities will fall into place faster" he explained.

Both Konstantin and Viktor were looking at Fedor as he spoke. "Once the water is fixed, we can move to the radio rigs." "Let the working radio be with me for now" Konstantin interrupted. "Han, our prisoner might be valuable from high command's point of view; we cannot let this information leak to them as yet. They will want to interfere and I cannot let that happen" said Konstantin.

Fedor nodded and did not question him further. "Well, that is for you to decide. Now, as for the material that is coming in, give me soldiers; I will lead them to the drop point and back. Also as mentioned, I need you to step up security around the Beast Bunker" Fedor concluded. "You heard the man Viktor, give him what he needs" Konstantin ordered. "Take as many men as you need, the Beast Bunker is secure enough" he concluded. "I can look into security of the arriving consignment my lord. Let him handle other issues here" Viktor tried to argue. Fedor was clearly acting out to be his superior as far as skill was concerned. "I will have no meddling in my affairs" Fedor curtly shot back. "Just provide what is asked for" Konstantin held out his hands silencing both of them. "Get to work Viktor" Konstantin concluded with a final authority. Viktor gave a short salute and dashed away in annoyance. This was already turning into a feud.

Fedor watched Viktor walk away to give further orders and procure soldiers. "What is arriving in the consignment?" Fedor coolly asked. The question caught him off guard and Konstantin considered Fedor for a moment before he spoke "Heavy water." There was a moment of silence as both locked eyes and held their peace. Konstantin was searching Fedor's face for some expression but it never came. If Fedor was hiding his surprise, he was very good with it.

"Why get nuclear material from Berlin?" Fedor finally asked Konstantin, breaking the silence. Konstantin was surprised at Fedor's knowledge. He pulled himself closer to Fedor as he spoke in a low voice. "I have an understanding with a German friend of mine. He had promised the delivery of these goods and other valuables. In the literal sense, it's not 'Heavy water' that we are getting. The material rests deeper inside Berlin and Marshal Zuhkov is fast gaining ground there.

As far as I know, he will win it by himself. Russian High command is hoping to soon lay their hands on the Kaiser Wilhelm nuclear center. That is why there's so much hurry" Konstantin spoke as Fedor intently grasped every word. "Clearly, the Germans have headway in nuclear warfare. Their research is incomparable and beyond our time. You understand the value of that, don't you?" concluded Konstantin.

Fedor nodded in understanding and spoke again "You mean to say that Stalin has no interest in Hitler?" "Hitler of course is a major concern for them. The politics of the entire world will change tide with Hitler's capture. Berlin will be ours in a few hours and then Hitler won't be able to evade us for long. Once they find him, the attention will be on his capture and we can put our loot to good use. My men have been able to secure entire study material from the German nuclear center and other smaller laboratories. That along with new found nuclear materials namely 'Heavy water' will help us greatly. All the other resources, we will have to leave behind for Marshal Zuhkov to find" he concluded. "What do you intend to do with the study material?" Fedor shot another question. "That needs to be decided. Whatever is arriving needs to be sorted out first, and then its fate decided accordingly." Konstantin didn't want to disclose more than necessary information.

"Are our scientists trained enough to handle whatever is headed our way?" Fedor shot another question. A small smile broke over Konstantin's face. "You are sharp, but my thoughts and visions are beyond you. I had the same concern before I set out to acquire these materials and studies" Konstantin said as he paused to look around the camp. "I have German scientists working for me, and working with them are a few of our researchers. I must say; they are the best scientists this world has ever seen! They will know exactly what is coming in from Berlin" he concluded.

Fedor nodded in understanding and was very impressed by Konstantin's foresight. 'No wonder, the Russian High command gave him his freedom' thought Fedor. Konstantin had been running this secret camp for nearly five years and the high command had cleared a lot of obstacles for him. He had managed to expand and set up an impressive fortress in a very short period of time. As they discussed further about the course of action regarding arrival of nuclear materials, Viktor marched up to them and stood in salute.

"The teams you asked for are ready. A convoy of fifty men awaits your orders" he said. Konstantin nodded in appreciation. "And the man you asked for my lord." Viktor called two soldiers who were holding a sorry looking fellow soldier. "I swear I tried my best to protect General Igor my lord" the soldier cried in fear. Konstantin looked at him and then around the camp. More than fifty men had assembled and stood around them. Konstantin swiftly got up from his chair and approached the soldier. "Somebody has to be accountable for the General's death you see. If you tried to protect him he shouldn't have died, Right?" Konstantin asked a direct question, his eyes boring into the soldier's. The soldier cowered in fear as he stood helpless in front of the towering Minotaur. Without warning, Konstantin attacked and held the man by his throat. Before the soldier could react, Konstantin clasped his massive hand around the soldier's neck. His fingers closed like an iron vice. The soldier was completely helpless.

Fedor, Viktor and the others watched in shock as Konstantin's fingers closed around the man's neck, snuffing the life out of him slowly. "You plotted against us and conspired to kill General Igor" Konstantin roared, so everyone could hear him. The soldier however couldn't even talk as the Minotaur's mighty hand closed around his neck. Slowly and painfully the life quenched out of him as he violently convulsed. A few more horrifying seconds passed and the soldier twitched for the last time. Konstantin bore into his inert eyes, daring him to react and flung the dead soldier away. The body fell with a sickening thud.

"Viktor connect me to the High command. I have grave news for them" Konstantin barked so that everyone could listen. Viktor nodded and dashed back to the cabin where their radio was housed. "The rest of you can get to work" he ordered. Concluding the merciless demonstration, he marched away from the soldiers and into his cabin.

Fedor called out to the fifty waiting soldiers and ordered them to assemble by the gate. Fedor wanted to leave more soldiers to secure the Beast bunker but he didn't dare defy Konstantin. He dispatched another team to fix the water supply. The security on the outer perimeter of the camp was now on an all-time low.

Konstantin barged into his cabin. Viktor was already there, busy on the radio. "Viktor" Konstantin barked. "This should be the only working radio in the camp. There will be no contact with high command unless I authorize it. No one speaks of Han or the arriving materials. Do you understand?" "Yes my lord" Viktor quickly replied. "The high command will soon want to interfere with this camp, and with General Igor gone it will be difficult for me to convince them otherwise" Konstantin spoke and sat as he waited for Viktor to connect the radio. Viktor was fumbling and trembled a bit. Konstantin's mere presence filled the room with fear. "Our German friend will reply soon" Konstantin spoke in a barely audible whisper as he closed his eyes and leaned back. The radio crackled to life and an urgent voice spoke from the other side. "Konstantin?" Viktor held the radio ready for Konstantin to talk into.

"Konstantin?" Konstantin took his time as he opened his eyes and slowly grabbed the radio. "General Igor has fallen" he spoke softly into the radio. His face was devoid of any emotion but his voice sounded low and depressed. "What? Talk clearly. What happened at the camp? Are we under attack?" The voice on the other end fired questions. Konstantin slowly spoke "General Igor is dead. A soldier from within our ranks conspired to kill him and succeeded. I have managed to capture the traitor and punish him." "Do not kill the traitor" the voice spoke with a rising urgency. "He will divulge information on the conspiracy" the voice said. "I have already finished him" replied Konstantin. "NO" The voice commanded loudly into the radio.

"We are sending General Vlad to your camp. You must report to high command with the documentation on this incident. It is a great loss to us that the death of General Igor came from the hands of our own soldier." Konstantin was trying to keep his anger low but the last order made his heart race. "I am not traveling anywhere from here" he barked into the radio "And Vlad can be put to better use, I assume" Konstantin spoke and waited for the reply. "General Vlad is headed to Berlin and we will then direct him to take command of your camp." The voice at the opposite end spoke hurriedly over disturbing crackles.

"We also need your help in closing the noose on the Nazi leader Adolf Hitler. We understand that you have friends in their ranks?" Konstantin closed his eyes and tried to compose himself as he replied "I have no clue of where Hitler is. Our troops are in Berlin, surely they can find him." "You cannot defy orders from your high command. Do as directed and stay alert for more information from us. You must travel to high command and divulge all that you know. We will establish contact again." The radio went dead as static build up. Konstantin settled back and a faint smile escaped his lips. "The high command is clueless about

Han. I need to connect with my German friend and strike the deals urgently. We have nuclear material and a very valuable Nazi to sell" he said.

Viktor nodded and understood where the conversation was headed. "What about Vlad my lord?" asked Viktor. Konstantin bore into Viktor's eyes and smiled. "I will personally talk to him. I know he can be convinced. In case I am unable to convince Vlad then find me another soldier. The General must meet an untimely demise too." Konstantin smiled and looked out his cabin window to see Fedor instructing a line of soldiers.

The burden of securing the camp was now on Fedor's shoulders, and this surely gave him more room to think of other matters. Trucks were lining up outside as Fedor formed teams to transport heavy water into the camp. Konstantin smiled, grimly.

Blood Haze

Crackles, followed by the shattering of glasses. Violent flames licked the house as heat engulfed the room. The door to the room opened up and Ralf burst out along with Falko.

"What just happened?" he shouted as Traugott dashed in from the opposite end to warn and gather everyone. "Hurricane fire, it's upon us" Traugott shouted through the noise, his words drowning out in the massive crash caused by the explosion. It sounded as if the missile had landed right on top of them as a portion of the ceiling began to sag and cave in under strain of explosions.

The people were screaming and scattering around trying to find a safe place. "Get over here" Traugott shouted and pushed a group of people to stand under the center beam. "Stay below this" he said, pointing up to the thick beam. People began gathering below it. By now, the children had gotten wind of the commotion in the air, as they cried out in fear; and they were inconsolable. 'This is wrong' Traugott thought as he saw the people scramble in fear. They would probably just die waiting in this shelter.

A few more explosions over them and the entire house would cave in. General Felix stepped out from the operation base. "Get inside everyone, NOW" he roared in anger. A small lantern was throwing light and it cast unusual scary shadows around the room as it violently swung overhead. General Felix's face was half covered in shadows with his scarred face looking menacing, the scary shadows further amplifying his set jaw. One after another, they rushed into a smaller room where the operating base was set up. Another explosion ripped at the grounds above them and they heard a massive crash. "Keep going deeper" Traugott shouted through the chaos. "Settle down wherever you find place to. I don't have time for this." General Felix was talking hurriedly with a commanding authority. The room was extremely cramped now. Nearly twenty people were crammed inside the strange looking operating base. General Felix looked frustrated. "Everybody fall silent" he ordered angrily. The chatter of the scared people fell down instantly. Somewhere above, the bombs exploded and they felt the room reverberate with tremors. Cold chills ran down their spines.

The operating base had a cross pattern wooden beam running along its ceiling length, from which loose dust fell over the people. Slowly the impact died down and a sudden silence filled the room as if everything around was listening to General Felix.

"The world is against us" Felix spat out the words as he addressed everyone in the room. He didn't have any other option but to discuss the strategy while civilians were piled into the room. All the lights were out and the radio hiss died with the electric supply.

"As you all might know, the Fuehrer has collapsed; and so has the Third Reich." General Felix's voice was eerie through the darkness. "We will all either be dead, or captured in a few hours. I am sure of that and I assure you the same fate but what we do now might ensure the freedom of Germania and her children for years to come."

Felix gestured to everyone in the room. Albert, in the meanwhile, lit up an oil lamp and hung it in the center. The light threw eerie shadows all around. Felix tried to gain eye contact with as many people in his audience as he could, in the small cramped place. An intricately detailed map of Germany was pinned on the wall behind him. The map looked rich and skillfully made; Felix ran his fingers over it as if it were alive with feelings. For a moment, he let his thoughts linger before speaking. "I had once discussed the ongoing war with our Fuehrer on this very map. The vision crafted was enormous, the magnanimity of which scared me too. Now, the people have faced enough hatred at their own hands and at that of others." Felix seemed possessed with an eerie madness as he addressed the few people. "We are to undertake a mission shortly, probably the last one we will perform together because after this we will either be dead or will be living a life of ambiguous identity."

Felix did not move and he kept his hand on the map as he continued talking. The room was silent and still as if no life existed, smoke wafted from burnt out cigarette butts; occasionally a deep rumble from far away blasts could be heard. The structures continued to creak and groan under strains of attacks. "I am assembling a team to go behind enemy lines" Felix spoke in a hushed but clearly audible tone across the room. The silence dropped down further by a few decibels. It was as if they were inside a vacuum.

"The others will have to fend for themselves as I cannot spare anymore soldiers" he said. The civilians looked up in shock as small clusters of chattering and whispering broke out through the tiny room. "Just stay back. We can live through this. You don't need to follow orders anymore. It is all over." A short woman from the center of the room spoke to Felix. "We just have to wait it out" someone else shouted. "What enemy lines are you talking about? They are right inside our cities" another voice spoke.

An array of questions and arguments sprung up from within the room. General Felix held out his hand motioning for silence. "We are not taking orders from anyone" Felix cut back the argument in a stern voice. He looked around, scanning once again, the faces of the people gathered in the tiny room. "I confide this information in you all because I do not fear treachery anymore. Most of us will be dead before the third quarter of the moon wanes out" Felix spoke as he moved away from the people and stared back at the map. Deep rumbling sounds were still audible within the room from reverberations that emanated from blasts. A few crashes were heard from the outside, indicating that the ceilings might have caved. "General Helmuth will give surrender orders as he sees fit and as of now he is the senior most person in charge of making political talks with other nations. If we find any relevant information before the political surrender, we might save or change the impending fate of many lives" General Felix continued speaking. "The team has members from within this room" he said. Pockets of disturbing silence lingered between Felix's statements. "If any chosen soldier wishes to back out or stay back in order to protect the civilians, he may say so now; and be done with it." A grave silence fell over Felix's last statement.

Meanwhile, Theodor and the two snipers had taken refuge in a house as missiles wreaked havoc on the streets. The snipers shifted the broken down structure and came out to travel further. This, they were sure of: more fire was headed their way. "You can stay underground with civilians. You'll be safer here" said one of the snipers to Theodor as they prepared to move further. "We must head back and report to our team" he concluded, half-running, half-walking.

Theodor nodded, acknowledging the urgency of the situation as he looked through the broken structure. He scouted around for a trap door to get underground again. In the darkness, he saw menacing fires headed his way through the skies. Theodor jumped into a cavity as massive fires razed the streets.

The overhead beams were creaking under enormous strain as General Felix was concluding his statement. Through the sound and chaos, the trap door burst open and two snipers fell through. Ralf and Falko instantly turned around with their weapons ready. Felix looked at the snipers and addressed them: "Gregor, Frank, any soldiers headed our way?" They nodded a no and moved through the ranks of civilians. Ralf and Falko lowered their weapons as they listened to what General Felix had to say. Felix nodded and continued talking as everyone settled. "As for the others" he said, looking at a few soldiers housed in the shelter. "You can choose to help the civilians by staying here or you can go your own ways. That I leave to you to decide. I do this to secure your freedom and..." Felix looked at the map behind him, with a grave look plastered on his face. "And I do this for Germania." With that he concluded his speech. A few people came closer to talk to him. The soldiers began gathering their equipment for the mission ahead; while Gregor and Frank pushed their way through the crowd to talk to Felix.

Theodor was curled up like a ball; trying to protect himself from the fires that ravaged the streets. "Are you a soldier?" someone spoke from the darkness. He screamed in reaction as he tried to make sense of the space that he was cramped in. His eyes saw the form of a woman sitting beside him. "Don't worry, we are civilians. We come in peace" said the girl. Theodor tried to get up and look clearly. "Who are you? How many civilians are in here?" he asked. "It's just me and my two brothers" she replied. Theodor felt something move around him as someone flicked on a lantern. Through the faint light, he made out three sorry looking faces.

On the other side of town; General Felix, Ralf, Albert and Falko lined up to march out of the room. The door fell apart completely as Ralf threw it aside to let everyone step out one after the other. Albert disconnected the radio wires and took a file with the codes in them. The outer room was a mess as parts of it had caved, in making their exit difficult. Ralf had immediately gotten to work. He along with the two snipers, Gregor and Frank started clearing debris while Traugott walked out and joined General Felix. They restored a makeshift ladder so the civilians would be able to leave. They stepped out and saw half the house blown away. The wrath of fire had destroyed the entire street and they were lucky enough to have survived this attack. One by one they piled out. General Felix along with the small army of men emerged and stood around the house. Felix, Ralf, Albert, Falko, Traugott, Gregor and Frank stood side by side.

"Your house has served us well Traugott, may it come out of this misery and flourish in the coming years" Felix spoke in his deep resonating voice through the darkness. Traugott acknowledged General Felix's words and looked at his ruined house. Memories, like lightning, flashed before his eyes in quick succession, merging into one another as Traugott gave a sad smile. Now, only those remained. His house was gone, devastated beyond repair. He looked at the shattered photo frames and burnt pieces of pictures. He drew a deep breath and walked towards the waiting men. The seven of them turned around and walked into the dense smoked filled streets and disappeared.

Theodor, on his end, threw open the trap door and climbed out. He had to keep moving, he told himself. The streets were unrecognizable; the missiles had destroyed everything in sight. He stepped out and checked for approaching soldiers, but all he found was death. "We will join you" a voice close to him spoke out. "Wherever you are going, we will come" said another man as he joined them from behind.

Theodor looked behind to see the girl and her brothers climb out. "This house won't hold another attack, we will move with you" the girl spoke. "I am going to find some hospitals and shelters around the area. I am looking for someone and hope to find her in this city" he said. The two men and the girl who crept out were looking at Theodor. "Then we will go with you, on the way if we find a safe shelter we will settle there" one of the men said. Theodor nodded in response. He was not sure if he wanted these people to follow him around. On his own he could have easily travelled unnoticed. Nonetheless, he began walking and trying to make sense of the streets. Theodor along with the three civilians moved through rubble.

They took a few detours and kept to the shadows of the city. Theodor's head throbbed momentarily as events from the past hour played out in his mind. 'Those soldiers must be really crazy to believe in this sniper and his information' he thought. He kept up his pace and walked a little faster than the tailing civilians. He didn't feel like talking to anyone or answering questions. They climbed over piles of rubble and kept moving through the devastation. Ahead in the distance they could see dark profiles of big buildings. Hopefully, one of them would be a hospital where civilians were hiding. Theodor was hoping against hope that they'd avoid any further encounter with Red army soldiers.

"What about the others in houses around us?" the girl asked. One of the men walking alongside them replied "They will be fine. As long as they remain there, the attacks won't harm them and they have no weapons either. Nobody will torture them; probably just take them as prisoners of war, if anyone barges in on them." Theodor abruptly held up his hand to silence the conversation. Up ahead in the alley, he heard shouts. Instantly, he ducked behind a pile of rubble and brought out his handgun.

Together with her brothers, the girl hid beside him. "Do you have any weapons?" He asked the men in a mere whisper. "We got nothing" they replied. Theodor frowned in frustration. He slowly chanced a look beyond the pile. There was a small group of Red army soldiers huddled around a broken truck. A jeep was parked alongside; in which they'd probably been traveling. They were reloading their guns and distributing ammunition amongst themselves. Theodor swiftly ducked behind the pile again. "We need to change our route. We are too close to them. Make no noise and start moving back, retreat till that point and take the turn" Theodor whispered as he explained the route they would be taking while pointing towards the turning.

As soon as he was satisfied they had got the description, Theodor got up and started moving. All three of them followed suit. As much as possible, Theodor wanted to put as much distance as possible between him and Red army soldiers. Gregor and Frank had come to his rescue once and he didn't feel like testing his luck too far. The two men were keeping pace with Theodor as they quietly made their way back to take another route.

The girl however, was a little slow. Theodor glanced back to check on her; and in her panic to keep up with them, she slipped. A yelp escaped her and rang clearly into the night air as she fell. Theodor cursed under his breath and armed himself. He pushed the men, "Go hide" he whispered. Theodor ran to the girl and lifted her, helping her back to her feet.

Beyond the pile of rubble, the Red army soldiers heard the distinct scream. Four of them gathered and ran across the street to check the source of commotion. They climbed up the pile and spotted Theodor and the girl running in one direction while two civilians ran in the other. "Get the rifle and take those two out" a Red army soldier ordered, pointing at the civilians. "That one is a soldier, we'll go after him" he gave the orders as he looked around. "Also keep the flare ready. If there are more Nazi snipers hiding around, give the signal to unleash fire" he ordered.

Theodor was running with all his might as he half pulled, half dragged the girl across the ruined streets. His heart was beating in panic. Suddenly, there were distinct gunshots and consequent thuds of collapsing bodies. The red army soldiers had fired fatal shots, killing the escaping civilians. Theodor pushed the girl behind a broken down building and jumped after her. She was trying to hold back her tears, her brothers were probably dead. 'They were still very close to the Red army soldiers' Theodor thought as he peeked through the broken wall behind which they hid. Another gunshot echoed in the night air. Theodor's mind was racing with panic stricken thoughts. 'This was going to be difficult now.' He was clearly outnumbered. A loud round of firing erupted from nearby. Theodor and the girl both ducked. They didn't know from which side they were being attacked.

The firing stopped abruptly and a deathly silence hovered over the surroundings. They heard a distinct click as a grenade flew and landed close by. The girl's eyes widened in panic and she cried out in shock pointing at the fallen grenade. Theodor hesitated but instantly pushed aside his fear, grabbed the girl and ran past the grenade. They ran into the open where Red army soldiers were probably waiting to gun them down.

Without warning the bomb exploded, throwing both the girl and Theodor off their feet. The sound disappeared from Theodor's world as he flew in an arc and crashed to the ground with a massive thud. The intensity of the blast had been too strong. He blinked and tried to get the uncertain feeling out of his head. A loud buzzing sound built up in his head as he felt someone lifting him off his feet and holding on to him. A massive punch landed on his stomach and he instantly crouched in pain as he spat out blood. His vision was still blurred. He tried to get up and suddenly the sound rushed back to his ears, letting in a terrible scream.

He rubbed his eyes and looked to see the girl pinned down by two soldiers. "Let her go" Theodor instantly yelled. "We come in peace" he said. The girl was struggling with her captors as Theodor also tried to break free. They were surrounded by four soldiers; two of them held the girl down while the other two pointed their guns at Theodor. The girl screamed once again, trying to break free. One of the soldiers bellowed in anger and whacked her on the head with his gun. Instantly, she passed out. A deep wound appeared on her head where the gun had been directed. Theodor pulled out his gun and shot one of the soldiers.

The Red army soldier fell screaming as the bullet struck his shoulder. The other soldier swore, and with a look of anger in his eyes, opened fire as Theodor rolled across the road and crashed into a pile of debris while another soldier lunged at him. There was no time to react and Theodor was easily overpowered. The soldier punched Theodor in the face. "We come in peace" growled Theodor "let us be so" he tried to reason as he dodged the blows. By now all the Red army soldiers were free to deal with Theodor. They had abandoned the girl and converged where the small wrestle was going on.

"Now he wants peace" spoke one of the Red army soldiers. "You Nazi coward" he yelled. Two of them pinned him down easily. 'This was his end' thought Theodor as he struggled against the soldiers. He settled within himself that this would be his end. He would certainly die here. A soldier walked up to him, gun pointing straight at Theodor's heart. "You will have peace soon you Nazi filth" he said. Theodor struggled to break free and unexpectedly the girl flung herself on to the soldier. He was very quick and moved back in time catching the girl by her hair and pulling her away. "You bitch" he growled. Theodor used the diversion and tackled one of them, a shot rang through the air, he turned around and the soldier dragged the girl by her hair pointing the gun at her. "Come save her now" he yelled, challenging Theodor. The girl had a look of deep set fear in her eyes and was breathing heavily. Theodor quickly brought out the hand gun he'd gotten from Traugott. Out of nowhere, a whack landed on his head and as the blood trickled down to his mouth, he felt the metallic taste on his lips. Instantly, he turned around and shot the soldier through the chest. It was a well-targeted shot, and perfect too.

He picked up the fallen soldier's gun and faced the remaining two. He was still out numbered but the Red army soldiers were alert and a hint of fear flickered in their eyes. The obstinate soldier moved towards the girl with a vile hunger in his eyes. He tore off her overcoat as she struggled to overcome them. They were urging Theodor to react. Now, it was one gun shot that mattered either ways. Suddenly there was a sound of an approaching vehicle. 'If more Red army soldiers were joining in, then he and the girl were finished for sure' thought Theodor. Even the Red army soldiers were concerned about the approaching vehicle. They looked around questioningly to locate the sound. Theodor heard a distinct whoosh as a flare went up and lit the skies. Everyone including the Red army soldiers panicked.

"That fool, what has he done?" The Red army soldier shouted in alarm. Theodor used the momentary distraction and fired. Multiple gunshots rang at once. The girl screamed through the dead air of Berlin. Theodor was late, she had been shot. He instantly picked her up and held her in his hands, she was gasping for breath, there was blood all over her shirt and a stream of tears was pouring down her cheeks. She clutched Theodor's hand tightly as he looked at her helplessly. He didn't dare break contact with her eyes as the sound of approaching vehicle grew louder. 'Let me die here too' he thought to himself. The Red army soldier laughed away into the night. "Now you both die" he growled. There was another gunshot, a screech split through the air. Theodor turned around and bright lights flashed across his eyes. He had absolutely no time to react as the oncoming jeep rammed into him. The sound of screeching tires and a few gunshots was the last thing he heard. Everything blacked out in a bloody haze.

Fallen Army

Traugott entered the makeshift runway and informally struck a conversation with the unaware guard. "Fabian told you I'd be coming right?" he asked. The guard was surprised to see someone walk up to him and strike a casual conversation. He wasn't too sure of this old man showing up like this though. "Fabian said you had money?" The Russian questioned back and loaded his gun intimidatingly. "Of course Fabian said that" Traugott retorted sarcastically through puffs of smoke.

Ralf swiftly moved through shadows and came up from behind the Russian soldier. His powerful arms clasped around the unwary soldier's head and in a single bone crunching twist, cracked the life out of him. Traugott continued smoking his pipe as usual and looked at the dead soldier. "I said I had money. I didn't mention I'd pass it onto you" he mockingly spoke to the dead body. The small army of men made their way into the waiting Russian aircraft and tackled the small number of remaining soldiers. The aircraft was yet to be loaded with supplies and Felix wanted to use it to their advantage. Within a few minutes, they were ready for lift off with Falko piloting the aircraft while others secured their escape.

Gregor and Frank took position to gun down enemy obstructions on the runway. Felix and the others settled in the aircraft cabin. Traugott walked up to Gregor and whispered "There is a guard manning the runway. Take him down." Gregor looked confused "I thought you paid him?" he asked. "What good is money once he is dead?" Traugott chuckled. "Now kill him already." Gregor looked away in frustration and aimed. The aircraft was a modified Russian Li-2 type carrier. No German aircrafts took off from Berlin in the past few days. Most of them were gunned down and only a rumored few made it out but no one knew for sure. Traveling in a Red army aircraft was their best bet to leave Berlin undetected and safe.

Somewhere in his distant memory, Theodor knew that he shouldn't be awake, or alive for that matter. Yet, he was. Or was this all a dream?

Theodor couldn't let the girl's eyes out of his sight as they kept glaring at him with an unnatural hue. The girl stared at him through her strangely still eyes. He held on to her as the wound bled and the color from her eyes began to drain. Theodor saw the blood pooling around her and he could do nothing to hold it back. It seeped out along with her life as her eyes desaturated. She had looked to Theodor for help; she followed him out of the shelter hoping that he could protect her and now, she was wounded. A sudden shooting pain erupted through Theodor's body. The girl was slipping away from his hands and he felt a terrible need to hold on to her.

Suddenly the girl started screaming, a loud dreadful scream. It penetrated Theodor's mind filling him with immense pain. He suddenly saw Adelheid sprawled in front of him, dead and bleeding. Theodor tried to scream and control these thoughts. He tried to help her and reach out but she slipped further away. He got up startled and drenched in a cold sweat. His eyes opened up to a vague surrounding. He had a nasty gash running across his face from the impact of the vehicle. He felt new painful cuts over his body as his vision adjusted and he looked around the place. There were small oval windows throughout the room and he felt a strange vibration surge under him. He blinked, trying to think straight and get his focus back. "That's twice I saved you soldier." Ralf tossed him a water flask as he spoke "Drink it. It's all we have here." "The girl, did she live?" Theodor caught the flask and asked in between short abrupt breaths. "I am afraid not" replied Ralf. Theodor felt more pain building up at the realization. He looked around and asked "Where are we? Am I back to your operating base again?" Ralf looked back at him, considered the surroundings and replied "Nowhere near Berlin." Theodor heard a low hum of an engine running somewhere and again felt the strange vibration surge through his body. He jumped out of his makeshift bed in alarm.

"Are we on an aircraft?" he asked. The room became clear as he finally registered the information and panic flared inside him. They were enclosed in a small section within the aircraft. Ralf looked at Theodor and nodded. "Yes, we are. The girl was in a bad shape and then we rammed into you creating a lot of commotion back there. The flares were up and hurricane fire was on its way" before Ralf could complete his sentence Theodor jumped onto him. Ralf was caught off guard and lost his balance. His head whacked against the metal door as Theodor pinned him to the ground and shouted in agony "I need to get off this plane. I have to be back in Berlin. This is not where I am supposed to be" he yelled. "Don't make me do this" Ralf yelled, trying to overpower Theodor. "We had to evacuate, there was no chance of you living if you'd stayed back in Berlin" he reasoned.

In the main cabin of the aircraft sat General Felix along with Albert, Traugott, Gregor and Frank. The same intricate map from the operating base was laid out on a table along with other detailed maps of the Russian territory. The remaining area was crammed with a pile of weapons. They heard abrupt sounds from the back cabin. "Gregor please check the commotion" Felix spoke without taking his eyes off the paper he was consulting. Gregor nodded and instantly got to his feet. Before he reached the door to check, it flew open with a loud crash. Theodor was sent flying across the length of the cabin and he crashed into the opposite wall. He fell to the floor as files and boxes toppled over him. Ralf stepped out of the room, red with fury and heaving slightly. Gregor was stunned to see the two fighting as others simply looked at him and then at Theodor. "We should have let you die in Berlin" said Felix. "Did he try to kill you Ralf?" "Not really General" Ralf replied in a short grunt. Theodor slowly propped himself up against the pile trying to sit straight. Tears were swelling in his eyes as his many wounds caused pain. Ralf stared at Theodor helplessly and spoke "I am sorry soldier there is no way to transport you back to Berlin. You are a fellow German and I cannot leave one to die out there. As soon as you passed out, the skies were filled with fire from the Russians. They had unleashed hell onto us and you wouldn't have lived" he concluded. Theodor stared at the lot of them, tears now freely escaping his eyes. Everyone was silent and uncomfortable at the situation.

General Felix turned and began discussing his plan with the others as if nothing had happened. "We enter here at the forest area, it's a massive range but we know it well. Enough records were collected with regard to this area by our intelligence agencies." He placed a pointer on the map as he explained the details. Ralf was now standing next to General Felix. "Once we enter the forest you two are on your own" he said pointing at Albert and Ralf. "You both on the other hand will provide us with a good diversion" he explained pointing at Gregor and Frank. "Though we cannot have too many people entering the Russian camp, you both can sneak towards it from the opposite end. Ralf and Albert, a small trek will take you to enemy gates and from there onwards you enter the camp. We on the other hand will hopefully have made it back to right about here" General Felix said pointing at Traugott and himself as he placed another marker on the map. "You both will meet an informer by the name of Fabian on your trek and he will reveal his findings on Han's exact location" concluded Felix. The aircraft jumped slightly as it passed through a storm cloud and the radio crackled to life with an urgent voice. Falko was handling it from the cockpit and he took down the message over a consistent crackle. "General" Spoke Falko. "We will be landing soon. Two vehicles have been assaulted and arranged for drop, they will be out and waiting as we land" Falko relayed the message, consulting the timepiece on his hand. General Felix nodded curtly and went back to mission briefing. "Once you have the location you will get Han out of there, we want him with us, also procure whatever documents left to him by the Fuehrer or any other vital information that he imparts. If you fail to cross over, destroy them completely. At a point within the camp, you Albert need to branch out and hack their radio. We will be waiting outside for a signal. You need to tell us if 'the shadow' is with us or not." General Felix kept up the constant flow of information.

"How we all get out of there and back to Berlin is still being worked out. Leave that to me and Traugott."

Everyone sitting in the cabin turned grave at this statement. It was too much of a chance to take but right now, what other option did they have? "If your mission fails do not disclose your German roots, you might be spared and can live a little longer than the others. In any case you make it to friendly land on your own, trust only General Helmuth and report directly to him. And if in any case the General too collapses, then keep the procured information safe. Read the signs and when the time is right use it to the nation's advantage, else take it to the grave with you. We need these three people dead, Hitler, Himmler and Konstantin" General Felix ordered; holding up three fingers. "They know that 'Blood Moon' exists. They are currently the biggest threat to Germany and to us." Silence settled over the aircraft cabin as Felix concluded his last statement. The low hum of aircraft engines was the only audible noise in the lingering silence. "You are right General" Traugott spoke in a deep voice. He had gone silent and was not his usual quirky self. "Hitler's death will not matter if Himmler lives. They must all die" he whispered.

General Felix nodded and replied; "If and when Germania rises from the ashes of this terrible defeat I hope the actions we take today will help coming generations to live a free and peaceful life." Felix too, was void of emotions as he spoke. "Albert and Ralf, you will be transported to the drop point, your supplies will be there. Whatever arrangements are being made, we have no clue of what and who will turn hostile at which point in your mission. So use your training and be on your guard at all times. Your records have been destroyed. From now onwards you are not German soldiers, so go out there and win your freedom. Everybody's records have been erased and as of now we are all without any identity whatsoever. We have no nation to go back to and we have no home." Everybody in the aircraft looked grave as they heard General Felix talk. "As for you" General Felix said, pointing at Theodor. "Lose your uniform. You are still vulnerable. What is your name?" Everyone looked at him as he sat by the pile of boxes. "Theodor" he replied. General Felix nodded in acknowledgement and looked away. "Very well Gentlemen" Felix said getting to his feet. "We are descending and shall land shortly, we will escort Ralf and Albert to their base and Frank and Gregor to theirs, the others are free to break out" he concluded. The aircraft dipped and they felt the jolt in the cabin as the air brakes were deployed. General Felix turned around facing Theodor who silently sat in the corner. "There will be prisoner and slave convoys heading into areas around Berlin. You may take one of them and head back but you are on your own. If you are caught, do not give any of us away. I trust you, soldier." Felix bore into Theodor's eyes as he spoke to him. The others stood rapt in attention not talking or speaking to any other as Theodor silently got up and held on to the safety belts that hung loose from the aircraft ceiling. There were tear stains on his cheeks as a miserable feeling built up inside him. The aircraft wobbled as it descended further to touch down. The landing gear was deployed and they felt the immense vibrations under their feet.

A thundering sound on impact was audible as the aircraft roared onto the runway. Everyone gathered their weapons and necessary equipment. Gregor loaded his gun and stood by the aircraft door. As he turned the lock around and flung it open, the roar of engines was massive. He quickly scanned the area around their landing strip and stepped back as General Felix came ahead. The General stood by the door, his hair and clothes rippling in the wind as he looked back and shouted over the chaos "It has been an honor fighting beside you; fine soldiers." All of them instantly went into a disciplined salute. Theodor refrained and hung his head low not daring to lock eyes with the General. Felix looked at each one of them, wanting to speak but men of war are known to emote by actions and not by words. An uneasy cold settled upon them as they stood erect and proud in salute to their General. Here, they clung on to the last dregs of hope for their homeland, while the world blew it up to smithereens. General Felix glanced back at them and roared over the mighty engine sound "This be the final stand that 'Blood Moon' takes. I announce you soldiers to be the Fallen Army."

Enemy Grounds

The small army of Germans descended from the Russian aircraft as General Felix led them forward. They marched towards two command jeeps parked by the runway strip. All around them was Russian territory and for miles together, they could only see mountains and forest covered terrain. Falko was an expert pilot; they'd landed in complete darkness and there were no lights on the runway strip or the aircraft. As the army stepped out into the dark, the sudden whiff of cold rain told them that they were at a higher altitude. They could make out faint forms of people around them by the feeble ambient lights as one by one they walked towards the jeeps. It was a spectacle to watch this small band of German soldiers walk onto Russian lands at such an hour into the war.

Germany had lost to the Red army and yet these soldiers had marched to rescue a fellow sniper. Side by side to a meticulous General Felix walked Traugott who was old, arrogant and wise. Trailing behind were Ralf, Albert, Gregor and Frank who were ready with their gear to breach enemy lines. Ralf was the tallest and most muscular of all, the two snipers composed and agile while Albert was the smallest one, who wore spectacles and as well, was the least muscular of the lot. Behind them followed Falko and Theodor. Falko seemed calm and alert while Theodor was scared and shaken from his bewildering journey. A man in his mid-thirties got off from the waiting jeeps and gave General Felix a swift nod as the men came to a halt. He had an unkempt beard and was shabbily dressed. The jeeps he had procured were typical 'type 82 jeeps', German made but taken over and currently used by the Red army. Theodor looked at the jeeps and thought about the solid metal that hit him. Two soldiers were dragged out from the back of a jeep and placed next to the waiting lot of people. General Felix eyed the gagged soldiers and asked "Are they important enough? Did they divulge anything?" "Maggots are better than these bastards." The man who had procured the jeeps spat on the gagged soldiers replying angrily. "All we know for sure is that Han is captured and within the camp. These two have no idea where he might be or if he is still alive. Also, the security is very low right now. More soldiers have been retreating further back into Russian territory" the man divulged all that he knew. General Felix observed him carefully before talking again. "Falko" he commanded. "You know what to do with these men." Falko instantly swung into action and dragged the bound Russian soldiers away from where the others were standing. He pulled out a hip flask and doused a wad of cloth with foul smelling fluid. He snuffed the gagged soldiers unconscious and dragged them towards the aircraft.

"Two groups" Felix spoke with complete authority as he addressed the soldiers. Theodor snapped back to his senses looking away from Falko. Everyone was intently listening to Felix once again. The wind had stopped, the forests were unnaturally quiet and the mountains stood still and looming as ever. The General had an unnerving knack of commanding attention as everything fell quite around them. "One takes this jeep and heads into deeper territory as planned. The other transports the snipers" he said. Theodor was confused 'How was he to get out of this mess now?' he thought. "Traugott, you will accompany Frank and Gregor to their vantage point. I will take Albert and Ralf to theirs" Felix gave the final orders and looked at everyone. The soldier who had procured the jeeps turned to General Felix and asked in a soft voice "What remains of Berlin, General?" Everybody silently looked at him. "It has been razed to the ground. The very air is filled with death" Felix replied. Everyone stood still, their eyes holding powerful emotions. Soldiers of war, soldiers of their homeland and now they were lost. Forgotten names, without any identity whatsoever, stood on enemy grounds hoping to carve the last change and hope for their kin. No one in the world was to know that a small army of German soldiers was making its way to a hidden undercover Russian camp to rescue Adolf Hitler's shadow.

Ralf and Albert loaded their ammunition and climbed into the jeep with Felix. Theodor stood there as he momentarily watched them settle in. He was still contemplating his escape, going ahead with the convoy would put him in imminent danger and by that, there was no way he would survive. Being on his own would help him be discreet; but for how long could he last on enemy grounds? Theodor noticed Falko who was bent low around a map, discussing something with the soldier who'd procured the jeeps. Falko consulted the map and drew lines over it to trace out a route.

He sensed Theodor approaching and without turning around he spoke "This aircraft is not heading towards Berlin Theodor." Theodor was taken aback at the abrupt statement. Falko turned to look at him. "I am sorry for your dilemma soldier. Ralf saved your life. You would be dead had he not put you on the aircraft. That is good and bad both for the situation that you are in. If you wish to fly with us, you may" saying this he went back to consulting the map. Theodor stood frozen in place. He was horribly stuck and could see no way out of this. An overwhelming sense of helplessness was gripping him from within. It was like being crushed under the burden of his decisions. He silently cursed himself for walking into the house and having met this band of soldiers. A clean death would have done him better than being stuck in this labyrinth of a situation. Every step he took now would put him through more trouble. Theodor stared at Falko as he plotted and then stole a glance towards the jeeps. Once both set of troops left, he was on his own and had no help to find a way back. His head was throbbing as he tried hard to think of a way to safely get back to Berlin.

At the end of the runway strip the jeeps hammered to life. Falko, Theodor and the soldier stared at the members in the jeeps. This was it, their final stand. It was an intense moment; their eyes held wave after wave of emotion and chances were that none of them would be seeing each other again. Theodor stood there, thinking to himself 'as to how this mission would end? How the others would fare and what the world would do to them?' All of this was a big enigma; one without any answers. Felix had discharged others from duty. They were free men and could now go their separate ways.

The two jeeps took off into the forest covered streets, General Felix in the lead while Traugott closely following them. Falko took charge and said "Let us head to the aircraft." He pointed towards the waiting plane and rolled the map. Theodor snapped out of his thoughts and looked at Falko. "I will fly with you. Wherever you head to, I will find a way back to Berlin from there" he said. Falko considered Theodor for a moment and nodded in acknowledgement.

In the spur of the moment Theodor thought that it was the wisest thing to do. Even if the aircraft took him further away from Berlin, he could still hope to survive and somehow get back. Hurriedly they walked towards the waiting aircraft. They heard a faint roar of an approaching airplane. "It must be the other aircraft" Falko whispered, "Hurry up and prepare for lift off." They all ran into the aircraft and pulled the unconscious Russian soldiers onto it. "We are going to fly low and descend over a village that is closest from here" Falko explained their journey. "We are behind enemy lines even now. Our only hope is this Russian aircraft that we are flying in. The flight should last us a mere twenty minutes. We might need these two once we land, so secure them properly" Falko ordered and pointed to the bound soldiers. "We hope to land into a nearby village. The villagers have been relocated and there are hardly any forces left. That should help us land safely" he said. Theodor nodded as he took instructions from Falko in rapt attention. "Nothing on this mission will work as planned, so everyone is on their own from here onwards" he said. "The other plane is headed for this runway strip and they will soon know that there is a missing aircraft, so let's fly." Falko clapped his hands and made a swooping motion. The soldier introduced himself as Edward and asked Theodor to help him drag the unconscious soldiers. Theodor helped as they dragged the sack of bodies and fastened them with belts. They felt a sudden jolt inside the aircraft as the engines roared at full throttle. The aircraft began to turn getting ready for takeoff.

General Felix was talking to Ralf and Albert as he drove through the darkness, his voice heavy and tense. "Ralf and Albert, you have mission briefings fixed in your heads. You will meet Fabian at the discussed site. He is posted there to brief you, once done you will follow his lead into the Russian camp. In any case you do not meet him; you are on your own. Do not abandon the mission; much depends on it. General Helmuth has sworn that he will provide safe passage once you accomplish this task" Felix spoke without taking his eyes off the road. "You will earn your freedom soldiers; keep your trust in General Helmuth." Felix hit the pedal harder as he concluded. Traugott followed closely as he kept up with General Felix's jeep. They were both driving minus any lights and were extremely vigilant. They dodged the rough terrain with utmost ease and precision.

There was a buildup of excitement at the Russian camp. The soldiers had piled into jeeps and trucks. They were to head to the landing strip to receive an aircraft loaded with "important supplies"; as instructed by their fiery new leader Fedor. One big convoy was heading straight to the drop point and two jeeps were to travel around the valley to check for possible ambush. Fedor had decided to go ahead with the main convoy. He did not want the material to be harmed or tampered in any way. A lean soldier by the name of Fabian entered a small jeep that was to do rounds of the terrain along with another. Both jeeps were allotted two soldiers each. The front gates of the Russian camp opened up and a convoy of vehicles emerged from it. A bigger convoy led by Fedor moved towards the landing strip and two jeeps moved in the opposite direction for their reconnaissance.

Within a few minutes, both jeeps, each of which was driven by General Felix and Traugott had entered deeper into Russian territory. The ambient temperature further dropped in cover of massive trees. The jeeps were going at a good speed, their lights were out and the only sound was that of crunching gravel and running engines. The roads went winding around the mountain as they drove deeper into enemy grounds. Traugott looked out into the forests. He could barely make out anything in the darkness. Once inside the valley, they were to break off from the other jeep and divert. They quickly covered the road that bended towards the valley and General Felix slowed down his jeep. As Traugott drove ahead, both jeeps were positioned side by side as they were being driven. Ralf and Albert both had their rifles out and were alert. General Felix looked at them and nodded in acknowledgement.

Traugott, Gregor and Frank went up in a short salute as their jeep took a sharp turn; branching off into the other route. The moon showed through the clouds and bathed the entire forest range in a serene silver glow. Here, in the middle of a dense forest cover; the two teams parted ways. Gregor loaded his rifle and took the front seat. He looked out to see the other jeep going into the deeper valley road and scanned around to spot any disturbances.

The aircraft ran the length of the runway and took off into Russian skies. Everyone inside was now tense and alert. Falko asked Theodor and Edward to take up arms and be on the lookout for trouble. They were flying in complete darkness. Theodor loaded his weapons and looked out the window to see moonlight cover the forest tops in a soft silver glow. The aircraft maintained a low altitude and flew a few feet above the tree tops as Falko cruised with expert precision.

The Russian patrol jeep headed towards forest covered lands. Fabian drove around the periphery of mountains. His eyes were steady and fixed on the road. They hit a narrow patch of road as they drove through the forests, scanning for signs of trouble. Fabian slowly turned around and looked at his fellow soldier. The soldier sat next to him with a loaded rifle in his hand. In a swift move, Fabian whipped out his knife and thrust it through the unwary soldier's throat. It was a quick, effortless and slick move; after which. Fabian continued driving through the rash terrain as if nothing had happened. The soldier twitched and his lifeless body fell off the car. Fabian accelerated and quickly drove to the topmost point of the terrain. He killed the engine and his surroundings fell unnaturally quiet as he got out of the jeep to scan the forests. An eerie sense of calm had fallen over the forests, and some leaves moved in tandem with Fabian's breathing pattern. His trained ears picked up the sound of a car and he instantly spotted an approaching jeep far below. He got his binoculars out and adjusted them for a better view.

He was right. A jeep was headed towards the check post. Was that another jeep that just caught his eye? Far away he could see it crashing through the forest and the convoy headed by Fedor which was moving in the opposite direction, towards the landing strip. He continued scanning the area when he noticed an aircraft flying low on the forest lands. He scanned once again and scowled in concern. There were too many activities going on around him and all of these hinted at trouble. His understanding with General Felix was that one jeep would arrive. He had no idea about the other simultaneous activities in the forests.

"Fabian has been informed only about you entering. He doesn't know that more members of Blood Moon will be around. It is necessary to withhold information at every point" General Felix whispered as he slowed down on the extremely narrow road. He continued driving through the rocky terrain and suddenly a gunshot echoed through the forest. They panicked and turned around searching for approaching soldiers. Far into the forest valley below, Ralf thought he spotted the other jeep. He panicked and strained his eyes to get a better view. The jeep was covering ground in haste and they were probably being shot at. General Felix floored the accelerator and sped into a dangerously narrow terrain leading towards their destination. A few more 'cracks' were clearly audible through the silence. Ralf's eyes widened in shock, 'the other team was probably being fired at' he thought.

Fabian looked through his binoculars in time to see that the patrol jeep had spotted an intruding vehicle. He quickly adjusted his binoculars to get a better view. He was confused as to which was Felix's jeep. 'The others' he thought 'will have to fend for themselves.' His aim was to get Felix and his team inside.

Fedor along with his convoy had reached the landing strip. The aircraft had arrived on time. It went a little off track while landing and there was panic build up within the soldiers. If anything happened to the contents of this aircraft, Konstantin would have their heads. The aircraft was parked close to the cliff's edge. The ground soldiers piled out of their trucks and circled the aircraft completely. Fedor walked up to the waiting pilot who descended from the plane. "Where is the other aircraft?" he asked with authority.

"Ambushed in Berlin" replied the pilot. "Must have flown off course too, we never saw it." Fedor was eyeing him suspiciously. "And the material to be brought" he asked "where is it?" "Everything that was asked for is secure with us. A few boxes might have been on the other aircraft but we have most of it" the pilot replied pointing at the aircraft. Fedor was not convinced of the situation. "Why didn't you radio?" he pressed his questions. "We did, there was no response from the camp" the pilot replied. "Damn Konstantin" Fedor muttered under his breath and ordered the guards to unload materials from the aircraft. The armored trucks were lined close to the aircraft and soldiers began to evacuate metal containers from it. "How many containers can you see?" Fedor questioned a soldier waiting at the aircraft gate. He looked inside, trying to roughly gauge the number of containers with his eyes. "Easily over a fifty" he replied. Fedor nodded in acknowledgement and spread out soldiers around the landing strip. "No one gets close to the aircraft or the containers" Fedor commanded. "Anyone who breaks ranks will be disposed" his voice abruptly stopped as his ears picked up a distinct loud 'crack' in the forests.

Gregor scanned the forest area as he avoided the frenzy of flying bullets. A lone Russian jeep was on their tail and Gregor could see bright sparks behind them as the oncoming bullets scraped metal. Traugott sped into the forest and went off road, taking the jeep deeper into dense terrain. Gregor and Frank were trying to precisely take out the soldier from within the enemy jeep; whereas the Russian soldier was ruthlessly firing.

Another gunshot echoed through the forests and a loud burst was heard through the commotion. Their jeep swerved out of control and scraped a tree bark as it sped through the forest with its rear wheel ripped. Bright red sparks emanated from the exposed rim of the wheel as it hit gravel. The jeep advanced up to a narrow clearing. In the meanwhile, Gregor managed to shoot the front wheel of the enemy jeep. The Russian jeep too spun out of control from the sudden onslaught.

Traugott was finding it difficult to keep driving with their burst wheel. On the other hand, Gregor and Frank were having difficulty aiming as the jeep crashed through uneven territory. Few more rounds of fire were let loose from the Russian jeep as it persistently caught up. Frank held his stance through the chaos and composed his breathing. He spotted the soldier through his scope and fired. It was an extremely precise shot which took the soldier down instantly. As he fell, the driver was left alone to tackle them now. The Russian slowed down a bit and this put a bigger gap between the two jeeps.

"I think he is slowing down" Frank shouted through the noise. Traugott kept up his reckless speed nonetheless. "This is not good. We'll jeopardize the mission" Gregor shot back. "We need to keep them busy till Albert and Ralf reach the camp" said Frank. "We are not here to merely distract them. We should have been more careful" Traugott replied without taking his eyes off the road. Suddenly out of nowhere, the Russian jeep crashed back towards them through the forest and the driver started firing.

Traugott instantly took a sharp turn to disorient the tailing driver. Gregor whacked his head on the roll cage of the jeep as it turned. Bullets rained on them randomly as the Russian inexorably fired. Gregor ducked, trying to avoid the oncoming fire and felt a warm liquid gush onto his hands. Before he came to a realization of anything, the jeep hit a huge boulder and went airborne. In the frenzy of chase; they had reached the edge of the valley and were now falling down through it. The jeep plummeted fifty odd feet into the gorge and crashed into a thick clump of trees. The front glass smashed onto them and they were suspended as the jeep came to a sudden halt. Gregor tried to get up and comprehend the situation as he adjusted his eyes to once again, scan the jeep. His head, where the roll cage had hit him was hurting and throbbing. To his horror he saw Frank, who lay defeated as his body fell forward, lifeless and cold. There was a deep bullet wound on his chest. Panic gripped Gregor as his current situation became clearer. A stray bullet had found refuge in Frank. When the jeep hit the rough patch on the road, Gregor was dislodged from his position and made way for the bullet to pass through and hit Frank. Gregor tried to calm down and look for Traugott. He slowly moved and chanced a peak downwards. Traugott hung in the air holding on to the front door of the jeep connected to a single hinge.

Meanwhile, oblivious of what was happening around them, Theodor, Falko and Edward were huddled inside the cockpit discussing routes on the map, trying to figure their best landing spots. Theodor's mind was working in overdrive as he scanned the map and tried to mentally place his routes to reach Berlin. They were engrossed in the map when a sudden loud gun shot rang and sparks went up in the cockpit panel ahead. Panic stricken, they turned around and ducked in reflex.

One of the Russian soldiers had regained consciousness and was somehow free from his bonds. He stood there; pointing a gun at them. Falko slowly shifted his hand towards his gun. The Russian had bloodshot red eyes and looked disoriented. A tense moment passed and nothing happened. Then, without warning the Russian soldier shot and before anyone could react the bullet hit Falko's arm. He screamed in pain and Edward instantly lunged at the Russian trying to tackle him. Theodor held onto the controls of the aircraft helping Falko steer and balance it through the low altitude flight. Edward was trying to tackle the Russian away from the cockpit to avoid bullets from hitting aircraft controls. The Russian however was resilient and kept up the wild firing. Bullets ricocheted off the fuselage interior and Theodor instinctively ducked as a bullet damaged the aircraft console.

Sparks emanated and the alarms instantly began to flash. Falko was losing a lot of blood but he held on to the controls as he tried to stabilize the aircraft. Before Theodor could react further, the plane jerked violently and he was knocked off his feet. The aircraft banked and turned out of control as Falko frantically tried to keep it steady. He turned the aircraft in the opposite direction to balance the bank. It took a steep turn and everyone slid in the direction of the bank.

Theodor was now out in the fuselage as he jumped to help tackle the Russian soldier. By now, the Russian had regained full consciousness and was landing swift, successive punches on Theodor and Edward. He picked up his fallen gun and fired at Theodor. Theodor dodged the ruthless assault as the bullets ruptured a few overhead pipes and a gate lock in frenzy. The Russian was facing two soldiers and was out of ammunition but before Theodor or Edward could react; he jumped and grabbed the gate lock. The bullet hit had made it weak and with the sudden force it gave away.

Theodor jumped forward to tackle the Russian and they collided as the aircraft jerked violently throwing open the gate. The sudden pressure fluctuations were fierce; throwing everyone off their feet. Theodor and the Russian soldier engaged in hand combat and crashed through the aircraft's interior. Falko and Edward were holding on to all they could to avoid being sucked out the door as the aircraft was now completely out of control.

The Russian soldier fell onto one side, holding on to the safety belts hanging from the ceiling. Everyone was being thrown around like rag dolls as the pressure varied and the aircraft experienced severe jolts. Alarms flared up as they rapidly lost altitude and were flying dangerously close to the tree tops. In a moment of confusion, both Theodor and Edward latched onto the Russian, landing punches on his face and belly. His hand let go of the belt as he crashed through the fuselage. The aircraft dipped further and banked out of control. The Russian soldier was desperately trying to hold onto something and he grabbed Theodor's foot. Theodor panicked as he fervently held on to the ceiling belts. The pressure fluctuation was intense and the belt gave away. Edward tried to reach out and help Theodor but he was too late. In the next instant Theodor along with the Russian soldier went crashing through the fuselage and was sucked out from the open gate.

The gun shots were clearly heard throughout the forest and Fedor was tensed. He quickly dispatched a jeep with two soldiers to reach Konstantin and give him an update on the state of commotion. Fedor was growing restless as he himself wanted to inspect the source and reason for firing. He obviously couldn't abandon this material and leave. "Hurry up with the containers" he ordered in anger. His eyes and ears were alert for any source of commotion and he picked up a low hum of an aircraft engine. 'Was the second aircraft approaching?' He thought and scanned the skies for oncoming aircrafts. Suddenly a huge explosion flared up and a fireball of smoke erupted from the forests below them. The soldiers took firing positions and Fabian ran towards the cliff to see the explosion. He stood at the very edge 'The plane that went off course was spotted' he thought. The forests lit up momentarily as the skies glowed red with fire that burst forth. Fedor felt an immense heat wave sweep through the burning forest winds.

Theodor was pulled out of the aircraft, instantly losing grip of the Russian soldier. They both parted as they flew a short distance and helplessly waited for gravity to finish its act. The Russian soldier disappeared somewhere in the trees and Theodor too felt the impact as his body smashed through the trees. His momentum instantly broke as he crashed through branches, trying in vain to grab something. Gradually he slowed down as the branches got thicker. He whacked his head against a particularly thick bark as he struggled to hold on to something. His vision blurred and he tasted blood as his hands gave away letting himself helplessly fall towards the forest floor.

A jeep reached the Russian camp gates and two soldiers ran towards it. The gates opened to reveal Konstantin already waiting there. "What happened?" he shouted in anger. "There seem to be intruders my lord" the soldier replied. Konstantin's eyes narrowed in fury at the statement. "Where is Fedor?" he asked. "He is guarding the consignment" replied the soldier. "Shut the gates, alert the guards and unleash our hounds into the forests." Konstantin's temper was peaking. "I will not have more Nazis' infiltrate my camp!" he roared.

The clump of trees creaked and groaned at the slightest movement. Gregor had managed to get out of the jeep. He reached a thick bark and helped Traugott climb down. They slowly walked away from the suspended jeep and had almost made it to the lower branch when a sudden noise ripped through the air. The branches holding the jeep broke and the jeep came crashing down. It plummeted towards the ground and hit the branch on which they were standing. The branch bent forward and sprung up instantly releasing its pent up energy. Both Gregor and Traugott were thrown into the air. They rose a few feet before they began their fifty foot fall. With a massive crash, they landed on the ground along with the jeep. The jeep lay there in a crumpled heap of mess as Gregor and Traugott fell right next to it, sprawled eagle on the forest floor.

Konstantin armed himself and strode in the middle of his camp like a predator on guard, daring intruders to come closer. Whatever temporary electricity had been restored was used to put lights around the camp area. On the landing strip, Fedor was standing close to the aircraft keeping watch over it with his unwavering gaze. Deep within the forests, Theodor lay on the floor, unconscious from his fall. General Felix, Ralf and Albert had abandoned their jeep and were waiting to meet Fabian at the check post. Traugott and Gregor were stirring back to their senses from the fifty foot fall. All of them had one thing in common. They were all on the same enemy grounds; grounds which were under Konstantin's vehement watch.

Wise Old Soldier

Traugott and Gregor swiftly gathered themselves; dusted themselves up and picked up their weapons from the forest floor. Both of them were shaken by the abrupt fall. Gregor quickly ran to the crumpled vehicle and pulled open the door. He dreaded the sight as he looked inside and pulled out Frank's defeated body from the rutted vehicle. Traugott too had come next to him as he helped get Frank's body out. There was a deep bullet wound and a trail of blood that flowed around the body.

Slowly and carefully, they laid Frank on the soft mud and closed his eyes shut. His body sank a few inches into the wet mud as the rain began to pour and soak everything around. Gregor crouched low beside Frank, lost in thought for a brief moment. Traugott was tapping his foot around to feel the ground. A few feet away, he found a small puddle of muck. Gregor eyed Traugott, trying to figure out what he was looking for. Traugott bent low to pick Frank. "Help me" he said as he grabbed on to Frank. Gregor exhaled deeply, uttering a small prayer under his breath before helping Traugott. They lifted Frank and carried him the short distance to lay him on the puddle which was the size of a full grown human. Gregor dashed back and took Frank's rifle from the crumpled heap of metal that was once their jeep. He kept it on his body and watched in disbelief as Frank's lifeless and defeated body sank into the puddle. Traugott pulled the rifle away from Frank's body. "Honor his life, use this" he said as he handed the rifle back to Gregor. The rain seemed to be pushing Frank's body down with its might. Gregor nodded and took the rifle as the muck slowly crept forward covering Frank's body. Within a minute, it completely disappeared from sight and sank into the puddle. A few bubbles erupted from the muck as the body made its way down. Traugott laid a hand on Gregor's shoulder. "We have to move" he whispered. The anger inside Gregor was building up. He had trained with Frank for so many years. They had worked as a team, protected the Fuehrer and now, here lay Frank. Defeated and disposed in a puddle of muck, miles away from home. Gregor was lost in his thoughts when a loud shout rang through the forests behind them. Gregor clenched his jaw in anger and told himself that 'he would do everything in his power to avenge his fellow soldier's death.' He and Traugott both gathered their weapons and dashed away into the dark forests.

Fedor was extremely restless; he dispatched a few more soldiers to inform Konstantin of the aircraft crash and random gunshots. He was burning in fury. Anything at all, that slipped away from his control bothered him endlessly. These gunshots and aircraft crashes were testing his patience to the hilt. On the other hand, the containers were heavy and taking forever to unload. The soldiers were trying hard to carefully get them into trucks but the rain made things worse for them. It also doused the sounds around making it difficult for him to keep track of movements in the forest range. The fire from the aircraft blast had died down and a thick trail of black smoke rose from the forests. Fedor could feel the burnt smell in the air as he sniffed. He was alert and constantly looking out for unusual sounds or sights around them. He kept moving around, his eyes scanning the forests hoping to spot something. Suddenly a crack was heard followed by a loud crash. Fedor quickly turned around to see that one of the soldiers had slipped from the aircraft staircase.

In the next instant, a series of sounds erupted through the forests. The soldier let out a yelp as the case fell from his hand and crashed to the ground. Fedor was so enraged that he didn't think twice. He pulled out his gun and shot through the soldier's head. "Shut up" he screamed through the rain. Every sound that his ear could pick up was important and the wailing soldier only made it worse. "You, outer line of soldiers, disperse into the forests and find the source of firing" Fedor hollered through the pounding rain.

The soldiers standing guard in the outer circle instantly got to action and ran towards the forests. "The second line, move ten steps back and secure the landing strip. The inner line, tighten the circle and let no one in. I will have your heads if you falter. Even if a fucking Nazi battle tank moves towards you, you will not falter" he commanded. The soldiers panicked but obeyed every command. They were alert and tense about the situation. They formed a human wall around the aircraft. In a single uniform clang they loaded their guns and stood guard. Fedor's anxiety was ebbing and he couldn't do anything but wait. He glanced around restlessly as the set of soldiers continued transferring material into the waiting trucks.

A jeep reached the camp and two soldiers dashed out of it. They ran towards the center where Konstantin was standing. "My lord, an aircraft has crashed. We saw it and on our way here we heard gunshots in the forests" the soldier spoke and stood in salute. Konstantin had his eyes closed and was soaking wet from the rain. He maintained his poise through the soldier's information. His features turned grim but he was trying to control his rage. The soldiers were too scared to address him further and waited for him to speak.

Viktor too had reached his side and was patiently waiting for him to react. A few seconds passed as Konstantin stood under the rain; he gently opened his eyes and clenched his fists. Blood still oozed from the bullet wound on his arm. "Reinforce the landing strip." He was taking measured breaths through the inundating rain as he ordered. The downpour seemed to be dissipating his anger as he stood there soaking in it. He slowly opened his eyes and looked up to a giant black light tower that stood in front of him. The soldiers were restoring electric supply to the tower so it could be functional. "Send a few men to inspect the aircraft and ask Fedor to hurry up with my consignment." Konstantin's hand quivered in anger as he gave orders. "Find me these Nazi bastards" he commanded and unexpectedly looked the soldier in his eye. The soldier froze at his menacing stare. "Take as many men as you need. I will personally stand guard to our fortress" Konstantin ordered. "Yes, my lord" was all that the scared soldier could mutter under Konstantin's cold stare. He gave his salute and swiftly ran away with the other soldier to recruit more men. Konstantin stood there, letting the rain soak into his very skin.

Both Gregor and Traugott were dashing through the dense forests. Three Red army soldiers had spotted them and were trying to take them down as they ran away from the campsite. Traugott was extremely agile and quick for his age as he dodged the trees with utmost ease. They hit a small protrusion and climbed up as fast as they could. Their plan was to lead the Russians away from the campsite so the other team could infiltrate, though they had no idea as to where the team had reached. The Russian soldiers were close on their trail and fired persistently. Traugott and Gregor were desperately thinking of measures to curb the assault. Gregor heard more footsteps through the forest. 'If more Red army soldiers were joining the hunt, it would spell instant death for him and Traugott' he thought. Suddenly there was a loud bustle in the trees and before they could react, from within the tree cover emerged Ralf, Albert and General Felix.

All of them were shocked to see one another but before they could talk or gesture, more gun shots followed. The company of men that had dispersed minutes ago was once again re-united. General Felix, Ralf and Albert had to abandon their spot because Fabian hadn't shown up yet and it was impossible to take the jeep further into the thick forests. It also seemed that the Red army soldiers were hunting them down in a pattern that led both teams to converge in the same area. The five of them dashed through trees dodging the attacks. No thoughts were going on in their minds but the very instinct to survive enemy onslaught. They didn't bother looking behind as barks of trees were being ripped apart by stray bullets. The bullets went whizzing past their ears at intervals as they ducked and stumbled but kept up the frantic pace.

A Russian jeep came to a halt at the landing base. More soldiers poured out of the jeep and a truck that followed. Fedor looked in anticipation, expecting Konstantin to ride out but to his relief only soldiers marched his way. He instantly directed them to the aircraft as more hands were always welcome to unload the nuclear material. Fedor was waiting for the batch of soldiers that he had dispatched to come back with answers. He checked the progress on the transfer and just one truck remained to be filled with material. Fedor made another small team of five soldiers and dispatched them to check the crashed aircraft site. He wanted to inspect the area on his own but was tied down until this material didn't reach the camp. He ordered them to fan the site, "whatever you find, report directly to me" Fedor's orders were stern and clear as the soldiers nodded in unison and dispersed.

Ralf, Albert, Felix along with Gregor and Traugott were running recklessly through the forests. Traugott noticed as General Felix slowed down in exhaustion. They were running dangerously close to the edge of a high rise mountain and if they kept up the chase, they would probably end up being cornered by Red army soldiers. Traugott fell back and ran alongside Felix. "We need to break ranks; General" he spoke in a whisper through the disarray and abruptly turned around.

It was a quick maneuver as he pulled out his weapons and fired at the Red army soldiers. Felix understood what he was doing and followed suit. Traugott cut through enemy defense as he fired from behind the thick tree cover. Felix covered the opposite side and made sure that the others got further away. The unaware Red army soldiers were falling prey to Traugott and Felix's sudden assault but the Germans could keep it up only till their element of surprise remained. "General, make sure they get in. I can handle them for now and don't let them corner you" Traugott shouted through the commotion of gun shots and rain. General Felix took out another Russian soldier and ran across to clear the way for his team. Gregor had fallen behind to help Felix as they teamed up and broke the line of approaching Red army soldiers. Felix chanced a look at Ralf and Albert who were now a good distance away and then he checked on Traugott who was putting up an impressive fight. The Red army soldiers were getting closer to Traugott and his fight had moved to a hand combat. Felix reloaded his ammunition and along with Gregor dismantled the approaching Russian units.

The soldiers were closing in on Traugott as he swiftly dodged and rained down bullets on them. More and more Red army soldiers were joining this battle now. Traugott, suave; was single handedly taking them out as he ferociously fought the swarm of Russians. General Felix kept up the merciless firing along with Gregor as they took out a good number of soldiers from their vantage point. Traugott tackled another Red army soldier; punching him squarely in the face. He kicked and rammed through two of them fiercely as they tried to tackle him from behind.

Felix glanced over his shoulder to see Traugott's aggressive battle unfold. Out of nowhere, a heftily built soldier jumped and smashed Traugott's side with a massive kick. They were fighting dangerously close to the edge and Traugott was thrown off his feet. In the small window that they got, another Red army soldier fired and the bullet hit Traugott's arm. He screamed in pain at the sudden attack and fell back from the assault. The Red army attack strengthened as they fired wildly to take him down. Traugott stumbled and fell off the cliff to evade the bullets. His face held shock and pain but the fire in his eyes was undiminished as he rose in an arc over the cliff. The wise old soldier traversed a few feet through air before disappearing silently behind the foliage and into the endless valley down below.

Howling Dawn

Theodor stirred as he regained consciousness from his massive fall. He opened his eyes to look around. How strange was it that each time he got hit on the head he somehow landed up in strange new surroundings? All around him, as his eyes adjusted to the darkness, were tall, ominous trees towering above him.

His entire body was designed with several cuts, from his head to his toe. As fresh blood oozed from each wound site, it stung, and he let out a little whelp. Soldier or not, he had pain receptors!

He felt some more pain. A few of the thinner wooden splinters had lodged deep into his flesh. Theodor moved sluggishly as he groaned in pain, sitting upright on the forest floor. His brain was fogged and disoriented from the constant trauma. He jolted back to consciousness and shook his head; pushing himself to his feet with all his might. Everything around was disorienting and he saw little stars fill up his vision.

He wobbled slightly as he lost control, afraid that he might have broken some bones. But his feet held true, he could stand on both his legs and he did so as he slowly regained awareness. With a sigh of relief, he sluggishly dragged himself behind a huge rock and held it for support. The soft foliage layer on the forest floor coupled with massive tree branches helped him survive the otherwise fatal fall. Theodor removed a small pouch from his belt and pulled out a flask from it. Without giving it a second thought, he uncorked it and poured the alcohol over his wounds. Stinging pain shot up through his entire body as cold fluid made contact with various wounds.

He removed his shirt and drenched his injuries in alcohol, biting his own fist in the ordeal to muffle his scream. He was breathing heavily and with great difficulty. Theodor looked around to see where he was. It was impossible to figure his exact location as he had no idea of where the airplane had turned and at which point he had gotten thrown out. The forests around him looked daunting. Suddenly, he heard a "crack" sound. It gave the distinct impression that someone had stepped over a dead bark. Theodor instantly ducked and crawled out from behind the huge rock. Slowly he gathered himself and ran away from the source of the sound.

'Were these forests guarded by the Russian army? Was he heading into the camp or away from it?' Thoughts raced in his mind and there was no way he could tell. He just kept moving, distancing himself from the noise as the forests stood terribly still otherwise. The winds were dead and damp with rain and everything else stood still under the massive trees. Theodor shivered as the cold penetrated his skin and he continued moving deeper into the forests. The stillness was killing him as it pressed on his mind. His senses were highly alert now; with his ears picking up the slightest of noises and his eyes, the smallest of movements. In the absolute silence, like a loud gunshot, he heard a menacing bark.

Theodor's heart picked up speed and was beating against his rib cage rapidly. 'Guard dogs, Red army guard dogs in the forests' he thought. Theodor didn't take another second to think or react as he instantly jumped and dashed into the forests. He dodged trees and rocks speeding past them in a blur of motion. The dog barks got louder and more distinct. He tried to put as much distance as he could between himself and the direction of barks. He dodged and ran around a few trees, hoping to put up a fake scent trail for the dogs. There was little rain and the damp grounds would hopefully make it difficult for those dogs to stay on his scent. His wounds were paining and stinging from the strain and cold. As Theodor became more alert, the actual intensity of pain began to shoot through his body. Nonetheless he kept up his relentless pace. The dog barks were crisp through the otherwise silent forests and he had no idea if he was running away from or into the Russian camp.

Far away in the Russian camp; Konstantin waited rather impatiently for electric supply to be restored to the main light tower which stood looming in the center of his camp. The team was just a few minutes away from fixing the supply as Konstantin inspected forces and stood guard to his camp. 'These Nazi's are like swarms of ants. No matter how hard you thwart them, they keep coming back' Konstantin was thinking to himself as he continued inspecting the area. Viktor came running to him and stopped in his tracks to give a quick salute. In-between breaths he spoke "There has been a lot of commotion in the forests my lord, requesting diversion of more forces. None of them have reported back as yet" Viktor reported and waited for a response. "Don't break ranks Viktor; that is exactly what they want us to do. If we draw everyone away it will be easy for them to enter. Take more men but make sure the shift changes are monitored. Brace yourself and be prepared for whatever intrusion this is, we will thwart them at all costs" Konstantin replied as he continued to inspect the thick wires that ran on the camp floor. "What about the surrounding area? Have you inspected it thoroughly?" Konstantin asked. "Yes my lord, it has been inspected and burnt to the ground. Any remaining dynamite, fuse wires or signs that Han might have laid would have been disabled by the fire that we spread through the forests" he replied. Konstantin nodded in appreciation as he watched the guards at work. The Red army forces had managed to restore water supply via a pump in the underground tunnels and now they were fixing electric supply throughout the camp. "My lord" a soldier shouted from far above. "The tower is ready to be lit up." A flash of lightening lit the camp area momentarily as rains picked up intensity once again. Konstantin smirked and looked up at the tower. Although it would be daylight in a few minutes, he wanted to flood the forests with light. He held his hand out signaling that the light be brought to life.

Theodor was tired from the relentless run. He slowed down due to exhaustion. The dogs however were still on his trail. Their intense barks were getting closer with each passing second. He came around a clearing of sorts and tried to catch his breath. The barking had momentarily stopped and rains were lashing down heavily. The cold was creeping into his wounded body as he tried to rub himself and generate some heat. In the next instant, a blinding flash of light met his eyes and he jumped to take refuge behind a huge tree. He fell from the abrupt movement, splashing into the muck as he flailed around. He thrashed through muck and climbed out of the small pool as he caught a glimpse of a huge tower that stood far away from where he was.

The massive beam of light was sweeping through the forests lighting up everything that stood in its way. The trees and forests looked even more eerie and intimidating through shadows cast by the beam. The barking was now dangerously close to where Theodor was. The Red army had protected their areas very well. Hunting dogs were strategically unleashed far away from the camp and were trained to drive intruders towards, rather than away from it. The barks continued to echo and move closer. Theodor panicked and closed his eyes to think straight. This really left him with no other option as he gathered himself and ran cutting through the trees and moving straight ahead. Not going towards the camp or the dogs, he ran diagonally. The dog barks were louder with every step he took and suddenly Theodor glimpsed a massive hunting dog running right at him. He dodged the trees and the beam of light as it swept at mechanical intervals.

In his frenzy, Theodor didn't realize a wire sticking out of the ground. His foot caught up in the wire and he stumbled. His heart pace quickened. 'If it was a trap wire, he was dead for sure' he thought as he crashed to the ground and slid along the foliage; his head ramming into something hard. Theodor waited for some sort of an alarm or an explosion to rip him apart any moment. His breathing was labored and he desperately tried to hold onto something as he slid through the steep downward fall.

He distinctly realized a burnt odor emanating from the forest floors. He came to an abrupt halt and desperately grabbed something from the floor. A loud menacing bark rang in his ears as his heart panicked and pounded through his chest. Before he could react, the dog landed squarely on his back. Theodor couldn't keep himself steady and fell to the ground along with the dog. He tried to whack the dog's face with what he grabbed and realized that it was just a hard bound leather diary. The dog was alert; he dodged it and attacked Theodor.

Theodor thrust the diary in the dog's mouth as the dog tried to bite. Theodor mustered courage and kicked the dog in the belly. Although the dog was massive, it was caught off guard and fell away, growling in rage. Theodor pulled the diary away from the dog's mouth and began running once again. As the light continued to sweep across the forests, Theodor noticed a cave like cavity up ahead. Without another thought he dashed for it, trying hard to run through the rain and away from the dog. He covered a little distance and the dog caught his foot. Luckily, Theodor wore heavy leather boots that prevented the dog from biting into his flesh. Theodor stumbled and kicked with his free foot again. The dog let go off his foot and barked right into his ear.

While he fought, Theodor picked up a rock with his free hand and threw it at the raging dog. Somehow, in his panic state, he was aiming precisely, with the rock hitting the dog's eye. The dog yelped in pain and fell back. Theodor mustered strength and ran towards the cave-like outgrowth. He reached it and saw an iron grill covering a round entrance. It was covered with foliage and one could barely comprehend the hidden cave. With all his might Theodor lugged at the gate, and mercifully, it opened up a little. It had been wedged shut due to muck and wild creepers that had grown around the grill. A loud ferocious bark emanated from behind Theodor as he swiftly turned around to see the dog closing in on him. He thrust all his force and groaned as the grill budged from its place. He threw in the book and slid inside half way. From the darkness, another dog appeared. As the dogs teamed up, both of them sprang into action and ran towards Theodor. He tried to squeeze himself through the barely open gate with all the strength he could muster. The dog yet again leaped into air to land on Theodor. He screamed into the darkness and pushed through the half open gate.

The wounds on his body scraped open further as he pushed himself in. He fell inside the cave as the dogs collided with the grill causing a massive rattle. The light swept the forests and Theodor backed further into the cave-like structure. He was panting and gasping for breath as his wounds hurt terribly. The dogs were snarling and trying to get in through the iron grill. Theodor pushed himself deeper into the tunnel out of fear and the light shone momentarily on the dog's face. The dog had one bloodied eye. Fresh blood was oozing out from the dog's eye as he menacingly growled at Theodor, challenging him to come out and face him. The other dog stepped back and howled loudly through the air. Night outside was giving way to sunrise as the dog dutifully alerted guards that it had found an intruder lurking in his master's camp. Theodor's heart thumped in panic. He looked behind him into the tunnel and then at the ferocious howling dogs outside. He knew there was just one way to go now as he sped away into the dark tunnel. He turned around to catch a last glimpse of the waiting dogs. Both of them were howling away as dawn broke over the Russian grounds.

The Deserter

General Felix and Gregor had effectively broken into the Red army's line of attack. Ralf and Albert were nowhere to be seen; if anything, that was a good sign. They traversed through the forests, curbing the Red Army's assault. Traugott's presence of mind was coming into good use as they broke through enemy ranks and disoriented the soldiers. Cold sweat was trickling down their bodies and their breathing laborious from the frenzied chase.

Everything was going horribly wrong; they had gone off track from their planned route and were being hunted down brutally. A massive light was suddenly sweeping through the forests; making it difficult for them to remain hidden. General Felix seemed extremely tired; he was panting as he did his best to keep up the pace. A few more gun shots were fired towards them as Russian soldiers inexorably kept up in firm pursuit. Gregor suddenly jumped through the air and swiftly kicked against a tree bark. He turned around in mid-air and fired towards the approaching enemy soldiers. It was an impressive feat to watch as his bullets seared through enemy ranks. One of the soldiers fell to his death and the other ducked in cover. Gregor landed on his feet and continued the attack. General Felix got an open window as he swiftly took out another soldier. They were effectively functioning as a team; throwing off their pursuers.

Ralf and Albert continued their frantic run as they branched out from the others. It was important for them to enter the camp. 'The others were sure to stand their ground but for how long could they hold on to the enemy onslaught?' Ralf's mind was racing with thoughts as he and Albert continued their run through enemy forests. Their aim was to either find Fabian or to get into the Russian camp on their own accord. A sudden rustling was heard from nearby trees and in the next instant a soldier jumped out; landing right next to them. Ralf instantly pulled out his gun to shoot. The Red army soldier curtly yelled "Blood Moon" and ran away from them. Realization hit Ralf and he refrained from pulling the trigger. Fabian introduced himself and dashed away in the opposite direction. Both Ralf and Albert instantly changed course and began following him. A wave of relief swept over Ralf on seeing Fabian run ahead. 'They might still be able to make it into the camp' he thought as he continued following Fabian.

A lone soldier was now tailing Gregor and Felix. Gregor saw a huge tree up ahead and ducked behind it. Before the soldier could change his course, Gregor came up from the other side and shot from the tree cover. The bullet hit the soldier in his arm as he screamed and fell. General Felix ducked behind a tree to reload his ammunition. The injured Red army soldier immediately got back to his feet and attacked Felix. Before Gregor could act, the soldier shot Felix. General Felix was slow to react and the bullet hit his shoulder. Gregor sprang into action and ran straight towards the soldier, ramming into him. Felix let out a scream and fell to the forest floor with a terrible wound on his shoulder. Gregor punched the soldier's bullet wound and tackled him down. Before the soldier could shout or scream, Gregor pulled out his knife and plunged it down the soldier's throat. The Red army soldier instantly fell silent and Gregor ran back to help Felix. The General's right side was hit and he was in terrible pain. The bullet had lodged above the shoulder joint and Felix could barely move his hand given the agony. Gregor lifted Felix off his feet and dragged him away from the sweeping light. They had to keep going to make sure Ralf and Albert reached the camp.

Ralf and Albert were blindly following Fabian through the forests as he ran towards a massive tree. They had never seen a tree so huge in proportion; it covered their field of vision almost entirely. Its branches spread out in all directions and thick, huge roots descended from the barks to support the ever growing tree. In the dark, it was difficult to entirely comprehend it's magnificence, but there was no question that it was a super large tree. Fabian continued running straight towards the tree, and for a moment they thought he would collide into the tree; but in the very next instant he vanished into the ground. Ralf and Albert tried to halt and watch what happened but their momentum was too strong. They faltered a bit and slid down a narrow crevice, disappearing underground.

The massive tree that bent forward had uprooted the forest floor and created a crevice in the earth. There was a wide space for them to slide in but one could see it only if they were familiar with the terrain. Otherwise, it was completely camouflaged by creepers and other elements of the forest grounds. Ralf and Albert thrashed through roots and other outgrowth in the narrow cavity. They slid down twenty feet into the earth; the broken tree roots scratched their faces and bodies as they slid uncontrollably. Suddenly they slowed down as the density of roots around them increased and without warning, they fell freely to the ground.

They splashed into a small trench filled with water that had accumulated from roots of the huge overhead tree. Fabian came walking from the opposite side, his weapon pointing towards them. Ralf and Albert were dripping wet as they held up their hands in surrender. "How many of you have entered? There were only two as per Felix's instruction" Fabian questioned them in a raspy voice while keeping a gun pointing straight at them. Ralf slowly lowered his hand and spoke "We are the two soldiers that will enter the camp. The others were a diversion." "Diversion?" Fabian shot angrily. "You have no idea about the chaos you created up there. An aircraft crashed, Russian soldiers are dead and Konstantin knows there are intruders in his forests. You are the clumsiest lot of soldiers I have ever seen. When Han entered, he didn't make any sounds or leave trails. In the past five years, he was the first one to breach this campsite with absolute ease" Fabian accused them. Ralf and Albert were eyeing him, trying to figure if they could relax and be off guard. Also, the news of an aircraft crash was bad indeed. Their fellow soldiers were probably onboard that aircraft. Fabian lowered his gun and crouched on the floor. "I will brief you on the directions and ways to get inside" Fabian spoke as he rolled opened a map, not wanting to waste time. He thrust a bunch of folded maps into Ralf's hands and started divulging information. "This is the area where you enter into the Russian camp. It is heavily guarded; thanks to Han. He made sure that guards now be put where none were before. But the catch is that there are not many men remaining to secure the entire camp so it's a strategic shift change that is being employed. More and more guards are being pulled into war while others here are restoring the camp. Also, Konstantin has some sort of consignment flying in from Berlin which has gotten him all worried. He has directed most of his forces to protect that."

Ralf and Albert sat next to Fabian listening to every word that he spoke. "Now the part about getting in, this tunnel behind us goes straight for a walk of about twenty minutes" he pointed into the darkness and continued explaining. Ralf and Albert both peered into the tunnel which now looked like their one way ticket to hell. Already, the mission was under so much strain. There was no assurance that they could ever walk out of this camp with the required information. "Take this route and keep walking until you reach a fork in the road" Fabian's voice cut through their thoughts as he continued to give instructions. "Take a right at the fork and continue straight. The Red army as of now, has no clue about these pathways so you should reach there unhampered. Once you walk further into this road" Fabian further explained opening the folded map and pointing out routes on it. "This leads up ahead" he said tracing his finger on the path. "From around this patch onwards the walk gets uphill and steadily climbs. This is where it gets tricky, the soldiers are aware of an opening here but they think that it ends into a small shelter here." Fabian was drawing circles on the map as he instructed. Both Albert and Ralf listened intently. "What they do not know is that it also opens up another pathway leading to where you will reach" Fabian continued his flow of instructions. "This area too is unmanned, just a lone soldier keeps watch every three hours or so. You need to be careful as you walk through this patch, beyond this you will be exposed for a small walk ahead which leads you to a point from where Han himself entered. It's a complete mess; it's been blown apart at every step. Once you are inside there is nothing much you need to fear, it's a maze from there onwards. We do not know the extent of damage Han has caused inside these tunnels so you are on your own exploring them. I have a pack of weapons and supplies ready for your use to open gates and doors. I am sure the ones which have come under the wrath of explosion are going to be stuck shut." Ralf and Albert did not even blink through the entire set of instructions. Albert appeared to be intently considering the pathways and trying to grasp in every detail. Fabian looked at their confused faces and spoke again.

"Try not to use dynamite while you are inside, it makes a racket of a noise, and chances are you will kill yourself. As you travel to this point" Fabian turned around the map as he showed the tunnel systems on the back side. He kept a finger on the map indicating the next move, "From there onwards you need to open into the bunker above, now this won't be easy. It's heavily guarded and there is a lot of activity going on here at all times. Even though the number of guards manning the outer territory is less, the guards within the camp are trained soldiers. How you get in here is a big question, use all that you have got. Han is housed in a suspended chamber within the beast bunker and no one has ever broken into it." Fabian paused as he considered the magnanimity of the situation that lay ahead.

"Konstantin, as you might know is the dreaded warlord in command of this camp. His personal guards are extremely sharp and ruthless. He has called upon his most trusted dog by the name of Fedor who wreaks havoc wherever he goes. The soldiers that Konstantin has at his disposal are some of the best. If you have the misfortune of crossing them, then just" Fabian paused in discomfort and spoke again, "Just run away from them." A hint of fear flickered in Albert's eyes while Ralf continued gazing at Fabian. "Now as far as I know; Han is still alive. So you need to get to him quickly" Fabian continued talking. "They are expecting some sort of a rescue mission but since Germany is defeated they do not flag it as a top priority task, which is true. Even I thought that General Felix will call off this mission." There was another uncomfortable pause in their conversation. "Daylight will filter through the forest soon; I think you should be gone. Get into the tunnels while it is dark. Once you are inside you can get to know them and strike from within. Even Konstantin doesn't know these tunnels completely. They are huge and have numerous openings throughout the forests. Some are covered by guards, some are not. There are a few undiscovered openings and a few have been sealed shut. This, you might be able to use to your advantage". As he concluded his set of instructions, Fabian got to his feet. Ralf and Albert too got up and packed their set of fresh supplies from Fabian. "I will go back and help Felix, I wish you luck" and as he said this, Fabian turned around and left. Ralf and Albert turned towards the tunnel, watching the endless dark that it stretched into. Without another word or thought they marched ahead.

Ralf and Albert walked through the tunnel with a tiny fire held high above their heads to throw light into their surroundings. They had travelled a good distance and were nearing the first fork as shown on the map. When they got to it, they headed in the relevant direction. Within a few minutes they would reach the other opening through which they'd travel into the Russian camp. They had to reach their destination before daylight; otherwise it would be impossible to get through guard ranks.

As they covered ground yet another fork showed up in their way. They stood for a while, a little confused. This fork wasn't on the map; neither had Fabian mentioned it. Ralf laid down the map and set his compass by it, trying to figure out the direction. "If we follow this one, it's the natural direction we should be taking to reach the opening as mentioned by Fabian. However, if we go into that one..." Ralf said pointing the other way, "we may end up getting out at this point here; but we cannot be sure of an opening or guards that might be manning it." Both Ralf and Albert considered the situation.

Albert traced his finger along a path on the map. "I guess we ought to stick to the normal route and see what lies ahead" he said. Agreeing to that; they both walked into the fork as they proceeded on the natural course. "How come Fabian doesn't know about this?" Albert questioned as he looked at Ralf. Ralf shrugged, "I thought of the same thing. If he knows the tunnels so well; why didn't he mention this?" They both looked puzzled as they considered the situation and continued walking deeper, unsure of what they'd meet in front.

Gregor and General Felix had walked deeper into the forest. It was becoming more difficult to keep going, bearing in mind Felix's massive wound. The General kept wincing in pain intermittently, yet he kept moving forward, with belabored breathing. The forests, on the other hand, swarmed with Red army soldiers and a bright beam of light that swept at intervals. A distance away, they could hear the barking and howling of dogs.

It was obvious that the Russians were fully at alert. Gregor forced his thoughts to remain focused on getting Felix to safety. He and Felix kept to the shadows; moving stealthily through dense foliage. They reached a patch which had a massive tree. It was uprooted from one side and its branches spread out in all directions through the forest. Up ahead, Gregor's eye caught some movement. He quickly pushed himself and Felix behind a boulder. From behind it, a soldier emerged from a cavity in the ground. Gregor observed as the soldier climbed out from some sort of a hidden opening in the ground. He was alert and ready to fire while Felix squinted so he could see better in the darkness.

The soldier brushed off some dirt from his uniform, looked around the forests and started walking towards them, unaware of the people hiding behind the boulder. As soon as he crossed them, Gregor pounced on him and punched him in the face. His scream was muffled as Gregor tackled him and put a knife to his throat. "Stop wait, Gregor" Felix called out from his hiding place as he saw Fabian. Felix let out a sigh of relief on seeing him and motioned Gregor to release his grip. Gregor pushed himself up and put his knife away. The three of them settled behind a huge boulder. "Fabian, where are Ralf and Albert?" General Felix whispered urgently through his pain. "They have been sent further on their mission General" replied Fabian. Gregor was crouching besides Felix. A wave of relief swept over Felix as he sat there holding his wounded shoulder. "There is hope after all, after the ruckus we created here, they might still be able to get to Han" Felix concluded and patted Gregor on the shoulder. Gregor nodded in acknowledgement and smiled faintly. Fabian looked from Felix to Gregor as he sat there.

"How do we go about the mission from here?" asked General Felix. Fabian looked around to see any approaching soldiers as he took his time to answer. The forests seemed to be clear around them. He pulled out his knife swiftly, a glint of mischief dancing in his eyes as he said; "the escape is pretty simple" and slipped his blade into Gregor's throat in a swift unannounced move. A mixed look of fear and desperation settled over Gregor's eyes in a flash. He made a slight attempt to fight back but merely twitched as life was mercilessly stabbed out of him. "NO" Felix screamed into the air. Thick blood pooled out on Fabian's hand as he pushed the knife deeper and let Gregor's lifeless body fall to the ground; with a loud thud. The world around Felix was spinning. This, was definitely not part of the plan. Felix tried to tackle Fabian with his functional hand; which Fabian easily dodged and punched Felix directly on his wound. Felix let out a terrible wail as the pain shot up through his arms while Gregor twitched for the last time and bled to death, his eyes forever open in horror.

Ralf and Albert were taking the upward climb, and although the distance was not much, the climb was arduous. Hopefully, they'd reached the opening where they ought to come out of; and before them stood a huge circular iron gate. This again was a matter of concern, Fabian had not once mentioned a gate. It was supposed to open into the forest cover directly. If they budged this gate open, it would make a racket of a noise for sure. Ralf handed the torch to Albert and tried to rotate the lock, it seemed to move smoothly. Ralf was confused. This is not how it should have been. Fabian couldn't have been so wrong, he was very confident while disclosing information about the tunnels. Albert continued to consult the map, briefly lifting up his face at intervals to view the sight before him, which sharply contrasted what was on the map. "I think we should back track a little" Albert spoke as he continued studying the map. "We should head back and take the other fork. It opens directly into the forest. We will at least know what lies ahead" Albert told Ralf as he traced a line on the map. "I should have seen this before" said Albert as he showed Ralf the map. Ralf consulted it and nodded in agreement. "Let's head back then" he said.

Fear gripped General Felix as he looked at the collapsed body of Gregor on the forest floor. "You are my ticket to freedom Felix, march straight ahead." Fabian held a gun at Felix's throat as he prepared to march him ahead. Felix got to his feet but was bent in pain as the wound sent spasms across his body. 'Traugott, Frank and now Gregor, they were all gone.' Several thoughts at once, coalesced in Felix's head. The General looked much older and frail, in light of his current situation. Fabian looked around to check for approaching soldiers. "Move General, we don't have much time. I am taking you to Konstantin directly. These clumsy soldiers will take forever to reach us" said Fabian. Felix held on to his wound and started walking. "Where have you sent Ralf and Albert? Are they going to be presented to Konstantin too?"

Felix asked through gasps of breath. Fabian was a little irritated by the questions. "They will be disposed properly. Don't bother about them. They are not important enough but you are; General" replied Fabian. Felix had no choice but to march ahead in despair. His mind was racing with thoughts, thinking of ways to escape and also, of possible ways to help Ralf and Albert. The pain from his wound was driving him numb and clouding his thoughts. Fabian kept Felix in the shadows as they made their way to the main camp. They heard shouts in the forests and Fabian pushed Felix further away from the approaching soldiers. He wanted to present Felix to Konstantin on his own and not with any other troops.

The last pair of Blood Moon soldiers, Ralf and Albert, had reached another opening which seemed to open above ground level. They were on their bellies, crawling through the narrow tunnel. Slowly, Ralf dropped out of the tunnel landing on his feet. He looked around to see two guards sitting in front of the adjoining Iron Gate. "Are you sure there is someone coming out of here?" asked one of the guards. "I don't trust the tip. Well I am leaving; you can wait if you want. The shift is over, if someone does come out, other guards can keep the loot. We better report back to base. After all the commotion in the forests, we don't want trouble on our hands." Ralf and Albert heard from the shadows as the guards conversed. They hid behind thick foliage from where they could see the soldiers. The Russian guards gathered their guns and began walking away from the gate. Ralf and Albert now had to crossover to the opposite side to enter the tunnels.

They slowly crawled out of their hiding place and looked around to see the territory completely unmanned. Stealthily, they crawled across the forest floor and reached the opposite gate. Ralf quickly got up on his feet and tried to open the lock. He turned the lock wheel around but it didn't budge. Yet again, he tried with all his strength and pushed the wheel, which made it to budge slightly. "Albert, help me unlock this" Ralf muttered and tried turning the lock again. Albert scanned the forest area to make sure no one was around and joined Ralf. The lock groaned as it moved inch by inch. It wasn't smooth and they had to exert a lot to turn it around. The forests were empty for now and they would have to hurry before any soldiers reached to man the gates.

General Felix turned around and looked Fabian in the eye as he brusquely stopped walking. Fabian was confused and questioningly looked at Felix. He kept his gun pointing towards Felix, "Keep walking General" he commanded. Felix kept his gaze fixed on Fabian, his eyes lit up in ire as he spoke "The dawn breaks Fabian. Blood moon will rise." A shrill swish was suddenly audible through the otherwise quiet forests and Felix swiftly ducked. Fabian was caught off guard as a huge tree bark whacked into his face and sent him flying off his feet. He crashed into a thick tree and fell to the ground. Felix noticed the wire traps on the ground and used them to his advantage. Fabian was moaning in pain from the impact. "Where are Ralf and Albert? I will ask only once" Felix questioned menacingly as he held a gun to Fabian's head. Fabian held out his hand indicating the direction where they would come up. Felix looked at Fabian and whispered "Since you know too much, I will let Konstantin discover you." at that, he pulled the trigger and shot him through the head.

Albert and Ralf had almost undone the lock. As the last turn ended, the gate was pulled open with a resounding clang and they prepared to march inside. "Intruders" a loud shout rang behind their ears and bullets came raining down on them. Both Ralf and Albert panicked and ducked from the onslaught of fire. A soldier had spotted them and was running towards them firing wildly. Ralf pushed Albert inside as he prepared to close the gate shut. He heard a scream through the forests and instantly recognized the voice. General Felix jumped from behind the foliage and fired towards the oncoming soldier. His precise shots took out the reckless enemy soldier and the firing instantly died out. They heard more footsteps and shouts as alerted Red army soldiers were converging around them. Albert held the gate open as Ralf dashed out to help Felix.

The Red army soldiers opened fire to take down Felix. Ralf swiftly pulled Felix through the chaotic attack and dragged him into the gate. Albert swiftly helped their General in, while Ralf closed the gate as bullets rained down on the heavy metal. Ralf shockingly looked at Felix and asked "What happened?" "Fabian turned us in" Felix replied in a labored voice. For a moment, they all looked defeated. And then, like soldiers, shoulders squared-save for Felix who still had one shoulder drooping, they continued to march deeper into the tunnels.

Honeycomb Maze

Theodor traversed deeper into the tunnels and ran through complete darkness. There was no way to figure out the direction he was running in or even what lay ahead. He blindly flailed his hands as he tried to decipher any obstructions in the blinding dark tunnels. From the moment he'd entered that house in Berlin, he'd kept moving from one troubling circumstance to another.

How he wished to turn back time and avoid the mess that he had gotten into! The darkness was pressing in on his thoughts; his mind was numb from the horrible events that kept on unfolding around him. He kept up his pace as he blindly ran through the obscurity. His wounds were screaming in pain as they stretched open to let fresh blood ooze out. The temperature within the tunnels dropped further and Theodor began to gasp for air. The interiors were damp and they smelled horribly of death. He could feel water leaking at places as a steady drip-drip was audible. At times he almost tripped over protruding objects in the tunnel joints but he didn't bother to stop nor inspect them. He had no weapons left with him and any sort of confrontation with enemy soldiers would spell instant death. Theodor continued his frantic sprint through the dark and suddenly collided into a solid wall. The resounding gong like crash reverberated through the tunnels.

Ralf, Albert and General Felix had run deeper into the tunnels. The Russian soldiers were on their tail as they heard various door locks churn and gates slide open. Felix was in a terrible state; he had lost a lot of blood and now; he simply couldn't keep up. His mental alertness seemed to be dropping and he appeared disoriented. Albert was leading the way as his mind calculated the course he'd take. Holding on to Felix, he helped the General through the semi dark tunnels while Ralf drew his weapons and backed them. The trio ran straight ahead and took a diversion into one of the openings. The tunnel had a number of such openings throughout and it was easier to dodge and put off any pursuers. They stumbled into a chamber-like cavity and came to a halt. Albert held the gate open for Felix and Ralf to enter. He closed the massive gate after them and turned the lock wheel to seal it shut.

"Traugott, Gregor and Frank have all fallen. The others have broken out" Felix spoke through his labored breathing. "Fabian spoke of an aircraft crash" Ralf replied. "I think we have lost them all" said Felix. Suddenly they heard muffled footsteps through the gates. They panicked and turned around loading their weapons. "Open this gate" a soldier shouted on the other side. "They couldn't have gone far" they heard more screaming. The lock began to turn noisily as soldiers on the opposite side began to open it. General Felix armed himself and looked at Ralf and Albert. "You both run deeper into the tunnels. I will tackle them from here. It is important that you reach Han" General Felix ordered in a tone awash with authority. Both Ralf and Albert opened their mouths to argue but General Felix cut them short. "It is an order soldiers. Bring the camp down if you have to" he roared, as he pushed them into the adjoining tunnel opening. Felix stood there armed and ready to face the oncoming enemies.

Theodor was recovering from the massive crash. The wind was knocked out of him as he had run into one of the gates. In the darkness he touched the gate and figured a lock wheel on it. 'Why did the gates have to be locked shut everywhere?' he thought. He put his entire weight on the lock wheel and tried to budge it. He strained under pressure and nearly screamed as the wheel finally turned. He released it, sweating from the strain. He caught his breath and clasped it again turning it with all his might. The wheel finally budged and began turning as Theodor relentlessly strained to unlock the gate.

The lock wheel turned and the gate burst open. Three Red army soldiers barged in and fired blindly. They found no one there as smoke settled and the sound of firing died down. General Felix quickly jumped from behind the gate and fired into the tunnel. The bullets ricocheted off curved surfaces, causing mayhem in the enclosed space. The Russian soldiers ducked to avoid the random and sudden onslaught. He managed to hit one soldier; swung himself out of the chamber, with his functional hand holding onto the gate. He closed it shut before they could react and tried to turn the lock wheel but the soldiers were obviously faster than him. They gripped the wheel from the opposite end and turned it open. General Felix ran ahead, trying to put a good amount of distance between them. The soldiers cautiously piled out and ran towards Felix. "Get him alive if you can" ordered one of the soldiers. "Konstantin will reward us well" he concluded.

As General Felix ran into the tunnel he heard more sounds from the adjoining gate. 'Probably more soldiers had joined the hunt' he thought and ran, effectively leading them away from Ralf and Albert's trail. Suddenly a gate next to him crashed open. Felix quickly pointed his gun towards the gate and was ready to fire. The pursuing Red army soldier had already caught up with Felix and opened fired from behind him. With no time to react, the bullet hit Felix and he crashed to the ground. As excruciating pain shot up his body, the General discovered that he'd been hit in the chest. He dragged himself against the tunnel floor and waited for the fatal shot.

Theodor stumbled out of the iron gate and was surprised to see Felix wounded and beaten. General Felix's eyes widened in shock; Theodor, the German soldier stood in front of him. Felix mustered strength and threw a gun at Theodor as he simultaneously opened fire at the oncoming soldiers. He pushed Theodor behind him and stood up to face the onslaught yet again. Another bullet ripped his belly but Felix continued to fire blindly. Theodor tried to dodge the fire and fell to the ground. He was yelling, terrified at the sudden battle that unfolded around him. He too; continued to fire blindly at the oncoming soldiers. The bullets were flying and ricocheting off tunnel walls in a deadly frenzy. The overhead light bulbs shattered on impact and lights around flickered as yet another soldier of the Red army fell. Only one soldier now remained; and he roared and charged towards Felix. General Felix dropped his spent gun and whipped out his knife. Theodor watched in horror and shock as he got to his feet to help the General. "Stay back Theodor" Felix bellowed. Even through his bleeding, Felix's command was sharp and loud. He stood there tall and alert with a knife in his hand, waiting to tackle enemy wrath. The Red army soldier lunged at Felix. Theodor had never seen such a swift move in his life. He stood there, frozen in place as Felix turned around and plunged the knife through the soldier's throat. The Red army soldier was completely taken by surprise as he rammed into Felix and crashed to the ground. Theodor pushed himself forward and rushed to help Felix. He dragged the General out from under the dead soldier and held onto him. Felix was breathing very heavily. Blood spurted out from his wounds as he drew labored breaths.

Suddenly General Felix gripped Theodor's hand and spoke in a soft whisper. "Do not dispose my body; let them find it, they do not know how many of us entered." As Felix struggled to speak, a thick pool of warm crimson blood collected around him. "Save Han, free Germania" General Felix drew his last breath and succumbed to his wounds. Blood pooled out in a steady stream as his heart stopped beating and he lay there, the mighty General, defeated in Theodor's arms. Dying an honorable death, just as a soldier would want to pass into the realm of the unknown. Fighting and saving his people before finally giving in to his wounds. The last words of the fallen General was wrapped in a burning desire to free Germania.

Theodor closed his eyes for a moment and prayed. He gently laid the General on the floor and got up. He gathered the weapons from around him and picked up the gun that General Felix gave him. It was a fine looking weapon, with an ivory handle and an exquisitely crafted barrel. There were tiny engravings on it which read: 'As always. The dawn breaks the darkness.' Theodor pocketed it and looked around the horrible scene. Dead bodies were strewn across the floor. Blood was flowing through open wounds that had accumulated around his boots. Theodor realized one thing, in that moment: he was in much deeper trouble than he'd initially thought. Not only was he on Russian grounds, he was now directly under the Russian camp and his only option was to find Ralf and Albert. There was no walking out of these tunnels. Red army guards were swarming in the forests and his only way out involved ;launching deeper into the camp. He turned around and looked at the endless tunnel. Theodor took in one full breath, and ran into the menacing honeycomb maze.

Iron Gates

The gates to the Russian camps opened as trucks led by Fedor drove in; one after the other. Konstantin was waiting in his cabin to receive a message from the high command. Viktor stood by his side waiting for his order to connect the radio. Konstantin was consulting a book as usual, which was spread out in front of him. "Connect the radio" he said without taking his eyes off the book. The intermeddling of the high command filled Konstantin with immense irritation. Yet, he had to put up a front of patience, in spite of his obvious impatience. As he looked through the book carefully and studied detailed drawings of some kind, Konstantin's eyes strained to take note of the small text. In the far distance, one could hear metal gates shutting close as the last of many trucks drove in. Konstantin looked at Viktor as he connected the switches and then looked behind him at the locked door.

The door had multiple locks on it and was made with reinforced iron. The crackling suddenly built up as the radio came to life. Before Konstantin could say anything a voice spoke over it "Konstantin?" This irked him to no end. He composed himself and spoke "Yes." "Congratulations comrade. Berlin is ours. As discussed, General Vlad has left for your camp. Before he reaches you, he will be visiting Berlin. Certain matters require his urgent attention there. The atmosphere back at the high command is jubilant. Victory has been declared." Konstantin seemed unaffected by the message of jubilance. "You have any other matter of importance to discuss?" asked Konstantin. The voice on the opposite end sounded taken aback. "Yes, you will leave the camp to General Vlad and report to high command. Before you do that, we need you to get in touch with your German friends. We need to confirm certain issues" the crackled voice spoke. "I need more time. There are certain matters that I must address before I leave the camp and fly to high command." Konstantin was trying to sound composed as he spoke. "Whatever needs to be done, you can hand it over to Vlad. He will take care of it; do not forget that we need your resources at the High command Konstantin. The reason for us contacting you urgently is that we have gifts flying in from Berlin. It is Hitler's dead body" the voice over the radio jubilantly spoke.

Konstantin froze at the statement. "We need your sources to confirm the body, no one's ever seen Hitler up close and the credit to his death will be Russia's to keep for years to come if we confirm it" the voice continued speaking. Konstantin was lost in thought and paid no attention to the voice. "Is that clear?" The voice over the radio was talking hurriedly. "Yes" Konstantin absent-mindedly spat and motioned Viktor to pull out the plug. The radio went dead as Viktor did the needful. Konstantin was brewing up his strategy, the news he got were a little out of place as per his calculations. "Filthy idiots" Konstantin raged. "What do I care about Berlin or Stalingrad? I need to strike my deals" he got up as he spoke. "Any response from our German friend yet?" he asked. "None yet my lord" replied Viktor.

Konstantin's concern was growing; his German friend being unresponsive was a bad sign for him. The deal was to hand over much more than just the nuclear materials. With victory being declared over Germany, Konstantin's chances of meeting his aid were turning slim. He absent mindedly eyed the book laid out in front of him as his mind contemplated all possible options. "Let's head out and inspect the nuclear materials" he abruptly broke the silence, closed the book shut; and strode out.

Fedor had the trucks line up outside the beast bunker for inspection. Soldiers were standing around the entire convoy guarding it from all sides. Konstantin walked towards them as Fedor jumped out from the truck. "My lord" he said, as he approached Konstantin. "What took you so long?" questioned

Konstantin. "The numbers are huge my lord, too many containers and very few soldiers to handle them" replied Fedor. "We have transported all of it safely. They will unload it into the beast bunker" he said.

Konstantin eyed him suspiciously and shifted his gaze to the waiting trucks. "Get the German scientist out and have him inspect these contents simultaneously" Konstantin said as he motioned a guard to fetch the scientist. The guard acknowledged and ran inside the beast bunker. Fedor moved closer to Konstantin and asked in a whisper "Our grounds are breached, request permission to hunt them down my lord." Konstantin eyed him again and spoke "Let the material get inside safely Fedor; then you may go. Even I am concerned about this intrusion." Fedor nodded in acknowledgement and stood by the Minotaur.

A harrowed looking man came running out of the huge iron doors. He was probably in his early fifties. He had white ruffled hair and wore thick spectacles. "Is it actually here? The nuclear material and the study we asked for?" The scientist asked, looking at the waiting trucks then towards the soldiers. Finally, his gaze settled upon Konstantin. "Forgive me, my manners. I am very excited to see this, my lord. That is what they call you right?" He extended his hand in greeting to Konstantin. Viktor and Fedor both moved a step closer to secure Konstantin. "I, I am Dr.Schmitz" the harrowed little scientist spoke as he held out his hand in anticipation.

All the soldiers along with Konstantin continued to stare at him; their faces stoic and mirroring Konstantin's unflinching gaze. Konstantin tilted his head towards the waiting trucks, indicating him to hurry up. The doctor shivered a bit under Konstantin's gaze and moved towards the truck. He climbed into the back and looked inside with awe. "We have a lot of material. How did you manage this?" he questioned and looked around. Nobody answered. They just kept staring back with a cold gaze. Konstantin gestured Viktor to hurry up. Viktor curtly nodded and went up to the doctor. "We need to secure the material, be quick about what you have to do, doc." Viktor threatened the doctor in a low and casual tone. The doctor looked around and was knocked back to his senses. "Have them empty the chamber." He pointed towards the beast bunker. "It all looks to be in order; we can only tell what's out of place once I start looking into each and every case" the scientist said. Viktor nodded and questioned him further. "Is there anything dangerous or reactive in nature, any special handling instructions to be given to the soldiers?" "You are smarter than the lot of them ehh... I'll have my team handle it. Just empty them inside the chamber" Dr. Schmitz replied. Viktor gave him a loath-filled look and strode back to Konstantin. "He wants them unloaded directly into the chamber" he said. "According to him, everything seems to be in order for now. Once inside, the research team will figure out what exactly has arrived" Viktor concluded.

Konstantin considered the situation for a moment and nodded. "Open the gates" he ordered. The guards sprang into action and turned the locks. The huge iron gates clanged open and moved. They moved aside, revealing a huge chamber from which a massive heat wave swept out and engulfed them. Two guards with gas masks stood in rapt attention in the chamber. A line of slaves stood by the side, squinting at the sudden light that hit their eyes. Rail-like tracks ran through the entire length of the chamber and a pungent odor wafted out from within it. Fedor moved a little closer as he tried to get a better look at the chamber. The trucks backed into the chamber to offload the material. "Now, what is the news of intrusion?" Konstantin spoke, surprising both Viktor and Fedor.

He held his gaze steady and still, watching the progress in the chamber. Both Fedor and Viktor plunged into details of the intrusion. None had a very clear idea about it, just what they had either seen or heard. The soldiers were not yet back from their rounds of the forests. The shift changes too hadn't been monitored yet. "My lord" a guard shouted from the light tower. Startled, they all looked up to the tower. Daylight had broken and filtered through the clouds and trees. The light beam was still functional and a faint light flashed as it moved in the tower. Viktor quickly walked ahead, "Any commotion?" he asked. "Jeep heading towards the camp" shouted the soldier. "Close the gates to the beast bunker" Konstantin roared into the morning air. The trucks instantly reversed into the chamber as the guards secured the gates shut. Fedor ran towards the entrance, he didn't want to miss this chance. Enough time had been wasted behind the material. He wanted to get to action and find who exactly these intruders were. Viktor gathered more guards to secure Konstantin as he stood alert and ready to face the oncoming jeep. Konstantin's faithful hounds were by his side, blood thirsty and hungry. He noticed a wounded eye on one of his hounds.

A signal went up to open the iron gates. With a rattle they slid open and from far away, their eyes made contact with an approaching vehicle. More than fifty soldiers stood guard as the lone vehicle made its way towards the camp. "Whatever comes in that jeep, you will hold your ground." Konstantin growled as his eyes remained fixed on the vehicle. A small and narrow pathway through the iron gates was all that separated the vehicle and the waiting squad.

The Emerald Signature

Ralf and Albert heard the commotion behind them and silently dreaded General Felix's fate. They hated themselves for having to leave him alone, stranded to fight the attacking soldiers. Albert had figured that the best possible way to head into the tunnel was to go straight through the main outer pipe. They broke out on the main section of the tunnel and stopped for a while.

Albert continued to consult the map while Ralf loaded his guns and readied the weapons for any impending assault. They were on their own now and directly under the Russian camp. According to the maps that Albert consulted; they had entered the Honeycomb maze, which was the most complicated tunnel systems ever built. They had to travel through these mazes and somehow manage to open into the Russian camp above them. With any luck, they would be able to get to Han and get him out of this place. They were not even thinking of any possible escape route as of now. If Felix and Traugott hadn't both fallen, that would have been their jobs!

The two soldiers only had two things on their priority list: to stay alive, and to locate Han. Suddenly Ralf and Albert heard footsteps approaching from the far end of the tunnel. They instantly took up firing positions and waited behind a gate. It was just one pair of footsteps; they didn't hear any other soldiers come behind them. Both Ralf and Albert were sweating from the heat as they waited for the attack. Time ticked as the footsteps grew louder, more urgent and echoed loudly. Their heart rates picked up in anticipation. Did General Felix make it? Were the footsteps that of a lone Russian soldier? A shadow appeared as the figure got closer. Ralf tightened his grip on the trigger. From the turning in the junction came a figure, and being cautious, he pointed his hand gun towards the turn. Ralf's eyes widened in shock, as he saw Theodor moving towards them.

Theodor came to a halt as he got closer and came face to face with familiar faces. Only a few hours must have passed since he had been separated from Ralf and Albert and here he was now, standing in front of them. Three faces were now visible in the tiny flickering light. They were blood covered, stained, scratched and dirty. Only their eyes shone brightly in the small dingy tunnel. "How is it that you are still here with us?" asked Ralf. "You saved me remember?" Theodor mockingly replied. "Well, here I am. Paying you back, now I won't die with guilt" he retorted sarcastically.

A smile broke over Ralf's face as he looked from Albert to Theodor. From the tiny underground room in Berlin to being here beneath the Russian campsite seemed like a long and dangerous journey. Ralf had never intended to put Theodor through this but it wasn't like he had any other option. Out of all the people involved in the mission, these were the three soldiers who actually made it under the Russian camp. Theodor relaxed a bit and told them everything about the aircraft mishap and how General Felix fought bravely to protect him. Ralf and Albert were listening to him in rapt attention and they too divulged Fabian's story of how he turned traitor.

A lot of their fellow men had died on enemy grounds. Many sacrifices had been made on this night just to get Ralf and Albert into the honeycomb maze safely. "Now it's the three of us left to carry out this mission, and we need to find Han and get out of here" Theodor concluded as he sat looking at Ralf and Albert. "Yes, it's the three of us in this godforsaken Honeycomb maze" said Albert. He had a map laid out in front of him and he had already sketched routes on them. Theodor glanced over the map. The tunnels systems were impossible to figure; they'd been rightly named the honeycomb maze.

Ralf, Theodor and Albert armed themselves and marched forward. They decided to go deeper and find a safe chamber to discuss their route. Marching into the never ending tunnel, they branched off into one of the openings. Albert had figured the best possible way to reach underneath the bunker where Han could possibly be held hostage.

They travelled into a cavity-like opening and went deeper. As they moved, they shut the gates behind them to throw off any pursuers and make it harder for soldiers to follow them. They entered a smaller chamber which looked fine to break off for a while. The three of them dropped their backpacks and weapons. Sitting against the tunnel walls, each of them let out a sigh of relief. Albert had some water in his pack which he allowed to circulate. All three drank from the flask, thankful for the water that travelled down their parched throats. Albert scanned the chamber and saw a broken down radio rig. "Who will I be looking to contact now? General Felix and Traugott were supposed to be waiting outside. Even if I hack into Konstantin's radio, whom do we divulge the information to?" Albert asked as he checked out the broken down radio.

Ralf and Theodor looked at each other as they considered the odds. "We will report to General Helmuth as discussed. As of now let's just focus on getting to Han" replied Ralf. Theodor nodded and looked at Albert who was busy fixing something in the radio. "If he is able to fix anything in that rig, can he hack into the frequency of the camp radio above?" Theodor asked. Ralf looked at Albert and replied "Maybe we can, let's see what he can do to fix it first." Albert was totally engrossed in fixing the rig and muttered something which sounded like "five minutes" under his breath.

Ralf had the map open in front of him and Theodor settled on the floor as Albert continued to work. Ralf's eyes were shutting out of exhaustion and he drifted in and out of a tired sleep. Theodor looked at Ralf and Albert. He couldn't afford to fall asleep. They were very vulnerable right now and he had to keep watch as Albert worked. Theodor thought about the events that had occurred recently. The crazy chase through forests, bullets flying all around and the fact that they were now under the Russian camp, everything weighed down heavily upon him as he sat there, staring at the faint light bulb. As he closed his eyes, Adelheid drift into his thoughts and Theodor felt an uneasy ache within himself. He couldn't stand the distance, the separation; he let out a sigh and opened his eyes. He slowly moved to inspect his wounds, thinking that it would take his mind off Adelheid for a while. His shirt was torn and blood-stained. He removed it and with a soft thud, a diary fell to the floor. He instantly jumped to pick it up. Ralf held the map with dazed eyes while Albert's head was buried in the radio. Theodor had totally forgotten about this strange diary that he'd found on the forest floor. He picked it up and studied it. It was blood stained, sullied and felt damp from the rain water. There were teeth marks from where the hound had bitten into it and it had charred edges. Theodor flicked through the pages, the writing was still legible. A few pages were soaked in water and ink had smudged at places but otherwise it was readable. The words were neat and slanting elegantly. Theodor flicked through it to see signatures or markings. He opened the first page, to find it empty. The second page had a single sentence scribbled on it.

"It is the fear of darkness and not the quest for light that leads mankind to concord." -The Noble Wolf

It was written in daunting black ink and the page around it had turned pale. The written words however stood strikingly fresh and commanding. Theodor turned another page, it was empty again. In anticipation he turned yet another page and found a striking green signature on it. His heart froze in mid-beat as fear gripped his mind. He couldn't believe his eyes; he couldn't believe what he saw on the page. He once again looked at Ralf and Albert to check on them. Ralf held the map in his hands while Albert continued fixing the radio. Theodor gently settled down and moved a hand over the signature. It was strikingly prominent and stood out against the pale page of the diary. Very neatly and symmetrically signed across the page was an emerald signature that read 'Adolf Hitler.'

Blue Eyed Boy

A small stone house stood over the hill, facing the village on one side and an endless forest on the other. A gentle breeze rustled the foliage on the ground, carrying stray leaves onto its porch. The sun was fazed and hid behind clouds, sending down streaks of warm light into the otherwise cold air. It was a serene setting, a village which seldom knew trouble. Peaceful folk settled here and farmed for eons together. Generation after generation lived peacefully, rarely deterring from their set livelihood. Wide open fields and clear skies were a regular feature of one's daily life in this passive village.

This warm stone house, belonged to the Hitlers', a small content family that farmed for a living. Alois Hitler, the man of the house, was a moody individual who seldom spoke to others. Klara, his wife, on the other hand; along with their kids, were warm and friendly with the village folk. From this house rose a narrow winding path covered with creepers. It further went winding through forests and opened towards a small barren patch of land at the cliffs edge. It was a path rarely used and the wilderness had taken menacing authority over it.

A thin boy with golden brown hair and loosely hung clothes stood motionless and as still as a statue; his feet digging into the earth and arms stretched out by his sides as though he were locking into an embrace with the world. The wind gently caressed his features as he stood dangerously close to the cliff's edge. Not wanting to open his eyes, he took in as much from the surroundings as he could via his senses. It wouldn't be improbable for a strong gust of wind to throw him off the cliff; but this young lad stood his ground, stoically. He let his mind wander around and take in every detail from the surrounding world. He felt leaves rustle in the distance, soft wet dew from grass strands touching his feet and a Heron passing him by in flight. He was breathing gently, his chest heaving up and down in a slow and composed rhythm. A bee buzzed around him before flying off to find a flower. The wandering air carried an occasional leaf causing it to gently scrape his feet; a few were parched while others green with life and he could tell just by the touch.

In the soil beneath his feet, he felt some warm rustling and looked down. An earthworm was digging into the soil, and soon enough, he felt wet cold life brush his skin. The sun played behind clouds; switching between momentary warmth and a subdued cold on his skin. Another flock of birds whizzed by and somewhere in the distance, a wheel barrow moved. A strong aroma of tasty, mouth-watering cooking wafted towards him; and he heard the mild gushing of water flowing nearby. 'Water' he thought. Gently he opened his eyes, flooding them with clear evening light.

Beneath where he stood was a steep fall leading to a serene water body. His eyes were as blue as the water far below, and he looked down wondering what it would be to take the leap, to plummet down into the vast dark blue chasm. But the calm blue water body always scared him. He never dared to jump. He looked around the water's edge; and saw a pack of wolves drinking quietly from the water body. These shy but fierce creatures would often be here; just like him. He watched them come and go just as they watched him from the opposite side. Adolf loved to lock eyes with these wolves. He watched them play and hunt almost daily. He always stood here, somehow feeling drawn to this place high on the cliff. Day after day, he would watch the wolves, the neighbors and their activities. He also watched the neighborhood boys run about and jump into water but he himself couldn't manage to do the same.

He could never muster enough courage to take the leap. His mind played games with him and he almost took the leap, yet he restrained himself. The still water appeared like a veil of ether, calm and blue, and the tiny ripples seemed to be calling Adolf, asking him to come and hit the surface. He spent hours staring at it and in times of great emotional turmoil, he even spoke to it. The tiny motion of ripples somehow gave him a soothing assurance. He had first wandered here to talk to the ripples after Edmund's death; the memory of his younger brother's death remained etched in his thoughts. 'Edmund's death was most unfair' he thought to himself. Such a small soul couldn't have done enough wrong to be snatched away by death. Edmund could easily take the plunge; he always jumped, not afraid of the water or the height. Adolf's thoughts slowly traversed back to the day it had happened. The day Edmund slept and never woke up again.

Adolf was waiting outside the church. It was a dull overcast day and everything seemed still and glum. His father had gone in to the church to make a few arrangements. Adolf didn't really understand the nature of these arrangements. He knew that something was wrong with his little brother Edmund. He wouldn't open his eyes, he wouldn't respond and his mother never stopped weeping. Adolf looked around, there was no one nearby; so he walked around the church and crept up to a cracked window on the back side. His father sat there, head bowed, with a man Adolf couldn't recognize. He couldn't see the face of this unknown man, only the old priest and his father were visible to him. "You see Mr. Hitler; it is not fair to the people here. If we let you burry your little boy, the people will feel cheated" said the strange man. "The people know nothing" retorted Alois. "I have proved my ancestry to the priest and it has been entered in official records many years ago. We were the Hiedler's, a proud and noble family. The old priest there was deaf and changed the name to Hitler. Surely that shouldn't be a problem to you." Alois was losing his temper as he spoke. "You very well know that's not the mistake I am talking about Mr. Alois" the unknown man spoke in a threatening tone. Silence hung in the air, nobody said a word. Adolf stood outside the window, hiding from the people sitting inside, looking up only enough to see and hear the conversation unfold. His father was fuming in anger while the priest sat there looking tensed. "I am no priest; I am just a keeper of the keys and records at the high church. I know the truth Mr. Alois. I know that your lineage has been tampered with." As the unknown man spoke on, everyone else maintained a steely silence. "I will bury my little son in the house farm then. I don't want any place on your sacred land" Alois spoke with a choked voice and tear filled eyes. "The high priest does not know of my visit here. I am sure there is a way to resolve this issue Mr. Alois." The unknown man was hinting in an undertone.

Alois abruptly got up from the chair fuming in anger. Adolf panicked and ducked behind the window. He ran around the church to get to the main entrance where he was supposed to be waiting. He heard people screaming through the walls. His father stormed out throwing open the church doors. "Adolf" he screamed; before grabbing Adolf roughly by his arm and dragging him away. The priest followed them as the unknown man stood at the door. "I know that your ancestry is doubtful Alois" he threatened. Alois tightened his grip on Adolf's arm. Adolf was scared, his father's anger was beyond control and he usually faced that wrath as a result. "Do not pay heed to him Alois" said the old priest in his feeble voice. "The church wishes you no insult or harm. We are all children of God" the priest's voice faded as Alois stormed away dragging Adolf along the path. They barged into the house and moved to the room where Edmund lay. Adolf released himself from his father's grip and ran to a corner.

Edmund Hitler lay still on a small bed. His mother was sobbing in a corner of the room, while his father settled on a small stool. The atmosphere in the Hitler house was cold and death like, for death had settled upon one of its members. Alois broke down as he stared at Edmund while Adolf stood in the shadows, extremely scared and disturbed by the events that he had just witnessed. Edmund Hitler slept, dreaming away endlessly into the day. The doctor had declared him dead following a bout of measles. Adolf kept staring at his little brother; unable to comprehend what just happened. 'Why would this strange man suddenly show up? Why would he not let them bury his little brother on the burial grounds?' he thought. The priest entered the house and stood beside them. He lay a hand on Alois Hitler's shoulder and gently spoke. Alois shrugged away and stood, watching Edmund sleep. "The keeper of keys and books are cruel people Alois. They are government agents pushed into our sacred churches, I am sorry" said the priest. After a moment of uncomfortable silence, the priest cleared his throat and began uttering verses; this went on for about a few minutes as Adolf sat on a stool with his head hung low.

Klara walked up to him and lay a gentle hand on him "it is time to say good bye to your brother now" she said with tear filled eyes. He hid behind his mother, clutching on to her dress and stealing glances at Edmund. Cold blue eyes looked at Edmund Hitler from behind his mother's warmth. Adolf failed to react or speak; he simply watched as they gently picked up Edmund and walked out of the house. He looked from the window as a small group of people joined the procession and made their way across the narrow road. Few villagers stood outside the house, silently acknowledging the sad demise. At the very end of the farm, a small company of men lay to rest Edmund Hitler, brother to Adolf and son to Alois and Klara Hitler. Adolf stood by the window, watching his father and the priest. A few more people from the village had gathered around them. Klara Hitler sat next to Adolf but he never really spoke to her. He just sat there in the comfort and warmth of his mother's presence. Adolf watched, tears rolling uncontrollably down his eyes. His little brother was gone, gone for good. And some cruel man wouldn't give him space for a grave. He sat there watching day turn to night. The cold winds didn't bother him much. He lost his only brother and they had to lay him down at the farm. Adolf fell asleep by the window, sore from crying and agony. Disturbing thoughts mired his dreams as he drifted in and out of sleep.

Adolf went about his work and school as usual from the next day onwards but something within him had changed for good. He tried questioning his father about Edmund's grave and why they were not allowed to bury him with the other villagers. His father refused to answer and forbade him from talking about this anymore. Klara Hitler too kept quiet about this issue and never spoke to him about it. Edmund's death and the talk with the strange man sent Adolf into a shell. He felt disconnected from his family; he knew that they were hiding something from him and that there was more to the burial. He started spending his days aloof from them.

He would stroll up to the cliff and spend his free time there. The other boys would snigger and laugh at him but slowly Adolf had grown distant from his friends and avoided most of them. His health was failing him; as he began skipping meals at home and a steady decline in his school interests was now evident. Adolf gave up his choir practices at school; he lost faith in God, the church, his parents and people around him; for no one had any answers. His thoughts were clouded for many a days, he was unable to think or reason and he let his mind go insipid in the process.

Adolf felt many emotions colliding within him but never did he find answers to any of them. Even the water that once soothed him now scared him horribly. Edmund could jump in easily, Adolf couldn't. Edmund was dead and gone, gone for good. Every few days; the vision of Edmunds death would come back to haunt him. His younger brother lay sleeping in peace, not moving or reacting to anything or anyone. No sign of life in the tiny boy, it seemed so unfair. He felt a hint of pain within himself and he couldn't explain what it was. 'The argument at church, what was it all about? What was wrong with his family? What did the doubtful nature of his father's ancestry mean?' There were questions exploding within his mind and absolutely no answers to be found. Adolf stood at the cliff's edge looking down at the water, searching for answers. The Gods had denied little Edmund sanctuary on their sacred lands what greater God would now help him resolve this conflict? Adolf stood there looking at ripples his blue eyes staring unblinking into the water, challenging it to give him answers.

Vagabond from Vienna

A dolf walked the streets of Vienna with hope in his heart, and a warm glow inside of him. As he traversed the streets and alleys, he took note of the brilliant architecture. Adolf came to a halt by the bridge and waited there, marveling at the richness of the place. He was waiting to meet his aunt here.

In a written note to her, he'd explained his predicament, stating how much he'd appreciate her help. Adolf wanted money to survive in Vienna. He needed a huge sum to be able to pursue his studies at the Academy of Arts from where he awaited approval any day now.

A few feet ahead, his aunt walked towards Adolf, and as he saw her, a grin colored his face. He was excited to see her; as they were meeting after a very long time. She was a fine lady in her late forties, dressed elegantly from head to toe. Adolf clumsily bowed down to her and kissed her hand. She smiled back, hugging him tightly. "My little boy" she cried out excitedly. "It has been a while since I last saw you" she said. Both Adolf and his aunt smiled at each other as they stood by the bridge. "So, my boy wants to become an artist eh? I am really happy to know that you have chosen the field of your interest" she said. Adolf nodded in response and smiled back. He was happy that someone in this world was with him on his choice of career and would support him through it. "I hope Klara is doing well?" Adolf's aunt questioned him. "Oh, yes mother is fine. She keeps going a little under the weather but otherwise; she's absolutely fine and happy" he replied. Adolf's aunt pulled out a little postcard sized photograph and showed it to him. "You are an uncle now, won't you come visit her?" She asked him handing out a picture of a small baby with big round eyes and an angelic smile. A wide smile broke over Adolf's face. "She is beautiful, little Geli" muttered Adolf. "I will come see her as soon as I can, do tell her that uncle Adolf is in absolute awe of her beauty and that one day she will grow up to be a fine young lady"

Adolf spoke as he stared at the photograph, mesmerized by the little baby. "I hope Paula is doing well under your care? She never even came to say goodbye to Edmund" Adolf asked and pocketed the picture. "She is well my dear boy, she misses you. Ahh, well she is better away from the tragedy you see" she replied. Adolf nodded and straightened up as he looked at his aunt. "I need your help auntie. I need you to help me with my education and expenses" he abruptly drifted into the conversation of his concern.

His aunt, taken by surprise at the sudden switch in conversation, quickly regained her poise and smiled gently. "You are my favorite little boy, Adolf. Study hard and spread your wings. I will take care of your education and living expenses. Don't you worry about them" she softly said. Adolf smiled and cleared his throat speaking again "I will need more money, much more." His aunt frowned a little and waited for him to speak further. "I want to paint and sell paintings, I also want to read and learn and visit new places" Adolf spoke with conviction as he described his grand plans. "We will do all that we can to fulfill your dreams my little boy" she replied with a reassuring authority in her voice. Adolf nodded but fell uncomfortably silent. "What is that you want to tell me Adolf? I feel there's something you have on your mind... be clear and say it now" his aunt questioned him, a little irritated at the situation. Adolf fettered a bit as he spoke, "Is it possible to give me my inheritance? The one that father left in your possession?" "You will get it all after I am dead, Adolf. You do know I am raising Paula too. Why such an unnatural demand?" his Aunt questioned, a hint of anger building within her. Adolf was taken aback at her sudden anger. 'Had he spoken too much?' "Unless you wish me an early death, I cannot give it to you yet" his aunt spat. "No no, I wish no such thing" he defended himself. The conversation wasn't going as planned for Adolf. "You seem to have turned greedy Adolf" his aunt's voice quivered with shock and anger as she spoke. Adolf was thinking hard as to how he could steer the conversation to a more subtle tone. "You boy, will have to wait. I will pay for your education and nothing else" her voice built up in annoyance. A few passing people were stealing glances towards them. Adolf tried to speak and make his intentions clear but his aunt cut him short. "Your father trusted me to take care of you. He left his money in my custody so that you wouldn't blow it all up at one go" she spoke in an angry tone. "I need the money" Adolf reasoned in a hushed voice not daring to look at his aunt in the eye. "And so, before my death you want me to hand over your inheritance to you? I might not agree on this Adolf" she concluded and puffed up in anger, no longer looking gentle or reassuring. "This demand is outrageous" she roared and a flock of pigeons flew away in fear.

Suddenly everything in the surrounding fell silent and still. Adolf was still looking around, trying to figure out a way to best tackle this situation. He kept stealing glances towards his aunt, trying to read her expressions and decipher how or what he could say next.

Adolf's aunt abruptly turned around as if to leave. "I am heading to the church" she spoke abruptly. "You may want to be a gentleman and walk me?" She prompted him to come. Adolf was standing there, his eyes moist and his hands trembling. "I will walk you to the city, I cannot go back to a church" he whispered. His aunt eyed him suspiciously and asked "Why so?" Under his breath and very softly; he muttered "Edmund." His aunt understood nothing of that for nobody but Alois knew of the story that unfolded regarding Edmund's burial. "The church was unfair to Edmund" he said. "Liar" Adolf's aunt spat back before he could complete the sentence. Even though they were standing in the middle of the road; she was unable to contain her anger. "You are as arrogant as your father and your grandmother. A Catholic liar, that is what you are Adolf. Why would the church be unfair to anyone? It is the abode of our God and forefathers."

She spat in anger and disgust. "The church means nothing to me and you know nothing." Adolf was trembling as he spoke.

"Have you called me here to insult and insinuate that I mean nothing to you? First, you want me dead and now you insult our church!" his aunt shot back and went onto a different tangent as Adolf stood there dumbstruck. He never said or meant anything of that. His aunt continued to hurl her anger at him. "You, your father, you get these thoughts from the wrong side; Adolf" she said. Adolf froze in place at the last statement that his aunt made. "What are you talking about?" Adolf asked as he clenched his fist and trembled in anger. "I have no wrong side to me" he spat on his Aunt's feet. His aunt's eyes widened in shock and disgust "Yes you do, you coward little thing" she roared back in anger, her skin turning a deep shade of pink now. Adolf looked away and began walking, trembling in fury.

"Maria Anna Schicklgruber" Adolf's aunt roared. Adolf stopped dead in his tracks. He had once heard this name before and it had given him a lot of sleepless nights. It was a very uncomfortable moment for Adolf; heat built up his body as he, facing the opposite direction, stopped dead in his tracks. None of them spoke or moved a muscle. People on the street were watching the argument unfold between these two. It was Adolf's aunt who broke the silence. "What are you running away from Adolf? I raised you, my favorite little boy. But I guess I know where such thoughts come into you!" she pressed on. Adolf didn't understand the context of this but a face flashed into his head. The strange man at the church, the argument over Edmund's death and the words 'illegitimate' flashed in his thoughts. Somehow this gave his aunt a wicked satisfaction, to see him helplessly stand there and not do anything.

"Adolf, you must know that your father was an illegitimate child" she said. "And his grandfather, well we don't know for sure but there is a distinct possibility" "You are a filthy old liar" Adolf roared back and cut her words short. His eyes were now watery and skin crimson red from anger. "You have no clue about what you say" Adolf was raging with anger as he roared, his breath coming hard and his chest heaving. He looked at his aunt with loath-filled eyes and turning around, he ran away. Adolf knew he should have walked out on his aunt a long time ago. He came back hoping that she might have changed but this time even that little association was to end completely. She had no business discussing his family tree in public, he knew better than to believe her knowledge on Alois's illegitimate ancestry. He ran as hard as his feet could carry him until he finally disappeared from sight.

Now, Adolf was truly left with no house to return to and no relative to turn upon. He ran endlessly into the streets, devastated by the statements his aunt had made. When he reached his apartment, an envelope awaited him. It was from the academy, and his heart thumped a little louder as he tore it open. His eyes travelled over formal salutations and settled on the one word that ripped him apart 'Rejected'. Adolf broke down completely; he crumpled the letter and pocketed it. He didn't bother to gather his belongings before running out.

Adolf ran as agony filled tears stained his cheeks. His life was now like that of a vagabond; with him spending his his nights on park benches and wandering about Vienna during the day. Adolf had a chunk of his savings left to him which he made no attempts to spend wisely. He spent his days on city streets buying painting materials and painting waterscapes. He would visit the opera at nights dressed in a coat, hat and with a stick in his hand, looking like a thorough gentleman. He would stroll through the city, sometimes like a wealthy businessman and on other occasions, like an artist vividly redesigning portions of it in his own imaginative talks; as he socially restructured civilization. His thoughts remained his own and he never really came out to anybody. He was without any friends or people to call his own at this point in his life. A steady decline in his lifestyle was evident and his elaborate spending went down by the day as reality dawned on him, the few water color paintings he made were obviously not selling at a great price. His expenditures went overboard and his income hardly filled the gap. Adolf had begun to sprout a beard by now and was emanating a stink like someone who hadn't seen a bath in days.

Very soon he was forced to sell off his overcoat to trade in for some food in return. He regularly slept on park benches, sometimes freezing to near death and sometimes bearing too much heat or rain. A few weeks into this lifestyle and Adolf was beyond recognition. Dirty unkempt hair, torn ruffled clothes, he was no different from the tramps that roamed the city. Hunger tore at his stomach and he had no option but to beg on the streets. He would go days without a proper meal and sleep stiff on freezing park benches.

His dreams were mired with ambiguous emotions; very often he would be back at the water's edge running through the green forest path and reaching the cliff. Even in his dream he wouldn't dare to jump into the deep blue chasm, his subconscious always stopped him from taking the plunge. It reminded him of how Edmund would jump and then his brother's dead face would come up in his mind. He dreamt of the argument his father had at the church and instead of the keeper of the keys; his aunt was the one accusing his father blatantly. He would wake up startled, hungry and frostbitten on the hard benches. Few of his dreams had a lady he didn't quite recognize but he was sure she looked a lot like baby Geli, his little niece.

Adolf had pocketed her photograph and kept it with him all the time. Over the days he had grown skeletally thin and he finally couldn't take the onslaught of harsh climate and hunger tearing at his stomach. He moved into a shelter for the homeless. Standing outside the shelter, Adolf read the names of wealthy people who made this shelter. It was run and managed by a wealthy Jewish family, giving shelter to anyone who walked in. as Adolf settled near the fire place, a bowl of soup was given to him, it was watery with a few vegetables floating in it. He didn't give it a second glance and gobbled it down in one go. He felt the hot soup travel down his cold hungry innards, and although he longed for more, this was all that was available for the day's ration. Stiff from the cold he settled on a bed and fell asleep instantly. For a change, the hunger and exhaustion made him sleep a dreamless sleep. Days passed at this shelter as Adolf lived under a roof, eating a decent daily meal. He regained a little bit of his energy and soon started earning a few coins that would buy him better meals. He lifted bags at the station, shoveled sidewalks for wealthy houses and cleaned toilets. This earned him his daily food and also some water colors. Finally, Adolf began to paint again.

On a fine morning, once Adolf was alone and had run out of work to do for the day, he sat at a park bench and noticed a battered book store which looked more like a library. He entered the store hesitantly, the tiny bell rang pleasantly and an old man appeared from behind the heaps of books. "Yes? How may I be of help?" he asked Adolf in a tiny voice. Adolf was baffled looking at the volumes of books that piled the shelves, he could read on and on with so many topics to choose from. The smell and sight of these books intrigued him. "Young man, may I help you?" The old shopkeeper was still looking at him questioningly. "I, can I read those books?" Adolf asked without taking his eyes off the vast volume of books. "Of course you can. You need to pay me though" replied the shopkeeper. "I don't have money" Adolf replied before the book keeper could finish his words. "Oh! I thought so" he said gesturing at Adolf's state. Adolf stared back at the bookkeeper, his deep blue eyes penetrating and commanding. "I see" he said. The bookkeeper observed him for a while; "you can help me out here in the store. You can clean the pathway and clear the back store" the store owner spoke as he waved his hands around showing him the area. "I can let you read a few of them in return. I do need help around but I can't pay you full time" he concluded. Adolf needed no better invitation to read these books. A smile flashed across his face as he happily took up the offer.

In the coming days, after Adolf finished his odd jobs, he'd come around to help the old book keeper who turned out to be a good mild mannered man by the name of Mr. Klaus. Adolf worked hurriedly on the tasks given to him and then he would go about digging deeper into every book that came his way, he read about each and every subject that he found interconnecting with the other. The deal was to let him read a few books but Mr. Klaus didn't really bother; as far as his work was being done. Adolf made sure he put in extra efforts and finished off his assigned work. He cleaned the sidewalks, tidied the counters, arranged the books order-wise and sneaked in a few books to read in between tasks. Within a few weeks of this routine, Adolf had covered a multitude of topics. He found himself hooked on various types of occult science books; he went about exploring various texts, some he understood, some he didn't and some he just discarded.

A very odd assortment of subjects caught his fancy and these books were like treasures to him. The shop had a small dingy room on the upper floor; and at times he spent entire nights poring over books. Mr. Klaus would usually retire to bed early; Adolf took full advantage of this. Under the pretense of arranging books, he would stay up reading. In no time, Adolf uncovered in this small forgotten shop, volumes of books that had either been banned or had disappeared from regular print. His fascination for strange arts grew, and he went about studying them one after the other. There were a few hand written books on occult sciences and practices that were apparently very dangerous to perform. Adolf wondered if Mr. Klaus even knew the value of these books that he had stowed away in his shop. On one of the nights, as he was reading through a heavy book on dream interpretations and their dynamics, his eyes grew drowsier and heavier by the minute. Slowly he drifted into sleep, his head lulled into the open book and he fell asleep, the dim light flickering and bouncing off his face emanating a soft glow.

Adolf was wandering in the forest, calm and serene with the green surroundings were inviting and warm. He heard a sweet feminine laughter in the nearby foliage. Curious to find the source, he searched around the shrubs, hoping to find someone. Whomever it belonged to, she was moving swiftly through the forest. As soon as he thought he had caught up with her, she would move away in a different direction and the laughter would emanate from somewhere else, farther away from Adolf. Chasing her through the thick forest cover, he reached a narrow path. The trees around were so dense and thick that light trickled down in small rays through them. He seemed close to the laughter now, he was moving slowly through the forest trying not to make any sound with his footsteps. This forest terribly reminded him of his home back in Austria. The strange girl seemed to be hiding behind a thick shrub as the laughter grew louder and more steady. Adolf moved towards the shrub and lunged at it, trying to grab anyone who might be hiding behind it. To his horror, the forest floor ended and he was falling freely through the air. Suddenly, Adolf was looking into his own dream from another perspective now.

The laughter died out and the air grew stronger as he fell through space. He glanced below and there was a calm blue water body waiting to engulf him on impact. He was afraid of the height and water. His heart was beating against the inside of his body as Adolf abruptly woke up screaming. Cold sweat trickled down his body, the lamp was almost dying out and it was time for dawn to break. He had fallen off his chair and was sprawled on the floor, his elbow hurting from impact. "What are you up to boy?" The bookkeeper screamed at him, his voice strong and full of authority. Adolf instantly got up, trying to gather himself. Mr. Klaus was now inside the room, arms akimbo, but with Adolf in a trance, he hadn't even heard him entering. "I saw you twitching in your sleep. What have you been up to?" The bookkeeper wanted answers as to what Adolf was doing holed up inside this dingy room. Adolf stared back at him with cold blue eyes, not answering or acknowledging his pressing questions. "You are going insane boy" his voice was now peaking, while Adolf maintained a ghostly silence. "I demand to know what you have been up to in my study." Mr. Klaus lost his sanity and roared at Adolf.

Locks of his neatly combed hair were falling loose over his face given the agitation. "You boy, you tell me right now what is it that you have been doing here? Is it some sort of black magic?" Mr. Klaus waved his walking stick threateningly. "Answer me boy" he screamed. A sudden smile crossed Adolf's face as he somehow enjoyed watching the bookkeeper fear him. He knew something that the bookkeeper didn't and this gave him a weird pleasure. It gave him an upper hand over the uninformed man. Slowly Adolf moved towards the door and passed Mr. Klaus as he walked out of the store. The warmth of sunlight felt good on his skin as he walked. He knew he could no longer come back to the store now that Mr. Klaus thought he was some maniac. Adolf laughed to himself and continued walking towards the shelter which was his only home. Adolf had now completely drowned himself in learning and understanding occult sciences, he would somehow get his hands on books through the black marketers who traded anything that was illegal and banned. He delved deeper and deeper into these sciences. The inmates of the shelter were getting uncomfortable around him and breathed sighs of relief when he spent some time outside the shelter. Adolf had stopped painting postcards and now barely got a meal a day. His hardships were piling up day by day but this was not the end.

A letter from home carried news of Klara Hitler suffering from a critical illness. Adolf, blinded by fear and pain, he abandoned everything and ran back home. With very little money to support his travel, he had to hitchhike most of his way back. He was hoping against hope to reach home on time and help his ailing mother. But when Adolf reached his doorstep, Klara Hitler was resting in peace; Doctor Bloch, their family physician having tried his best but failed. Klara had crossed yonder beyond from where there was no return. Adolf was shattered; everything around him came crashing down. He looked at her, resting there, calm and serene.

The warmth of the only woman he had known in his life was gone forever. He felt cold, angry and helpless. Adolf cried into the evening, his insides tearing apart, screaming in agony, he wept. He felt dead from within, a silent scream emanating from his broken soul. When he fell asleep at his mother's side he never knew, it was evening and the few villagers had left the crying boy alone to moan over his beloved mother's demise. Adolf woke up, tears still streaming silently from his eyes. He put on a candle with trembling hands. It cast an unnatural glow over the entire room with shadows lashing at everything present in the room. Adolf silently latched the house door and emptied his bag. From the few contents strewn on the floor he took out his sketching canvas. He set it up in a corner and started sketching out a portrait of Klara. She lay there sleeping for all eternity, her pale skin glowing in the eerie light from the candle and Adolf continued sketching. Tears were pouring down his eyes while he sketched a portrait of his dead mother. The sun was sinking as the light and warmth from Adolf's world waned. The rays of the sun disappeared as he put the last stroke on the canvas before passing out on the floor out of grief, hunger and pain.

Adolf now walked the familiar path leading up to the cliff. Way too much had changed since he was last here. He lost his mother, father, brother, aunt and friends. Alone he stood there, facing the water. He had abandoned his home for good, left everything that he held dear behind. His bag had his father's war photograph book and in his pocket, he carried his mother's picture along with Geli's. Adolf stood by the calm blue water, watching the ripples. His blue eyes hunted for answers, and hunted for solutions yet he found none. The villagers observed him from far away; they had disowned him, for he had grown into a weird little man. Under their breaths they muttered, there he stands; "the vagabond from Vienna."

The Beginning

Pain! Pain, beyond measure surged through Adolf. In his unconscious state, Adolf twitched and whimpered in pain. He opened his eyes, only to be hit by darkness. Immense pain coursed through his body as his skin, filled with blisters, had turned yellow and inflamed at different spots.

He exhaled blood from his nose as a result of which his breathing became labored and slow. In the pit of his stomach, Adolf felt extremely painful cramps; enough to send convulsions up his throat as he tasted a vile acid crawling up his mouth. A putrid stench filled his nostrils and he couldn't fight it away, it lingered around, threatening him. He was no longer that young man who was mourning his several losses. As time passed, Adolf had taken up arms to defend his country. He seemed happy and focused as he fought in the Great War, following orders and executing them responsibly. He felt a sense of achievement and fulfillment as he served.

Within the past few days of his drifting in and out of deep pain and semi consciousness; Adolf had gathered a few stray words. He lay quarantined in the warfare injury ward, probably alongside those who'd suffered the same fate as him. He had also heard more words that hinted at loss, betrayal and defeat. He screamed out in agony, as more pain surged through his body. There were hurried voices around him, but they made no sense. He felt a warm hand grip his cold sore wrist and then came a prick in the pit of his arm. At first he resisted the sensation; and then images from the last battle flickered on in his mind, he had been delivering instructions to the front line soldiers. A few soldiers were reaching to back them up in the trench; 'Germany would win this war for sure' Adolf thought to himself and that was when it happened, the familiar stench. The enemy attack came, they were coughing and their insides burning, he heard screams, there was smoke all around them and a huge deafening explosion rocked the trenches.

Slowly, those images began to fade out as he drifted into darkness. Adolf twitched again as the sedative worked its way up his mind, waking him up to a dream but the pain never left. It engulfed him instead and became one with his subconscious, and although he felt his body give in to sedation, the pain lingered on. Vivid images began flashing in his mind, he was trying not to fall asleep but the medication was winning against him and he slipped into a dream.

Klara Hitler's painting flooded his mind, her dead face, her cold skin, her frozen eyes. He remembered another painting that he made before leaving home for good. Adolf walked into the dark corridors. These corridors were familiar to him, 'school' he thought. Adolf's catholic school was housed inside a castle-like cloister. The brilliant architecture dated back to nearly the eleventh century, with numerous stone corridors running through the building. They were adorned with majestic archways and symbols etched onto the walls. He used to wander around after school, studying these symbols and engravings. One particular symbol caught his attention more than the others. A cross with the arms bent at right angles, this was the 'Swastika'.

Adolf moved through the empty school building with a wistful look around him, any school or academy now reminded him of rejection and humiliation. His eyes were sore from crying and the dearth of sleep had taken its toll on him. The villagers had abandoned him after his mother's death and he packed his belongings to move for good. Adolf wandered like a ghost through the corridors making no sound at all. He removed a bottle of red paint from his bag and came to a halt before a giant coat of arms engraved on one of the walls. It was the same fascinating symbol, the Swastika. He started painting; throwing blotches of red paint on the dark black stone walls. The red paint collided brilliantly against the hard stone; and he spent an entire evening in bliss, painting the engraving red. Tirelessly he worked; he dipped his tiny brush into the paint jar and threw color as high as he could. The entire engraved symbol stood massively on the stone wall. It was huge and menacing, Adolf couldn't reach the top but he jumped and threw paint blotches as high as he could.

So engrossed was he in his art that he didn't even notice that the entire day had been spent. The sun was beginning to set at the far side and very little light crept into the corridor where Adolf stood. The warm glow from dying rays hit him as he stood back and observed what he had created. His face and clothes were covered with tiny red dots of paint. Spent bottles were lying across the floor dripping left out paint. He moved back, staring at the huge stone wall with his tiny paint brush clenched tightly in his grip. The entire engraved portion was painted red in random disturbing strokes. The huge red coat of arms had a circle drawn around it and looked quite magnificent against the absolutely black stone wall. He stood there watching, his magnificent blue eyes searing through the walls. A massive blood red 'Swastika' stood in the center as Adolf stared at it. He stood still, staring at it until the last rays of light went out and the entire corridor sank into cold darkness.

Adolf yet again opened his eyes. Faint and far away blobs of lights began to flicker in his vision. He didn't know how much time had passed since he'd last opened his eyes. Tears were sliding down his face; he let them flow without even attempting to wipe them off. His body was rigid and tense. For most of the succeeding days, he would sleep alone, facing a plain white wall, not even turning around to acknowledge anyone and refuting all attempts to make conversation or even eat.

The doctors were of the opinion that his loss of sight had traumatized him so much, and he hadn't yet come to grips with it. The conversations he heard around him were much clearer and made more sense to him now. He drew conclusions that Germania had been defeated and that it lay in shambles. He felt betrayed, his army men had fought and died in vain. Adolf momentarily felt the same pang of betrayal he'd felt when the doctor couldn't save his mother, the same when he was rejected from the academy, the same when his father forced him into technical school. Edmund's dead face, the stranger at the church, his aunt… 'Your father is an illegitimate child.' The words rang in his ears. 'You cannot have a place on the sacred lands.' All of this pain was stored in one place in Adolf's confused mind.

One again, the pain jostled him back to his current reality. In the pitch darkness that was now his world, Adolf tried to fight back the pain, or at least, suppress it, albeit unsuccessfully. He did not bother to move for days together. Periodically, Adolf felt pricks in his arms; the pain and hatred didn't bother him anymore. He let it grow inside him; he let the hurtful emotions take over him. His state of semi consciousness continued for a few more days as he kept drifting in and out of dreams under the influence of sedatives. Defeat was painful; it was a painful betrayal to his fatherland. He felt the darkness return and engulf his thoughts.

Adolf drifted in and out of dreams; with many things flashing inside his head. He slept for several days on end, not bothering to attend to the hunger tearing at his stomach. Even when he did, he threw up all that he tried to eat and digest. His insides were filled with anger but all he could do was hope to recover. He fought his injuries, his body fought, and little by little, some vision crept back into his eyes. Yet another needle prick and he slept, even through heavy sedation, he could feel the constant pain lingering in his body. He drifted into sleep once again and opened into his dreams. This time around, Adolf was able to control his mind. His dreams were pushing him towards the blue waters but he resisted. He could sleep peacefully without those dreams disturbing him much. He drifted into a deep slumber. For more than seventy hours he slept, not getting up for food or water. In those deepest of slumbers, Adolf remained lost.

Over the next couple of days, Adolf made peace with the pain inside him. He felt a surge of energy flowing through him; and his vision was almost entirely back; with his senses being alert. Even in the darkness of the night, he could see around the hospital clearly. He held his left hand, the cut on it was still tingling and blood oozed out onto the bed but he did not bother. He got up and easily evaded the staff around; his left hand was dripping blood on the clean and shiny hospital floor. He stepped out into the night air and took in a deep breath from the surroundings.

It instantly felt better to be rid of the putrid stench that filled him since the gas attack. For a moment he closed his eyes and thought about home, his favorite spot on the cliff, the calm blue water calling him, the wolves at the edge of the water. Adolf waited there in the night air, calm and breathing slowly. Klara Hitler took up his thoughts. She appeared as she lay there, sleeping in eternity. The cut on his left hand was healing, the wound sealing itself slowly. He thought of the strange girl from his dreams, he knew who she was. Adolf slowly walked onto the streets and into the night. The boy Adolf disappeared into the darkness, never to return.

The staff in the hospital was in a state of shock the following morning; they saw the empty bed and a patch of blood on the white covers. They had searched the entire hospital to locate the patient but he seemed to have disappeared. The nurse noticed strange drawings on the wall next to his bed. They seemed to be drawn in blood, also explaining the red patches on the bed. They were random and blotched at places, but it was clear who the 'bloody' artist was. The drawing was that of a cross with arms bent at right angles within a circle. They were all tilted at an angle, striking and disturbing against the plain white wall. The hospital staff gathered around to see the strange symbol and empty bed where a screaming patient by the name of Adolf Hitler had lay, only a few hours ago. He had drawn these swastika symbols on the white walls with his blood. Where had he disappeared to? None knew, save him. And truth be told, for Adolf Hitler, it was a new beginning.

The Beast Bunker

Theodor tore away from the pages of the book he'd immersed himself in. He couldn't comprehend the happenings penned down in the diary. These thoughts and words made no sense whatsoever; they were strikingly different and ambiguous from what he knew about the Fuehrer. 'Were these written down by Adolf Hitler? Or was it penned down by someone else?' thoughts were racing through his mind. 'Was it even real?'

Theodor was thinking hard and too many questions arose concurrently. Ralf stirred a little, he had fallen asleep with the map open in his hands and Theodor snapped out of his thoughts. In the time he'd been reading this book, which was at least 20 minutes, they'd all been stagnant. He was filled with a sense of urgency. They had to move deeper into the Russian camp, else they would be found. Albert was still busy with the broken radio set. Theodor rubbed his eyes, blinking momentarily as the faint light source exhausted his eyes.

He flipped the book again to check for a date or some other markings but the only substantial thing he found was the signature reading 'Adolf Hitler'. Theodor felt a mixture of anger and fear surface within him as he held an artifact that probably belonged to the Fuehrer himself. Though it didn't matter to him, he and everyone else were in their current situation because of Hitler. Theodor had no family to go back to and Adelheid was away from him because of this one man. His thoughts clung on to Adelheid as she crept back into his mind and before he knew it, cold grey eyes were once again staring back at him. He thought of the dead girl and noticed dried blood and dirt on his wrist; 'the girl's blood' he thought, as a feeling of gloom settled over him.

Theodor's eyes travelled to the diary which was blemished in dark crimson stains. He flicked a few pages and thought to himself about the importance of such a document. 'If this really did belong to the Fuehrer, it could win him his freedom. A document of such importance could make all the difference in his life. Theodor was thinking hard, 'but he had to get out of the Russian camp first, for they wouldn't bother less about a few pieces of paper. If he got onto friendly territory he could bargain his way out with this' he thought. He scanned the book again, thin scrawled writing stood out; intimidating and alluring at the same time. He felt a pang of fear every time he opened the diary, as if he was listening to the Fuehrer himself.

It felt as if Hitler was directly talking to him through the pages and he couldn't prevent himself from wanting to read on into the narrative. 'What if Adolf Hitler still lived? What if he would resurface?' More and more thoughts poured into Theodor's head. 'If Hitler ever knew that a common German soldier was in possession of his private diary, he was sure to face a horrible death.' He pondered over the consequences and a small grin escaped him, 'either ways; he would die' he thought. Carefully he stowed the diary into a bag on the floor and got up.

He was shaken from the events that had occurred in the past few hours. He glanced at Ralf and Albert, Ralf was still asleep with the map in his hands. Tired and battered, he slept on. Albert was still trying hard to fix something in the radio set. 'Should he tell them about the diary?' he wondered. He noticed Ralf stir a little from his sleep. 'There was no bargaining with the Red army at this point' he thought. They wouldn't just let him walk away. Similarly there was no point disclosing this to Ralf and Albert just yet. He would tell them if the situation arose. Theodor felt a pang of guilt build up inside him but he pushed away the thoughts and tapped Albert on his shoulder. Albert was startled at Theodor's touch. "No luck with this radio yet" he said as he pulled himself out from the jumble of wire and sat there covered in sweat. "I can probably fix it if we get more material from other broken down radios" he said.

Theodor nodded and woke Ralf from his deep stupor. All three of them looked around and saw where they were actually trapped. It wasn't the bad dream they'd probably wished it was; this was their reality. Three German soldiers trapped beneath the Red army camp, hoping to save Adolf Hitler's shadow. Ralf looked at both of them and spoke, "we need to get going if we have to get to Han." Theodor and Albert nodded in acknowledgement. "Any luck with the radio?" Ralf asked as he sat down and opened a map in front of him. "None at all, it is beyond repair for now" Albert replied. "For how long did I sleep off? Why didn't you wake me? There is no time to waste, the alarms must have gone off and they might have sent search teams to look for us." Ralf was angry at himself for falling asleep as he kept blurting out. Albert and Theodor just stared at Ralf. All three of them were in a sorry state with their ruffled hair, labored breathing, blood stained faces and multiple injuries. But it was hardly a moment to sympathize, the world around them was in a worse state and there was no running away from the truth. Ralf got to his feet and removed the map that Fabian had given them. He spoke as he unfolded the map and pointed out routes. "We can enter here now" he said, his finger showing a path that led to an opening under an air raid shelter. "Or we can move from here" he pointed.

The other path was living up to its name; the honeycomb maze. It was a network of innumerable pathways that connected to each other. "We will have to surface at least once to figure out Han's location. He is rumored to be kept somewhere here" he pointed towards a bunker at the center of the map. "We also need to make sure if Han is alive, only then can we proceed further" said Ralf. "I have been studying these tunnels, and the paths are not really difficult" Albert interrupted. "They only look complicated; the turnings are pretty easy to remember. I suggest that we don't take either of the paths that you mentioned." Theodor and Ralf simply stared back at Albert as he reasoned. "We need to go this way" Albert pointed out as he moved the map closer to him. He pulled out a pen and traced a line on the map. "This path here, will lead us to a chamber under the Russian cabins. Entering under the bunker directly will be of no use. Since we know Han is their prisoner, it will obviously be heavily guarded. So we need to break open near the closest cabins and surface. From there onwards we can figure what to do and how to reach the bunker." Both Ralf and Theodor were pretty impressed by Albert's research on the tunnels. Albert had proposed a third route which led to numerable chambers and had vertical openings too. The better option was to open up under the cabins and not directly under where Han was held. But the convoluted Honeycomb maze was a big concern to Ralf and Theodor. Albert on the other hand was pretty confident of taking them, "If we somehow do get to him, how do we intend to get out?" Theodor asked. They looked at each other and a steely silence hung over them. "We will have to figure that along the way; right now we can't do much in terms of thinking up an escape route. Also, in any case if Han is dead we will have trouble finding documents that he has left behind, if there are any" replied Ralf. He stood up gathering the map and his backpack.

"We will travel along the path that Albert suggests then? The tunnel which opens underneath the cabins" he said pointing straight ahead of him. "From there on we can surface and figure out a way to either break into the bunker that holds Han or otherwise do whatever the circumstances demand." All three of them got up on their feet and prepared to march into the tunnel. Theodor took Albert's backpack and swung it over himself. "I'll carry it; so your hands are free to read the map" he said. Albert wasn't sure but nodded in response. "Also, before we leave, we need to pay our respects" Theodor suggested.

Both Ralf and Albert looked at him clueless as to what he was talking about. Theodor pulled out a hand gun from his pocket. "We need to honor Felix, Falko, Traugott… all of them" he said. Albert and Ralf looked at Theodor; surprised at the gesture. Theodor held out the General's hand gun, which was his last remaining memory. Albert and Ralf nodded as they moved closer to where Theodor stood. Theodor dug out some loose mud from the broken floor, Albert too helped by digging around riveted junctions of the tunnel. There were broken rivets and cracked pipes from the explosions that Han caused. Ralf, Albert and Theodor stepped out into the main pipe to lay down the gun. They didn't want to make it easy for anyone who was on their tail to follow them. Theodor gently placed the gun on the floor and Albert covered it with mud, the small blood covered gun had saved Theodor in his near-death experience. The three soldiers bowed their heads in respect. "To loyal and fierce soldiers, to loyal and faithful friends" Ralf said and raised his hand in salute. The three of them stood there in salute to the lives that were laid down. Felix, Traugott, Gregor, Frank, Falko were mere names now. It was because they laid down their lives that Ralf, Albert and Theodor lived. The last remaining members of Blood Moon were now deep inside the Russian camp. They turned around, gathered their belongings and began their journey into the tunnels.

Ralf led the way, with Albert tailing him and Theodor taking up the rear. They marched into the tunnel, alert and determined. It was dark and devastated throughout; there were burn marks and heavy dents at places. The tunnel had faint lights at irregular intervals. They did not provide much illumination but were enough to see in the otherwise dark sections. Some of the light bulbs were shattered and broken, hanging loose from the ceiling while a few had open wires dangling dangerously close to where they were walking.

The three of them looked in wonder at the magnitude of these tunnels. They must have taken expert engineers, massive equipment and many years to build. The tunnels turned and opened into one another with striking precision. The door locks and hinges were massive and glided open with absolute ease. Some junctions had reinforced concrete around the pipes while some others had metal couplings. Their purpose and utility remained a big mystery but they were surely coming into good use now. Ralf, Albert and Theodor looked at the heavy dents that came up at regular intervals. They were probably caused by of direct contact with dynamite placed within the tunnels. If Han was responsible for this damage, there was a slim chance the Russians would have still kept him alive. The dynamite had ripped apart doors, junctions and rivets, rendering certain sections completely useless. There were no cave-ins or collapsed tunnels but it affected their freedom of motion within them. Certain doors were locked shut while few were blown open and lay spent. They kept moving deeper into the maze as Albert consulted the map and took turns at relevant intervals.

Theodor and Ralf on the other hand were pretty lost. They just relied on Albert to lead the way. It was worse than a maze; the tunnels kept convoluting and getting darker as they moved forward. At times they felt a slight air brush them. There were no openings or vents that they could see but surely there was some sort of a forced ventilation system in place. They found many indirect openings but still couldn't figure out the source of seeping air. There were overhead ducts and vent-like protrusions which were sealed shut. They marched monotonously into the tunnel, seldom stopping to examine openings or odd dents caused by explosions. They didn't hear any noises or notice other activity; this was a good sign. The farther away they were from the Russians, the better. If they didn't encounter any trouble along the way, they would be at the base of one of the shelters within a few hours.

As they moved deeper into the tunnel, they were also traversing deeper into the heart of Konstantin's camp. The air began to grow heavier and a rotting stench was faintly building up around them. As Ralf came to an abrupt halt within the path, Albert nearly bumped into him and Theodor looked around to see the reason for his halt. In front of them lay a dead soldier, charred and completely burnt. The stench was extremely strong and unbearable. The three Germans looked around to see if there was anyone else nearby, it was empty except for the dead body. Ralf inspected it to see any markings or unused weapons.

They didn't find anything of significance but the body looked freshly burnt. He seemed to be a soldier, based on the torn bits of uniform that covered his burnt body. They once again inspected their surroundings. There was a small vertical tunnel leading upwards. It had no ladder but it definitely opened up on the grounds or somewhere accessible to the top. That was probably from where the dead body had made its way down. The three of them looked at one another and carefully avoiding the dead body, skirted around to move ahead. There was no way of surfacing upward from that long tunnel. It was a good fifteen feet high to just get to and then the climb. Minute by minute, hour by hour they walked deeper into Russian territory. They infrequently came across odd things, just one dead body, a few scattered broken objects and two gaping dents in the tunnels where dynamite might have directly affected it.

Ralf and Albert consulted the map again while slowing down a bit, as up ahead was a diversion which meant they were pretty close to the cabins now. Theodor rested against the tunnel wall for a few minutes. The gate at the diversion was completely charred and dented; all three of them were sweating from the immense heat inside the enclosed tunnel. They consulted the map and continued on their relentless march into darkness. Theodor heard a buzz in his ears as he walked; could it be that the heat was making him hear odd things now or was there truly another source of the buzz? He tried looking around for the source of buzzing, but couldn't see anything. The tunnel just stretched on minus any openings or other anomalies as they relentlessly covered ground.

As they approached a chamber, they noticed another massive explosion that had ripped apart the area; it was heavily charred and burnt with deep dents in the tunnel. Here, the dynamite had affected it enormously, to the extent that it had ripped apart a section of rivets on the tunnel couplings. A little bit of earth was creeping into the tunnel and their eyes met a sight which was impossible to completely make out in this isolation. A small creeper was growing into the tunnel through loose mud. It had a small white flower on it and was growing towards the earth where gravity pulled it. It looked strikingly green and fresh. 'How was it possible?' Theodor thought. 'There was no sunlight, how did this life form possibly grow here.'

Again, Theodor heard the strange buzz around him. 'He sure was losing his mind now' he thought. But the source of buzzing was changing its locus constantly. 'It couldn't be his mind playing these tricks?' Suddenly out of nowhere a bee flew in. All three of them noticed it fly around their heads as they stood there watching it hover. It moved around the plant, making a buzzing sound through the air. Such an uncanny sight to behold within this tunnel was a bee hunting for nectar. They watched as it hovered around the plant and finally settled on to it. They snapped out of their thoughts and marched ahead into the dark damp tunnel.

They had lost track of time, but the trio trusted Albert to keep consulting the map and lead them in relevant directions. Both Theodor and Ralf were alert and took firing positions at every turn and bend. The tunnels were getting darker and darker, the air inside growing damp and heavy. Their breathing was labored and their brains were shutting down due to the lack of oxygen. "If anybody attacks now, I don't have the stamina to stand and fight" Theodor whispered. "Keep walking soldier, just keep walking" Ralf muttered as they strode through the dark tunnels. They took another turn through the tunnels and opened into a chamber. It had a massive door, nearly fifteen feet in diameter. It stood locked and intimidating in front of them. This section seemed bigger than the rest of the tunnel and looked like a junction of some type.

There were two more small doors by the sides, one of them charred shut from the explosions and the other soot covered. "Good thinking Albert. Whatever made you think that we should take this route helped us" Ralf said as he inspected the other doors. The three of them silently moved up to the bigger door and pressed their ears against it. A deep whining sound met their ears; it was humming and at intervals emanated a strange rattle. Surely it was some sort of machinery operating on the other end. Ralf touched the lock wheel to check. It was tightly shut. "This is the only way ahead now" they settled into a huddle as Ralf spoke.

"If we do encounter any soldiers beyond the door, we have only one option and that is to take them out. The distance from this adjoining chamber to the camp opening is large. Even if they know we are here they cannot cover the distance." The three of them stared at each other as Ralf explained the attack. "I think there will be ways to enter the adjoining chamber from above"

Albert was looking at the map and talking. "The fact that they have placed machinery in the room should mean that it has multiple access points" said Albert. "He is right" agreed Theodor. "But nothing shows up on the map that we have here" Ralf argued. "So we march in and be quick about it, even if there are vertical tunnels; they won't be able to travel that fast. We are no less than thirty feet below ground level. You and Theodor would enter with ready firepower. Weapons ready; gentlemen" Ralf gave the orders as he geared himself for what lay ahead. They pulled out their guns and strapped on the extra ammunition. Ralf held his hand gun ready and looked at them for acknowledgement. They nodded and Ralf swung into action. He pushed the lock wheel with all his might while Theodor and Albert took up firing positions. Ralf heaved the lock wheel as it grunted and turned around making tremendous noise. It took several turns to open the lock completely, not wasting any time; Ralf pulled the massive door open and ducked instantly. Both Theodor and Albert jumped into the opening, their guns aiming into the chamber and senses highly alert.

A flash of light met their eyes. A bright bulb hung from the ceiling. It was powerful and the intensity blinded them. Theodor and Albert ducked and fanned around to confirm if there were soldiers. Ralf was the last to enter as he scanned the chamber. The three of them relaxed their guard and looked around. It was a huge chamber, the center of which was occupied by a big motor and another door stood on the opposite side. No other openings were visible in the room. The machine was making considerable noise so there was no need to panic or keep their voice down if somebody was at the other end. Theodor looked into the machine to see water gushing through a turbine. The chamber had wires running on the floor and stray pieces of pipes thrown around. It looked as if they had just shifted this motor and gotten it running. Two massive pipes were running in and out of the room. They were absurdly huge and had been freshly clamped into place which was obvious from the heat marks and fresh rivets on junction couplings. Albert found a bunch of maps and circuit diagrams discarded on the floor. He collected them and looked through to understand the functioning of this strange room.

Ralf went to look at the opposite door and pressed his ears against it. He couldn't hear anything but the machine whine in their chamber. He turned around and looked at them questioningly; Theodor and Albert instinctively took firing positions and aimed at the door. It was a similar looking door through which they had entered, Ralf turned the lock but this one didn't budge at all. Ralf looked at Theodor and Albert, gesturing them to be alert. He tried turning it again with all his might, straining his muscles to move the lock but it remained stuck. Theodor kept aside his gun and helped Ralf move the lock. Their combined effort also didn't help; with the lock remaining shut. Panting for breath they fell back a little. Ralf searched around the room and picked up a long metal pipe from the floor, which he wedged in the lock wheel. Once again they heaved together, Ralf using the pipe as a lever and Theodor with his bare hands. Ralf's muscular arms flexed as he put pressure on the wheel.

The metal pipe began to bend as Ralf kept up the pressure. Both he and Theodor exerted pressure trying to turn the lock wheel. Suddenly the pipe bent and slipped from Ralf's hand. Theodor instantly ducked to avoid the flying metal. It flew and hit the overhead pipe with a loud clang and fell right into the turbine. Ralf fell back as he slipped from his stance and Theodor was already on the floor. With loud and scary jolts the entire turbine started vibrating, making loud crunching noises. Theodor jumped to dislodge the pipe from within the turbine. It was stuck and was being crunched into the motor by the powerful gear teeth of the turbine. Ralf too got up and rushed to help Theodor. The machine was now whining loudly and heating up. There was too much friction as the gears tried to push and the pipe remained stuck in-between. Smoke began emanating from the fuse box and Ralf was still attempting to pull it out in vain. Albert quickly saw the wires running on the floor, he pulled out the diagram that he found and made a quick note of the wires. He caught two wires from the floor and ran his fingers along their length, reaching the junction. Albert pulled out his pocket knife and cut the connection. Instantly the motor died down and Theodor and Ralf both looked back to see Albert holding severed ends of the wires. The motor and tremendous noise died down instantly as the turbine came to a complete halt. Both Ralf and Theodor let out a sigh of relief. They were panting from the effort of pulling out the wedged pipe. Albert's quick thinking coupled with his ability to study maps and diagrams was getting them out of tight spots.

"Let's get back to opening that door?" Ralf mockingly questioned as he and Theodor both tried again to pull out the metal pipe. The gear teeth had eaten into the pipe; dragging it inside, making it impossible to wrench out. Albert was looking around the tool box and at the scattered equipment; there were more floor plans and working drawings of the entire Russian camp. He went through them and studied the pipe lines. "We might be able to reverse polarity and make it turn backwards. That might throw the pipe back out or at least get it back enough to pull it out from the gear teeth" Albert spoke as he consulted the diagrams laid out before him. Ralf and Theodor simply nodded, happy that Albert had figured out a way. "Yes Mr. Decoder. What did you eat when you were young, circuit boards?" Ralf mockingly asked.

Suddenly Albert held out his hand motioning them to keep quite. He opened the map that he was studying. "Come here" he called out to Ralf and Theodor; a striking urgency in his voice. They both huddled around him and looked at a circled out point on the map. It read 'the beast bunker'. "Fabian mentioned this bunker" said Albert. Ralf moved closer nodding in acknowledgement. "You are right" replied Ralf as he too studied the map. "This is where Han is held captive" he said. "I am afraid not" interjected Albert as he continued studying the maps. "Look at this impossible feat of engineering. He is housed inside a suspended chamber within the beast bunker. He obviously has to be housed in something which provides maximum security and this chamber seems impenetrable" Albert went on talking without taking his eyes off the diagram. "And if you roughly consider the placement of this beast bunker" he spoke in a barely audible whisper. "We are exactly under it!" he concluded as the three of them slowly raised their heads; looking up at the ceiling, hoping to see through the layers of metal and concrete and gaze at the massive feat of engineering rightly known as, the beast bunker.

Water

The room was saturated, filled with wafting smoke and steam. A tiny man sat smoking a pipe and lazily looking out the window. "Konstantin will join you shortly." A guard placed some rum on the table and spoke to the small bald man who was sitting in Konstantin's cabin like he had not one worry in the world. Konstantin was out with Fedor and Viktor.

The atmosphere was a little less tense at the Russian camp. The approaching jeep was that of General Mark; an old ally of Konstantin. He was well placed within the government and passed important information to Konstantin. His arrival had eased the atmosphere and Konstantin was relaxed. General Mark was on his way to Berlin to raise victory flags and report back to high command. His visit here was not authorized and as such, was to be kept a strict secret.

Konstantin welcomed him into the camp and asked him to settle while he finished pending matters. Viktor was standing by Konstantin's side with a guard who reported the firings in the forests. Fedor too, waited for orders as he stood anxiously to get into action. "These are not Nazis" Konstantin spoke with rage. Both Viktor and Fedor were confused. 'Not Nazis'? Who else would want anything from a Nazi sniper,' they thought.

"They are a secret group called the Blood Moon. We have little information on them. If along with Han we can capture more of their kin, we might be in luck" said Konstantin. His mind was thinking of better possibilities already. "Han is secure enough; we must let these intruders get closer so as to capture them alive" he said. Viktor and Fedor were shocked to hear this. Konstantin actually wanted the intruders to get closer to Han. "Viktor, order the guards to fan out and give me a detailed report of the intrusions. I want to know from which side they entered and how far into our territory they currently are. Fedor, you gather the resources you need and track them down. Do not kill them yet." Konstantin was deep in thought as he gave the orders. "I shall go meet General Mark now, report to me as soon as possible and be extremely vigilant" he concluded. Both Viktor and Fedor nodded, bowed down and dashed away to carry out their orders.

"Mark" Konstantin happily roared as he entered his cabin. General Mark was happy to see Konstantin and greeted him with a big smile. "Congratulations, my old friend. We are at Hitler's doorstep. Now all I want is to see his miserable dead face. What a victory we have achieved!" Mark looked tiny in front of Konstantin as he happily boasted. "What a victory I have achieved, General" Konstantin replied as he sat in his chair and flexed his arms. His wound was still bleeding and the blood trailed down his massive arm. "Bloody sniper bullet" he cursed under his breath as he looked at the wound.

"Come on Minotaur. Our soldiers are fighting in Berlin. It is our victory" Mark retorted. Konstantin stared into Mark's eyes. "If I had not bought out their key associate, this would have never happened. I won the war for Russia, not us" Konstantin banged his fists on the desk with a final authority.

The entire table trembled under his hand and the glass of rum toppled over spilling into the map. The rum seeped forward, turning everything into a dark shade of maroon. The tiny figure of General Mark looked insignificant as compared to the towering figure that Konstantin was. "Viktor" Konstantin barked. "Get the General some more rum, will you?" "Some hot water too if you don't mind. My throat hurts so much, since I had to inhale a lot of ash from your surrounding areas" said Mark. Konstantin smirked "It was important Mark, to wipe out certain evidence" he said as they continued talking. Mark lit a pipe and asked "What about Vlad now?" "What about him?" Konstantin retorted. "He will want to interfere, obviously. He will want command of this camp" Mark asked cautiously. "I will give away the neighboring land General, but will retain this portion, this camp that I have made. It will serve us well. Heed my words" Konstantin replied with authority and open arms showing off his camp. "Vlad needs a marker on the map for high command to see, he will have it. But I will not give up this camp to him" Konstantin pressed on as he spoke. "Had Hitler's orders been followed with regard to the Russian offensive, the war for us would have been over with them winning it easily. Hitler is shrewd and his strategy involved surrounding our lands from all sides. I made sure his orders were relayed for a head-on attack instead. With great efforts and at terrible personal risk, I managed to buy out Nazis. Nobody back at the high command sees this, they do not understand that it is I, Konstantin that has led them to victory. I single handedly turned the tide in Russia's favor. My German friend has helped me a lot and I wish to hear from him any moment" Konstantin concluded, pointing to the radio expecting it to crackle to life.

He was playing his cards with perfect ease. He knew exactly how and where to nudge people into listening to him. "Berlin, as I hear is in a mess right now, so communications are down. But you must go back to Vlad and convince him to leave this camp alone. Tell him to leave it in my command. They will have plenty to loot from Germany now" Konstantin reasoned. A soldier entered and placed a glass of rum on the table. "I am sorry my lord, Viktor is away on duty, I will assist you in everything that you require" the soldier said. Konstantin nodded, not bothering to look at him. General Mark lifted the glass and drank from it. "The soldiers spoke of some disturbance around the camp? What was it; who were they?" asked Mark.

Konstantin smirked as he replied "Nothing to worry about, just some soldiers who went astray and a few prisoners we suspect." Konstantin maintained a straight face and easily convincing Mark. "I asked for some hot water, didn't I?" Mark questioned the soldier. "Sir we have run out of water, the problem is being fixed and I will get it once it is available" he replied. The General nodded in frustration as he lifted his glass and drank the rum at one go. Konstantin held out his hand to silence the soldier and General Mark. "What is the problem with the water supply?" he enquired, his voice quivering with suppressed anger. Cold silence fell over the room as Konstantin waited for a reply. "Supply has stopped sir" the soldier replied. "I have asked for someone to fix it" he said. "I see" replied Konstantin through gritted teeth. "Get me Viktor and Fedor, Now" he roared and got to his feet. A few things fell off the table as he abruptly got up. General Mark was surprised at his reaction. "A little bit of hot water doesn't bother me Konstantin. It is absolutely fine" Mark tried to calm him down. "Silence" Konstantin hollered as he loaded his shotgun.

Viktor instantly dashed into the room, he was panting from the run. "This part of the bunker area is supplied with water from the new thermal pump I assume?" Konstantin fired questions at him without waiting. "Yes sir" Victor nodded in agreement, taken aback by the abrupt question. "Which means it is practically impossible for water supply to stop, right?" he asked. Viktor's eyes widened in shock and understanding as he replied "Yes my lord." "Where is Fedor? Connect me to Igus right now" Konstantin roared. Viktor dashed towards the door. He shouted orders to the guard to hurry up and fetch Fedor.

Viktor dashed back inside and started fumbling with the radio. Igus had been gotten on the other line. Konstantin snatched the mike from Viktor and spoke into it. "I think we have a situation, is the chamber safe?" after a few moments a voice broke over the radio. "Yes it is." "Step up security around the bunker. I will come to see you once I finish matters here" Konstantin concluded and disconnected the switch. He looked at General Mark who was dumbstruck and did not understand a thing from what was going on. "I think it is best if we act now, times are bad and once the allied forces reach these areas we will have great difficulty covering up our activities. Trust me and act today General, keep Vlad out. You must convince him" Konstantin pressed on, keeping the topic diverted. It was important to keep Han's capture a secret and Mark was now completely confused.

The door flew open and Fedor strode in "I heard you need me my lord. What is the situation?" Fedor asked and stood rapt in attention. "The water supply here has stopped; it comes from the new thermal motor. Intrusion is closer than we think" hinted Konstantin. Fedor clenched his fist in anticipation. "We discovered bodies in the forest, our soldiers and Germans too" reported Fedor. Konstantin jumped onto Fedor and held him by his neck. "You fool, when will you report the same? What were you waiting for?" Fedor was calm and unaffected by Konstantin's rage. "I just got the information; I haven't confirmed it and hence didn't bother you."

Saying this, Fedor calmly waited for Konstantin to release him. His gaze was unflinching as he bore into Konstantin's eyes. "The forests have been fanned, the mazes remain" Fedor told Konstantin as he loosened his grip. "Get me a map of the underground" Konstantin barked. Fedor dashed away in an instant. "Viktor, alert guards at all openings and secure the areas tightly. We are going to weed them out. They are much closer than I anticipated." Konstantin was forming a strategy in his head as he instructed. Fedor dashed back into the cabin while Viktor nodded and gave orders to be relayed further. Fedor rolled open the map, the General was on his feet standing by the table dumbfounded. "Viktor, you have been inside the maze post devastation; tell me which areas directly open into the thermal motor compartment" Konstantin questioned.

Viktor took a pen and traced out areas on the map. "Here you see the straight tunnel, this one and the one on other side opens to our shelter. This is guarded now, for the new rigs are housed here and here." Viktor was marking areas on the map as he explained the layout of new rigs and their installation. "There are two possibilities, either this straight one here or the opposite one on this end are both long patches, one of them is where we last sent Mr. Krammer" said Viktor. Both Konstantin and Viktor glanced at each other while Fedor eyed the map keenly. "I see" Konstantin nodded, "that traitor met his downfall there. Krammer conspired and killed General Igor, we set him straight but we lost the General." Konstantin looked at General Mark and explained the situation to him. Viktor nodded in acknowledgement and continued. "There are vertical entry points here and here. We can send soldiers down from both points and intercept intruders. Even if this is just a problem with the fuse; which is highly unlikely our teams can reach within twenty minutes" Viktor continued explaining and drawing points on the map. "How likely is it to be a fuse or wiring problem?" questioned Konstantin. "Chances are less my lord. Our team did a good job with the installation," before Viktor completed his sentence Konstantin banged his fists on the table and roared "It's them, they are inside." Konstantin's anger was peaking. He studied the map for a while and his hand reached out for the book that he kept consulting.

He momentarily eyed the metal door in the cabin and spoke, "We will stamp them out with their own plan then." Konstantin suddenly appeared gleeful and possessed. He snatched the pen away from Viktor and drew on the map. "Reverse water supply from this section and route it back to the pump. Open floodgates from camp reservoirs and run them. There are two pipes that connect the pump right? Reverse them both. Let the water flow out through the pump. There are half connected pipes in this section too. Flood water in both the chambers" he concluded. Viktor, Fedor and General Mark appeared dumbstruck at the magnanimity of Konstantin's statement. "They won't stand a chance. We will run water for around ten minutes. That should flood these pipes enough to fill them completely. Once that is achieved we will receive them at the camp opening. If we send in our forces, they will have enough time to disappear in the endless mazes. Deliver the orders NOW" Konstantin bellowed, as a content smile spread across his face. "I want you to fan the areas Fedor. Any activity that is out of place, anything at all; we must know. Lock all openings from the outside and station guards all around them. Put guards to man the hatches too, unleash our hunting squadron in the forests."

Konstantin was gripped with a maniacal energy as he gave the orders. "Go flood the tunnels" he concluded. Fedor and Viktor both nodded and ran across the room disappearing behind the door. Konstantin patted General Mark, gesturing him to follow "Come General, let's weed out some German flesh" he mockingly said. "There are Nazi intruders this deep in our territory? You have kept this a secret from the high command?" Mark spoke in surprise. "Konstantin, you dare to put us all in this mess and danger!"

General Mark was wide eyed and dumbstruck at the news. Konstantin laid a heavy hand on the tiny General's shoulder and gripped it tightly. General Mark seemed to buckle under the weight. "You will now walk with me and watch me maim these intruders with nothing but water" Konstantin concluded, a wide grin plastered on his large face.

Death Like

Ralf, Albert and Theodor kept trying harder to open the door and cross the chamber. Going by the map, they were pretty close to the area labeled Beast Bunker. If they, somehow, could manage to ascend vertically, the three of them could actually make it to Han in very little time.

Theodor was trying to displace the lock and open the door while Ralf tried to pry out the wedged pipe. Albert sat on the floor drawing out routes from maps that he had acquired. The pump had stopped working and short spurts of water were stemming from within the turbine. Albert was in awe of the suspended chamber's design. He was studying the possibilities of getting in once they got closer. A few minutes passed by as the three were individually occupied with their activities. Suddenly, a deep gurgling sound echoed through the room. Ralf and Theodor continued their activities but Albert froze in place.

He rolled up the maps and looked around for the sound. "What was that noise?" before he could complete his sentence a sudden spray erupted from one of the pipes leading into the motor. It drenched Ralf from head to toe and he stepped back, dripping wet from the spray. It was a short but powerful spray. The water was extremely cold and Ralf was shocked as he rubbed himself to keep up the heat in his body. Albert dashed across the room and pressed his ear to the pipe, he caught distant gurgling sounds. He looked up at Ralf and Theodor, frozen in fear. Both Theodor and Ralf looked at him questioningly. "What is it?" They asked in unison. Theodor pressed his ear to the pipe trying to figure what Albert heard. "I think they know" said Albert. "What do you mean they know?" "What do they know?" Both Theodor and Ralf questioned Albert trying to make sense of his statement. "This is a thermal pump. It regulates water from one point to the other and it is basically used to maintain constant supply along with temperature of the water so it doesn't freeze" Albert was talking hurriedly and he seemed scared. "Water just gushed out from it, which means they have already or are activating a pump somewhere else, which is pushing water down to us. I have disconnected the wires here, this one can't start" Albert concluded; pointing at the spent wires and pump.

Konstantin along with his guards was at the control cabin. They were cutting out electric supply from sections of the pipes which they wanted to flood. If they ran water along with electric supply it would cause electrical malfunction and overload the main circuit breakers. Konstantin checked his watch. "Flood them, will you?" he ordered impatiently. His men responded by switching off required power units and opening up the massive reservoir gates. Far away, a huge churning sound was heard as the gates grind open letting the water loose.

The three Germans stood in absolute darkness, unable to even make out their own faces. They had packed their maps in the bags and had their guns out. Theodor found rubber insulation straps on the floor with which he wrapped the diary and shoved it into his backpack. Albert too, was packing the maps into bits of rubber and shoving them in the bag. Ralf pulled out a flash light from the extra equipment that Fabian had given them. He put it on and checked the pump. Another loud gurgling noise was heard and a massive spray of water burst out of the turbine. This time, the water pressure was so high that it nearly touched the ceiling. All three Germans were thrown back from the force. It was such a massive gush that the entire pump shifted from the pressure. They heard a metal clang and the wedged pipe came loose. "Good news, the pipe is out" Ralf shouted through the commotion. Before they could register the events, another pipe burst open and water flew into the chamber with an equally massive force. The rivets simply gave away and let gushing water flow through the chamber. Albert struggled to see through jets of water now flowing in fury within the room and rushed to the fuse box. He pried open the box and disconnected the wires. In any case, if they put the electricity back on, they would be electrocuted to death. "They are flooding the area, they know we are here" Albert yelled, trying to recover from the onslaught of water. Theodor abandoned his post, Ralf pushed him back "let's open this, it's the only way we can go, if we go back we meet a straight tunnel leading out of the camp which they will cover for sure and the other door is charred shut and dented. Heave" Roared Ralf and they applied their strength to nudge the lock. Albert looked around trying to see the burst pipes.

The spray of water increased two-fold and was now bouncing off the ceiling. "Wait, leave that door" shouted Albert. He pulled both Ralf and Theodor out of the chamber. "What do you think you are doing?" Ralf yelled in anger. "Leave that opening alone. We need to get out and seal this door shut!" Albert shot back pointing towards the door from where they entered. The plan actually made sense as Theodor and Ralf registered the information.

The three of them jumped out from the chamber and pushed the huge iron gate shut. The water was already flowing out of it and it took quite a lot of effort to lock it shut. They grunted through the effort and closed the door. The three of them caught their breath as they leaned against the gate. They heard more grunting and groaning through the tunnel systems and before any of them could speak, huge explosions were heard. It echoed through the tunnels and rang in their ears. They froze in place as they heard more gushing and pipes above their heads burst open. They were instantly drenched in water and the force of spurting water increased. The water, they noticed, was bitter cold and it cut through their skin, freezing them in place. Ralf grabbed both of his allies and pushed them forward. "Run" he shouted through the sprays of water.

Konstantin had ordered his guards to assemble near the gate while he went into the beast bunker. He had dismissed guards in and around the bunker. He climbed into the trucks that were lined up and checked them one by one. All of them carried the promised nuclear material from Berlin but Konstantin was looking for something else. He patiently climbed into each one of them and inspected the canisters. One of the trucks shouldn't contain nuclear material as per his knowledge. He climbed into another one and checked the canisters. He opened one and a light began flashing. It was a pressurized container and liquid gushed out from it as the canister was opened. Konstantin stood there unaffected by the spray of unknown fluid.

A smile crossed his face, he knew these decoy canisters. He unscrewed the container further and a flash of gold met his eye. A satisfied smile crossed Konstantin's face. His German friend had sent him the entire collection. Each canister in this truck was filled with gold. He had finally procured the broken down parts of the legendary Amber Room. The mysteriously lost treasure which people had been hunting for ages was finally in his hands. Konstantin rummaged a little deeper. He found box after box that held the entire remnants of the Amber room. A satisfied smile sat on his face as he walked out and got into the driver's seat. He hit a switch before entering the truck and a floor panel opened leading to an underground tunnel. The tunnel was big enough for a truck to enter. Konstantin revved the truck to life and drove into the underground cavity.

Theodor, Albert and Ralf ran through the tunnel trying to dodge water. They covered a small distance before hearing another pipe burst open as more water poured into the room, the massive force ripped apart joints and rivets that held the pipes together. Water was now flooding the tunnels from multiple open pipes. The three of them ran through freezing cold water as the levels rose threateningly. They hit a straight tunnel which they were to traverse through initially. Water was accumulating at a fast pace and they could feel it rising above their ankles already. Ralf put on his torch to check what lay ahead, but all they saw was an endless tunnel which stretched into obscurity. Suddenly they heard a sharp crunch followed by a resounding crash. Ralf quickly glanced behind to see a huge wall of water headed their way. The iron door had ripped apart from its very hinges by the intense pressure. The flood swept them off their feet as it moved with a mighty fury. Albert yelped as he helplessly flailed forward with the waves. Ralf was the first to get up as he tried to withstand the oncoming tide.

He swiftly helped Theodor and Albert to their feet. Panic clouded their minds as they stood drenched in icy cold water. Ralf pushed them ahead in panic, running was their only option now. "We need to go all the way back from where we started. We can enter the other section from there onwards" he said recalling the routes on the map. "Hoping that there will be a functional door there, we can seal it off and head further into the maze. It is the best we can do right now" he screamed through the chaos. The force of gushing water increased and they were fast losing the battle against its rising levels.

Theodor's thoughts were racing at a crazy pace, he had never felt so helpless in his life. Everything was falling apart. He hoped against hope to reach the intersection and find an opening. The three of them were slowing down considerably as they waded through water. None of them spoke or stopped, they just glanced around to make sure everyone was on their feet and running. Momentary flashes of light were visible from top openings but none were feasible enough to reach out or climb into. The flashlight that Ralf had was still working and it showed them the way through floods. All three were tired and wet to the bone already. Their muscles were screaming in agony as oxygen levels dropped to an all-time low.

Red army soldiers were yet again in a state of frenzy as they secured gates, shouted orders and took up their positions. In the space of a few hours, the Russians were facing one intrusion after other and they knew Konstantin's temper was peaking. Konstantin finished securing his treasures and came out to personally inspect security; standing with his shot gun at the entrance of the tunnel. The gate was closed shut, and water was already leaking from within it at irregular rivets and joints. He consulted his watch and stood there, patiently. Viktor stood beside him armed and ready along with an array of guards. Soldiers stood on top of the tunnel, long range shooters were placed in the trees and hounds were waiting at the gate. Fedor didn't want to take any chances with these intruders. If they were proficient enough to breach their security, there was no telling how dangerous they were. He had all unknown tunnel openings sealed. The Honeycomb maze was a huge system and it was impossible to know which opening would lead where. He couldn't take chances and so, he set out with a batch of guards to overlook any lapse in security.

Theodor, Ralf and Albert were now struggling to keep above the water level. Gasping for breath, they were being pressed against the tunnel ceiling by the flooding water and tried their best to keep afloat. Theodor was feeling dizzy and perplexed, he couldn't think properly as the lack of oxygen was shutting down his brain. A faint buzzing sound was building up in his ears. This, he thought was the sound of approaching death for sure as water levels were up to their necks and within a few minutes they would drown. However they kept pushing through the tunnel strenuously.

The buzzing sound was growing more prominent and was audible over the splashes. Albert gave up as he came to a halt trying to stay above water. Theodor and Ralf looked at him and waited. The three Germans floated there gurgling water as their cruel end approached. Albert closed his eyes and was drawing the last breaths of his life. "No matter how this ends I salute you both" Ralf spoke in a gentle tone. Albert and Theodor looked back at Ralf, not knowing what to reply. Heartlessly the water rose and the buzz in Theodor's ear grew stronger. Theodor closed his eyes and shut out sights of their current dilemma. Eyes of the dead girl instantly flashed into his mind and looked at him, urging him to help. Adelheid drifted into his thoughts, he felt her gentle touch, her radiance, her warmth. Theodor was silently weeping in his mind. He wanted the last memory in his dying mind to be of Adelheid.

He heard sounds around him, sound of ever-present water and the irksome buzzing that grew louder. The sound suddenly shifted to his other ear. Theodor abruptly opened his eyes and turned; this didn't seem to be the buzzing caused by his ears. It was something totally different and then he saw the tiny bee hover. It drifted gently over water, its reflection breaking up on ripples just below its sting as it swiftly flew around. 'This small life form must die here with them' thought Theodor. The bee buzzed and flew up into a tiny hole in the ceiling. That's when Theodor noticed a burnt area above his head. "Ralf" he half screamed half gurgled under water. Theodor fumbled and punched the ceiling, Ralf came splashing towards him. "What is it?" he asked. "The bee, it went through" Theodor said pointing at the hole, "it looks like a grill but it's charred and dented" he explained. They touched the ceiling and clung onto it. It seemed to be a hatch. Their fingers dug into the small openings. The water on the other hand rose, touching the ceiling and submerging them completely.

The three of them swam holding their breaths. Ralf and Theodor held on to the grill, jabbing their fingers through the grime that covered it. They lunged at it, mustering strength, it moved a bit, releasing a small line of bubbles around them. Theodor's lungs were getting uncomfortable and he exhaled into water. Both Theodor and Ralf turned upside down within the tunnel and pulled the hatch. They thrust their feet against the ceiling; giving them enough leverage and finally the hatch fell loose from the opening. It was adhering to the walls with slime but as it came off, they could see an opening. Along with it fell a few oddly shaped objects that looked like rotten body parts. Sticky fluids mixed into the water along with pipes and bones. These odd objects floated eerily in the water around them.

Ralf threw himself out of the water, Theodor was about to do the same when he saw Albert drifting away, lifeless and ghost like. He froze on the spot. Albert drifted along in the water, not moving or reacting. Theodor swam and held him by the waist. He tried swimming back up as the strength in his body failed him. The force of water was thrusting them away from the opening.

Theodor's lungs were protesting in anguish, they were over laden with emptiness and were waiting to exhale the buildup of carbon dioxide. A stray snake like pipe tangled around his foot, constricting his movements as he tried to swim up. He was losing consciousness as he tried hard to propel himself but the weight was too much and his vision blurred. He saw the eyes looking back at him, unblinking and open. They turned into Adelheid's eyes. He twitched and tried to push himself up but there was no energy left in him. Everything around them turned calm, blue and composed as Theodor and Albert floated like ghosts in the cold, death-like water.

Map Reader

Konstantin was stroking a hound that waited beside him. The dog had one bloodied eye, and he growled uneasily at the gate. Konstantin glanced at his watch again. "Yes my mate, we will rip their eyes out and feed them to you" he said to the growling hound. He rose to his full height and looked at the leaking water. His gaze turned to Viktor as he nodded; it was time to open the gates.

Theodor was floating in the water, lifeless and ghost-like . A line of bubbles escaped his open mouth as water filled his lungs. His foot was entangled in a floating pipe that held him in place. Slowly, life was creeping out of him. "Theodor" Adelheid called out to him as everything blacked out. He suddenly felt immense pain in his chest. Someone was probably punching him. Another blow and the pain shot up two fold; he couldn't bear it anymore.

'Didn't the enemy understand? He wasn't there to steal any secrets. He was there by a terrible mistake. He just wanted to get back to Berlin. Only if they stopped beating him, could he explain.' The pain that came next was unbearable. He screamed his lungs out and his eyes opened up. Theodor was pulled back to his senses. He vomited as soon as his eyes opened and welcomed the air into his dying lungs. His breathing was extremely labored and abrupt. "Listen to me Theodor, hold on to this rung. Albert is missing; I need to find him okay." Theodor understood bits and pieces of what Ralf shouted panic stricken into his ear and his hands grasped the slimy rung. In one swift motion, Ralf jumped into the narrow cavity and disappeared sending up a massive spray of water from his jump. Theodor's vision was still blurred as he tried hard to steady himself and breathe through the pungent surrounding air.

Fedor and Viktor stood, guarding Konstantin. Red army soldiers stood armed and ready at the iron gates. General Mark was still dumbstruck and he stood by the trees with a fleet of guards around him. 'Nazi scum, this deep into their territory and no one knew about it.' He was baffled and angry with Konstantin for withholding this information. If he could keep quiet about this, what else was Konstantin hiding from the rest of them?

The Red Army stood still, aiming every bit of fire power at the iron gates. The winds were dead, forests were quiet and the soldiers' raspy breathing was the only audible whisper through otherwise killing silence. Two soldiers turned the lock wheel as it grunted open making a racket. The last turn was undone and the gate flew open. The soldiers were thrown back from the force of water. "Arm yourselves" roared Konstantin and in a uniform motion, the Red army soldiers loaded their guns as more than fifty fingers curled around the deadly curved metal. A huge wall of water came gushing towards them from the tunnel. "Stop pumping water" Konstantin ordered and a soldier ran to relay it further. His guard dog was growling and sniffing the air.

Suddenly a heavy mass floated out of the opening, and the hounds began barking as they sniffed death. Konstantin lunged forward and grabbed the floating mass, it was a dead body. The long range shooters were alert, waiting to fire at the slightest movement. Within that moment, another body floated out and hit his feet. The soldiers gathered around and lifted the body. Konstantin easily lifted up the first body to eye level with one hand. The body was decayed and rotting. Observing the dead body closely he spoke, "Ah! Mr. Krammer, I pity your demise. Throw him away" he flung the body mercilessly as it fell with a sickening thud.

The soldiers held up the other body for examination, he was a Red army soldier who'd been on duty. Konstantin's features contorted in fury as he looked at the dead soldier. Before they could register the events, yet another body floated out from the tunnels, 'more Red army soldiers' Konstantin was shivering in rage, too much had gone unnoticed and the Blood Moon kin had wreaked havoc. General Mark stood disturbed beyond belief. 'So many dead soldiers, looked like a lot of Nazis' infiltrated Konstantin's camp tonight' he thought. The Red army soldiers lined up dead bodies on one side. Konstantin stood waiting for more bodies to pour out with the water. Another floating mass could be seen. Konstantin lifted the body and held it close.

This one was different. It was a German intruder, and numerous wounds mired his body. He handed it to the soldiers. "Keep it aside" he ordered. Almost all water had poured out from the tunnels. Konstantin was raging in anger. These Germans had infiltrated deeper than he thought. No other bodies came out of the opening as they waited by the open gate. The surrounding areas were soaking wet from the water and these dead bodies held no answers. Fedor was standing by Konstantin as he observed the bodies. "Give me a team to man the exits. I will fan the tunnels alone and report back to you in an hour" he softly spoke. Konstantin eyed him suspiciously as he contemplated the odds.

Ralf climbed the narrow cavity where he had left Theodor to recover. Theodor looked at him as he climbed the ladder alone. He seemed exhausted and his face was discolored from exertion. Ralf laboriously climbed the rungs as he came close to Theodor. There was very little light filtering down to them from the hatch above. Three small openings were letting down a pale blue light on their faces. The faint blue light hit Ralf's eyes. They were red and sore as he looked at Theodor. "I couldn't find Albert" he said softly. Theodor was petrified from their near death experience and now, they'd lost their map reading spectacled friend. Without him, their chances seemed even bleaker.

Call from Berlin

Konstantin smoked his cigar as he walked through the beast bunker. He was shivering in rage and fury; desiring sharp answers to every question he posed. How could so much have happened under his watch? First, Han landed up at his camp and now more soldiers were trying to breach in; either to get Han or for some unknown reason. His German friend was still absconding and this got him really worried.

The guarding soldiers opened the gate and let Konstantin pass through a corridor on the second floor. "Get all the soldiers out and lock the gates until I am back" Konstantin spoke in between heavy puffs of smoke. A guard nodded and shouted orders to evacuate. The gate rattled open as Konstantin stood there, waiting for soldiers to pile out. The guards that piled out were huge and menacing. They were as tall and broad shouldered as Konstantin. A single light bulb hung at the very end of the tunnel, the entire walkway was otherwise dark and unnaturally silent.

All the soldiers stepped out and waited as Konstantin entered. There was an abnormal step in between and the floor rose up by a feet. The gates shut behind him and he heard the satisfying rattle of locks. Konstantin drew a deep puff from his cigar and slowly started walking towards the light source. Each of his steps echoed threateningly through the empty tunnel. The entire chamber was a suspended cube built into the beast bunker. It was used to house valuable materials during past years but it currently housed Han.

This chamber was invincible to attack; no bullet or bomb could penetrate its iron walls. It was suspended within the bunker and was engineered in a way that allowed it to be air lifted through an opening in the roof. There were air ducts connected to it at strategic points to maintain air supply. It was vacuum sealed at times when volatile nuclear materials were housed within it. This was a one of its kind chamber engineered by Konstantin himself and scientists that worked under him. The entire chamber reverberated with his heavy steps as Konstantin reached the very end and stood under a light bulb. He looked around for a switch but didn't find any. He was running out of patience and was irritated by the impending situation. He calmly reached out and held the hot light bulb with his bare hands. He looked at the door in front of him, this room housed their prized possession. His fingers tightened around the bulb and the glass cracked. He felt a slight wave of current surge through his hands and the heat of the bulb burnt on his thick skin as he pulled the wire from the ceiling. The surroundings instantly plunged into absolute darkness.

A loud uncomfortable screech ripped through darkness as the locks slid. Everything remained dark while the door groaned open and Konstantin walked into the vault-like prison. The door swung back and was locked shut. The chamber was extremely hot and dark. A faint glow from his cigar was visible as Konstantin pulled out a metal chair and sat on it. The chair groaned under his weight and sank a little. He drew a raspy breath before he spoke into the darkness. "You have caused me great trouble and I will do the same to you. I will break you and make you weep. I will seek pleasure in it as I watch you beg for death."

Konstantin released yet another puff of smoke into the absolute darkness. "Actually, all of that might not affect you. You are strong, I know and respect that. You and I are not very different you see. Discarded and taken for granted by everyone, with no family to go back to. No country to fight for. I just couldn't buy you out you bastard. Your loyal ass didn't let you budge" Konstantin spoke as he drew another long puff from his cigar and waited for some reaction. There was darkness, silence and an uncomfortable feeling that hung in the air. "But I know exactly what will affect you. I found out you filthy bastard, I found your secret and that's exactly why you came hunting for me. Didn't you? I know what will break you from inside and I know the path to that" Konstantin concluded his threat and sat back with a smirk on his face. There was another raspy and labored breath suddenly audible in the room. Konstantin let out a bark-like ring of laughter. He clapped his hands and continued laughing through the darkness. Loud and menacing; it rang disturbingly, his laugh echoing back and forth through the suspended chamber.

Viktor was running through the camp with a portable radio in his hand. He dashed through guard ranks and entered the beast bunker. He got his security cleared and entered the second level. He was sweating in tension with his features contorting in panic. The guards stopped him there. "I need to enter now" Viktor ordered. The guard forbade him and stood in front of the gate. He was twice Viktor's size and covered the entire door as he stood. "You will stand right there and not move a muscle till Konstantin comes out" the guard warned Viktor.

Konstantin took his cigar and touched it to his prisoner's flesh. It burnt a hole through the skin and blood oozed out of the wound. A burning smell of skin and flesh wafted around as the prisoner twitched at the intrepid touch. As Konstantin abruptly got up, the chair fell backwards with a loud clang. He moved around the room, with his heavy footsteps being the only audible noise. "I will give you some time to think over your decision to keep quiet. Tell me where my friend is, give me answers to all that I ask you and your secret will live on. I won't enjoy killing you. I will keep you and your little secret alive, unless of course you want me to spill it out" Konstantin threatened and looked towards the corner of the room.

He flicked a lighter and his eyes narrowed from the sudden light. A small table with various contraptions used for torture was set up. There was a crude switch waiting to be activated, and he moved towards it, flicking it on. A small motor whirred to life and began pumping fluid from a canister. A small glass capillary tube pumped liquid through it and onto a nozzle on the prisoner's head. A small drop of liquid formed on the surface as the prisoner's head lolled sideways in a semi-conscious state. The liquid drop got heavier and as surface tension gave away it fell onto the prisoner's chest. Smoke began to waft from the skin surface as the membrane burnt. The fluid trickled down on his flesh, leaving a trail of etched skin. Konstantin flicked the lighter off as he was satisfied with his method of torture. "You will talk. If not for yourself, you will talk to keep safe that which you guard" Konstantin whispered through the darkness. "By the time that starts etching into your lungs through the breast bone you will talk" His voice was abruptly cut as he heard commotion around him.

He stopped in mid-sentence and looked around. He swiftly marched out of the room securing the door shut behind him. The voices grew louder as he approached the other gate. He banged his fists on the gate, commanding them to open it from outside. The commotion quickly died down and they opened the gates. "What is going on?" roared Konstantin as he stepped out from the darkness. Viktor was arguing with the guard and he stopped abruptly as they saw Konstantin march out. A guard was holding Viktor back from entering the chamber. Viktor looked at Konstantin and held up his radio "Vlad is in Berlin. He has asked to connect to you urgently" Viktor concluded.

Freedom

The forests were flooded with water that flowed out from the camp. It was as if a cloud had burst over the forests; as abundant water ran into the foliage and seeped into a cavity around the massive tree. The surrounding was dark and damp in the cavity under the tree as a torrent of water, flowed down from above. A small light flickered in the area illuminating the place faintly. A man wearing a prisoner uniform sat huddled in a corner. He was shivering from cold and looked around in fear as the faint light threw eerie shadows around him.

"You know the number of soldiers that are at camp?" A deep and stern voice spoke through absolute darkness. The prisoner couldn't see the face of the man who was speaking. Dense smoke wafted through the small cramped place. "I have been inside only once. I am lucky to be alive but no, I do not know the exact number" the prisoner replied in a soft voice. "Where are the other prisoners?" The deep voice asked. "They are scattered within the camp. There are posts outside where they are held. Some go into the camp and never come back" the prisoner replied to the darkness.

"How many able bodied prisoners are in the outer periphery right now? Can they fight?" The unknown voice asked yet again. "Not more than thirty. The number of prisoners is more than hundred but most of them are nearly dead. They just give us enough food so that we are able to exist" whispered the prisoner. Silence lingered in the damp space under the tree. Water continued to flow down as another prisoner walked through a cave-like opening and stood by their side. "How did you get out?" The deep voice asked again as he considered the situation. "I slipped from the gates as they were pilling other prisoners. I was able to fall through the half open bars of the cage" he replied. The prisoner did look very thin and frail, just like skin wrapped tightly onto a skeleton. There was no visible flesh left on him. "We need to recruit these able soldiers that you speak of" the voice cut sharply from the dark corner. "We are going to break into the camp. You, I and all those prisoners who can join us, it might spell imminent death but it's not like we'll live happily ever after anyways" said the unknown voice. The prisoner was confused and scared.

He tried to look through the darkness trying to catch a better glimpse of the person that spoke. "The war lord Konstantin is merciless. He... He does things to people, Bad things. I saw with my own eyes. I see them wail and ask for mercy with my waking eyes. I shouldn't even be living. They chose death over this torture" the prisoner concluded. The figure in the dark shifted uncomfortably. The prisoner standing by the cave opening held out his hand and cut through.

"Have faith brother; there is a lot of commotion going on up there. We might be able to escape after all. Have faith in god" he said. "If there is a god, he will have to seek my forgiveness first" the prisoner retorted in a barely audible whisper as tears swelled his eyes. A steely silence hung around the area as no one spoke. "Sad stories, my brothers but Konstantin doesn't scare me" the deep voice abruptly cut through pressing silence. "Being scared of someone; now that scares me. Cowering and living a life in fear, now that scares me" the voice spoke as more smoke wafted forward. "It is easy for you to say these things. I've burnt my family to ashes with my own hands. I've seen their dead bodies being used for experiments" the slave responded and fell silent as he broke down completely, weeping on the floor. "Who... who are you? Why are you doing this?" he mustered courage through his sobs and asked the unknown figure.

"I am nobody to the world, but to you I will reveal myself. I cannot talk you into joining me and neither do I care much about such. Recruitment was Felix's job. I am doing this for one simple reason. Freedom! Although revenge would be a far fitting word, but that is for cowards" he spoke in an intimidating tone. The smoke shifted and a face appeared through the dark corner. The flickering light threw scary shadows on his face. It was scarred and bloodied; and many cuts on his face looked fresh as they oozed blood. There was a deep gash on his right arm where a bullet had seared through. His eyes held the same undiminished fury that was evident in his voice, while his hands held onto a chipped ivory pipe. "I want to live a free life and my freedom lies in getting into this camp and breaking Konstantin from within. You need to get back to your god, I need my freedom. You keep your reason and I will keep mine" he said. He gazed into the slave's eyes and whispered softly. "My name is Traugott and I fight for freedom. Are you with me?" he asked. The slave maintained Traugott's gaze, and gave a faint nod. Traugott smiled, giving a curt nod in return.

Departure

Theodor climbed the small ladder that led to the only opening and hope for them. Ralf was behind him and a little slow as he was still breathing hard from his futile hunt. They still couldn't believe that Albert was gone. Just like that, the cruel water had swept him away into the obscure tunnels. Step by step, Theodor made the upward climb through cramped space. With Albert gone, they were clueless about their whereabouts.

Their backpacks were drenched and any chances of them making use of maps was unrealistic, in light of Albert's absence. Moreover their only way out now was this tunnel. The water had suddenly disappeared from beneath them again. 'The Red army must have opened the tunnels to hunt for them' they thought. Risking the tunnel again was no longer an option as they were sure Red army soldiers were hunting and would probably reach them soon enough. Theodor held on to the slimy and dirty ladder rungs. They had to take efforts to hold onto them as they continued their climb.

Their breathing was extremely labored as oxygen levels were down to nil. Theodor's vision blurred and his muscles ached in protest. The last hour had been an excruciatingly painful run with death constantly on their heels. As time crawled ahead, they reached the top and looked at a circular overhead opening. Where had they landed themselves?

"I don't know if our weapons will work now. They are drenched in water. Nonetheless, we need to keep moving. There are people searching for us in the Honeycomb maze, our cover is blown" Ralf spoke in a whisper as he moved closer to the top opening. Theodor simply nodded in acknowledgement, he didn't know what to do or think. He just wanted to get out of this situation alive. His thoughts were stagnated and his mind blank. "Listen soldier" Ralf spoke looking into Theodor's eyes. He knew Theodor was rattled from the near death experiences. "We need to get out of here alive. We will do it, trust me; we will" Ralf assured Theodor with a pat on the back. With no working weapons on them, they climbed upwards ready to push open the circular hatch and surface out on the Russian camp.

The circular hatch was heavy and didn't budge easily. Theodor braced himself on the ladder rung and pushed hard. It budged a little but still felt heavy. Ralf came close to him. "What is it?" he asked. "I think there is something obstructing the hatch. It doesn't seem to be locked but it's pretty heavy" Theodor replied, trying to look through a small gap in the metal hatch. Theodor pushed it again and tried to look through the opening, with his heart in his mouth. It was very possible to end up under a Red Army soldier, but he sincerely hoped that he wouldn't find himself in that position. The hatch opened enough to let Theodor see through, and as he did so, his eyes locked with another pair of eyes staring back at him. He froze in place, neither could he close it nor push further. He stood there frozen to the bone and staring at a pair of glinting eyes. There was a weird blue light that reflected back at him through the eyes. Theodor blinked but out of fear stood rooted to his pose. Ralf held out his hand to help Theodor hold the hatch open. Theodor snapped out of his fear and slowly pushed Ralf down, closing the lid.

"There is someone up there; he just saw me" Theodor whispered hurriedly. Ralf too froze in place, "But why didn't they react? They should have come charging down on us" he asked. "Let's open it again, if they spotted us they would surely have reacted. Are you sure you saw eyes?" asked Ralf. "Yes I did" spoke Theodor as he braced himself to open the lid again. Both Ralf and Theodor were now pressed in that narrow cavity as they climbed up and slightly pushed open the lid. Ralf lifted it and instantly his eyes met a powerful flash of blue light, He ducked out of reflex but didn't close the hatch. The blue light cast an eerie glow over the room as it swept mechanically. Theodor and Ralf both looked through the half open hatch to see more than a hundred eyes staring back at them.

Konstantin was back in his cabin. Viktor and Fedor stood by the door guarding it and he was heatedly talking on the radio. "I will not abandon this camp to you Vlad" he spat. "Respect Konstantin, Respect. I know all about your experiments" The voice on the radio was calm, composed and heavy with authority. Konstantin seemed unnerved by the speaker and his poise. "You will now fly to Berlin on my unofficial orders. I think we have found Adolf Hitler. I also need to discuss certain matters with you" Konstantin was listening intently to the voice.

"Now" said Vlad. "General Mark has an interesting story to tell me." Konstantin's eyes widened in shock, he had completely forgotten about Mark. 'That wretched bastard' he thought. Konstantin released his hand from the radio and spoke to Viktor. "Where is Mark?" he asked in a frustrated voice. Viktor was dumbfounded at the question. "He said he would wait in his jeep" replied Viktor. "Does he have a working radio in the jeep? Or is he sending birds to communicate with Vlad?" Konstantin roared into Viktor's scared face. "I will have it checked right away my lord" Viktor's voice quivered in reply. "Stay right here. The damage is done" Konstantin spoke through gritted teeth. Fedor smirked on the side, enjoying the confusion. He didn't care about these political motives. "What is the matter Konstantin? Your silence says you seem troubled?" Vlad spoke mockingly over the radio. Before Konstantin could reply, Vlad spoke again. "Prepare to leave now Konstantin and report back to High command. I am heading to take command of your camp. The war is won, we can't continue running your little fantasy camp anymore. Get General Mark, fly to Berlin with him and report straight to me." Static build up over the radio as Vlad ended his conversation abruptly. Konstantin was shivering in rage, angry at himself for letting Mark slip from right under his nose. He flexed his muscles threateningly and the wound opened up again, allowing fresh crimson blood to ooze out of his injury.

Both Theodor and Ralf threw the hatch off their head and climbed out of the cavity. They were prepared to face the forces and surrender; for there was no other way out of this mess. They climbed out and a pungent smell hit their nostrils. The image which presented itself before them was that of the cold blue eyes of hundreds of dead bodies that hung mercilessly around the room. Theodor looked around and each dead pair of eyes reminded him of the dead girl in his arms. Everything around him began to spin as his vision blurred and he fell to the ground. He vomited all over the floor as excess water purged out of his lungs and the repulsive stench filled his senses. Ralf stood there speechless and disturbed.

All around them was nothing but death. They were surrounded by dead bodies, heaps and heaps of them, some with open staring eyes while others had been badly maligned. Some of the bodies were bare while some others were covered in rags. Some were split open and their innards spilled out. Bodies hung from the ceiling on a rack while many others were strewn on the floor. They had a calm look etched on their faces as if they accepted their fate and walked into this hell. Just their biological selves now remained, rotting away silently under this strange blue light. Ralf looked over to the corner and saw a heap of piled babies. Theodor had managed to get to his feet and was standing next to Ralf. Their hearts froze in place as they stood in this "Death Chamber" looking at the horrific scene of boundless dead and scattered bodies.

Konstantin, Viktor and Fedor were sitting at the table. Viktor was extremely uncomfortable and scared now that Konstantin was at the peak of his anger. Fedor sat there poised, calm and smirking slightly. "I am leaving for Berlin" spoke Konstantin. He was trying to keep calm as he drew deep breaths through his cigar. "Vlad will try to interfere and want command of this camp. I cannot let that happen." Konstantin looked uncomfortably at his injury as he spoke. He had removed all the bandages and was now wearing a tunic that exposed his huge muscular arms. "I like to look my enemies in the eye as they fret" he spoke as smoke wafted from his mouth and his gaze fixed on the wound. Dark red blood crept down his bronze skin as he flexed his arm. White sinew was visible through the dark wound. He took another deep puff from his cigar and spoke further, "You both are in charge of this camp while I am gone. I will look Vlad in the eye and deal with him as I see fit. I don't want to do this but if the situation calls for it, I have no choice but to dispose of him." Both Fedor and Viktor tensed at the last statement.

"It is time to break off from the High command." Konstantin studied their reactions as he spoke. "Can I trust you both?" He asked. Viktor and Fedor instantly nodded in acknowledgement. "Yes my lord" they replied in unison. A smirk crossed Konstantin's face as he leaned forward on the table and spoke. "Prepare to transport our prisoner. Get the flying squadron in place. Round up the scientists and get the study material packed. All our research goes with us, scientists can be eventually disposed. I hope to meet my friend in Berlin and accordingly I will strike the deals."

Konstantin had thought this through and was delivering one order after another to Viktor and Fedor. "There is a truck in the underground chamber. It contains highly volatile nuclear material, prepare it for transport. We need loyal guards for ourselves. We will evacuate this area if need be but I will burn it to the ground before I hand it over to high command." Viktor's eyes widened as Konstantin spoke further. "Yes Viktor, unlock the control room and procure the dynamite switches" he ordered. Both Viktor and Fedor were disturbed by Konstantin's sudden plan to pound the camp to dust. "What is the final report on infiltration? How many of the Blood Moon? How many of our own prisoners have been involved?" Konstantin casually asked as he settled back into his chair.

Viktor fumbled as he replied "The reports are in my lord. Three of the bodies are suspected German soldiers. None of them have any markings or artifacts to confirm the same. Our soldiers too have been killed and we have no idea of their motive yet. The aircraft sight as well, has been investigated. We found our soldiers and suspected German soldier bodies too. If they were hoping to get to Han it was a very crude plan as they obviously didn't succeed. The entire attack seemed disoriented and vague; we found bodies far and wide. If the group had any other motives, then we are still unclear on that front. We have absolutely no information on this Blood Moon group that you talk about my lord" Viktor concluded his statement as he kept a file in front of Konstantin explaining the details of infiltration.

Konstantin flicked through the pages clumsily and looked at Fedor. "I want the remaining infiltrators weeded out by the time I am back. Viktor you will secure the materials and arrange transport. Fedor, you will put an end to this infiltration. The forces are in your hands and at your disposal." Konstantin got to his feet as he concluded his orders. Viktor and Fedor also scrambled to their feet, and stood in attention. "Prepare my guards; I am hoping to be back from Berlin soon. Vlad is a fool; time has come to branch out. We will now act independently from high command. Viktor, procure keys for the control room, I will need access to it once I am back" Konstantin ordered as he walked out of the room. Fedor walked behind him to hunt while Viktor dashed away to procure keys to open the control room as the Minotaur prepared to head to Berlin.

The Fallen Twins

Theodor and Ralf scouted the huge hanger-like place; with its frosted windows and dim blue lights placed at regular intervals. "These blue lights or whatever they are, have been installed to maintain sterility I suppose" Ralf muttered, half speaking to himself, and half speaking to Theodor as he inspected the lights. Theodor nodded as he noticed a pair of tracks running at the periphery of the room and travelling through huge iron gates which were closed shut.

Ralf carefully moved towards the windows, which were not made of normal glass; instead, it was thick, frosted, probably unbreakable and sound proof. Theodor knelt on the floor and emptied his bag. He pulled out the drenched map, opened it and Ralf scooted over to his side. They were safe for a while; at least, until someone came into this chamber. Theodor and Ralf exchanged silent looks. With Albert, was their steadfast map reading comrade gone; dealt with by the ruthlessness of the Red army, they had no choice but to go through the maps themselves to see if anything would make sense to them. Theodor opened up the maps on the grimy floor. "Well, death seems to be on our heels and here we are now, in some sort of a death chamber" said Ralf, breaking the uneasy silence as he looked around.

"What are these?" Theodor asked as he too studied the dead bodies. The bodies were maimed, ripped and damaged in innumerable ways. It was clear that these bodies hadn't just been tortured- they'd been maimed, horribly malformed beyond recognition with a few of them having bizarre contraptions running through them. "They seem to be running some sort of an experiment here" Ralf spoke as he inspected yet another dead body. It was still and lifeless, with eyes staring into void and mouth leaking body fluids. The entire floor was covered with sticky grime and the room emanated an unnatural stink. The two of them could hardly comprehend these inhumane conditions, but when one is running away from death, even the worst conditions turn out to be a sanctuary; as this death-hub was for them in the moment. The dimly lit blue lights somehow helped them calm down from their near death experience.

Theodor's eyes tore away from the dead faces and looked at the open maps. They were drenched and useless; all of the maps which Albert had hastily collected, destroyed. A few faint lines that he had drawn over them were still visible but it wasn't of much use since most of the markings were wiped out. Theodor rummaged through the bag to find other important things that could help them. As his hand touched the diary, a cold shiver ran down his spine. Theodor remained frozen from the diary's touch. "Ralf, I have something to tell you" he spoke in a soft whisper. He held the black diary and pulled it out slowly for Ralf to see. Theodor swallowed hard as he spoke "I found this in the forest when I was running away from Red army hounds. I should have given this to you before but I didn't, I didn't trust you enough." Ralf was observing Theodor intently. "So, you trust me now?" he asked. Theodor was taken aback by the question.

"Albert's dead, we might be dead soon. If there is a way to make this mission a success, this" he held the diary up for Ralf to see "this might be of help." Theodor tossed it at Ralf. Ralf caught it and ripped the rubber covering off it. He opened the pages and surprisingly, the book seemed to have survived the onslaught of water. He saw Adolf Hitler's signature and read through it. Theodor observed Ralf, waiting for him to react. Painfully silent minutes passed as they sat in the death chamber surrounded by bodies and an unnerving cold. "This book probably belongs to Adolf Hitler" said Ralf. Theodor merely nodded in acknowledgement. "This might be one of records Han has, and you found it at the very beginning of this mission" he questioned as Theodor nodded silently. "I understand your dilemma soldier" said

Ralf. "A document of such importance should be kept safe." Theodor relaxed a bit at Ralf's statement but was confused. "Any of the maps helped?" Ralf asked. Theodor was surprised at the abrupt switch in conversation. He felt guilty for hiding the diary from Ralf.

The response he'd expected from Ralf was one of fury, but instead of the man to burst out in anger, he'd casually continued the conversation. "These maps are useless now" Theodor replied, trying to let go of a little of the tension he felt inside. "Albert probably had the maps fixed in his head but with him gone, we are stranded" he said, straining to make sense of the sodden maps. Ralf got to his feet and began inspecting the room again. "We need to find a way out of here to begin with" Ralf spoke as he looked at the strange room, trying to figure a way out of it. "Keep this diary safe with you, Theodor. Once we get to Han we will decide what to do with it" and with that, Ralf tossed the diary back at Theodor.

Both Theodor and Ralf spent the next few minutes inspecting the room. They found two set of gates which had no locks or mechanisms with which they could open them from inside. A strange set of tracks ran from under the gate and out of the room. They curved around the room, entering from one gate and exiting through the other. The room had innumerable pipes that entered from outside and ran through the ceiling. Both Theodor and Ralf contemplated ways to break out from the chamber but each idea seemed less feasible than the previous one.

They couldn't break the windows and step out for they didn't know where they were. They had no weapons on them and their maps were ruined. If they went down the hatch again, they were sure to encounter Russian soldiers. They could hunt for more hatches but there was no saying where they would lead them to. Ralf picked up the drenched map and tried to trace their route on the poorly visible markings. "We were here when we got swept by the water. We approximately travelled all the way here" Ralf was explaining as he thought of possibilities. Theodor tried to make sense of the wasted map when a sudden shrill alarm rang near them and a loud rattling sound kicked off behind the walls. They panicked at the abrupt sound and fixated their eyes on the gate as it began to open. They instantly gathered their strewn belongings and sprinted towards a pile of dead bodies. The massive automated gate opened with a disturbing rattling sound.

Ralf and Theodor had only one option; which was to hide, they both jumped into the pile of dead bodies. They felt cold, bare and lifeless skin touch them. Their faces were inches away from the inert eyes around them as they hid with bated breath. A huge cart moved on the tracks and entered the room; with two soldiers standing guard on it. They were entirely covered in uniform and wore gas masks. One of them had a gun ready and pointed it towards the bodies while another handled the cart and slaves that were riding along with them.

A bunch of slaves were wearing the same uniform as some of the dead bodies. The soldiers scanned the area to check for any movement as the cart came to a slow, calculated halt in the center of the chamber. The guards dismounted and opened the railings to let the slaves off. "We need to pile up as many bodies as we can. This chamber has to be cleaned up immediately" a soldier shouted orders. The other soldier pulled out scythes and threw it to the slaves. "Start piling" he ordered and stood guard while the slaves got to work.

Theodor and Ralf were watching the unnerving situation unfold in front of them. "We need to get out before the gate closes" whispered Theodor. Ralf nodded in acknowledgement as his eyes remained fixed on the unfolding activities. The slaves were using scythes which looked like pick axes and were plunging them deep into the bodies. They hauled the bodies mercilessly and piled them onto the waiting cart. Blood splattered with every plunge of the scythe. Ruthlessly, the bodies were thrown onto carts and piled; with a few of them ripping apart from the mouth as the scythe made contact with their faces. Children through whom the scythe went through, women and men; were all being heaved heartlessly. They only piled bodies that were strewn on the floor and didn't touch the ones that were suspended.

A few bees buzzed around Theodor's head as they hid in the pile, watching the cruel scene unfold. A few more heartless minutes passed as the cart filled up. "Fill the cart to its maximum capacity and line up" shouted the guard as they climbed onto the cart and ordered the slaves to march out. It looked like a routine for the slaves as they marched ahead, unflinchingly, and the soldiers rode the cart. The gate began to open with a disturbingly loud rattling noise as the cart and array of slaves made their way towards it. The soldiers looked around to see if everything was in place. They looked exactly at the point where the Germans were hiding. The pile of bodies looked untouched and Theodor and Ralf were nowhere to be seen amongst them.

Konstantin finished inspecting the bodies that were found in the forests and tunnels. The German soldiers seemed unrecognizable. They checked their records and none of the faces matched with those of the intruders. "Keep checking records and see if you find any names. Also, get in touch with our informers and try gathering information on this Blood Moon group" he ordered and walked out. Konstantin strode out into the open and reached the waiting convoy. A total of four guards and a pilot were dispatched to take him and Mark to Berlin.

He couldn't afford to take a bigger array of guards because of the unofficial nature of his visit. A guard came running to him with a freshly ironed uniform. He stripped his soiled clothes and put on the crisp uniform as soldiers watched in awe. Konstantin's body was well tanned. It was a massive bulk but it'd been well-crafted by years of discipline. There were numerous cuts and scars on the warlord's bronze body. The bullet injury continued to leak fresh blood. Konstantin adorned blurred and faded tattoos across his arms and back that he had gotten made while his years in prison. The nature of a prison tattoo was different from an ornamental one. Prison tattoos were made under the most contaminated environments and to live through them was by itself a feat of great pride.

Konstantin got into his uniform and his medals were put up for show. The shirt sleeve instantly turned a blotch of red as blood smeared through the fabric. Konstantin looked around at the watching soldiers. "I am going to raise the final victory flags. I am hoping to get you many Nazi heads as gifts" he spoke in a deep authority filled voice. The soldiers roared in unison at the statement. Konstantin held out his hand to silence the cheering. "Hold the fort while I am away" he roared. The soldiers shouted in unison and raised their weapons to salute their warlord. Konstantin looked around, boring into the eyes of each and every soldier. Daring them to conspire against him, daring them to touch his camp while he was away. He raised his fist into the air and growled in response. The very air stood still in attention to the warlord as the soldiers kept their weapons raised. He gave them one last look before settling in elegance into the waiting jeep. The iron gates were thrown open to let his jeep pass. Both Viktor and Fedor stood in salute as Konstantin's vehicle passed through the gates and disappeared.

As the cart carrying dead bodies entered the central chamber, it came to a slow halt. The prisoners had lined up and were standing by its side. The two soldiers jumped off the cart clumsily and stood there looking around. The massive gates had shut down and the only way in or out was to activate them from outside. The slaves stood in line, waiting for their next order. One of the slaves broke the silence and spoke "I think the guards are sleeping." "Those wretched bastards never sleep" said another slave. "Then why won't they start the incinerator?" The slaves could barely see as their vision was destroyed by the toxic fumes that they were made to inhale. The two waiting guards looked around and then at each other. They were the only ones in the massive room as they slowly removed their gas masks. With their ruffled hair and sweat laden faces, Theodor and Ralf stood in the very center of the Beast Bunker.

Fedor and Viktor had assembled the guards in the camp. Fedor had taken charge of security, while Viktor was in charge of other matters. The flying squadron was instructed to be on standby for lift off with the suspended chamber that held Han. Two helicopters were positioned on top of the Beast bunker; heavy metal ropes were coupled to the chamber which would facilitate them to fly out with it. Viktor checked the time on his watch. He would dispatch guards to pack up the nuclear material once he finished other matters. Fedor had stationed guards around suspected openings and was studying on a map that lay in front of him. Konstantin, in an act of wisdom, had kept them in charge of independent activities, knowing the hatred that festered between Fedor and Viktor. Viktor was worried about the keys that he had to hand over to Konstantin, while Fedor was desperate to weed out these intruders; they were getting on his nerves now- how could they have evaded him for so long?

Theodor and Ralf looked around the room to see where they were. While in the chamber, they had skillfully tackled the guards. They had run out from behind the pile of bodies when the gate opened. The rattling camouflaged their footsteps as they ran through and took out the unaware soldiers. Theodor plunged his knife through a soldier's heart while Ralf used his bare hands to crack the unsuspecting soldier's neck. It was a swift and silent move.

They were now out but skeptical about the slaves and their vision. They could definitely see, but not clearly enough. One of the slaves came forward and asked them. "Are you the infiltrators that everyone has been talking about?" Ralf and Theodor froze in place at the direct question. They looked at each other for approval, they were not sure if they could trust these slaves. "Yes" spoke Ralf. "We have broken into the camp to save our companion" he concluded. "We thought as much" another slave spoke. He had a heavy voice and was bulkier than the others. "You didn't take away our scythes, you didn't push us around and you didn't activate the switch" he said. "What switch?" asked Theodor. The near blind guard walked towards a lever and activated it. The cart on which Theodor and Ralf came out sprang to life and began moving towards the opposite end of the room. "That switch" said the slave. Theodor and Ralf were taken by surprise at the abrupt motion of the cart and they stepped back. Heavy iron gates on the opposite side opened up and they felt a massive heat wave sweep over them. Both Theodor and Ralf looked dumbstruck. Huge menacing flames licked the room from floor to ceiling while burning hot ambers crumbled on the floor. The heat wave created horrifying illusions in the chamber. 'It was an incinerator' realized Theodor. The cart slowly moved through the gates as they began to shut. They saw the bodies catch fire instantly. A few of them began bursting as trapped air from them was released. Suddenly a small trapdoor opened up in the floor. Both Theodor and Ralf jumped and prepared to fight.

A small looking man dressed in a white lab coat emerged from within. He was harrowed and looked disoriented. His hair was thick, white and ruffled. He didn't even bother looking at Theodor or Ralf and simply walked towards the death chamber. Ralf and Theodor had put on their gas masks to protect their identities. "You soldiers gather a few slaves and get them here. I need more subjects. The bodies have to be fresh and supple. I told them to keep my subjects alive but no, why would they listen to me? My test results are going wrong one after the other" the mad looking scientist spoke to himself as he remained completely disoriented. He then took out an identity card of some sort and showed it to Theodor and Ralf.

Ralf held it as if checking it and nodded. It read Dr. Schmitz, head researcher. "Slaves line up" shouted Ralf through his gas mask. Dr. Schmitz rolled his eyes; he was annoyed with the entire checking procedure that they had in place. "They keep changing the shift all the time" responded the scientist on hearing a new voice. Ralf and Theodor looked at each other and escorted the slaves. The slave hit a lever and the gate opened up. It seemed like the slaves had decided to be accomplices to Theodor and Ralf, God knew why.

The doctor walked inside to inspect bodies. "Pick that one and that one" he ordered as the slaves picked up bodies and piled them out. "Ahh twins, I like them" the scientist shouted in glee as he ordered the slaves to pick up two small bodies. The scientist kept looking at them closely to check how fresh the human subjects were and ordered the slaves to remove a few more bodies. "Careful as you pull out the needles from their veins" shouted the doctor. Theodor and Ralf realized that there was some sort of pipe connected to the dead bodies that were hung. The doctor walked out of the room where Theodor and Ralf were waiting. "Get these bodies down to the lab. Hurry up now, I don't have all day" saying so, he disappeared into the underground trap door. Ralf and Theodor removed their masks. "What was he up to? What does he use these bodies for?" Theodor asked one of the slaves. "They use it to run experiments. We will end up like them once more prisoners are brought in and our vision vanishes for good" the slave replied. "Are there soldiers down there in the lab?" Ralf asked one of them. "No, soldiers only man the outer territory" replied the slave. "They come in once every few hours to check but they are not allowed inside. Even your shift will change. You are safe for the next hour until another batch of guards comes and replaces you" he explained. The slaves knew pretty much everything that went on around the camp. Ralf had a plan up his sleeves. He took Theodor aside and explained. "Let's get the know-how from these slaves and that mad doctor. This is the closest we will get to Han. We have enough time before the next batch of guards open doors for inspection" suggested Ralf. Theodor was already nodding in agreement as he comprehended the plan. Even he knew that the only way to get out of here was to get to Han; for only he might be able to transport them further away and out of this mess. Ralf and Theodor armed themselves and opened the trap door without hesitating. They both jumped into the opening and landed right into Dr. Schmitz's lab.

The doctor was taken by surprise at the soldiers jumping in. "What is it? If Konstantin needs me, tell him I will talk to him later. Right now I am about to discover important antibodies" he spoke without taking his eyes off the microscope viewfinder. They had never seen such a set-up in their lives. The lab was cold due to the regulated temperature and there was an array of machines set up inside. Various units flashed and beeped through the otherwise eerie silence. There were massive circular doors all around them which probably opened into different sections of the Honeycomb mazes. Human subjects were suspended in huge glass canisters as various fluids were injected into them. Ralf looked away from the machines and walked up to Schmitz, punching him squarely in the face. The scientist went flying and crashed into a pile of files.

Before he could scream or react, Ralf pointed his gun towards Dr.Schmitz. "Speak up and co-operate; or I will kill you" he ordered. Ralf stood there as Theodor took his side. The scientist surrendered and they propped him up on a chair. He was bleeding from a torn lip and nose. Ralf was powerful and a singular punch from him had knocked the senses out of the tiny, spectacled researcher. "Where is Han? Konstantin's prized prisoner" questioned Ralf. The scientist slowly looked up to answer "I knew something was out of place, I heard bees buzzing in the cold room" he spoke with a maniacal glare in his eyes. "What you look for is housed in the suspended chamber. You will never get to him, there is no way" Dr.Schmitz smiled as he answered Ralf.

"You see I partially built the chamber ventilation systems. All that you see here are my brilliant creations." The scientist held out his hands showing off his lab. Ralf and Theodor looked at each other and then at the scientist again. "If there is a way out, there is surely a way in. Do not test my patience." Ralf tightened his grip on the trigger as he yet again questioned the scientist. Someone in the room suddenly screamed as the scientist got up and ran. "That looks like an emergency now, the sedation on this woman is wearing off. Interesting, very interesting you see" he spoke pushing Ralf aside to pull open a curtain. There were beds lined with live human subjects. They had missing limbs; and a few had various pipes running in and out of them.

There were small babies that were stitched together at places and were still alive and breathing. Ralf and Theodor were dumbstruck at what they saw. Live twin fetuses were suspended in canisters filled with liquid. The canisters were interconnected and so were the twins. "Stop right there or I'll shoot" Ralf screamed pointing his gun at the scientist. The scientist raised his hands and stopped dead in his tracks as he looked towards his subject. A heavily pregnant woman was moving in her bed. A tube was inserted into her stomach as she twitched and without warning began to thrash violently. "I need to tend to her" shouted the scientist. "Do not move" Ralf yelled through the woman's screams. Dr.Schmitz seemed possessed and reacted quickly as he ignored Ralf's threat. He picked up a tray and whacked Ralf on the head with it. Ralf threw up his arms to protect himself from the mindless assault. Dr. Schmitz lifted a syringe and lunged at Ralf. Theodor jumped in to tackle the attack. The needle pricked his arm as he punched the doctor in the stomach. He yelped in pain and shouted "You will not interfere in my experiments." He seemed to be possessed by a maniacal energy.

He picked up a dissection knife as he dodged Theodor and plunged it straight into the woman's stomach. Both Theodor and Ralf froze in place as a spurt of blood erupted from the woman's stomach. The pain must have triggered her back to her complete senses as she opened her eyes in horror and screamed in pain. Theodor locked eyes with her as he saw the cruel scene unfold. The mad doctor jumped and ripped her belly completely. Ralf lunged at the doctor and they both crashed to the wall. An overhead pipe burst and a foul smelling gas leaked from it while blood gushed out in torrents from the woman's belly.

Theodor felt uneasy as he saw yet another life slip away in front of him and the prick in his arm felt weird. He tried to help her as he saw two babies fall from the ripped belly. They fell to the floor with a sickening thud. They moved a little with the life they had in them, their mouths open in a horrific silent scream. Their sterile bodies were getting infected and their ghastly death approached. Theodor's world was spinning, he lost control of his muscles as his body gave up and he collapsed on the floor. Theodor fell right into the endless pool of plasma and passed out. The last thing he remembered were the woman's eyes, the foul smell and the fallen twins on the floor. In all his life, he'd never seen a crueler sight.

The Black Diary

Ralf threw open the trap door and climbed out of it, exhibiting inhumane strength for he easily scaled the ladder using one hand while carrying Theodor in the other. He was quick enough to have put on his gas mask as he battled the mad doctor. Both the doctor and Theodor had passed out due to the fumes which they inhaled. Ralf tied down the mad doctor securely as he didn't want to take any chances.

They were still in the Russian camp and not even halfway through their mission. His mind had gone blank and he couldn't think clearly. He climbed out, panting and gasping for air. The slaves were waiting in anticipation. "Please tell us you killed that doctor" one of them asked as Ralf stepped out. "He won't bother you. I have tied him up, let him rot there" replied Ralf. He pulled Theodor up and propped him against a wall. Theodor was alive and breathing but had passed out completely. The injection and gas fumes were potent sedatives by the looks of it. Ralf walked to a table and gathered the slaves. "I need to get to Konstantin's prisoner" Ralf told the slaves. "Why should we trust you soldier?" asked one of them. "I have seen my family die in front of my eyes. I piled their bodies and burnt them to ash. If you are helping Konstantin's prisoner you must be a Nazi, and I am in no mood to help one" replied the slave. He whipped out his scythe as his voice peaked in anger. Instantly, all the slaves removed their scythes and pointed them threateningly at Ralf. Ralf slowly moved away from the table. "I am not a Nazi" he replied and kept his gun aside. Blood stained and beaten, he stood there in surrender to the slaves.

He was tall and muscular, he could have easily tackled all of them at one go but he chose not to. He stood there hoping to gain their trust. One of the slaves stepped forward and asked "Why are you doing this then?" there was a dead silence as the slave fired a question. "I am not doing this for anyone. I am doing this so that when I die, I know that I made a difference. I will know that I didn't live in vain. I fought for a reason and that reason is all of us. I do this for everyone, not because I don't have a family to bury but for those who still have families. I fight for freedom." Ralf fell silent after his reply and so did the slaves. The slave who had questioned him stepped forward and looked at Ralf in silence. He slowly raised his scythe to him and said "In that case you have my scythe." He stood there in service to Ralf. "These are my companions. If they choose so, they too will stand by you" he said pointing at them. Slowly, all the other slaves followed, they stood there with their scythes raised and in service. Ralf nodded back in silent acknowledgement to his new companions.

Ralf gathered them closer to discuss the best way of saving Han, because falling out into the open even under disguise was too dangerous. The slaves could help, but their involvement was limited and they couldn't fight or overpower trained Red army soldiers. They knew the routes and secret pathways but none led to Han's captive chamber. Ralf was listening intently to one of them describe the suspended chamber. He had never seen anything like this before. The entire chamber was suspended and there was only one way to enter it which was heavily guarded.

Ralf was at loss of ideas; he just couldn't figure a way to get into the chamber without being caught. Meanwhile, Theodor was still unconscious from the trauma. Ralf had propped him against a wall to let him recover. A pang of guilt flickered within him as he looked at Theodor. It was because of him that Theodor had gotten dragged into all this. Suddenly a loud rattling sound brought Ralf back to his senses. The incinerator gates opened up and the cart was pushed out. There were two carts, one cooled as the other was ready to take the next batch of bodies. "Let's burn that doctor alive." One of the slaves came up to him and mocked. Ralf got to his feet and looked into the incinerator. "You get the next batch of bodies from the chamber" he instructed them and looked around. It was a massive furnace, red hot from heat and burning with dense fumes. He got closer to see the pipes running inside it. 'What material withstood that amount of heat?' he thought. Ralf was trying to breath in a composed manner. There was too much death around him, too much at stake and just no answers. Practically, Han was right above them in a suspended chamber but there was no way to get to him. 'Breathe Ralf, breathe and think.'

Ralf closed his eyes as he ran the structure through his head. 'The chamber was suspended; the pathway to it was guarded' Ralf thought of the entire layout as he continued plotting. His breathing was finally getting even as he thought about the metal couplings, the walkway, the ventilation pipes and what else connected the chamber? He opened his eyes in a flash. He stood there in front of the incinerator looking at the metal pipes. 'Breathe he thought, of course breathe.' A voice rang through his thoughts. The mad doctor had mentioned a ventilation system.

Ralf dashed to the prisoners and called one of them to inspect the idea. "What is it?" the prisoner asked. "This section here provides air supply to the chamber that the prisoner is suspended in" said Ralf, pointing to one of the pipes that ran through the incinerator. Ralf was trying to make sense of his own thoughts as his mind functioned in overdrive, trying to comprehend the possibilities. "There is one duct that opens through here" Ralf explained it to the prisoner who was quick to grasp what Ralf was trying to say. "You might be correct" he said and pointed towards a huge silver metal pipe that ran close to the roof and disappeared into the incinerator. "That pipe runs through the incinerator and splits into two, opening into the suspended chamber" the prisoner concluded the explanation on behalf of Ralf as they both stared at the silver pipe.

Ralf pulled out the ruined maps from their bags and drew a route. It was a very good and possible way to get to Han, the biggest glitch being the extreme heat that he and Theodor would have to face through the chamber. "What if we shut down the incinerator?" asked Ralf. The slaves looked at each other. Ralf didn't notice that others too had gathered around them as they discussed. "It's never been done in the past four years but we could try. The exhaust systems can still be working as they are not interlinked. You still have over thirty minutes before the guard shift changes. You can climb into the chamber, but your cover will be blown because as soon as guards open the gate to change shift they will know what's happening" concluded the slave.

Ralf nodded in acknowledgement, it was time to get Theodor into his senses. They were really close to Han now, and this might be their only chance to get some substantial work done. Ralf got up and asked the slaves to arrange for as many clothes as they could find. He would use them as padding against the extreme heat. The slaves dispersed to shut down the incinerator and to procure clothing for Ralf and Theodor. Ralf walked up to Theodor to wake him up. He saw Theodor's open bag and the black diary jutting out from it. He hesitantly picked it up and flicked it open. If this was really the document that Han had, they were risking their lives further for no reason. He anxiously flicked the pages trying to read something important. 'Thirty minutes' he thought as he glanced at Theodor who was knocked out by the sedative. Ralf scanned his surroundings for any other disturbance; but all around him spelt quietness and peace. Once again, he flicked through the intimidating black diary, once a fond possession of Adolf Hitler.

Maiden in the Wilderness

Many years had passed since Adolf Hitler walked out from the hospital and into an endless night. The German political landscape seemed to have changed rapidly. Hitler's National Socialist party was escalating upwards at an unimaginable pace. There was no stopping this party that was poised to be forerunner in German politics, at all cost.

Many influential international dignitaries had also commented on Hitler's phenomenal rise to success and his ability to bring people together in such harsh times. The Nazi party garnered support in large numbers, growing strong day by day. The top stratum leaders of Germany were considering using Hitler as a pawn to keep power intact.

Hitler himself had risen from ashes. He had come a long way from being a helpless little soldier in the First World War to stepping up his progress through government hierarchy. He was single handedly changing the tide in favor of his people. Within his company of men, he was highly respected and commanded them with an enigmatic verve. He had already gathered an impressive array of followers. Somehow, his charm and exceptionally superior oratory skills had won over scores of people and they had sworn to ride along with him to the very end. Though Hitler was at a nascent stage of his political career, his vast and expansive agenda made him the one cohesive force that united people.

Throughout the journey, Hitler sat still, in a tense mood. A phone call awaited him back at the hotel. He was lost in thought, an unnatural tension building up inside him. He let out a deep breath as he looked out the window. 'His dream was coming true' he thought 'It was finally shaping up.'

Hitler's hand brushed a half opened envelope lying next to him on the seat that held a copy of his book. He ripped open the remaining portion and pulled it out. It was doing phenomenally well, the copies were selling fast and they were already reprinting. Hitler pulled the book closer and felt the fragrance of newly printed manuscript. He closed his eyes and allowed the smell of new books to infiltrate his senses. He used to do the same while he was writing his book, back then those pages smelt of ink and sweat.

Nine months he'd spent in prison; but he never felt trapped, for his thoughts and visions wandered endlessly. His many nights in the dingy book shop had given him strength to hold on to his dreams. His own dreams, he'd been able to sift through them as and when he wanted. It was a remarkable ability and he used it with ease. He now knew who the lady from his dreams was. "Geli" he whispered under his breath. His breathing was getting heavier and he felt the knot in his chest tighten.

Hitler wished that the driver would just hurry up. as he looked out at the approaching building. He had just concluded his meeting with the head of states. Throughout that meeting, he'd sat with a troubled mind and an uneasy feeling inside his head. He wasn't sure of the feeling but suddenly, even the weather had seemed to agree with him. The sun hid behind clouds and an unusual cold swept around him. 'Nuremberg was getting exceptionally chilly for a day in September' he thought. The skies were otherwise clear; leave aside a few patches of clouds. The air suddenly carried along with it a cold that wouldn't go unnoticed by one's skin. It was weird for the cold to linger around at this time of year. The guards at the hotel were confused at Hitler's arrival. He had left for Hamburg; why would he return back abruptly? They'd wondered.

As his car reached the parking area; Adolf Hitler felt the inclement air and feared that it was an omen of grave news. He was sitting in the car in complete silence, trying to sort out his thoughts and calm himself. His recent spate with Geli troubled him the most. "Geli" he whispered under his breath yet again. These days, she constantly pervaded his thoughts. As soon as he thought of her, he also kept having unusual dreams, dreams that took him back to the cliff. Hitler seldom thought of home these days, it troubled him as it reminded him of loss.

The car came to a slow calculated halt at the parking. Hitler snapped out of his mixed thoughts and reached out for the door handle. Hitler looked at the driver through the rear view mirror and ordered "stay here." He hurriedly climbed the small flight of stairs and dashed into the corridor. The waiting guard connected the line as Hitler reached out for the phone, "Yes" he spoke into the receiver. He calmly listened to the voice on the other end.

Turning around, he faced the door from where he had just entered. The light hit his eyes; they were dark blue and stood out magnificently. A little sheen was building up in them as he patiently attended to the speaker on the opposite end. His face held no expression whatsoever. Hitler took a deep breath and handed the receiver back to the guard and in an abrupt unannounced motion stormed out of the room. He got to his car and ordered the driver out. The driver stumbled out of the car and stood aside as Hitler slammed the door and got in. He revved the car to life, floored the accelerator and sped out of the parking bay.

Hitler drove on like a maniac, he felt possessed by urgency and a desperate urge to reach Munich. He never shifted a gear down and cruised through the open roads. He noticed another car tailing him. 'Probably, the security set up by Himmler was following him' he thought. It was very unlike Hitler to act like this. He generally remained calm and composed, handling all situations with immense patience. He was yet again intrigued by the cold air and now it made sense to him. The unnatural chill was indeed a bad omen, it brought death along. He drove non-stop for around two hours before finally reaching Munich. Adolf didn't slow down and in his possessed fervor rammed his car into a waiting police vehicle. He jumped out of the car and strode up to his apartment. There was a bustle of activity in and around the house as his personnel lead him inside. Hitler's heart hammered against his ribs as he approached the apartment. Hitler entered and saw the entire staff lined up, waiting for him. A few of the maids were in tears and sobbed away in muffled voices. Hitler turned his attention towards the bedroom door as his heart sank deeper with sorrow. He took a few shaky steps and stood in front of the door, slowly lifting up his hand to touch the knob. He turned it and took a deep breath before finally opening the door.

He noticed the air in the room, it was warmer than the world outside; Hitler entered and closed the door behind him with a faint click. He felt Geli's warmth and presence in the room. On the floor were deep crimson stains and a massive pool of blood. The stains were red; full of life and warmth. Geli's clothes and effects were strewn all around the room. It felt as if she would step out from somewhere and use them any time now. Adolf sank down to his knees and picked her shirt from the floor. He looked at it longingly and inhaled deeply from it. The sweet perfume was intoxicating and he already missed her. A strange sensation stirred within the depths of his heart. It was pain, immense pain. He couldn't believe this was happening. His eyes bore at the blood lying on the floor as if searching for answers, searching for a reason in that deep crimson pool. He felt giddy and closed his eyes as silent and painful tears escaped him.

Ever since Adolf had dreamt, ever since he had heard that laughter in his dream, he knew. The blonde girl running away from him and disappearing over the water's edge was Geli. He obviously had never mustered courage to cross over, not even in his dream; he didn't dare jump into water. Years later, when he saw Geli Raubal standing in his apartment blossomed into a fine young woman, the first thought that struck him was the unknown laughter. He had spent several sleepless nights in deep thoughts over the connection and repeatedly, he dreamt of this girl in the backwoods. Hitler opened his eyes abruptly as he clutched Geli's shirt. The room flooded was with light erratically. The light from beyond the window seeped in as the curtains shifted with the slight wind. He was covered in sweat and was breathing very hard. He looked around with tear-filled eyes. He couldn't believe that Geli had shot herself. He cried, painfully writhing on the floor and in Geli's blood. His clothes stained from the crimson pool. His face touched the blood that was lying on the floor as endless tears escaped him. Adolf Hitler, leader of the Nazi party. The dynamic new hero of the people lay on the floor, crying uncontrollably and in a complete wreck. He tried to compose his breathing, closing his eyes and hoping for the pain to pass. Slowly he pushed himself up on his feet. His clothes, hands and face were smeared all over with Geli's blood.

He walked towards the door, glanced around the room and noticed a Walther pistol lying next to the bloody pool. He reluctantly lifted it off the ground. Little drops of blood hung from its barrel tip, the surface tension increasing along the length of merging drops. They hung there, clinging onto the pistol. Adolf wiped his hand over the pistol, letting it stain further in warm crimson liquid. 'In Geli's blood' he muttered to himself as he opened the barrel to find a lone bullet inside. Slowly, he pocketed the gun, looked around once again and inhaled deeply the perfume that she usually wore. An immense emotional surge rose inside him. He looked at both of his hands; they were soaked in Geli's blood. A sick feeling gradually built up inside him; he glanced around the room one last time and walked out.

His members of staff waited outside, taking in the gloomy situation. They knew; a deeply disturbing incident that had befallen their leader. Everyone knew about Hitler's affair with his niece but no one dared to speak of it. He stepped out into the hall. "I need time to myself, everyone leave!" he said. It was an eerie sight to watch Hitler blood stained and disturbed. The staff abandoned whatever they were doing and hurriedly left the room. Himmler lingered on, awaiting orders from Hitler. Hitler noticed Himmler standing in the far corner. "I want that bullet, the one that pierced Geli" he spoke with a quivering voice. Himmler nodded in silent acknowledgement. "You will see to it that this room remains locked. Nobody enters it or touches anything around" Hitler concluded and fell silent. He pulled a chair and sat by the window. Himmler understood that his work was done; he'd been summarily dismissed.

Hitler sat there, alone and lost in thought. His eyes brimmed with tears. He looked at his hands, at the blood dripping from them and cried. Geli's sudden and gruesome absence from his life was unhinging. He wanted to go back to his favorite spot on the cliff, what he'd give to stand there once again, he'd probably jump off to meet the cold water this time. So much had happened between when he was last there and now. He'd totally jump off and become one with the ether, meet Geli and his mother and Edmund. Hitler slowly closed his eyes as thoughts troubled him to no end. The faint laughter continued to echo inside his head, inside his thoughts. She evaded him, Geli; his little niece that he loved to death had become nothing more than a maiden in the wilderness. A distant dream, one he couldn't hold on to; that's what she was.

Prisoner

Ralf was flummoxed from what he read in the book. None of it made any sense to him; as his eyes wandered over the text. Throughout the book, there wasn't a singular handwriting pattern, it changed from page to page. He randomly flicked through its pages. 'What sort of a document was this?' he thought. He reflexively checked his watch; a good ten minutes had passed. It was time to gather their belongings and wake Theodor. He carefully wrapped the book in rubber and stowed it back into Theodor's bag.

Fedor studied the nature of possible infiltrations and now the camp was an impenetrable fortress. With Konstantin gone, he was the head of security. He gathered an array of guards and divided them into teams. They were all to search the camp thoroughly and capture intruders alive. Fedor had other plans up his sleeve. He knew the intruders wouldn't be lurking around openly as he walked around and eyed the beast bunker. Two helicopters were parked on top of the fort-like bunker. 'Viktor was making his arrangements as per Konstantin's instructions' Fedor noticed. He was going to enter the Honeycomb maze himself now; as it was time to take charge of the situation. He stood outside the maze; looked around and walked into the dark tunnels armed with just his rifle.

Viktor had assigned soldiers to check records and come up with information regarding their identities while he had other matters on his mind. The helicopters were parked on the Beast bunker and were anchored to the suspended chamber, ready to fly out at a moment's notice. Viktor was also ruminating over the keys that Konstantin had asked him to procure. They were dangerous in Konstantin's angry hands. The entire camp was built in a way that the cement was laced with dynamite. If Konstantin, in his rage triggered dynamites in the control room and brought down the camp, then it made no sense. He stood at the window in Konstantin's cabin as he pondered over the issue. Another guard entered the cabin and Viktor turned around. "Erik" he said. "I am going to hand the keys and dynamite controls to you. Can I trust you with this?" he asked. Erik nodded a yes as Viktor eyed the radio, preparing his next move.

Icy cold water splashed onto Theodor's face. Gasping for breath, he struggled and opened his eyes to adjust his vision. Ralf was standing before him and Theodor saw in his eyes, a look of relief that he'd finally woken up. "Why is it that every time I pass out and my head hurts" Theodor was pointing a finger at Ralf as he spoke. "I feel that you are the reason for all of this" he said. A smile broke over Ralf's face as he helped him to his feet. It was true though. In the past few hours whenever Theodor got to his feet from an attack or injury, it was Ralf who had saved him.

Theodor looked around the chamber disoriented. The fumes and injection prick had made him heavy in the head. "Any luck with Han yet?" he asked. A few slaves had gathered and were standing next to Ralf. "We are going to get into Han's chamber in the next five minutes" replied Ralf. Theodor froze; there was silence all around him. 'They were actually getting to Han' Theodor thought. Ralf and Theodor exchanged silent looks. It had been some journey to reach this point. Ralf cut short the uneasy moment and rolled open a map in front of Theodor. He spent the next five minutes explaining what he had discovered and how they would have to pass through the incinerator to reach Han. Theodor was dumbstruck but was prepared for the worst. After all that they had been through, this was just the last step to get to Han. The slaves gathered around them and dumped a pile of clothes on the floor. Ralf and Theodor had to use them as padding to get through the heat. Some of the slaves even gave up their own shirts to help the two Germans.

Fedor was walking through complete darkness, fanning the tunnels. He swiftly covered ground as he moved through the damp maze, and with water dripping all around, it was extremely humid in the enclosed space. The honeycomb mazes were now a complete mess. First, the explosions ripped them apart and now floods. They were slimy, dented and broken. Fedor quickly covered quite a stretch; albeit it was uneventful and nothing relevant was found or hinted at any sort of infiltration. Fedor picked up his pace and swiftly ran through accumulated water in the tunnel as he whipped out his flashlight to see better through the darkness. He was running and covering ground quickly when his foot suddenly hit a battered metal cover.

Fedor stumbled and looked behind to find a soot-covered hatch on the floor. He quickly scanned the area to see where it would have come from. The top of every tunnel section had a cover like this. He flashed his light on the tunnel tops and this cover matched the ones on top. He calculated the odds and moved faster through the tunnels. He doubled his pace as he frantically checked the tunnel junctions and joints. Fedor looked for any opening or intersection that might have a missing cover. After a few minutes of uptight searching, he reached a section which had an open ceiling. A gaping black tunnel stretched above the opening. He put away his flashlight and in one straight leap, hung onto the first rung of the ladder. He seemed inhumanely strong to have jumped so high in a single leap, and Fedor swiftly climbed up the ladder. He reached another metal cover and pushed it open. Now, he'd entered the Death Chamber and in true fashion, abhorrent fumes met his nostrils as soon as he inhaled. Fedor looked around and a possibility struck his mind that the infiltrators might have escaped from here and into the camp.

The incinerator was now cooling down as Ralf and Theodor were preparing to head into the pipe. They were layering themselves with extra clothes because even if the incinerator did shut down for nearly an hour, it was still bound to be extremely hot. Ralf geared up and put his weapons in order, handing out a pack of them to Theodor. They gathered their belongings and waited for the slaves to open the iron gates that led straight into the incinerator. The slaves flipped a lever and the gate slowly rumbled to life. A massive heat wave flew out dauntingly as if waiting to burn them down. One of the slaves came ahead and spoke softly "It is time; the shift will change in a few minutes." Theodor and Ralf exchanged looks as they stood facing the incinerator. They looked heavy and puffed up; what with all the insulation that they'd layered themselves with. These would hopefully delay the heat from burning their skins as they travelled through pipes. They wore the heat and gas protection suit over the padding which they'd procured from the dead Russian soldiers. This was probably the wildest plan that they could ever come up with but the odds were pitted against them, if they did not get to Han through this, they might as well give up altogether.

Fedor ran out of the tunnel at breakneck speed. He had to get to the beast bunker and by all means possible, find the intruders. There was no way to open the Death Chamber from within and yet again, the Honeycomb maze surprised him. Fedor never knew of this vent that led down into the maze from the Death Chamber. He came out of the tunnel and shouted to the guards to head to the Beast bunker. A few of them ran while others hopped on to jeeps and raced towards it. Fedor leaped onto a moving jeep, his anticipation building.

Within a few minutes he reached the entrance to the incinerator zone. He jumped off and ordered the guard to open the door. The guard was given clear instructions by Konstantin not to let anyone in if they were out of routine. "I cannot let you pass yet, you will have to wait for ten more minutes" the guard said checking his timer. "I said open it" Fedor came within two inches of him and spoke through gritted teeth. "The heat wave will burn you down, I said wait" the guard replied with equal angst. Fedor looked away in disbelief; refusing to be the one to take any orders at all from anyone. In a swift move he smashed the soldier's head with his gun. The soldier fell to the ground, twitching in pain as Fedor pulled the switch. The door opened up to reveal the near blind slaves standing there, waiting to change their shift. Fedor noticed that many were without their clothes. He held one slave and asked him "are you always without your shirts?" The slave was in no mood to give him a straight answer. "You don't give us food, what good will shirts do anyways?" he mocked. Fedor was irked beyond limit; and he stabbed his blade eight inches into the slave. The slave let out a howling cry of pain and fell to the ground, spraying blood through his open wound. Fedor instantly activated the alarm; he intuitively knew that a lot of things were out of place and the intruders were definitely nearby. He stepped into the chamber cautiously looking around, his knife and gun ready for any assault. The guards followed him and fanned out to secure the area.

Theodor and Ralf were drenched in sweat. With their clothes almost entirely torn, there were burn marks all over their exposed skin and as well, their eyes watered excessively from the rampant heat. Their calculations were horribly wrong; the pipes hadn't cooled down at all. They were sweltering hot and this slowed them down considerably. Slowly, they made their way up the chimney that would lead them directly into the suspended chamber. They were already exhausted and their dead weight increased two-fold with the clothes catching their sweat and getting damp. They struggled to go up, with Ralf closely behind Theodor in the chimney-like pipe, if Theodor missed a step, Ralf was best suited to hold on and catch him from falling to his absolute death. Time was running out, the fire would restart in a few minutes as per camp routine. Theodor looked down to see a bend in the silver pipe. In a sudden moment, something around rumbled, making a brash wailing noise and the heat intensity increased. Ralf looked up to Theodor and whispered "Hurry up. I think the incinerator is on."

Fedor was standing at the gate, anger glinting in his eyes. He watched as a gigantic tongue of flame licked the incinerator walls in fury. If there was any way for intruders to move, it had to be through the conduit. His team of soldiers had secured the other areas throughout the zone. Fedor turned the heat intensity to maximum and with a satisfied leer on his face; marched towards the upper floor where Han was. The gate of the incinerator was slowly closing shut as fires erupted inside with a bellowing fury.

Theodor climbed as high as his hands would let him. Ralf followed suit and did the same. They had reached the bend from where they would take another vertical climb. It was getting extremely difficult; with them being unable to get enough footing in the pipe. With the heat increasing rapidly, they began to slow down. Theodor's heart began to panic, his brain was flashing visions. All the deaths, all the people that he'd seen dying in the past few hours flashed before his face. "Hurry up will you?" Ralf shouted, a hint of panic in his voice.

Ralf was the last one to panic in any situation but the growing heat was getting to them. If their grip gave away they would both fall onto the glowing red hot ambers and burn to death. Theodor kept making desperate attempts to keep up his pace through the vertical climb. He lunged at the burning hot couplings one by one and continued his upward climb. The cloth padding had almost completely worn off and they were now touching the hot pipes with their bare skin. Theodor lunged again but this time, his hands couldn't take the heat. He fell down the vertical pipe and onto Ralf. Both he and Ralf went down the pipe, landing on the red hot junction. They screamed in agony as their bodies began to burn. Theodor couldn't think of anything at this point. He screamed out in fear and pain. Ralf too was howling as his skin touched the glowing hot pipe.

From out of nowhere two hands came down and grabbed Theodor. He blindly held on as he was pulled up with a jolt and thrown onto a concrete platform. The unknown hands came down again and Ralf grabbed them as he too was pulled up and thrown onto concrete. He landed with a crash but the heat was less intense here. Both Ralf and Theodor's exposed hands were thoroughly burnt. They were sweating profusely through the heat as they turned around to see their savior. It was a familiar spectacled face; they couldn't believe their eyes. Albert stood there, along with a well-built prisoner who'd pulled up the rope.

The Shadow

Cold winds moved across the valley with a bellowing fury. The entire camp was covered in snow; and a few soldiers along with new recruits were making their way into a shelter while Nazi officials sat still, observing the entire proceeding. The camp was a secret training facility which had been set up on practically inaccessible mountains. It was a small camp with only the barest minimum facilities at their disposal; only the topmost Nazi officials were aware of its existence.

A lone boy sat in the far end of a trench; all other recruits had run into the shelter after performing their tasks. This boy, probably in his early twenties; was sitting alone with his hands cupped over a flame which emanated from burning wood on the icy floor. He did not withdraw his hands or even flinch when naked flame arising from the burning amber licked his frost bitten palms. He rarely blinked as he looked over the vast landscape that lay in front; his green gaze stern and fixed on the skies stretching far ahead. A blizzard was slowly but surely building up and he showed no signs of the cold penetrating his body. Unflinching he sat there, gazing ahead into the vast emptiness of the snowcapped lands.

The company of people watching him from the shelter curiously awaited the outcome of his task. While all other recruits had put up their performances and he was the last one to do so. Just one recruit had performed satisfactorily and now this boy remained to be judged. The commander of the military camp stood alongside a few guards and deputy general who had flown in with his aids.

Occupying the middle ranks alongside Heinrich Himmler stood Adolf Hitler. They were keenly observing every movement the boy made, though he seldom made any. Hitler was in an arcane mood as he sat there quietly, looking at the brilliant landscape. His penetrating blue eyes were gazing far and wide as if searching for something. Himmler knew that Geli's death had unhinged him in some way. The camp commander too had expected him to be angry since almost all of the recruits had failed at the assigned task. Although the time span given to them to train these marksmen was extremely short, they'd still been expected to deliver. Suddenly from far away a screech was audible as it echoed through the valley. It was time for the test.

The Eagle had left its nest and was now the boy's turn to hunt down the master of the skies to prove his worth. He was probably the youngest recruit in the training camp. The eagle soared high into the landscape, circling mountain tops like a true ruler of the world. Unchallenged, it soared through the blizzard. The boy had his hands cupped over red hot ambers. The blizzard made it impossible to see through and flashes of the eagle flying by were visible, it encircled the mountain area once again and without warning dived into the valley. The audible screeches it made were the only way to trace its activity.

The boy moved, taking his hands away from the ambers as he firmly grasped his rifle. Back in the shelter, Adolf Hitler stirred a bit and craned his neck to get a better view. The boy loaded his rifle in a swift effortless motion and took his position. He was completely covered in snow now, but he held on to his rifle with an iron clasp. Each recruit was given one shot, just one round of fire to prove themselves. Another screech and the eagle came soaring up, whizzing past the mountain. The boy noticed a kill in its talons as he persistently followed her through the eye piece. Time was pressing and it wouldn't be sky bound for long.

The boy pressed the trigger and a loud shot echoed through the mountains as sound waves travelled far and wide. A bare silence hung over the campsite and the people sitting in the shelter tried to get a better look at the scene unfolding before them. Another loud screech pierced the silence, the eagle lived. The blinding blizzard had rendered all the training useless as the boy failed his test. The eagle was truly the master of the skies for no bullet could take her out.

Adolf Hitler had had enough. He gathered his coat and with Himmler and the guards by his side walked out of the enclosure. "You have disappointed us greatly" Himmler spoke as he faced the camp commander. Himmler was trying to study Hitler's reaction but none came from him, he was quiet and at peace. "They need more time to become proficient, my training is at par with the standards set by you" the commander argued.

Hitler looked around but surprisingly didn't make any further comment. He gave one last look at the commander and walked out towards his waiting car, Hitler glanced over the trench to check on the boy, only to see that he had disappeared from sight. The camp commander thought he saw a hint of a smirk cross Hitler's face. Himmler got into another car along with a batch of guards while Hitler sat in the one behind his.

It was a regular security measure to travel in different cars, as it helped in hampering assault motives. The camp commander felt helpless, and moreover Hitler did not comment on anything, an outburst of anger would have done better than his silence. He got on to his motorbike to escort Hitler till they both reached the end of the camp area. The blizzard was now frantic. The convoy started heading towards the gates and the front car picked up speed. Hitler's car was moving at a slow pace, side by side to the camp commander's bike. Hitler was sitting alone, he had ordered the driver to fall back and go slower than the car ahead.

The convoy was slowly winding down the mountain as snow made it difficult to see and ride through the terrain. More than half way down, the boy was spotted walking up the mountain. He had his rifle strapped on to his back and was walking through the snow covered terrain with his head ducked against the winds. Hitler asked the driver to stop the car. The boy also took note of them and stood by the window of Hitler's car. The camp commander came to a halt and pushed him aside, "get to the camp, I will meet you there" he ordered. The boy gave a cold look and held out his hand. A dead rodent hung from his hand; it had a deep wound running through its tiny body. Hitler stepped out on to the snow covered road. "I will handle it sir please be seated" the camp commander instantly got off his bike. Hitler smirked; "I thought I saw you take down the rodent" he spoke, removing his gloves. "You saw right" replied the boy. "You failed to follow orders though and that is a serious offense when it comes to military discipline" said Hitler.

Himmler along with two guards came running up to the spot where they had stopped. "What is the matter, why have we stopped here?" He was panting heavily as he asked and looked at the boy. The boy looked at Himmler and then back to Hitler and spoke "I wouldn't dare kill a master of the skies, if it's my skill that needs to be proven, I have this for you." He dropped the dead rodent by Hitler's feet. He had managed to kill the trapped rodent in the eagle's talons. "Boy, do you know whom are you talking to?" Himmler spat turning an angry shade of red. The boy gave Himmler a steely stare. "The master will decide my fate" the boy replied; giving Himmler a loathsome look.

Himmler was burning in rage and the camp commander intervened, he held him by his arm and tugged him away. "Enough. You get back to the camp. I will see to it that he is punished appropriately" said the camp commander. "Yes, he better learn some respect" said Himmler. Yet again the boy stared back at Himmler and spoke "Demand respect and you shall never have it. Command it; and it will be yours." He stared back at him with his green eyes. The commander slapped him squarely on the face, the frost bite was hard and a mild cut appeared on his face as fresh blood oozed out. Hitler held out his hand signaling the commotion to end instantly. "Send him to me, training starts soon" said Hitler. "I object" Himmler intervened. "He needs to be disciplined, no matter how good a marksman he is, it won't matter" he argued.

Yet another smirk crossed Hitler and he reached out patting the boy. He then held out a hand and rested it on Himmler's shoulder. "We are going to build a new Reich, a new hope and future for our people. Let us together get to doing that" he said studying the boy's dog tag. The metal was cold on his bare hands, it was scratched and worn out but the letters were visible through the heavy scratches, it read Han.

Disturbing noises emanated from the room, it comprised of a mix of heavy thumping on metal and banging of some sort. Han was flitting in and out of a trance but as soon as he opened his eyes, a surge of pain rushed through his body. He screamed, loudly and non-stop but nothing seemed to help. The pain never ceased and he tasted blood, it had been a long time since he'd tasted any food at all. He was wounded and in a very bad state, not able to move much. He managed to bend his feet slightly but his hands didn't budge. The voices were getting louder, 'What were they?' He thought to himself. He tried moving once again, but the pain was immense. A loud crash was heard somewhere in the distance and he tried to open his eyes a little. He saw blobs of light and could make out some movement in the distance.

Theodor, Ralf, Albert and the prisoner had managed to reach the chamber. They moved into the chamber, dripping in sweat and covered with burn marks all over. Albert dashed towards the only door within the room and bolted it shut from inside. Theodor and Ralf scanned the room looking for escape routes or any way the Red army could get in. The room was built with thick iron walls on all sides and a huge iron door on one.

It had a tiny window to see through which Albert was hammering on to dent shut from the inside. There were small grills on one of the walls for forced ventilation; these were covered with thick barbed wires. Theodor, Albert and Ralf gathered around in the center and looked up in disbelief. Suspended from two corners of the ceiling, huge rusted iron chains were clasped around the wrists. The entire body was covered in blood and grime; with burn and incision marks all over the subject of the Red Army's fury. Down below was a pool of blood that dripped from the body. A silver chain and an oval dog tag were left on the body, along with a small cloth that covered him below his torso. Every other piece of clothing had been stripped off him, and his bare skin was sore from inflicted torture. In this tortured and nearly dead form, lay the great German sniper. Behold, Hitler's shadow.

Fuehrer Bunker

T he city of Berlin, covered in looming black smog, rumbled with tremors from far away explosions. It was seemingly impossible to see or breathe clearly through clouds of dust and smoke. The piles of debris and dead bodies all around increased by the hour as an uneasy calm settled over Berlin. She was dead, razed and defeated. The happy announcements were made. "Adolf Hitler, leader of the NAZI party was dead." The Nazis' were defeated, their cruelty destroyed and their regime finally put to an end. Newspapers and radio broadcasts were carrying triumphant news all across the world.

Through the chaos, an unidentified aircraft descended over the smoke filled skies of Berlin. Massive engines roared past as guards stood alert on the small makeshift landing strip. General Yakov stood still by a guard who took down details of landing aircrafts. He eyed the aircraft as it came to an abrupt halt on the small landing strip. The rubber burnt on tarmac to give out a pungent sulfurous smell. Russians had captured everything in Berlin, including the skies and nothing occurred without their knowledge anymore. Yakov kept a hand on the guard's shoulder. "This plane never landed, Vlad's orders" he said and stood there with an array of guards to receive the important delegate.

Yakov tightened his stance as the aircraft door opened and he tried to get a better look through the smog. A huge figure descended from the aircraft and walked down the stairs with his coat bellowing in the wind. Two soldiers tailed him, both of whom were armed and with one of them was carrying a portable radio. As the smog cleared, Yakov strained his eyes to see a huge figure walking towards them. The Minotaur was in Berlin.

Yakov gave a short sharp salute to Konstantin as he neared them. Konstantin nodded in acknowledgement and saw Mark descend from the aircraft. The jeep door was held open for Konstantin; and he turned around to his personal guard. The guard drew closer, waiting for orders. "Fedor, Viktor or any other correspondence from the camp, do not wait, report instantly to me." In the slightest of whispers, Konstantin spoke to his guard. He looked around to see others. General Mark prepared to settle in and Yakov stood on the opposite side waiting for Konstantin to sit. Konstantin looked at him and then once again, looked in the direction of his guard. He kept a hand on his guards shoulder and drew the dumbstruck soldier closer. "A man by the name of Heinrich Himmler might contact you on this radio. The information is very important, take it down and report to me immediately. Do not delay the flow of information" he spoke, inches away from the guard's face. The guard could smell Konstantin's foul breath as he nodded in acknowledgement. The Minotaur concluded his orders and settled into his jeep followed by Yakov. The small convoy of jeeps drove away from the landing site as Konstantin's personal guard settled back into the aircraft.

As the jeep travelled through the broken city, Konstantin looked around. General Yakov was a little uncomfortable sitting next to him. The Minotaur's reputation throughout Russian ranks was extremely notorious. Yakov didn't know if he had to strike a conversation and glanced sideways, contemplating having to strike up a discourse. Konstantin looked at Yakov, daring him to talk as he himself was in no mood to discuss anything. He closed his eyes and sat through the small ride. His mind was calculating the next moves; Vlad, Hitler, his prisoner Han and Himmler were all causing him trouble. His thoughts stopped at Himmler, as his anger ebbed. He wanted to meet Himmler anyhow. It was of utmost importance to find out if he'd succeeded in carrying out their plans. Konstantin's thoughts took him back to his first meeting with Himmler, Hitler's most trusted man and how easily he'd won him over.

It was a cold grey day. Konstantin was sitting in his cabin, twirling a piece of paper in his hands. He looked a tad younger than he was now; a heavy muscular body well-toned by discipline. The young Konstantin wore a satisfied smirk on his face as he sat there thinking 'His plan was finally working.' This would get him close to riches and victory, very close.

That same evening he set out alone, and in his jeep he drove through water logged forest roads. The rain poured down in fury. He drove through the muddy terrain, taking a few detours with the aim of throwing anyone who wanted to be on his trail off his path. After almost an hour of driving he reached the spot as decided over a brief telephonic conversation he had with his aid. Konstantin parked his jeep under a tree and disembarked. He walked towards a parked vehicle and glanced around the area making sure it was unmanned. The jeep was waiting for him, parked on the opposite side of the rain washed road. It bore no markings, even the mandatory number plates were missing from it. It was battered and seemed unused. A little closer inspection of the jeep told him that it was probably Russian made.

A faint smile crossed his face. 'His aide was smart enough and he might strike gold with this deal' he thought. The door opened and a soldier stepped out, motioning Konstantin to take a seat within the car. Konstantin got in and closed the door with a soft thud. The jeep sank a little under his weight and as soon as the door closed shut, they were plunged into darkness. The glass of the jeep was covered with black slate like fittings. Only the windshield allowed some light to get in. A faint light flicked on from a lighter that the guard held. "Shut that please" a soft eerie voice spoke. Konstantin looked around to see a Nazi official sitting calmly on the side. He was a medium-built officer wearing a thick coat over his uniform; a stiff collar visibly jutted through the overcoat. He wore round rimmed spectacles and had sharp facial features. In the next instant the driver turned around, his gun pointing at Konstantin. Heinrich Himmler faintly nodded his head and a smile broke over Konstantin's face.

The guard still had the gun pointing at him. He looked from him to Himmler. Konstantin did not budge or move, he was unaffected by the guard or the gun that was pointing at him from a few inches away. "I forgot to greet you now, did I?" Konstantin asked in his deep commanding voice. In a swift motion, Konstantin clasped the hand gun by its barrel and pulled it closer to himself. "Shoot. Go on, shoot" he spat intimidatingly. Konstantin's hand crushed the cold metal barrel and bent it. The guard was trying hard to wrench his gun free from Konstantin's hand. Himmler waved to the guard to put his gun down and step outside. He obeyed and clumsily stepped out, closing the door behind him. "Why did you get another soldier along with you General?" Konstantin asked, pointing at the waiting soldier. "I don't like to drive in the rain. It is a waste of time. He will be disposed, do not bother" Himmler replied. "Well then, you pay heed to my offer?" Konstantin drove his conversation straight to the point.

Although Himmler seemed a bit unnerved, and looked lost, nonetheless he wanted this to work. Konstantin, sensing Himmler's nervousness, felt he could use this to his advantage. Konstantin's brain was formulating different possibilities. He was happy at the fact that Himmler was actually sitting here in front of him. If he bought Himmler out today, the war was just a little away from Russian victory. "You are very brave, I must say General. You are here in secrecy; and that takes some courage" Konstantin pressed on. "Hitler usually maims and kills the people who conspire against him, I have heard." Konstantin was playing with Himmler's mind. "So, I ask you again" said Konstantin. Himmler composed himself; there was a moment of silence as rain thundered outside. The very trees shuddered at the rain's fury and swayed spraying excess water all around. Even the rain seemed to be shaken by Himmler's audacious move to dethrone his master.

After an uncomfortable silence, Himmler finally spoke. "You must know the risk involved in this is tremendous. If things go wrong or if information leaks, the magnitude of the situation will be too grave to even think of. If Hitler has a hint, even a whiff of my being here, discussing this with you" "I know, I know" intervened Konstantin "he will have you killed." "Killed is an understatement" retorted Himmler and fell silent as they both locked eyes with each other for a brief moment. Himmler did not want Konstantin to think that he was scared of doing this although he couldn't hide his nervousness. "So you will carry out these experiments that I ask of you, in your facility?" Himmler was now excited as he pulled the conversation in the direction that he wanted. "You see it has been my dream to study these beings for so long now and Hitler just dismissed these ideas; saying that I was losing my mind." A hint of anger flitted Himmler's voice. "He won't understand, he still insists on deporting thousands and thousands of the populace out of Germany when I can use them to carry out experiments on genetics. To breed a new race of humans designed to do my bidding!" Himmler spoke with a fanatic energy in his voice. "I'll have a team of doctors sent along to set up and monitor labs within your camp. You will carry out these experiments and dispose the unwanted people effectively. You see; we can literally raise a slave army here, we can control the population. We will decide if new life should be born or not, we will decide the fate of coming generations and make sure only the purest breeds survive" Himmler concluded his insanely fanatic plan. Konstantin was grinning and nodding in acknowledgement as he replied "I will carry out these experiments that you want me to General, no one will know about them and you will be sent detailed reports of every experiment that goes on here. This secret will be kept safe between the both of us, to our deaths. No third person needs to know what we do here." Himmler eyed him for a moment and asked "How will you have such a free hand under the Russian high command? Surely no one will let you do this legally." Konstantin bore into Himmler's eyes and a smile broke over his face. "I will do it exactly the way you do it. Surely your high command does not know you are here striking a deal with me, legally?"

Konstantin asked and sat back with a satisfied smile over his face. He had played along extremely well. Himmler, short of words but with a glimmer in his eyes, nodded silently. "It will all be yours, given you deliver what I want" Konstantin pushed the conversation further in a low commanding tone. Himmler became a little serious and spoke in his eerie soft tone "Yes it will be delivered. All the military tactics, attack plans, military data, layouts of all the factories. Nuclear material, their relevant studies and treasures will be delivered as planned" promised Himmler. "I do not want any treasure, Himmler" Konstantin cut him short. "I want the Amber room specifically" Konstantin's eyes had a glint like never before; as he made his demand. There was silence between the two yet again as the rain storm wreaked havoc.

The Amber room was a lost treasure that had disappeared from sight and over the years, had been totally impossible to trace. The Nazi intelligence had somehow acquired it and now, Konstantin wanted it from them. It was priceless and if Himmler managed to deliver this, the Minotaur would be in an excellent position of power within his ranks. Konstantin shifted and bore into Himmler's eyes as he spoke. "And I need something else from you too" he asked. Himmler looked at Konstantin, he wanted to break away from his gaze but couldn't. The fiery black eyes kept him held. "Yes" replied Himmler. "When the time comes, you'll have Adolf Hitler." Konstantin let out a bark-like laughter that rang through the small cramped space. "Remember, I want him alive" he demanded.

Himmler nodded in acceptance and smiled uncomfortably. "I will need a safe passage once the hand over happens. I wish to take over complete leadership of Germany once you dispose of Hitler" Himmler spoke uncomfortably. Konstantin smiled back. "Give me Adolf Hitler and you will have Germany to rule" he promised. Himmler finally broke into a smile at the last statement. "How do you intend to capture him?" Konstantin further questioned. "Well that remains to be seen, and carefully planned. There is a hurdle in our way. Hitler's personal sniper, his shadow they call him. He is difficult to break" Himmler explained as he continued to stare out the windshield. I am going to slowly but surely start placing my trusted aides around Hitler. Once I dispose of Han, our path clears up and when the situation is in our favor, I will have Hitler meet a Russian dignitary under pretense of a pseudo peace talk. He will buy it; that I am certain of. More than anything, he wants to capture Russia" said Himmler. Konstantin's expression turned grave at the statement. Himmler, noticing that, spoke quickly in his own defense. "I obviously will declare peace once Hitler is taken out. I wish to befriend such a great nation at all costs. Only a fool, namely Hitler would want to attack Russia" he concluded. Konstantin moved close and spoke in a whisper "We will rule side by side, Himmler. Give me Adolf Hitler; and the path for you becomes completely clear to become supreme leader. Not to forget, by then we will be breeding our own army of slaves."

Konstantin unconsciously stroked the car seat. Now, he realized the reason these thoughts were coming to him. This car was very similar to the jeep he sat in all those years ago. He looked out the window, they were nearing their destination. They abandoned the jeep a few meters away and walked towards a compound wall. Yakov walked alongside Konstantin, showing him the exact places. There was a small house-like structure in the center, filled with rubble and dirt. Konstantin stalked the roads of Berlin, a faint sneer flickering over his face. 'We managed to pound our enemies' He thought. 'He, Konstantin, had managed to pound them to dust.' Of course everything was still not working out as planned, they had hoped to get to Hitler alive but news had come in claiming his death. Konstantin marched along with his guards; his visit was a fiercely guarded secret; he was not supposed to be here walking freely in Berlin. But what did Konstantin care? Right in the epicenter of the world's greatest battle, he strode in with absolutely no fear in his eyes. The soldiers around him wore gas masks to enable them breathe through dense smog and dust but it barely affected him. He walked free and unhindered as if he was meant to walk through all the devastation and hurt with absolute ease.

Although his primary aim here was to check on Hitler, he secretly had other plans brewing in his mind. More grave decisions to take, more people to meet. It had been a few years since the meeting and ever since, he and Himmler corresponded over radio or coded letters. After a point, the communication had gone bleak and Himmler began to act strange.

Now, Konstantin stood in the premises of the Fuehrer Bunker which was completely cordoned off by Red army soldiers. Frantic searches were being conducted throughout the bunker, one hoping to find Hitler and the other trying hard to procure whatever documents and treasures they could find. A set of soldiers carried two bodies and lay them down on the ground. "These might belong to Hitler and his mistress" they discussed. Konstantin bent low and studied the dead bodies; they were half burnt and oozing fluids. It was impossible to tell or confirm who they were, just by looking at the corpses. "We can never tell" a deep menacing voice spoke over Konstantin's shoulder.

Konstantin slowly turned around, the voice jutted at him with such clarity; he could never have mistaken it for another's. He wheeled around to find his commanding officer and only living relative standing there. As tall and well-built as Konstantin, they looked like brothers. "Of course we can" retorted Konstantin as he walked closer to face Vlad. Their faces held wave after wave of angst and unspoken emotions. "The world will now believe what we tell them. We have won the war, Vlad." Konstantin was trying hard to talk normally and was holding his anger back with great difficulty. Yakov gave a short salute to the commanding officers and disappeared.

Konstantin wanted to establish contact with Himmler at all costs and for that he had to play along with Vlad. "Last I heard, you were up to a lot of chaos in that camp of yours. A lot many filthy experiments!" Vlad drove a knife through Konstantin's thoughts. Konstantin maintained a straight face and didn't react. He looked around the devastated bunker. "The war is coming to an end Konstantin" said Vlad. "Right here, below your feet lays Adolf Hitler, dead and defeated. The other forces won't be far away. Though, what you suggest is right, we will tell the world that we have Hitler." A smile crossed Konstantin's face. "Well said, commander. Let's click a picture, a victory pose. Right in the heart of Berlin, over a probably dead Hitler" roared Konstantin and with a massive thud; stomped his foot on the ground. He waved out to a camera man who was collecting pictures for evidence. "I am afraid I cannot do that" Vlad cut him short. "Your visit here is not authorized. Only I know that you are here so once you head back, prepare to dismantle the camp. Remember the plan; your camp belongs to the Nazis'. So make sure it looks like that" said Vlad. Konstantin bore into his eyes. "I am afraid you will, Vlad" he muttered in anger. He called the photographer and asked him to click a picture. Konstantin pulled Vlad closer. One hand rested on Vlad's shoulder while the other remained in Konstantin's jacket, clutching skillfully onto his knife. Vlad felt the steel brush his ribs.

"You see my dear brother. Things are falling apart for us all" Konstantin spoke in a barely audible whisper as he posed for the picture. "Your high command won't bother me much now. You cross one line and I'll have you killed. I can drive this knife into your lungs right now."

Both Vlad and Konstantin stood still for the picture. A small bead of sweat trickled down Vlad's face. "Empty threats brother" spoke Vlad. The photographer clicked as they stood in the devastated Fuehrer bunker. Konstantin let Vlad go and dismissed the photographer. "I got you out of that miserable prison, don't you ever forget that Vlad." Konstantin held fury in his eyes as he reminded his elder brother of their mutual past. "Konstantin, I keep you in that camp against orders from high command. If anyone has a whiff of you still operating under me, we'll both be thrown out for good" spat Vlad. "We will end up right where we started from, in prison." Vlad spoke with a vehement hiss in his voice. "I don't care about them anymore. Along with Hitler, Stalin too shall pass. Choose what you want commander Vlad" Konstantin spoke with suppressed anger as he openly threatened to break free from reigns of the high command. "What is the progress here? Is there any actual trace of Hitler?" asked Konstantin. He diverted the topic before Vlad could react to his threat. Vlad looked away in despair. "None that we can truly confirm, he seems to have vanished. We have checked all possible exits. Berlin is sealed but there is no Hitler. A lot of reports have poured in of people seeing him and killing him. None are true though, he has simply vanished. All of this is going to move to a secure location within the next few hours." Vlad pointed at the bodies and artifacts that were being packed for transport. "We have a pile of dead bodies from this bunker but there is no way to test or confirm if it is Hitler" he said. Konstantin looked at the bodies that were being brought out. "The reason why I called you here Konstantin is that you need to securely transport two cadavers. They might be the bodies of Hitler and his mistress" Vlad spoke in a whisper. "If there is any possibility that Hitler died here in this bunker, the bodies we have procured are the only proof" he said. Konstantin was considering the odds. 'Was this actually happening?' he thought. Even though Himmler was missing, Konstantin was being handed over Hitler's dead body. "I will fly down to your camp from here to decide what to do with the bodies" Vlad's words snapped Konstantin out of his thoughts. "As much as I do not want to trust this in your hands, I have no other option. Only your camp remains a safe house as of this moment and you must personally transport them" Vlad spoke on, in hushed tones, as Konstantin continued to look around. "Why trust me then? What if I turn you in brother?" Konstantin questioned Vlad again. It was highly unlikely of Vlad to act like this. "There is a rumor Konstantin, a very peculiar one that is doing the rounds. Someone has spotted the Amber room" Vlad softly addressed Konstantin with a hint of accusation in his voice. Konstantin shot Vlad a look of mild disgust. "Let me know when that rumor turns true" concluding his retort Konstantin walked away to look around the bunker premises. "That is not all Konstantin" said Vlad. "They have spotted Hitler's shadow. That rumored sniper and the Amber room were spotted very close to your camp" he concluded. Konstantin stopped in his tracks. 'General Mark knew more than necessary and he disclosed even more' Konstantin's thoughts raced as he walked around the bunker. Han was a very well-kept secret that he was planning to put to good use. Vlad's knowledge of these happenings was pretty much accurate and was of grave concern. A soldier came running to Vlad with a file full of papers. Vlad addressed the files as Konstantin took liberty to walk around. Konstantin's visit was turning out to be futile as far as Himmler was concerned. Either that Nazi bastard had ended up dead or he had disappeared. No Hitler, no Himmler and this was an absolute waste of time. He looked around at the devastation with a satisfied smirk though. It was because of him that Russians were able to march right into Berlin. But who knew this apart from Konstantin and Himmler?

A soldier ran through the pile of debris. Konstantin stopped him abruptly. "Found anything soldier?" "There is no sign of him sir" replied the tired soldier. Konstantin interrogated him further "Are you sure? Alive? Dead? Nothing?" "Yes sir; we have fanned the bunker. There are more dead bodies but none confirmed to be Hitler" he said. Konstantin considered the situation for a moment. He came close to him and asked softly; "Did you by any chance find a German high command officer by the name of Heinrich

Himmler?" The soldier thought for a second. "I can check the records and let you know my lord" he replied. "How long will that take?" asked Konstantin. "I can assign someone to get the records to you" replied the soldier. Konstantin nodded and agreed. "Have them sent to me while you continue the search. Let me know if you find something" he said. It was a tough call for Konstantin now, in a short while he would have to travel back; disappointingly, there was no sign of Himmler. Vlad was extending a hand of friendship and handing over apparent dead bodies to him. The equations were changing and he would have to find his own buyers. Out of all of these problems, Hitler still eluded them all.

The Red army soldiers were piling up trucks with important Nazi artifacts and the remaining data that they could find within the bunker. Konstantin absentmindedly looked around and thought about various possibilities. How could he be sure if the body was of Hitler or not? Vlad had come back and now, he stood beside Konstantin. "Are you able to recognize any of the bodies?" he asked. "No Hitler and no Eva Braun. That much I can tell for now" replied Konstantin. "How do you know Eva Braun so well? Have you seen her up close?" asked Vlad. "Well I slept with her and bore a few kids with her. That's why I know her" Konstantin replied, mocking Vlad's question. Vlad stepped close to Konstantin, his anger now peaking. "You get back to your filthy rat hole of a camp. I'll arrive shortly and take charge of it. Get your reports ready and prepare to be thrown back to Stalin's mercy" Vlad spat.

Konstantin turned around in cold anger. "I am taking the bodies back to my camp because you want me to. Know this brother; I have a way to figure out if these belong to Hitler. Now you listen to me and stop being an idiot" Konstantin retorted. "The high command doesn't know anything yet. Marshal Zuhkov is far away from here and he has other matters to settle. If I you assure a way to identify the bodies, you and I can split the loot" Konstantin said, offering a straight bribe. Vlad was not concerned with any bribe as of now. There was no way of telling if these bodies belonged to Hitler and Konstantin's methods, although untrustworthy, seemed to be his only choice. "We can't evade the high command for too long" whispered Vlad.

Konstantin was contemplating what bait to throw next and then suddenly, he spoke up. "You are right; I have the Amber room." Vlad was shocked at the statement. "How can I be sure?" he asked. "You are transporting your sorry self to my camp aren't you?" Come see for yourself" Konstantin replied. Vlad considered the offer but didn't look convinced. "I have Hitler's shadow; his name is Han and is currently held captive in my camp. Imagine the price we can fetch on him?" In the faintest of whispers Konstantin made his final move. Vlad was now dumbstruck. "Keep them safe and don't be up to anything till I reach. Such valued prisoners need to be dealt with care. If Hitler is dead, this is his only body. I am sending a decoy corpse back to Stalin. The High command will trust my word on this and will think they have Hitler's corpse. I will carry more loot and fly to you soon" said Vlad.

Konstantin smirked and walked towards his waiting jeep. He settled down in his car, waiting to head back to the camp, his mind now working in overdrive about the situations. He had definitely secured himself a better deal here. Himmler was not going to turn up anytime soon and Konstantin had to take action. A soldier was running towards his car with a bunch of papers. "Sir, these are the confirmed people that we have found in the bunker" he said flipping the pages. He handed out another bunch of papers and explained "These ones are the speculated lot of people that were seen in and around the bunker." Konstantin flipped through the pages and photographs that the soldier had presented to him. "And these are the missing people" said the soldier. Hitler and Himmler topped this last list. He was flipping through the endless list. Morell, Speer, Goebbels... the list went on. Konstantin flipped and abruptly stopped at a picture. It was Han. "Which list did you say this is?" asked Konstantin. The soldier checked and replied "Missing people sir." Konstantin looked further and saw the name Eva Hitler. His mind began racing. "Eva Hitler?" He asked the soldier. "We found witnesses who confirmed their marriage my lord. No official records as yet though. And the body that was found along with Hitler's is burnt beyond recognition. Unless someone personally knew her, it's impossible to tell. But if Eva's body is confirmed, then the other one is Hitler for sure" the soldier concluded. Konstantin was smiling to himself as he flipped through the papers, his mind lost in thought. There was another list that read 'top secret.' It was from Nazi records and showed a list of people to assassinate. He flipped though and found another familiar face that read General Felix. Konstantin strained his memory to remember this face and like a jolt of lightening, it came up in his thoughts. 'The dead body that they found in the honeycomb maze, it was General Felix' he thought.

Konstantin was thinking hard now as he read through the papers. 'Associated with secret organization Blood Moon' was printed along the bottom. A faint smile settled over Konstantin's face as he sat there, deep in plot. The time had come to wrench the information out of Han; Konstantin had to break him anyhow. He turned around to the driver and spoke. "Drive to the aircraft as fast as you can." The jeep hammered to life as the driver nodded, the soldiers had loaded coffins into the jeep. Konstantin handed the records back to the soldier with a curt nod as they sped away from the Fuehrer bunker.

Raging Fires

Han was on the floor. Ralf, Albert and Theodor released his shackles and in a team effort, undid the straps that held him in place. He was in a sorry state and couldn't move freely due to blood flow constraint. His chest had a deep acid wound blotched on it, while his bloodied eye was unable to maintain full focus. There were innumerable cuts and burn marks all over his body. Ralf flicked on a lighter to see better in the darkness. Han had numerous wounds on his body and his thigh had turned purple. Sore veins throbbed around a probable bullet wound and a deep wound on his side which still bled.

Theodor and Ralf helped Han steady himself and get to his feet. They gave him water to drink and ripped their own clothes to cover him up. "Han, I am Ralf, this is Theodor and Albert. We are here on General Felix's orders" he said. "We are members of the Blood Moon and are here to rescue you" he hurriedly spoke. Han was listening to everything that Ralf spoke. He carefully tried to open his eyes and adjust to the sudden light. Both his eyelids opened with great strain as he looked around at the soldiers standing by him. Han had never known a family, Blood Moon was his only kin and here they stood by him now.

Through all the torture and pain inflicted on him, Han exhibited an unbroken iron will that reflected through his actions. He looked at Theodor, Ralf and Albert and flashed a faint smile, appreciating the severe risk he knew they'd taken to get to him. Han finally began taking deep steady breaths and tried to stand on his own. He felt immense pain surging through his wounds. The acid burn through his chest, the cuts, the cold water splashes, it all came rushing back to him. In a sudden gush, he vomited blood on the iron floor of the suspended chamber. He crouched low on all fours as pain erupted through his lungs and chest. Foul smelling vomit pooled around him as he tried to steady his breathing. He slowly rose to full height, bending the pain to his will and standing with an iron spine.

Albert had a plan in mind; he had timed an explosion around concrete couplings that held the suspended chamber in place. They suddenly heard locks being dislodged around them. Footsteps and commotion echoed through the iron walls as expected. "I locked the door from inside. They can't get in for now" Albert said as he looked around in panic. He had opened up a map to show it to others. Ralf and Theodor heaved sights of relief, what would they do without Albert on their team? With surprising strength and co-ordination, Han walked towards Albert. "Leave those maps alone, we need to get out of here via the ducts" Han spoke with a deep composed voice, a voice so serene and commanding that one had no option but to listen to him. The three of them were surprised at Han's ability to live through the torture. A sudden loud bang told them that the door was being broken open. They heard other muffled voices around the chamber too. "Mr. Han" Albert tried talking. "We must try and get out of here through this duct, the incinerator is functional and there will be an explosion any moment now."

While Albert explained his plan, the prisoner that had helped them through the ducts tried to draw their attention. "We don't have much time…" his voice trailed off as a massive explosion erupted in the distance. "I tasted the concrete and found out that it has been laced with dynamite. Some sort of a hydrogen compound, probably peroxide mixed with an adhesive poured into the cement" Albert said, cutting through the chaos. "You are eating cement?" Theodor asked him, disgusted. "Licking is the right word, I presume. " replied Albert. "You are licking cement?" Ralf asked, even more disgusted by the fact. "That's the reason you both are alive" retorted Albert. "Mr. Han, the incinerator fire will reach peak temperature and if we removed the coupling, it will self-trigger an explosion around other couplings too" Albert went on, trying to explain his plan. "Will you shut up? Yes, we are proud of you and very happy that you are alive" Ralf shouted as he armed himself. Someone was trying to break down the iron door as the chamber slowly began tilting onto one side. "Is this supposed to happen Albert?" Theodor asked as he tried to steady himself. "Well a little bit of a tilt is fine" Albert replied, concerned by the sudden shift. "Everybody move to the opposite side now, slowly; just walk" the prisoner cut through. Han looked at him and acknowledged as they slowly slid towards the opposite side. Without warning, the entire chamber abruptly tilted, they were thrown off their feet and smashed into the iron walls.

Viktor had panicked at Fedor's alarm and initiated 'Code Falkon'. He ordered the helicopters to lift, thus breaking the suspended chamber from couplings and causing it to rise from its sanctuary within the beast bunker. It was the highest security measure within the camp, one which up until now, had never been used before. Viktor ordered it to be transported to a Russian safe house deeper within the forests. 'Konstantin or Vlad' thought Viktor. He was going to shine through this and rise above Fedor. The two transport helicopters were positioned at a calculated distance from each other as they rose. Iron ropes were attached to the bunker via a pulley system to facilitate easy lift off. A series of metal spacers maintained distance between the ropes to avoid entanglement. "You fool. Stop the helicopters" Fedor yelled from the bunker gates. "The couplings have to be undone or the chamber won't rise" he shouted. Viktor didn't pay heed to what Fedor was shouting. The chaos and noise around them was too much to understand anything that Fedor said. Viktor had a satisfied smirk on his face as he saw the helicopters rise.

Han, the prisoner and the trio were being thrown around the suspended chamber mercilessly. Yet another explosion rocked around them and they felt a massive jerk. "Albert?" Theodor shouted angrily through the chaos. "Is this all part of your brilliant plan?" Before Albert could reply, the chamber rolled over and they were thrown to the other side. The air circulation pipes had broken loose from their sources as they felt pressure fluctuate in the chamber. They tried to cling on to something, anything; but even that seemed rather impossible. There were no protrusions to hold onto. Suddenly the entire chamber jolted and came to a standstill. They were thrown towards the wall and crashed into the metal sides.

One of the air circulation pipes wedged itself in a crevice and got stuck there. It remained connected to the chamber but gave away from the other end. The helicopter pilot was unprepared for this. As per the design, all couplings were supposed to give away and let the chamber loose. The pilots pushed the rotors to full throttle and tried to rise. There was an evident strain on the helicopters as they tried to lift the chamber. Before they could lift it to full height, one of the metal ropes suddenly gave away. It snapped from the coupling and rolled around the pulley. The chamber slid to one side while its entire load shifted onto one helicopter. The chamber smashed through the bunker walls as it lay suspended on just one coupling.

The connecting pathway of the chamber crashed through the bunker and into the incinerator. Red army soldiers retreated back from the suspended corridor as it swayed dangerously. A few of them fell from the sudden motion and crashed all the way to the ground. The helicopter pilot was unprepared for these sudden jolts and he swayed out of control as the chamber pulled the helicopter downwards. The walls collapsed around the chamber as it smashed through them. The helicopter flew off course and swerved close to the bunker top as the pilot tried to stabilize its motion through this sudden strain. The suspended chamber was heavy and was designed for lift off with the combined power of two helicopters. It sank deeper hanging over the incinerator and pulling the helicopter down with it. With a thundering explosion, the helicopter crashed on top of the beast bunker and caught fire. The other helicopter steered abruptly to avoid impact and hovered away from the bunker top.

The massive explosion sent pieces of pulley system flying through the air; one of the pulleys flew straight into the rotor of the hovering helicopter. The pilot tried to steer clear off the debris; but was too late. The metal smashed through the rotor as the helicopter swerved out of control. The guards scattered, slaves as well, ran loose from the open bunker walls as they saw the helicopter fly out of control. With a deafening crash it rammed onto the camp grounds; engulfing everything around it in a huge explosion.

Viktor watched in horror as the chamber fell freely into the beast bunker. The walls of the bunker were breaking from impact as fire swiftly spread through, multiplying the blasts. The massive concrete walls cracked and chunks fell loose as blasts ripped through in rapid succession. The suspended chamber plummeted right into the epicenter of the blasts. Explosions erupted through the beast bunker as the dynamite laced concrete triggered a wide wave of fire. Fedor dashed towards Viktor, running away from the blasts. "You bastard, do you have any idea what you just did? Konstantin will have your head for this" he roared into Viktor's face as they both helplessly stared at the devastation.

Somehow, Ralf managed to sink his fingers into a small crevice as the entire chamber rolled and crashed around. They felt massive heat within the chamber and were sweating profusely. Finally, after what seemed like forever, the chamber came to a violently abrupt halt. They were tossed and thrown into a corner as it stopped spinning. Ralf and the prisoner instantly got to their feet and tried to nudge open the door.

With all their might they pulled at it. The heat was building up and they couldn't hold much longer. Theodor too joined in the effort as they kicked the heavy metal door. Ralf's kicks were denting the door at places. The slave and Theodor wedged their hands into the dented sides and applied their combined strengths to rip it open. Ralf charged and rammed into the door and finally, it gave away from the hinges. They pulled it aside and looked to see that they were right in the middle of the incinerator. The fires licked their chamber from all sides and the buildup of heat was immense.

The guard turned on the radio as the aircraft passed through minor turbulence. "Code Falkon has been initiated on Viktor's orders." As Konstantin heard this over the crackle, his blood boiled with rage. He got up from his seat and entered the cockpit. In a swift motion, he pulled the pilot out and pushed him away. Konstantin gunned the engines to full throttle. There was too much turbulence outside but he could care less. Konstantin's vile energy surged through the very aircraft as he pushed the engines to roar at maximum speed. At breakneck speed, he travelled furiously with the aim of reaching the camp as soon as possible. The cockpit was dark and glows from the dials threw faint light on Konstantin's face. The radio operator and pilot stood behind, scared and dumbstruck. A far away lightening pulse lit up the cockpit. Konstantin's eyes were bloodshot and his angry face contorted in rage as he expertly piloted the aircraft through horrible weather.

Surprisingly, Han stepped forward through the fires that were erupting all around them. "Follow me soldiers, do not stop and do not look back" he ordered as he ran headlong into the flames. Ralf, Albert, Theodor and the prisoner blindly followed Han through the piercing heat. Han dashed through the flames with inhumane energy. The rest followed suit, dodging explosions and fires as they ran through the incinerator and into the bunker.

Fedor had his rifle out and was trying to look through the chaos. His heart froze as he saw the German soldiers being led by Han and running through raging fires.

Han's Army

Han led the pack as they ran tirelessly through erupting fires. The incinerator walls had collapsed, leaving gaping holes in the bunker. The air was filled with ash and dust from recurring explosions and fires which rapidly engulfed the entire bunker. Ralf, Albert, Theodor and the prisoner ran blindly behind Han. Avoiding the flames and blasts was an herculean task, yet they had no other option than to keep up their frantic run. The heat was so intense that their skins burnt and their dripping wet clothes caught fire randomly. Somehow, Han knew the route by heart; and he kept his fast pace which was surprising considering the amount of torture inflicted upon him. He easily stood strong and ran through broken corridors with boundless energy.

Viktor routed the guards and procured water supply to douse the raging fires. His heart hammered against his ribs. He had to take control before Konstantin arrived. Fedor panicked as he entered the beast bunker with a team of guards. He didn't care as much about the fires; his utmost intent was capturing these infiltrators that had dared disturb the sanctity of their camp. Fedor was extremely angry with himself and Viktor. The infiltrators were right under his nose. 'How could he just let them slip away?' he cursed under his breath as he entered the Beast bunker.

Viktor gave orders to douse the fire and assembled his own team to enter the raging Beast bunker. He had to restore the mess created under his orders. The Russian camp stood devastated right now. Two destroyed helicopters, their most protected beast bunker up in flames, the suspended chamber completely blown off, slaves were on the loose and most infuriating of all; Han was out again. Viktor shuddered to even think of Konstantin's reaction to this mayhem. The camp had been an impenetrable fortress under Konstantin's watch and now a handful of Germans had broken through its very heart. Viktor ordered Erik, his next in command to step up and evacuate the beast bunker of all study and nuclear material. To Viktor's luck, the nuclear material was housed in a separate room and was still in the canisters. Erik took the orders and instantly got to executing them. He had to douse fires, evacuate material safely and try to restore bunker walls so it could be gated shut.

Han burst through a locked wooden door. He wrecked the door to pieces as he rammed into it and fell through. The others followed suit and came to a sudden halt within the room. Han quickly looked around and saw his effects. He took the burnt rags off his feet and grabbed his clothes and boots. Everyone was busy dousing minor flames all over their clothes and boots. They collected weapons and prepared for the impending battle that lay ahead.

Albert fell to the floor as the sole of his boots burnt through his very skin. Han quickly helped Albert to his feet and noticing his dilemma, offered him his boots. They were heavy, black, tailor-made boots that adorned an engraved eagle insignia. Han turned around and faced the lot, "We need a plan. General Felix? Traugott? Anyone gathered outside? Can they help us?" he asked. At these words, the trio froze. This was the moment. Everyone thought that Han would have a plan; that he would have answers to how they could break out from this camp. Han looked at them, waiting for a reply as he concealed his wounds. "They fell to their deaths when we tried to break into the camp. We are on our own; getting out of here alive is our sole responsibility". Ralf replied. Han's expression didn't change one bit at the statement. "Is there any chance that you saw a Nazi official when you got here? Heinrich Himmler? He was rumored to be here too" Han questioned them further. "We came up through the Honeycomb maze and reached you. We have no idea about what might be happening in the camp" Ralf replied. "Himmler is missing. Konstantin has been trying to get in touch with him but he hasn't responded" said Albert as he put on the boots and loaded his weapons. Everyone questioningly looked at Albert for an explanation. "I hacked into their working radio. They were trying to get in touch with him but there was no response" Albert clarified. "I also know that Konstantin was supposed to leave the camp and travel to someplace. I think he is away at the moment" Albert concluded. "How did you do all this? Didn't you die in the tunnels?" asked Theodor. "David saved my life. We went through another path in the tunnels and reached a radio that could be fixed" Albert concluded and looked around. They could hear more explosions and soldiers shouting around them. "We need to get out of here and onto safer grounds" Han abruptly cut in. The four of them looked at him helplessly, imploring him to have a solution for their escape. They had come this far, a lot of sacrifices had been made along the line and now they stood here, not knowing what to do next. Their gazes were fixed on Han, hoping he would now lead them out of this. "There is no way to get out of this bunker and face the soldiers outside. There are too many of them; and we have no ammunition. But if Konstantin is away as Albert says, we stand a chance of getting out. Once we are on safer grounds, I need to eliminate Konstantin" While Han spoke, explosions continued with the heat around them growing intense. Han was trying to find something in his jacket as his hands fidgeted with the pockets. "There was a diary, a document that I hid in my jacket. We need to procure that from Konstantin's cabin" Han said as he continued his search for the diary. He was sure that Konstantin himself must have taken it away. Theodor and Ralf eyed each other. Theodor pulled out his backpack and held the diary. "Is this the one?" he asked. A wave of relief spread over him as he eyed the diary. Before Han could get his hands on the diary, the entire room trembled with an explosion. "I know a room where they store weapons" said David. "We can arm ourselves effectively before marching out. There is a small prison camp where more slaves are held. We can get there safely," another explosion rocked the bunker as David spoke. There was urgency in his voice as fires spread within the chamber. "Lead us to the room" Han commanded through the chaos. "Theodor" Han ordered. "Keep the diary safe with you." David broke into a sprint and shouted "Follow me" as Han and the trio followed, trusting blindly in David's sense of direction.

Erik was evacuating nuclear material from the bunker. One by one, the trucks were being pulled out and parked as far away as possible from the fire. "Sir, there is a hatch-like opening. Should we check inside it?" One of the soldiers asked. Erik didn't know of any such openings; but if there was inflammable material down there, it was important to get it away. He thought for a few seconds before replying. "Open it up. If you find any more unknown hatches, open them and get all the material out safely" Erik gave the orders.

The soldiers in the camp were divided into ranks, only a few of them had ever seen the inside of the beast bunker. The others usually manned the outer territory. Given the current dilemma, Viktor had no option but to use all the resources at his disposal. Erik had ordered for water supply to be redirected. Massive jets were now ready to control the fire in the beast bunker. On his orders, the water was let loose and the jets sprayed to life. Thick, black smoke rose up from the camp in an endless looming cloud as water doused the fires.

Fedor was already running through the patch where he saw the Germans escaping from. He didn't want to fall behind. A small team of soldiers who he'd taken in along with him tailed him. Viktor, on the other hand, entered on the lower level and was fanning the areas. David opened into a room and showed them the pile of stacked weapons. Han eyed them and instantly began to arm himself. It was just a matter of time till they would have an head-on collision with Red army soldiers and by then, it would become a pure test of will. "We have no time to lose. We march out in battle against Red army soldiers and disperse into nearby forests. David, you lead the way to this prisoner site that you talk of" Han ordered as he effectively took lead. Suddenly a door burst open as more prisoners piled in. "Ralf" one of them shouted. Ralf and the others turned around, startled to see the prisoners. "We lay down our scythes for you" the prisoner spoke. "We will fight by your side!" they said as Ralf looked dumbstruck from Han to the prisoners. It was an intense moment.

These German soldiers had braved their way into Konstantin's camp and now the prisoners were fighting alongside them! "So be it" Han muttered to the others and in a swift motion loaded his guns. "Ralf, you lead them" said Han as he ran ahead, kicking the door open in one swift moment. Han roared and jumped out to face the Red army. Ralf, Theodor, Albert, David and the prisoners followed suit. Far away, the Red army soldiers panicked to see so many people charge at them. The battle had begun; the Red army was up against Han's army.

Endless Tunnels

One of the camp prisoners was running at breakneck speed through the forest. He looked around for guards, they were shouting and pooling around the main camp. There was frenzy all around and loud explosions were audible throughout the surrounding forests.

He easily evaded Red army soldiers and ran through thick tree cover. The Red army soldiers were heading towards the camp to tend to whatever was causing these massive explosions. The prisoner kept to the shadows as he moved cautiously through the darkness. He knew the area very well; and he kept ducking and hiding effectively behind thick tree covers. He reached a massive tree and jumped into the ground. He held his hands up to protect himself from the outgrowth of roots as he crashed through them and slid into a narrow crevice.

He fell through and landed into a pool of water under the massive tree. It was a routine for him as he easily got up and ran into a small dark cavity to come face to face with Traugott. "The beast bunker has been infiltrated, Konstantin is out and there is a lot of commotion at the camp." He was panting heavily as he reported. Traugott's eyes widened in shock and amusement as a smile broke over his face.

More than thirty odd prisoners had amassed in the cavity below the massive tree. Traugott was hatching a plan to infiltrate and the prisoners had been very helpful with their insights. "We don't have enough guns to tackle these soldiers" pointed out one of the prisoners as he stood before Traugott. "True enough, but we have an unmatched will, there are more than thirty of us right now and heavens will help. I am sure more will join us once the word is out" Traugott spoke as he heard the deep rumble of explosions above him. "We have the biggest weapon with us; the fact that we have nothing to lose" he roared. All the prisoners listened in rapt attention as Traugott walked amongst them; looking into each one's eye. "Your families are dead, you are nearly dead. Most of you have thrust a scythe through your own blood. You have much more than what those cowards have up there; you have an unmatched anger, you are blood-thirsty for revenge!" he said.

A few of them chuckled and nodded as Traugott tried to charge them for the battle that lay ahead. There was unmistakable fire in their eyes. "Right now is the best time to attack, they are not expecting this assault, they are already busy fighting and by the sounds of it; our friends are wreaking havoc. I want us to fight in teams of two each. The stronger one with the scythes will rip Red army flesh while the swifter ones will swing scythes far and take them out from a distance." Traugott paced the dingy tunnel as he spoke to the prisoners that had pooled in to fight. "Swing and rip, your aim is to leave none alive. We have only one motive and that is to kill. For we gentlemen have nothing more to lose but this very life itself" Traugott's sentences went up in a puff of smoke as the tunnels shone with hopeful glinting eyes.

The prisoners were gathering their scythes and pairing up in teams. The plan was set; a team of them were marching into the Russian camp from one end while another marched in from the opposite end. Traugott's wound was strapped with a torn cloth as he led the third group of prisoners through the daunting Honeycomb maze. This was pretty much their final attempt to get in and help the others. If they didn't succeed now, chances were; they never would.

All prisoners held their scythes tightly and marched into the Red army camp. They had effectively divided themselves as per Traugott's instructions. Since the camp's inception, this was probably the worst infiltration it would ever face and with the mighty Minotaur gone, it was literally crumbling apart. Traugott was walking ahead as a deep rumbling sound emanated from the surroundings. They stood still, trying to figure what was happening. "Whatever stands in our way, we fight. We do not fight to our deaths; soldiers. We fight to our freedom" Saying that, Traugott ran into the endless tunnels with infinite energy surging through his veins.

Konstantin

F edor stalked the beast bunker like a ghost; as major fires were dying down from sprays of water that flooded the bunker. He was drenched from head to toe as he stealthily moved about, trying to find a vantage point. His team was disoriented and slow but what did he care? They only functioned as a distraction. He positioned himself at a spot in the bunker from where he could see them. His mind raced on with calculations. Fedor saw through the scope of his rifle, scanning the areas from where he sat. He saw a prisoner running through the fires, dodging and jumping them.

A disturbingly loud shot rang through the bunker as David's head burst open and a bullet ripped through his skull. Han instantly pushed others behind at the abrupt sound of the gunshot. Albert screamed in disbelief and ran forward, firing blindly with his hand gun. Theodor tried to hold onto him but Albert had broken lose. Theodor instantly ran behind him, "Albert, wait" he shouted trying to stop him. Han could see more soldiers pouring in through the broken bunker walls as he sneaked around to help Theodor and Albert. Ralf had ordered the prisoners to open a three pronged attack.

One team charged forward with Ralf while the other two came up from the sides. "Arm your scythes and cut through Red army guts" Ralf screamed out orders as they charged ahead. Han understood the sound that emanated. 'They were being hunted by a sniper' he thought as calculations ran through his mind. He looked towards the source of sound and a small glint told him that there was a scope in the far end of the bunker. Without a second thought, Han jumped; crashing into Theodor and Albert. The three of them along with David's dead body fell. They plummeted twenty feet and crashed onto the lower floor of the bunker. The explosions had ripped apart sections of the bunker and there were exposed areas as walls collapsed around them. Han quickly got up on his feet and spotted a sniper on the opposite end. No matter how good or bad one was on their feet, there was no dodging a sniper bullet. Han pushed Albert and Theodor into a room through a broken door.

Ralf's army of prisoners had a fire in their eyes that made the Red army cower in fear. Ralf read the tag on his opponent's shirt as he launched his massive blow. The tag read 'Viktor', Ralf sneered, he was no match for this guy. The massive German smashed Viktor's jaw into two as he punched straight through his face. The prisoners used their scythes to rip open Red army soldiers who were unprepared for so many of them. The Red army was taken by surprise; before they could effectively attack, they fell prey to the prisoner army. Ralf swiftly picked up a machine gun and fired it at oncoming soldiers. Many of them fell to his bullets while others scattered, trying to hide. The prisoners fought with an iron will; unleashing their scythes onto the Red army. Few of them were mighty impressive with their fighting techniques as their scythes went right through Red army skulls. The prisoners had been forced to use these on their own friends and families once; now, it was payback time. Facing their enemies, their scythes easily penetrated deep within their bodies with hate filled precision.

Fedor had taken up another position on the ledge. He watched from above as the battle unfolded all around him. He loaded his rifle to take out the German that was fighting Viktor. Through the scope, he saw the huge figure. The Red army soldiers were being thrown around by him single handedly as a team of prisoners backed him up. The scope was fixed on Ralf and Fedor curled his fingers with anticipation around the death unleashing metal.

Another deafening shot echoed through the bunker; followed by a series of gunshots. Han was airborne. He leaped into the air, his eyes looking through his rifle scope. It was impressive to watch Han as he fired through his jump. He couldn't take Fedor from such a far distance, that much he knew; and so, he fired instead on the metal wire that held the platform in place. Han landed on his feet as he concluded the jump and waited, looking at a confused Fedor. The shot that was fired from Fedor's rifle took out a Red army soldier instead of Ralf and the platform gave away from under his feet. Fedor fell from his vantage point and crashed to the floor as a pile of debris collapsed over him.

Theodor and Albert dragged David's body inside a room and laid him to rest. "While life crept out of me as I floated unconsciously in those maze like tunnels. David came to my rescue and nursed me back to full health. He was a good man" Albert murmured under his breath. Theodor kept a hand over his shoulder. "We must join the others" he whispered. Albert tightened his stance and picked up the scattered weapons. "Let's do this Theodor" he said. Both Albert and Theodor loaded their guns and crept out of the room.

Ralf was busy fighting the pool of soldiers that marched in. The fight had now moved on to a disorganized gunfight, as everyone moved in hurried frenzy. The prisoners and Ralf were scattered behind broken walls. Having picked up weapons from dead Red army soldiers, the prisoners were firing at a batch of new soldiers that had just arrived. The prisoners were obeying Ralf unconditionally and were coordinating better. Ralf was razing down soldiers efficiently, and any soldiers that survived the firing would fall prey to his wrath. He was sweating and his tunic was off his torso. The massive chiseled German attacked and ruthlessly took down Red army soldiers. The prisoners too were fighting bravely as their scythes cut open anyone who stood in their way.

The entire bunker was a mess. The walls were further collapsing, random fires erupted in several places and the constant downpour of water now began to accumulate in the bunker. The incinerator had completely cooled down; it was a disturbing sight to see countless dead bodies piled up in the rooms. The death chamber that had saved Theodor and Ralf lay exposed and bodies spilled out into the bunker. They looked eerie and disturbing in their ghostlike state. The machines that had been pumping saline through them had stopped and now, they oozed fluids onto the entire floor. The stink was unbearable as blood mixed with water and spread throughout the bunker. Three floors of the beast bunker were broken beyond repair and crumbled from impact.

Han caught hold of a prisoner and dragged him behind a broken wall to protect themselves from the onslaught of bullets. "There is a prisoner camp on the outskirts, how do we get there?" Han asked. The prisoner had been working as an assistant to Dr. Schmitz and knew the place quite well. He suggested two options to Han. The first was to open fire and charge out from the collapsed walls while the other was to go underground and take the tunnels. The tunnels opened on forest grounds from where they could easily get to the camp. Han thought for a while, 'opening out in attack would be tantamount suicide. On the other hand, returning to the Honeycomb maze was an option; but they were endless and confusing. It was almost impossible to know exact directions down there' his thoughts were racing as the attack multiplied.

Albert and Theodor had joined Ralf in combat. They made use of their hand guns and a random assortment of weapons that they found. Red army soldiers were now getting stronger as they coordinated their moves and entered from strategic points. "What was that book you found?" Albert questioned Theodor. Theodor looked around to check if anyone was near them. They were firing from behind the debris as they conversed. "It's Adolf Hitler's personal diary" he said. "What on earth...?" Albert was dumbstruck at the statement. They both ducked as a soldier went flying over their heads. Ralf was at it again. He smashed through the ranks of soldiers that charged in and took them out with ease. Within the next instance, Ralf crashed over the debris with another soldier. They were engaged in combat but he was no match for Ralf; who smashed the soldier's head with his fist. Ralf crawled up to Theodor and Albert. "Having a good chat are we?" he asked them. The three looked at each other as a smile broke over their faces. Now as they stood untied, it all seemed possible from here onwards. They had managed to rescue Han and with him by their side, their chances of leaving the camp were actually better. They all had an adrenaline surge as they watched another body go flying by. Ralf easily tackled a soldier, Albert and Theodor fired to take out the entering batch of soldiers. The trio was coordinating an effective counter attack and pushing back the Red army.

Viktor's face was plastered up in a white band which held his jaw in place. Ralf's punch had cracked his jaw bone. He was waiting outside the bunker along with a radio operator by his side. Viktor had sent a jeep out to the landing strip to receive Konstantin. He was in extreme pain; but his fear was worse. Once Konstantin came in contact with the mess, nothing would stand between Viktor and imminent death. The only way Viktor could save himself was to capture the Germans.

A mechanical sound echoed into the evening as Viktor painfully turned around to see the marching soldiers. He had called for a battle unit to march in. More than thirty odd soldiers marched in an orderly fashion towards the beast bunker. Viktor stepped aside and a megaphone was handed to him. He gave orders, his voice sounding eerie, as he was unable to move his broken jaw. He ordered a batch of soldiers to form a ring on the outer periphery and another to open attack in smaller units from all sides. He confirmed with Erik if the material had been cleared from within. "Show no mercy. Do not slow down, I give you fifteen minutes. Get me those Germans" Viktor concluded and a massive roar filled the air as Red army units charged into the beast bunker.

Han had devised a counter attack with the help of some of the escaping prisoners that had pooled around. As he scanned around, he saw that the collapsing bunker could be used to their utmost advantage. They had managed to gather decent amount of ammunition and now, they were gearing up for the attack. Han, along with Theodor was to lead a ground army while Ralf and Albert were attacking from the upper floors. The floors were disjointed and broken; so they could use those segments as vantage points. All of Albert's studies on the map were coming into good use and Han sent a team of prisoners to break open hatches that would lead them into the Honeycomb maze.

The battle was to last only a few minutes and as soon as the hatches were ready, they would disappear underground and escape into prisoner camps. There was no room for anything to go wrong in the plan, they had to execute it to perfection. They heard the shouts of Red army soldiers as they attacked. Han and Theodor took charge of the ground army and opened a counter attack against them. They fired rounds of artillery on the oncoming Red army soldiers. The first line of soldiers was caught unaware and fell to their deaths.

The next batch was a little difficult to counter; they'd opened with bomb attacks. Small but lethal explosions erupted close to where Han and Theodor were. Ralf and Albert were firing from upper floors of the bunker. They managed to take out a few of the unit commanders and let their soldiers run haywire. The batch of prisoners that were locating hatches and opening them were already running behind on the planned timeline. The debris was massive and they couldn't move it on their own. They found only three accessible hatches as opposed to the fifteen odd ones that they were supposed to find.

Viktor was growing restless, he wanted instant answers. The clock ticked; Konstantin was on his way. The relay soldiers were not yet bringing good news. The Germans were in there, they had somehow managed to get those wretched prisoners on their side and together; they were actually putting up a good fight. 'It was preposterous' he thought. He ordered more firepower to be drawn into the battle. More bombs were to be brought in and a machine gun placed at the entrance to tackle the mindless prisoners.

Han and Theodor had retreated behind, along with a few prisoners. Their ammunition was running out and the hatches were still not functional. The prisoner team reported back to Han with only a few functional hatches; those too were in danger of sealing shut if they didn't hurry. Ralf and Albert were dodging and jumping onto the ledges from upper floors. They were stealthier than the ground forces; and were at an advantage but the Red army was quick to adapt and more soldiers were brought in to tackle the upper floors.

Viktor ordered more soldiers to enter the beast bunker as its walls further collapsed and crumbled into the premises. He was desperate to lay his hands on the Germans; when suddenly, a massive roar filled the skies. The sound grew louder as the seconds passed by. The war in the Beast Bunker came to a near standstill as an aircraft closed in on the camp. Viktor looked on in horror as it deployed airbrakes and prepared to descend right onto the battlefield.

The black smoke and meek fire from the beast bunker glowed in Konstantin's eyes as he expertly positioned the aircraft into a near-impossible landing space. With a deafening roar, the rubber burnt over tar as the aircraft stormed by. Brakes were deployed and it came to an abrupt halt right in front of the beast bunker. A loud crack and spasm that rippled through told them that the fuselage had fractured. But what did Konstantin care? He left the pilot's seat and stood in front of the door for a few seconds.

The soldiers inside helped him take off his over-coat and strap on his ammunition jacket. Everything around fell silent for a moment; Konstantin closed his eyes. Shivering in anger and clenching his fists, Konstantin loaded his shotgun and ordered the door to be opened. Given his massive body size, he was extremely swift; he jumped out of the aircraft and landed on the wing. Viktor looked in horror and the entire Red army stood, frozen. Konstantin had returned to take charge of his camp. The prisoners far below ran to take cover as they saw the threateningly huge demon-like form of Konstantin rise above them.

Minotaur's Fury

Konstantin opened fire on the prisoner army. His shotgun was lethal; splicing through anyone that stood in his way. The unprepared prisoners fell mercilessly to Konstantin's ire. His mere presence filled the Red army with enough vigor and stance to continue fighting. He roared; charging forward like a battering ram. Red army soldiers roared in unison and opened fire with a fresh fervor.

Han and Theodor retreated deeper into the broken bunker. The onslaught was terrible and Han's army had to retreat underground now. They had almost run out of ammunition; and with no way to stand up against this assault, they had to retreat. Albert had come down to Han and Theodor who were now holding off the soldiers with the limited ammunition that they had. Albert spotted Ralf on the upper floor, he was fighting against more than ten soldiers single handedly. Theodor instantly rounded up a few slaves and jumped out of the debris to help Ralf. Theodor landed punches on Red army soldiers as he broke their ranks and joined Ralf.

Viktor was losing his patience and was scared of Konstantin's presence. He frantically ordered a rainfall of grenades into the beast bunker. Before Theodor knew it, the upper floor cracked under the strain of the oncoming explosions and gave way. The heat was intense; cement exploded all around him. He jumped onto the opposite ledge to break his fall but the explosions instantly multiplied and the ledge broke loose. Theodor had no time to react, as he fell freely to the lower level. The fires were once again out of control as fresh explosions rocked the bunker.

Albert rounded up a few prisoners; they were huddled in the center of the bunker as Theodor recovered and joined them. The Red army had surrounded them from all sides and closed in rapidly. Ralf ran towards them from the upper ledge. He jumped and landed on the same floor as them. Gunshots were being fired all around as the prisoners continued to resist the Red army. Had more prisoners joined the battle? It seemed so. The concrete under their feet was heating up and Albert was worried about it exploding. There was no saying if the entire concrete was dynamite laced as the trio retreated and fell back.

A huge explosion ripped through the Beast bunker. The dead bodies went flying in air, splattering blood and body parts all over. Konstantin moved closer to the bunker and looked straight into the eyes of Theodor and Albert. They froze in place, eyes locked with the mighty Russian warlord. Through the rain of bodies; they saw Konstantin, the massive Minotaur who stood, uncowering, ready to take them down to the last man. Han was dashing through the ranks; aiming with every step, to get closer to Konstantin. He had to take him down anyhow.

A loud and prominent gunshot rang through the chaos as Theodor and Albert ducked, trying to avoid the lethal shotgun bullets. They crashed to the floor; taking refuge behind a broken wall. From behind their shelter, they saw Ralf standing at the far end. He merely stood there as he looked at Theodor and Albert. Theodor was shouting for him to take cover. "Get out of there, jump the debris. He is right behind you" he yelled. Theodor couldn't understand why Ralf wasn't moving. As Ralf turned around, his comrades looked with wide eyes as a wound was carefully positioned on his chest. Theodor bellowed in agony, he couldn't believe his eyes. He ran from behind the rubble to help Ralf. Seeing this; Albert also ran out, blindly firing away and screaming.

Konstantin was flanked by a host of his guards as he stood on the upper level. A few of them fell to Albert's mindless firing but Konstantin stood there; unflinching and unmoved. He stood unaffected by the flying bullets as if he was sure they wouldn't affect him in any way. As Theodor locked eyes with Konstantin, his rage equaled that of their enemy. Han noticed what was happening and he knew Theodor and Albert wouldn't stand a chance. He abandoned his position and ran to help them. Konstantin reloaded his shotgun, aimed and fired. Ralf was still conscious; he lunged towards Theodor, pushing him back into safety and took another shot squarely in his back. Han reached their side and instantly collided with them; he caught Theodor and Albert as he pulled away from the point of explosion. The very earth was cracking and exploding under strain and bullets flew in frenzy around them.

A stray bullet ripped through Theodor's arm. He screamed in agony as it seared through his ripped flesh. Albert's calculations were correct; the entire ground gave away as concrete exploded. Theodor and Han went head first into the opening, followed by Albert. Theodor locked eyes with Ralf for the last time as he disappeared through the opening. The Beast bunker collapsed with a massive crash and caved within itself. The three of them were now buried inside the hatch.

Hitler had probably slipped, Himmler was absconding, and now; Han was escaping from his clutches. Konstantin was enraged beyond limit as he held his shotgun. His soul's only consolation now, was that he managed to kill at least one of them. The walls of the beast bunker had completely given away; the last set of explosions had wreaked havoc in Konstantin's camp. The prisoners were shouting and running in frenzy and Ralf lay defeated; finally fallen at the Minotaur's furious feet.

Fedor's Hunt

Konstantin roared like a lion atop the broken bunker wall. With his gun aloft, he declared victory over the dead German. "Round up the prisoners and show them hell!" he roared. The beast bunker had collapsed within itself and the ground had cracked open. Even under the parked aircraft, a few blocks of earth had opened up and one could see inside. The massive iron pipes of the Honeycomb maze were visible at places where the earth had split open. The Red army soldiers rounded up the remaining prisoners who were trying to escape. Many of them jumped into gaping holes in the middle of the beast bunker to escape within the mazes.

A very scared looking Viktor headed in the direction where Konstantin stood. The Minotaur walked down from the broken bunker walls and stood there spitting fury. Konstantin turned around and before Viktor could speak or react, Konstantin punched him in the face. The blow was so massive that it broke through Viktor's plaster and completely dislodged his jaw. Viktor screamed as he flew a short distance and crashed to the ground. The entire Russian camp watched him writhe in pain as his face lost all shape and half his jaw was thrown out.

Fedor walked down from the building covered in dust and rubble. He bled from several parts of his body, principally was his head and nose as he picked Ralf's body and dragged it all the way. Konstantin looked on with fury as Fedor dared to walk towards him. Slowly and painfully, Fedor reached Konstantin and let Ralf's body fall at his feet. Konstantin was raging in immeasurable angst as he looked around at the mess that was left of his beloved camp. He lifted his foot and crushed Ralf's head under it. In a fit of rage, he repeatedly stomped his foot over the dead soldier's face and screamed out in vehemence. "To all who stand here" he roared and looked at everyone who was standing around him. All activity instantly stopped and everyone turned towards him in rapt attention.

Only the burning fire made noise; the ebbs of the fire didn't seem to pay homage to Konstantin. There was an occasional fall of debris. With both his arms open as if calling out in an embrace, Konstantin spoke "Here you see fallen Nazi filth before your eyes. He will rot here, trying to protect his fellow soldiers. His master is dead. Yes, Adolf Hitler is dead and rotting away his innards right now as his corpse is being transported back to our country. We have won this war" He shouted and raised a fist in the air.

At this gesture, the soldiers hailed and raised their weapons into the air with a deafening roar. They were hooting and cheering in victory, and their caps and weapons went up triumphantly. Konstantin smiled and held out a hand to silence them. "We will soon evacuate and move into another camp. There will be time to celebrate, as we once again emerge victorious for the entire world to see!" he concluded and stomped his foot over Ralf's face yet again. Ralf's face was disfigured beyond recognition and his skull cracked to spill out the innards. The camp stood still, death-like and silent as everyone watched on. He abruptly turned to Fedor and punched him in the stomach. Fedor fell back from the blow. "You ripped apart my camp" Konstantin growled. "Viktor did it" retorted Fedor as he painfully got up on his feet spitting blood. Konstantin turned his shotgun over and whacked Fedor in his face with the butt of his gun.

Fedor spat more blood but stood his ground. "So you watched as Viktor brought it down?" Konstantin spoke through gritted teeth. "Let me go alone. Let me go right now and I will bring them to you in an hour" Fedor spoke breathing heavily. "You really think you can get me Han?" Konstantin mocked Fedor's failed attempt. "You let them slip from your clutches and now you'll go fetch them again... Are you a dog?" Konstantin spat on

Fedor's face as he insulted him. "They say Han is the best sniper this world will ever see. I am forced to agree with them" he said as he turned around and walked towards Viktor. Fedor was furious but he had no option, he had to deal with Konstantin's anger.

"Get that no good filth up here" roared Konstantin as he pointed at Viktor. Two soldiers helped Viktor up. Viktor looked at Fedor who stood there, waiting for Konstantin to finish what he'd started. The soldiers helped Viktor walk and stand next to Konstantin. "Give orders to evacuate immediately" Konstantin told Viktor. Viktor was bleeding uncontrollably and couldn't talk. "You can't talk; is it?" Konstantin mocked him in anger. "You feel the pain Viktor? I feel it too" he said. "This camp is a part of me; I have made it with my own blood" Konstantin spat and was only a few inches away from Viktor's disfigured face. Viktor was in immense pain as he stood there, listening to Konstantin. "The nuclear material and underground truck have been damaged or evacuated?" asked Konstantin. Viktor couldn't talk anymore and merely nodded. "They are damaged?" asked Konstantin. Viktor shook his head from side to side. "So they have been evacuated" he said, relieved.

With great difficulty, Viktor stood there. He bent low in pain, unable to stand to his full height, and with hot tears brimming in his eyes. In an unexpected move of power, Konstantin turned around once again and punched Viktor in the face. The punch was massive; sending Viktor sprawling on the ground in pain. He howled as his lower jaw completely gave away. Konstantin bent low and howled back at Viktor mocking his pain. "How did you manage to let them escape? We now have three Germans on the loose and just one dead" Konstantin spat at Viktor.

Tears were pouring down Viktor's face as he writhed in pain. He was right next to Ralf, the dead German soldier. He was also as good as dead, before his master. "Get up Viktor and check the soldier for important artifacts" Konstantin ordered. Viktor tried to get up but failed; collapsing back to the floor. Konstantin clenched Viktor's head with his bare hands and lifted him off the ground. "I just gave you an order Viktor. Follow it." Konstantin's eyes held a fury like never before as he roared into Viktor's face.

Viktor attempted to let out a scream, but no sound came out of his mouth. The entire Russian camp was watching this merciless demonstration unfold. "You defy a direct order from Konstantin and you know the repercussions to that?" Konstantin hollered in Viktor's face and tightened his grip. With that, in one final blow, he crushed Viktor's skull with his bare hands. Viktor's skull cracked and his face deformed further. Konstantin looked him in the eye as Viktor thrashed in pain. Thick blood oozed out onto Konstantin's hand as he let him slip and fall. With a sickening crunch, his broken head hit the ground and a pool of blood splattered around his body.

Konstantin looked at his blood soaked hands as he motioned Erik to come forward. "You evacuated the material?" he asked. "Yes, my lord" Erik bent low in respect and answered. "Give orders to evacuate and destroy the landing strip. I don't want any incoming aircrafts. Viktor had a set of keys to open a room within my cabin; locate them and get them to me. Do everything as mentioned and report back in five minutes" Konstantin concluded his orders and looked around the camp-site. He noticed the smoke, fire and the devastated building. Ripped apart and defeated, it was crumbling to the ground. The suspended chamber where Han was held captive lay broken on the floor. The walls had given away; exposing the incinerator as well as the Death Chamber. He noticed hundreds of dead bodies strewn around the camp.

Konstantin stood there looking around at the camp. This camp had served him well over the years, but now time had come to abandon it and move forward. He looked down at the dead German soldier; Huge and well-built his face was now bloodied and broken. Konstantin was burning with rage and fury. His hound came by him and barked as Konstantin stared. "I promised you their eyes, feast" he said. The hound merely growled and sniffed the body. "So he is not the one who took your eye?" Konstantin nodded as he spoke to his blood thirsty hound. If only he could pry the information out of Han, this would get a lot easier. All around the camp-site, soldiers were evacuating and gathering their belongings in a frenzy. The mood within the camp was good as they had won the war but deep inside, Konstantin remained in a pensive mood. He had single handedly engineered the war from this camp for a very long time; now he was going to abandon it. "Han" he thought was his closest possible answer to the dilemma regarding Hitler and Himmler now.

He looked around, sniffing the air. "You can't hunt them alone" Konstantin whispered to Fedor. Fedor was silently waiting on the side for further orders. "They will escape from our clutches. Han is way better than you are" he said. Fedor came closer and spoke. "I will go after them alone my lord. I assure you..." "You cannot assure me anything you imbecile fool!" Konstantin cut him short and began walking towards his cabin. He burst open the door and walked to a smaller room within the cabin. He rummaged for something in the many drawers and pulled out a small key. Fedor stood there awaiting orders. "The faster I go, the better my chances at getting them" he tried to reason. Konstantin held out his blood covered hand indicating silence. "Watching Viktor's brain ooze out didn't teach you anything?" Konstantin whispered as he looked at the key. Erik dashed into the room with a wooden box. He was panting from the run as he stopped and gave a short salute. "My lord, the keys you asked for" he said. Konstantin nodded and dismissed Erik as he opened the box. He pulled out three keys from within the box and held the fourth one. He gave two keys to Fedor and asked him to insert them in the slots. Fedor understood what it was, the door needed four keys to open and they had to be turned precisely at the same moment. Konstantin and Fedor both turned the keys and the door clicked open.

The room was filled with a huge console that had an array of switches. A beautifully crafted topographical map had been laid out on the center table. It was a three layered map of the entire Honeycomb maze, the camp on ground level and exploded views of buildings and chambers. "You won't reach them on time Fedor; which is why I have to curb their movements." Konstantin studied the layout as he spoke. He activated a few switches and looked at Fedor. "This is the last chance I give you. On your way out, send Erik. Go hunt; you dog." Konstantin dismissed Fedor. He bowed down in salute and sprinted from the cabin, hoping to please his master this one last time. A smirk crossed Konstantin's face as he thought to himself, 'And so begins Fedor's futile hunt.'

Mr. & Mrs. Hitler

Traugott and his small army of slaves heard the unmistakable explosions rumble above them. They were running through the tunnels to reach openings from where they could surface. The other two teams that Traugott commanded were running through different routes and gaining much ground rather quickly. Yet, Traugott's worries grew with each passing moment. "Hurry up" he shot back at the prisoners. "The battle sounds are getting more intense" he said. The prisoners nodded and quickened their pace. They had horribly miscalculated their movements within the tunnels and sadly, they were still far away from the camp grounds.

Erik dashed back to Konstantin's cabin and knocked at the half open door. "My lord, you sent for me?" he asked. Konstantin stood there studying something Erik couldn't make sense of. "Erik, you will take two soldiers and unload coffins from the aircraft that I arrived in." Konstantin; studying topographical maps spoke without taking his eyes off the maps. He was writing something on a piece of paper as he studied the layouts. He had the same book laid out in front of him as he studied from it. Erik hesitated and asked "What do they carry my lord?" Konstantin paused for a second and still; without taking his eyes off the layout he spoke, "Those coffins carry dead bodies as all coffins do!" he replied trying to keep his anger under control. "Be extremely careful. Don't talk about it to anyone; be back in five minutes" ordered Konstantin. Erik nodded and dashed out to procure the said coffins and boxes. He shouted out to two guards "Get a ladder and follow me" and ran towards the aircraft.

The guards propped up a ladder and Erik climbed onto it. There was a strange stench building up in the aircraft cabin. Erik looked around and found two wooden coffins in the far end of the aircraft cabin. They were anchored onto the aircraft base with wood and cloth straps. As they moved closer to the coffins, the stench became unbearable. Erik tried to protect himself from the strong smell as he ordered the guards to lift them carefully and take them to Konstantin's cabin.

The guards got to work; they undid the anchor fasteners and let the coffins loose. One by one, they lowered them out of the aircraft. The coffins were cold to touch and a cool chemical-like fluid leaked from the edges as Erik wondered whose bodies these were, and why they were even here!

Konstantin stood over the massive console. He was done writing and studying the map. He gently laid his hands over the switches and waited. He composed his breathing, this was going to be a difficult task for him; yet it couldn't go undone. The door opened up and Erik came in with two guards who carried the caskets. Konstantin strode out, "Open them" he ordered. Erik was scared but nonetheless, ordered the guards to pry open the coffins. With a crunch that ripped the nails from wooden casing the coffins lay open. The bodies were drenched in liquid and a pungent stench wafted through. "Adolf and Eva Hitler" Konstantin muttered. 'Eva Hitler' Konstantin thought to himself. 'Interesting, very interesting' He turned around and without another word, pulled out his hand gun. He shot the two guards through their heads. They had no time to react and they fell instantly. Dark crimson blood slowly pooled around their spent bodies. Erik stood there, eyes wide in shock. "Cover them and get the scientist to do something so they remain preserved. Come back for further orders immediately" Konstantin casually gave orders and marched back into the cabin. Erik gave a short salute and yet again, ran away to fetch the scientist. Konstantin held the switches in his hands and one by one flicked them over in a calculated order. Small indicator lights flashed as they blinked to life. There were three indicators, the primary ones had flashed while the other two would flash as soon as the unit drew enough power to relay the trigger. As ordered, Erik came back running towards Konstantin's cabin. "Sit Erik" Konstantin said as he motioned towards the center cabin. "The scientist is on his way my lord" Erik replied as he pulled a chair to sit down, remaining guarded. Konstantin settled on a chair across the dead soldiers and coffins. Their boots were dipping in blood that steadily continued to pool around their bodies. Erik seemed a tad uncomfortable to be sitting right in the middle of so much blood. "We need to get our hands on those Germans" Konstantin spoke. Erik nodded in response, still sitting still. "We will have to weed them out; one of them in particular was held in our suspended chamber. We need him alive" Konstantin spoke as he tapped his boots in the pool of blood around him.

Erik was sickened by the sight and sound around him. Blood continued to splash all around. "Is this the body of Adolf Hitler, my lord?" Erik questioned Konstantin with a hint of fear in his voice. A faint buzz was suddenly audible from the inner room. Konstantin looked at Erik and smiled. "Yes, it is and we have power" said Konstantin. The unit had drawn enough power to trigger the motors as deep rumbling sounds were now audible through the cabin where they sat. It sounded like someone was shifting something heavy underneath their feet. Erik was confused as he looked around, trying to make sense of the sound. "Now they either rot down there or come right to me" Konstantin said with a satisfied smirk.

Traugott stumbled as he tried to hold onto something. The sudden momentum dislodged him and the others. He looked ahead in awe as the junction of the honeycomb mazes turned. These mazes were the most advanced feat of engineering they had yet seen. If people thought they were mere mazes, they hadn't seen them function yet. Each junction of the maze was housed on a high torque motor that could turn and couple with new sides. Every junction was self-powered by individual motors and the entire layout could be changed at will. The tunnels formed a huge circuit by themselves and innumerable pathways could be opened or closed as required. Konstantin knew the tunnels through and through as he calculated the number of junctions on the detailed topographical layout and made the necessary turns. Even blasts didn't affect their functioning as the motors were housed beneath the junctions. The Germans had disappeared right under the bunker and he knew exactly what sections to cut off so as to keep them trapped, with absolutely no other way out. Whoever was confined inside the tunnels had only one way to come out now; and that way opened right in the center of his camp. The outer junctions had disconnected from the tunnels further up. Either his prisoners would keep running in circles or open up exactly where he wanted them to.

It was no longer the honeycomb maze; it was now Konstantin's labyrinth. Traugott helped the others to their feet and they retracted back towards the exits. "Get up, fall back" he shouted to the prisoners. Up ahead, a huge pipe turned and locked itself with another junction. Ahead of them now lay a completely new tunnel. "That wretched Minotaur, he played this one perfectly" fumed Traugott.

Konstantin heard the rumble with a satisfied smirk. The tunnels would re-orient and lock themselves in a matter of minutes. The Germans had no chance this time. He was happy to have finished work on these tunnel sets. His plan was to do this to the entire honeycomb mazes but they were insanely vast. His team had managed to power the ones that were on the outer periphery. They had been smuggling in prisoners through these tunnels over the years. The illegal activity had to be kept off the map and Konstantin literally did that by housing everything underground. There was a knock on the door as a harrowed looking scientist walked in. Konstantin eyed him as he broke out of his thoughts. "Where is that white haired freak?" he questioned. "He was found dead in the labs; my lord" the scientist replied. "Good. I didn't like him much anyways. Open those coffins and preserve whatever is inside them" Konstantin ordered. The scared looking scientist lifted the casings off; and came face to face with the dead bodies of Adolf and Eva Hitler.

Han's Mistake

Han and Albert continued to drag Theodor through the tunnels. Theodor was losing a lot of blood as he tried to steady himself and keep up pace. They suddenly stumbled and tried to hold onto something as the entire section turned around with an unexpected jolt. Albert looked at Han; searching for an explanation to this absurd movement in the junction. The gate on opposite ends remained locked as they looked behind them.

The tunnel through which they were running had completely disappeared from sight. Han quickly turned the lock and opened the opposite gate. He understood what was going on and instantly jumped to action. Han wedged himself between the tunnel and rotating junction. Albert looked around helplessly; wondering what to do next, this was completely out of his knowledge. Han strained with all his might to keep the junction from re-orienting. "Call out to the prisoners; Albert. We need help." Han yelled through the strain. He seemed immensely powerful as he tried pushing the junction back with his bare hands. Albert nodded and tried to squeeze in through the narrow opening. "We are here. Hurry up" he shouted. Theodor too mustered enough energy to help Han. He pushed the junction as his wound strained; causing more blood to ooze out. They heard footsteps and looked up to see a vast number of prisoners running towards them. Han and Theodor both strained to keep the junction from rotating and locking them out completely. "Theodor" Han called out, "Jump through the gap, you are losing too much blood. You need to stop straining that wound" he ordered. A prisoner was running to them and would soon reach to help. The motor strained under pressure as it whined loudly; trying to turn. Albert took up Theodor's place and pushed him through the small gap into the adjoining tunnel. As Theodor slipped through, the strain on Han's hand increased before Albert was able to provide enough support. Suddenly; Han's hand slipped and he fell through the gap as the junction violently turned. The prisoner anticipated this and threw a metal rod through the gap.

It wedged right in between the open space, as the junction came to an abrupt halt, crunching the rod. Albert fell as the junction violently turned. Han and Theodor were on one side of the tunnel and the prisoner was on the other; while Albert remained stuck in the junction. Theodor was in extreme pain; he had lost a lot of blood and was fast moving out of consciousness. He sat on the cold tunnel floor and looked at Han. "Albert!" Han shouted through the gap. "Yes, I am here. We need to turn this around" Albert replied from within the junction. "Have the prisoners reached the other side? We can't do this alone" he said. "I have a better plan Mr. Han." Albert said, as he looked through the narrow gap and spoke. I might be able to slip down below the junction. If I can reverse the polarity and make it turn around, we can easily open it up" he suggested. "We don't have that much time; Albert. I'm pretty sure that The Red Army is on its way now" Han retorted. "But if all junctions have been re-oriented, we might not be able to get out of here. We will keep running in circles; or we might just end up surfacing at a point that Konstantin wants us to. If I instead, figure a way to reverse these; we might be able to chalk a way out of here" he argued. Albert's plan made sense as Han considered the odds. "Okay you take ten minutes to get under and figure out the polarity. I'll get the bullet out of Theodor. Ask the prisoners to keep guard and cover us" Han gave his orders before turning to Theodor. Albert replied with an "okay" before getting back to work.

Theodor's vision blurred; he was in terrible pain and he moved his hand with great difficulty. They had tied a crude bandage around his arm to restrict the blood flow but it wasn't helping much. "Alright Theodor, I am going to prop the bullet out of your flesh. We need to get going in a few minutes" Han spoke as he sat next to Theodor; taking out his knife to get the bullet out. "I need to go after Konstantin, Theodor" Han spoke. "Stay with me, listen to what I have to say. It is important that you hear me out" Han spoke, dabbing at his wounds with wads of cloth. Theodor had strained way too much and was almost unconscious. If the blood continued to flow at the current rate, there would be no chance of him surviving. "I am going behind Konstantin; and you will go back to Berlin" Han spoke as he studied Theodor's wound. The bullet seemed to be wedged into his bone; this was going to be difficult. Theodor slouched and gave up as his mind shut down. He barely mustered enough strength to remove a letter from his pocket and slipped it into Han's hand. He managed to form the words "Adelheid" in a whisper before collapsing with a thud. "No, no Theodor; listen to me" Han screamed.

He pushed him flat on the tunnel floor and raised his feet trying to keep the blood flowing to his brain. Han removed his clothes and covered him up to keep him warm and breathing. He constricted the flow of blood to his arm and prepared to take the bullet out of his wound. "Listen soldier, you cannot give up. You have come this far, you need to push yourself further. You need to know something Theodor; there is something that you must take out of this camp with you" Han spoke as in a swift motion he plunged his blade into Theodor's arm. The pain made him react as he twitched but still; he remained unconscious.

Theodor was barely breathing as Han tried to evacuate the bullet from his arm. "I've made a terrible mistake Theodor, and you must know this before you leave from here." he said. "I have no past and probably no future" he spoke trying to keep Theodor conscious. There was no telling if he registered the information but he was grunting from time to time. "My first memory goes back to the days when Adolf personally picked me up from the camp. I remember nothing of my life before the training camp, I was lost and broken. One day I opened my eyes and I woke up with a rifle in my hands. Faint flashes of memory did come to my mind at times, but sadly, I've never been able to build something strong out of it. I was forced to become like this. Just like Hitler, who was forced to leave home and disappear; but he survived and so did I... I found myself to be like him in so many ways."

Han spoke as he tirelessly worked and finally pulled out the bullet from Theodor's arm. "I made a terrible mistake soldier; and you must know" said Han as he dropped the blood covered bullet on the cold metal floor.

The Noble Wolf

The day Geli died, Adolf made himself a promise, he would return to his roots in Austria. He'd waited for so long to sit by the cliff's edge. Han had watched Hitler spend sleepless nights planning political buyouts and tactically acquiring information. The night when the final battle plan was drawn, Hitler expressed a wish to actually see the battle progress from the warfront. Han considered this to be an outrageous demand. "It was too dangerous" he said, trying to reason with him but to no avail. The Generals too called it a preposterous idea but Hitler held his ground and expressed a desire to ride to the warfront.

Hitler wanted to March along with his army and win Austria. Han tried making a valid argument against such a move; reasoning that his rifle would be useless against aircrafts and enemy tanks. Hitler laughed it out and patted him on the shoulder in reply. Finally, Han and the Generals gave up on trying to convince Hitler and began planning along his thought pattern instead. A day before the orders were to be given, arrangement was made to secure Hitler on a cliff overlooking the border.

The troops were ready to march on the ground and air force was ready to cover the skies. The plans and orders were being read and re-read to Hitler. Hitler's insights into war dynamics were profound and extremely detailed. From memory alone, he spoke about the number and types of assault machinery that had to be dispatched. An air journey was first considered to transport him to the cliff. Han, however, pointed out the dangerous implications of air travel while they were so close to the war front. Eventually, that plan was dropped and Hitler had to travel by road. Two decoy drops were put into place; these would curb assault motives. Han alone knew the location and mode of transport that Hitler would use; as all preparations were double-checked before the final day. It was time to march into battle.

Early in the morning, Hitler stood on the cliff from where he could see the Austrian border, flanked by his entire staff, Generals and obviously Han. Tents were set up to accommodate Hitler and his Generals; no one knew how long the invasion would last. All required equipment was transported to this make-shift camp-site. Radios, weapons, files and everything of consequence to the war was brought up to the cliff. A convoy of cars had lined up on one side and tents were put up on the other.

Hitler's war ministry worked its way up the ladder of the Austrian government ranks and pressurized them to yield. They dispatched ministers to negotiate; hoping to avoid a conflict. Hitler's war propaganda ministry in the meanwhile, had flooded Austrian citizens with peace talk and an idea projecting collaborative efforts of the two nations if they stood united. There were a lot of Nazis' in Austria, usurping peace and demanding that Austria become a part of Germany under Hitler's rule. Dedicated teams worked tirelessly to get every piece of the puzzle into place and the one man who was waiting to walk into Austria stood on the cliff's edge. Hitler hardly slept the night before, his mind an avalanche of emotions and now he was here, close to home!

The company of men stood beside their leader on top of the cliff. Hitler, along with his generals, stood in complete silence while Han waited in a jeep, few feet behind them. He had thoroughly secured the area with Hitler's personal guard spread out in surrounding forests. Han had split them into tiers and they formed multiple levels of protection against any possible onslaught. Han had also arranged heavy ground artillery. They were terribly close to the warfront and if the battle got intense, he would need every backup possible.

Han had also leaked false trails of Hitler's whereabouts. Apart from a selected few, no one knew where Adolf Hitler really was. It would eventually be obvious, but before the war began, it was a necessary precaution. Somehow, Hitler appeared extremely composed and serene. He knew the outcome of this battle and had it sorted out within his head. Far away into the horizon, the company of men saw the sun's first rays travel across space and hit earth. The atmosphere around began to change as skies swelled up in a riot of colors. The stars began to fade as shades of crimson build up from the velvety blue. Hitler looked towards his generals and asked "Any news from our ministers?"

A soldier ran up to them; a paper was in his hands. The general took it in his hands and read from it "The ministry has been appropriately infiltrated." Hitler nodded with a broad smile and looked away into the horizon. In a soft whisper, he spoke: "It is time." The general left his side to radio codes to go to war. They had given an extension to the Austrian government but Hitler knew better, he had to do this.

Nostalgia erupted within Hitler. He closed his eyes; he imagined himself to be standing on the cliff near his house. He was going home, just as he had promised himself. A lot of disturbing years had passed and he had not been able to stand on the cliff. After Geli's death, he really yearned to be there. He wanted to lament her death and be at the cliff's edge to look for answers; but he had to wait. Now, he could win his home back. Just as the junior Adolf stood on the cliff, Hitler closed his eyes and soaked in the surroundings. He could feel everything around him as his senses opened up. Just like his childhood days when he would stand and observe, he felt the rush within him as he heard the sounds, it was a blissful moment of enjoying nature. An unfamiliar drone met his ears. The drone grew louder as if approaching him. 'This was not water' Hitler thought. He drew a deep breath and waited as the drone steadily grew louder.

Han walked away from the jeep and towards Hitler, looking up into the skies as he walked. His rifle was loaded; ready to strike. A huge black cloud seemed to be moving towards them. Han closely observed the approaching black mass. Thousands and thousands of aircrafts encompassed the German skies. Sunlight hit the aircrafts and the company of men standing on the cliff. Strong and random flashes were seen as the light hit the glass panes of the aircraft cockpits and reflected off them.

Hitler's eyes were still closed; instinctively his hand went up in his legendary Nazi salute. The Generals saw this and went up in salute as they stood side by side. Han flung the rifle over his shoulder and stood in salute by his Fuehrer. The swell of emotion was so overwhelming; none could resist becoming a part of this great moment. All soldiers who were spread out on the mountain and surrounding forests stood in salute.

It was a historic moment as each and every one stood there awestruck. Hitler opened his eyes; they were moist and glistening, portraying powerful emotions. He was going home, he was going back to the bones and ashes of Klara Hitler and he was going back to his cliff. He would see Edmund and his school. 'They didn't have space to bury Edmund' he thought. Adolf Hitler was going back to claim Edmund Hitler's rightful place.

The drone became a deafening roar as thousands of aircraft engines roared from behind Hitler. This demonstrated the might of Hitler's Germany as planes flew over their lands and into the Austrian border. Hitler and his men stood watching the spectacular display of strength and power that Luftwaffe put up. The aircrafts flew over Austria and instead of dropping bombs, they flooded the morning skies with peace feelers and paratroopers that would land and talk peace. Thousands and thousands of feelers were dropped into Austria. Hitler was here to take them under his wing and like a true 'Fuehrer' he had marched into battle; along with the Luftwaffe the ground army moved ahead in peace. A line of motorbikes roared alongside battle tanks and jeeps. They all had the Nazi flag; with the tilted Swastika that Hitler adorned. Hitler smiled to himself as his master plan unfolded right before him; falling perfectly into place. Austria, Adolf Hitler's home was now a part of Germany.

A few days later; the Fuehrer's car was passing through a huge waving crowd. Adolf Hitler stood atop his Mercedes, waving out to the cheering crowd. Women came forward, holding their kids up in the air. People bowed down to him as he stood in salute to the peaceful people of Austria. Huge crowds were cheering as the convoy passed through. Later in the day, Hitler went to a country tavern and sat there with his troops. Han had the most difficult time as he squeezed through throngs of troops that desired to meet with Hitler. Members of the German army, Austrian army and townsfolk gathered around the tavern to catch a glimpse of Hitler. He was sitting inside on a small stool, biting into freshly baked bread and sipping hot beverage.

The people around him were piling up and hoping to talk to him. Between mouthfuls Hitler spoke "We are born in great times. I have always maintained this." Han had managed to get inside and sit right opposite Hitler. Another Nazi soldier too, had sneaked in along with Han as a backup. Such instances proved most difficult to control as Han was helpless against huge crowds. Hitler was now talking to a teenage boy who had probably joined the army at an early age as he looked too young to be serving yet. "I ran away from school and had nowhere to go. My father couldn't afford my studies, so I dropped out early." In a small squeaky voice he spoke to Hitler. "I failed at my studies, boy" Hitler roared. "The mark sheets were circulated and they were ridiculous. I had failed at everything, each and every subject" he said. The crowd fell silent, not knowing how to react to the news of Hitler's prior failure. "That very day, I used the mark sheet as toilet paper and sent it back to the school's principal" The crowd roared with laughter along with Hitler. "But that didn't mean I hated school. I merely hated what they taught me" he said. People were still laughing and listening intently. "So I promise you education my boy. I promise you schools that will teach you things that you want to learn. So you can go to school when you are meant to, and not just when you have to. You will love the schools, your subjects and your teachers. I promise you better education" Hitler concluded. The people in the small tavern cheered and hailed their new leader, a leader who sat with them as a commoner, eating and drinking the same food as them. Their talks continued as Hitler spoke about the new Reich that he would build and how he hoped to drive Germania out of the humiliation and loss that had been inflicted upon them post World War one. Han observed as Hitler easily won the hearts of the people who had gathered around in the small tavern. He was awestruck seeing Hitler address and make note of the problems that people had, from schools to jobs to working conditions and economic crises. The meeting concluded and everyone rose in salute to the Fuehrer. "All Hail Hitler!" they roared as Hitler waved back and acknowledged them smilingly. Hitler had won Austria, he won the people of Austria and those who stood up to him were long forgotten.

Later on, as everything settled, Hitler told Han to make arrangements for him to visit his house. Hitler prayed and bowed down by the grave of Klara Hitler; he wept silent tears by Edmund's side and looked around his old house, taking note of the refreshing and nostalgic memories that came with each picture. Hitler carried a small suitcase with him as he made his way to the cliff, alone. The familiar path, the same grass covered road led to his favorite spot on the cliff. Only Han followed from the shadows. Though Hitler's whereabouts couldn't be kept a secret anymore, Han tried his best to keep the crowds away. Hitler took the path he'd taken every day as a kid and walked alone as he looked around with his bright blue eyes.

Hitler now stood on the cliff's edge, a deep calm water body stretched below him. Hills stood in the surrounding and gentle winds caressed him like a mother would, her kid. He closed his eyes and stood still, breathing, taking in the nature that surrounded him. He opened the small suitcase and pulled out Geli's shirt. He held it dearly in his hands, gently sniffing the perfume that lingered on in her shirt. Adolf Hitler silently wept as he un-bottled all the emotions he'd kept within. He never loved another woman as he loved Geli, but Geli was gone for good. Edmund, Klara, Geli. Adolf had lost too much and today, he stood here for them. For all the losses, for all the love, he stood by the cliff's edge. Far away on the opposite side, he saw wolves, as always they'd come to have their drink. Han and many of the villagers watched from far away. Many years ago, the pictured they'd seen was of a small malnourished vagabond standing by the cliff's edge and weeping. Today, at the same cliff stood Adolf Hitler, leader of the Nazi party. Villagers watched in awe as Adolf Hitler's moist eyes wandered across the landscape. Under their breaths, the villagers muttered "the Noble Wolf."

Ancestry

I t was a clear day; laced with bright blue skies and ample sunlight. The atmosphere was relaxed and elated as Hitler sat nestled in his chair while his troops stood guard at his outhouse. A few months had passed since they had secured a brilliant victory over Austria. The Nazi's were ever since expanding their territorial boundaries and seemed unstoppable. Hitler looked outside to see hordes of people passing by. They were far away from his house but amassed to have a look at their dynamic new leader.

Hitler was now a beloved Fuehrer as he single handedly lifted the nation from the depth of defeat and humiliation. People stole glances at Hitler; each time he caught an eye, he smiled and waved back to them. It was an unusual day, a lot of foreign as well as German dignitaries had dropped by to visit him and congratulate him on his achievements. As Hitler waved out, he noticed a few kids jumping the barricade and running towards him, carrying flowers in their hands. The guards moved forward and tried to stop them from reaching the Fuehrer. Hitler immediately got up from his chair and called out to the guards motioning them to let the kids pass.

Han's grip on the rifle instinctively tightened in tension. He sat hidden in the topmost room of the house. Han was one of Hitler's best kept secrets and sat hidden in shadows most of the time. Hitler wanted Han to function only under his orders and have no meddling from other superiors. The staff and close associates obviously knew of Han's presence but rarely acknowledged it and never dared question the Fuehrer about it. Han glanced below and saw that Himmler had also arrived to greet the Fuehrer. Han's enmity for the man had cropped up the very first time they met at the training facility. Han's true identity remained unknown to anyone but Hitler and Himmler. The training camp had been dissolved two years after Han joined their forces. Himmler had argued with Hitler in a fit of rage; trying so hard to coax him to keep the facility running. The plea however fell on deaf ears. Han had proved every bit of his mettle while performing his duties. He had exceptionally procured information from behind enemy lines and had taken out prominent opposition personnel.

As such, Hitler had grown to trust him and his word completely over the years. This gave Han access to Hitler's every move and plan. Be it a meeting or an official visit, Han tailed Hitler like a shadow. The two closest aides to Adolf Hitler were now Han and Heinrich Himmler, although that too was another concern for Hitler. Han and Himmler absolutely hated each other and Hitler rarely put them together on a common mission. Han had his expertise on issues of security and military functioning whereas Himmler was an exceptional diplomat. Himmler always enjoyed the free reign that Hitler gave him. All through the years, Himmler had taken liberty to overrule Hitler and pitch the stakes higher than required.

Han continued watching from the shadows as one hand gripped his rifle while the other held a cup of hot beverage. All dignitaries stood back as Hitler reached out and accepted flowers from the kids. He warmly shook hands with them and bent low to talk, asking them for their names. A small boy was the last to reach them and he handed a bunch of white flowers to Hitler. He accepted them and gently lifted the kid off the ground. The kid was delighted and laughed aloud. The crowd of people were waiting and looking at what was happening. The small kid too, had strikingly similar blue eyes like Hitler. Hitler looked at the kid and spoke, "I promise you a great nation to live in little one. You are the future of this nation and us. You are the blood of my blood" he said. Everyone stood in awe as they watched Hitler lift the kid high above him. Adolf Hitler's face broke into a smile and so did the kid's, revealing a couple of missing teeth. Everyone from security guards to the Generals smiled at the gesture. Han noticed Eva Braun, she had peeped out to assess what was happening. She was graceful and elegantly dressed as always. She stood by a security guard, vying for Adolf's attention. Hitler let the kid run back to his parents who were waiting in the crowds. Han was sure the kid must have not understood a word that Hitler spoke but nonetheless looking at the crowds gathered to meet Hitler; the kid surely was privileged. As soon as the kid reached his mother, he delightfully jumped into her waiting arms. The parents waved out in appreciation to Hitler. The charismatic leader that Hitler was, he faced the huge crowd and stepped forward slowly, extending his arm in salute. The crowd roared cheerfully. Elated, they waved out to him; smiling and awestruck at his gesture. Han scanned the area keenly. Such loud noise levels made it very easy to cover a gunshot and if anything was out of place, it was his duty to notice.

Hitler turned around and made his way inside to greet the Generals and other dignitaries who had gathered around to see him. Victory on the Austrian front was very well received. People from all over the world were congratulating Hitler on this phenomenal rise. Hitler interacted with each and every one present at the gathering and addressed their talks. "You seldom have time for me, my Fuehrer" Eva spoke softly as she lingered around him. Hitler smiled at her, his penetrating blue eyes boring into Eva's. "My little one" he whispered. "Any amount of time spent with you is miniscule, for you and I are not bound by time but by life" he said and smiled. Eva smiled too as she could never get enough of the Fuehrer and his charisma.

Himmler kept on dodging people throughout the party, intent on speaking with Hitler. He kept skirting around, hoping to strike a conversation in private. Hitler moved around with Eva by his side, the two of them stealing whispering conversations. Finally, Himmler snaked his way through the crowd and stood next to Hitler. "My Fuehrer; what a wonderful victory we have achieved" he said. Hitler nodded in approval. "Yes, yes indeed" Hitler spoke as he looked around. "I was wondering if we could talk in private" Himmler abruptly spoke and there was a certain urgency in his voice. Hitler looked at Himmler and studied him for a while. "What is the matter, my fine man?" Hitler questioned

Himmler. Uncomfortably, Himmler looked away and answered that he wanted them to speak in private about a grave situation. Hitler eyed him once again and finally, led him away from the crowd. They entered the study and closed the door behind them. Hitler had carried his plate into the study and now, he kept it aside as both he and Himmler settled down. Wagner was playing in the background and it resonated through the high walls. Himmler struck a conversation straight away. "You have been avoiding meat my Fuehrer. Is your health fine?"

Hitler didn't bother to look up and replied, "Meat somehow reminds me of Geli's dead body. I cannot eat it. As soon as I see it, I see Geli flash in front of my eyes." Though he had never seen her dead body, it had somehow formed as a picture in his mind. Hitler saw that Han had entered the floor above along with them. It amazed Hitler as to how he could always get to places before anyone else and how intent Han was on watching his back. Hitler cut short the uncomfortable talk and spoke "Obviously you didn't bring me here to question me about my eating habits, Himmler? Fire away, what is this situation that you speak off?"

Himmler looked dumbstruck as he was caught off guard. He nonetheless cleared his throat and spoke "My Fuehrer, since we have gained dominance over Austria I was hoping to talk to you regarding the population there." "Couldn't we talk about this later?" Hitler was a little blunt and cut short his conversation. "I understand what you mean but there are a lot of people escaping from the borders" said Himmler. "So?" Hitler casually asked. Himmler shifted uncomfortably in his chair. He was usually confident and gave clear headed ideas but right now, he seemed a bit ruffled. "I was wondering if we could put the unwanted population in its proper place. I have mentioned to you about my plans and advances in medical knowhow. It is of utmost importance for me, that we look at those and we need more people to test them" he said. "I do not want to dirty my hands Himmler. You know this very well. The propaganda against certain Jewish population is one thing, deporting them is another but I can't let you kill them. I won't have their blood on my hands. I won't let them reside in my nation either" a hint of anger edged Hitler's voice. "If they are escaping and evacuating on their own, it is good for us. That leaves us with less work to do" Hitler concluded. Himmler was getting more uncomfortable and continued to make restless motions while still seated in his chair. Hitler noticed this and spoke again "I leave that decision to you Himmler. Round them up and deport them but we do not want them dead. If such tactics leak out, it is extremely bad propaganda for us don't you understand?" Himmler nodded but his features were stern. "My Fuehrer, I do understand your views on this but you never have to worry about secrecy. I will make sure nobody knows about it. The experiments will be run in complete privacy and moreover, the findings will be of great advantage to us. The impetus this will provide our industries will be magnanimous" Himmler coaxed his ideas. Hitler studied Himmler for a while in complete silence. "No. I will not agree to this, Himmler. You know my hatred runs deep but my answer remains the same" he said. Clearly the meeting was not proceeding as Himmler desired it to. "What you do with them is your problem" Hitler continued talking. "I have bigger problems to look at, bigger wars to wage and even bigger victories to achieve." Himmler nodded in reciprocation "absolutely my Fuehrer" he said. Himmler looked away disappointed, but he had this planned as he got up from his chair and walked towards the window. The subdued light hit his face and his eyes glistened menacingly from behind round rimmed glasses. He did not wait for the topic to digress and pushed it ahead with his well-planned motive. "I received an anonymous letter my Fuehrer. It was sent to you by local post. Since all letters addressing you come under me first, I had it scanned" Himmler spoke softly as he did not dare lock eyes with Hitler who heard him out silently. "It questioned your ancestry my Fuehrer. I read through the entire letter and the findings are shocking. It concludes in a rather unpleasant statement and leads one to believe that your ancestry is……" Himmler let the words linger around for a moment and then concluded softly "illegitimate, probably Jewish."

Silence hung over Himmler's last words. Han moved slightly out of the shadows to get a better view of the unfolding conversation. Hitler's face was turning red with anger; remembering with great fury, the day he had found out a similar possibility. His aunt too had once believed in this which led to their bitter fallout many years ago. Himmler now turned around and looked at Hitler with concern-filled eyes and knew that he had touched upon a nerve. Wagner's music killed the silence that otherwise hung over their conversation. "Who sent you that letter?" Hitler finally asked. His voice was stern and heavy, ebbing with anger. "There was no signature but I can have it traced, my Fuehrer" Himmler spoke carefully. Hitler eyed him for a moment and spoke again. "This ghost will haunt me forever Himmler. Find out who did this, find each and every one who is behind this and bring them to me within a week" Hitler concluded, trembling with rage. "I will have them at your mercy" Himmler confidently spoke as a faint smile appeared on his face. "Well, that concludes this meeting Himmler. Get them to me and as for your experiments, whatever you do, be discreet. Our victories are at stake" Saying this, Hitler marched out of the study. He flung open the door and stood there for a second. "Eduard Bloch. You won't touch him or his family. He once tried to save my mother. Also a book shop owner in Vienna. Mr. Klaus, he will live. Get me all the books from his shop" Hitler concluded, as he walked out. Himmler wore an extremely satisfied smirk on his face as he composed himself and walked out of the room. From the shadows, Han lurked out and considered the happenings. Himmler had played this extremely well; turning Hitler's unknown ancestry against him.

Himmler House

Hitler waited impatiently for this rather long meeting to come to an end. It had stretched on for the past two hours, and he'd lost concentration. He never usually lost concentration in a meeting, making sure he looked into the minutest detail of the plans being discussed.

Today, things were quite different. He forcefully pulled his mind back to the meeting. In an hour's time he would meet Himmler. Early in the morning, he had called to convey that a Jewish family had been hunted down and by the evidence pointing towards them, they were the ones claiming to be related to Hitler. Himmler confirmed that by early afternoon they would all brought before him and could be dealt with as he saw fit. Since the time Hitler had come to know about the letter, he was troubled. The gravity of this situation unhinged him devastatingly. It was a small letter written in blue ink over a rough parchment, it read "The propaganda you have begun with regards to the Jewish population is fruitless. For one cannot run away from his own roots. In pure context of me writing this letter to you I must point out that you and I are related. By the records that I have produced along with this letter, I can say that we are cousins. Many people in my vicinity have urged me to write to you with respect to this situation. Since your propaganda, many of my immediate family members have had to evacuate their shops and houses and flee in fear. You are inflicting this much pain upon your own brethren. I would request you to please consider this situation and go through the records that I have produced. With great difficulty I have exhumed these from credible sources."

There was no signature or any other marking on the letter. It had neither a salutation nor a signing off identity. Hitler immediately pulled out the enclosed parchment that had a family tree traced out on it. Hitler read his name at the bottom-most branch of the tree and as he went up, it traced to Maria Anna Schicklgruber. Every name had a small balloon next to it; confirming the source of information. The bubble next to Hitler's father read Illegitimate. Hitler traced it and saw his grandmother's name along with two names of Jewish origin. Alois from there onward was a Hiedler for many years, but over time, the records were tampered with and Adolf was born a Hitler. The unknown man at the church, Adolf's aunt and all those little hints and accusations came back to haunt him once again. He boiled in anger as he read from the parchment. He saw more information written next to his father's name. 'Church records tampered with.' His blood boiled further in anger as he tried to contain his fury. Hitler wouldn't take this lying down. He wanted to set this problem straight and fix it once and for all.

Hitler was still sitting inside waiting for the meeting to conclude. He had both the letters with him placed in a folder that he carried along into the meeting. He could not come to terms with the fact that he had Jewish ancestry. Not because he hated them, but because they were the reason his family history was mired. His father went down as "illegitimate" only because of a bunch of wealthy Jewish men. Hitler's mind was teeming with these thoughts as he sat through the never ending meeting.

He didn't yet know how he would deal with the man who wrote this letter to him, he didn't even know if it was a man or a woman. Hitler decided he had enough with the meeting and as if sensing his thoughts, the door opened and a guard walked in. He came and whispered in Hitler's ear "He is here." Hitler needed no better invitation to end the meeting. He abruptly rose from his chair and announced, "Gentlemen, an urgent matter needs my attention" he spoke addressing the people seated around him. They were discussing economic conditions and the best policies to deal with them. Hitler found such talks to be a waste of time anyways. If one had to overcome these situations, they needed to produce material solutions that could put the entire nation to work. Talks behind closed doors and inventing policies would never help. Hitler always maintained the need to think long term and these economists merely bought time until another crisis befell. All the people around were flummoxed as they stared at him. "My sincere apologies to you all, we will resolve this issue at the earliest" he concluded and walked out of the room without waiting to exchange pleasantries. His personal staff sprang into action and surrounded him. "When and where is Himmler meeting me?" He asked. In the very next moment Himmler strode in looking happy. He gave a salute and spoke "They await you my Fuehrer. We have been questioning them since morning and all evidence gathered proves the origin of that letter. That is his name" Himmler said as he passed a small parchment to Hitler. Hitler took the parchment and read the name scribbled down on the parchment. 'A. Frankenberger' was scribbled on the small parchment. "Lead me to them" Hitler stated and they walked out.

Han sat outdoors polishing his rifle. It was a relaxed day, Hitler had a meeting which would last till lunch and he could while away his time. Security was in place as they were housed in a government building and Han didn't have much to look into. He had seen Himmler walk in and was expecting them to walk out any moment. Hitler's schedule post-lunch had been called off. Himmler had managed to find the family that claimed to be Hitler's Jewish cousins. Han deeply doubted Himmler's motives but he had no way to prove otherwise or act against him. Hitler and Himmler emerged from the building as Han got to his feet, ready to stand by Hitler as always.

Hitler looked around and ordered Himmler to lead the way. "Where are you holding them?" Hitler asked as the cars drove up to them. "At my place, it is safest to hold them in personal spaces lest the information leaks out, my Fuehrer" Himmler replied in the most flattering way possible. Hitler nodded and replied "Good move." Himmler opened the car door for Hitler as the driver stepped out and stood aside. Han had already moved forward to take the driver's seat. He kept his rifle beside him as both Himmler and Hitler settled in the back seat. Han turned on the ignition and the car roared to life.

The Mercedes was cruising through the open roads. The three of them were seldom alone in any situation. Hitler knew that Himmler and Han hated each other; yet this was one mission they would have to undertake together. It couldn't be left to chances, for any reason at all. The trio was silent as Himmler's house got closer with each passing moment. There were no convoys or security cars tailing them. Somehow Hitler felt anxious and scared at the same time, he wanted to get rid of them but something in the back of his mind was holding him from doing so. His thoughts were engaged in a conflict. 'A lot was at stake if this man turned out to be speaking the truth' he thought. All that Hitler stood for would be destroyed. He felt miserable and looked out the window to divert his thoughts.

The landscape was gorgeous as the sun shone brightly on vast lands. Hitler moved his hand so the sunlight could reflect on it. The warm sun felt good on his hands, it almost felt like Geli was touching him once again. They were headed to Himmler's country side house; the safest place to conduct such affairs. Hitler slightly rolled down the window to breathe in the sweet, fresh air. He could have painted this magnificent view and preserved it on canvas. He imagined a younger Adolf standing on a rock capturing this landscape. The car slowed down and took a sharp turn as Hitler snapped out of his thoughts looking at the approaching house. They slowed down and drove around the muddy road to reach the gates. The huge and commanding house was covered with high walls all around. The car came to a halt and Himmler got off to open the gates himself. He had dismissed all house help and security guards to keep this visit a well-covered secret. The car made its way through the gates and Han parked in the driveway. Hitler and Han both got out as Himmler closed the gates and bolted them shut.

The three of them moved into the hall. "They are out in the atrium my Fuehrer" Himmler spoke and gestured towards a door; waiting for them to go ahead. Himmler was closing and bolting all doors as they passed through. "Do you wish to question them further?" Himmler asked. This question came as a surprise to Han. Hitler considered the question for a while and said "Let me see them." Himmler smiled and led the way as Han interjected abruptly. "Have a look through the records. We might be able to find some information" Han whispered into Hitler's ears. Hitler walked on, not paying heed to Han's statement. All the while, Han had stayed quiet but now he felt the need to intervene. 'How could Hitler blindly trust Himmler? What was the proof that the letter was written by these bunch?' thoughts raced through Han's head. Hitler seemed to have already made up his mind and he didn't want any explanations regarding this situation anymore. All he wanted was to get rid of this problem.

More than anything, Hitler, for the first time was feeling fear, he was afraid of how his world would turn out, should this be true. He did not want to come to terms with the connection whatsoever. It simply couldn't be; he repeatedly told himself. Himmler's huge house was lavishly done up, Han noticed as they walked through it and reached the atrium. They moved towards the opening and saw four people tied up and gagged. Their hands were tied behind their backs, wads of cloth were stuffed into their mouths and their heads covered with a black cloth. The four captives were left on the floor and were tied to an elaborately carved pillar that rose from the ground. The pillar adorned the Nazi insignia and the imperial eagle perched on top.

Himmler had moved everything else away from the surrounding and cleared the area. Hitler looked at them with loath-filled eyes and slowed down as they finally approached them. He slowly walked towards them and in a swift motion, removed his hand gun, steadily pointing at one of the victims on the floor. Hitler pointed it towards the bigger body that was the male who was tied up in the middle. There was a woman and two children by their sides, girl or boy he couldn't tell. They had realized that someone was around and so they tried to move but were tightly bound by the ropes. Han panicked at Hitler's sudden move whereas Himmler enjoyed seeing Hitler lose control.

Han moved ahead and tried to reason. "Just for once you should consider their lineage, check their papers. They might be innocent" he spoke in panic. "Uncover his face" Hitler ordered through clenched teeth, ignoring Han's plea. Himmler bent low and removed the face mask. The man looked up and squinted from the sudden outburst of light. He moved a little and saw Hitler towering over with his gun pointing straight at him. Hitler was furious, he saw fear build in the man's eyes. Han yet again intervened and gently pushed Hitler's arm down. "My Fuehrer, consider the situation for once. This man might be a liar, he might not be related to you" he reasoned.

"This is no way to talk to the Fuehrer" Himmler spat in anger as he faced Han. Both Han and Himmler were eyeing each other with utmost hatred. Han knew that Himmler was driving Adolf to kill the man, for some reason. The three men stood there as time ticked. Han was still holding Hitler's hand, hoping to avoid unwanted trouble. Himmler moved closer to Han. "You filthy sniper, you dare stop the Fuehrer from fulfilling his wish. This filth lying on the floor lives to tarnish our Fuehrer's lineage and questions his heritage" Himmler spat in anger. Hitler, standing in-between the two was boiling in rage, his eyes locked on the helpless man sitting on the ground. In an abrupt unannounced move, Himmler threw a punch at Han, he instantly let go of Hitler's hand and recoiled.

He dodged the punch and kicked Himmler in the stomach throwing him back by a few feet. Han being stronger and quicker could easily overpower Himmler. He lunged at him and threw him away from where Hitler was standing. Hitler did not budge though; his eyes were still locked on the man tied to the ground. The man stared back in fear as he saw the gun pointing at him. Hitler bent low and pulled out the wad of cloth from the man's mouth. He screamed in fear. Han and Himmler both turned around in shock at the sudden cry. "You cannot run away Adolf Hitler. Every word in that letter is true!" said the man as he faced Hitler and looked him in the eye.

A loud gunshot echoed through the house. Hitler's hand was shaking and the man lay dead at his feet. "No" screamed Han as he let go of Himmler and turned towards the fallen man. Before the man could speak another word, Hitler had shot him. He dropped his gun to the floor and sat down on a small chair. Han was at a loss of words and didn't know what to do. Himmler appeared battered from the fight but was happy nonetheless. He got up and placed a hand on Hitler's shoulder. "You did the right thing my Fuehrer" he said. "Han" Hitler spoke, "Finish the remaining three." Han froze in place. He looked at the other prisoners and then back at Hitler. They were shivering and crying through their black veils. "No my Fuehrer" Han softly replied.

"Since the day you recruited him, I have warned you against him my Fuehrer" Himmler spoke spitting anger at Han. Hitler was still shivering as Han looked from Hitler to Himmler. "Such filth should be done away with my Fuehrer; there is no room for sympathy. Those who stand as traitors to the Reich or to you must be killed; for they are a disease. Like gangrene they infest the entire nation and cripple it" Himmler spoke as he tried to convince Hitler. Hitler looked at Himmler with blood shot eyes. "Pick up the gun and finish them" He ordered, as anger pulsed through his body. Han blocked the way to argue and instantly Hitler rose. "Han wait at the gates, it is an order" he said. Han stood between Himmler and the remaining people of the family. Himmler pointed his gun towards Han's chest. "I am your superior Han" he said. Step aside or I will shoot."

"Han" Hitler sternly spoke and gestured towards the gate. Han eyed Himmler with a burning rage. He knew that Himmler was playing his cards very well and that now, Hitler wouldn't rest until he finished off the family. Han walked away from them and marched towards the gate. He hurried through the house, opening one bolt after the other. He wanted to get himself away from this mindless murder that was unfolding right in front of his eyes. He reached the car and punched it in anger, still thinking of how to avoid this manslaughter. A few minutes later he heard three gun shots fired, one after the other. He flinched at the sound of each of them. For a sniper, it was second nature to kill people, but snuffing innocent lives out for no reason? That gave him concern. 'They were innocent civilians' he thought. Killing politicians gave him a sadistic joy; he felt he was in a way helping others by weeding them from social strata but this right here, was unacceptable. He tried to control his breathing as he stood there waiting.

Hitler and Himmler walked out from the atrium to where Han was waiting. "We must finish this here; I want no more questions to rise regarding my ancestry. Regulate the media and what they print. If anyone claims any further evidence to these theories, eradicate them" Hitler spoke to Himmler as they approached the car. Hitler was still mad with anger. He was sweating profusely and his uniform had blood splattered over it. He looked at Han from the corner of his eyes as they approached him. "That man there spoke of procuring records, find out from where. Trace them back to their sources and have them destroyed. Destroy the records, their copies and sources too. He also claims that the villagers knew of this and urged him to write, round them up and finish them. Burn the entire village if you have to" The words came out of the Fuehrer's mouth in rapid succession, he certainly wasn't thinking any of these orders through. His eyes were red and bloodshot and locks of hair fell loose. Han saw Hitler in such a state for the very first time. Himmler had succeeded in his motive and for that reason, Han's hatred for him intensified with every passing second. Han saw right through Himmler but Hitler was blinded by fear and turned a blind eye towards Himmler's actual motives.

Back in the atrium of Himmler's house, four bodies laid strewn on the floor a male, a female, a small girl and a boy. Their eyes were wide open and staring into a void. Himmler had removed their masks before taking their life. Blood slowly pooled around them, thick and crimson, it crept forward as the sunlight shone brightly over the massacre at the Himmler house.

The Architect

Germania now shone brilliantly on the global map as it pushed its boundaries and developed at an astonishing rate. Countries of the world eyed this growth with a grave concern as there was no stopping them, they grew and they conquered. The people of Germany were happy to have work on their hands and food on their tables. It was indeed, a beautiful sight.

The embarrassing defeat of World War one was slowly and steadily being left behind and forgotten. The cruel and harsh treaty that had been put in place to avoid another war and to stomp Germany out of the map was crushed by Hitler and his party. He had effectively increased Germany's military strength and had added significant war machinery to their air force and navy. All demilitarized lands were once again populated by military forces. Hitler single handedly defied governments of the neighboring countries and brought about these changes with immediate effect. This made him the people's favorite leader and he ruled Germania with panache.

On the other hand Himmler was slowly but steadily influencing Hitler's mind. Hitler had a circle of people around him that formed an interesting hierarchy. He remained in the center and in absolute power while others surrounded him in tiers of ranks. They took undue advantage of their closeness to Hitler and the freedom that they enjoyed under him. Goebbels, Speer, Bormann, Morell... the list was endless. These people had numerous industries under their command and their profits were phenomenal.

To a certain extent, they were able to warp Hitler's mind to gain their free hand under his command. But amongst all of these, Himmler understood Hitler like none other. He warped Hitler's thoughts and instilled fear into him. The question of his ancestry rose surprisingly over the years with rising frequency. All across the world, people began to question the credibility of this truth. Hitler would keep an eye on such information and curb the news instantly. Foreign writers and ministers too were extremely curious to understand the truth behind this matter but it never came out clearly. Behind all the propaganda concerning this information was Himmler.

He had sent anonymous letters to many countries claiming Hitler's half Jewish inheritance. Such information could change the war completely and give the information holder an upper hand instantly. He kept half the truth hidden though, astutely he leaked only the curious parts and withheld the ultimate answer to none but himself. It was unclear though if he himself did have any answers but he flaunted the subject with an extremely mysterious air around it and held the impression that he knew more than others. He effectively played with Hitler's mind as and when he wanted.

Immediately after he pushed Hitler to kill the small family, Himmler produced innumerable reasons to wipe out the town from where they were. He had convinced Hitler that the letter writer had leaked information to people around town and it was of utmost importance to curb it. To which a grave and troubled Hitler replied "Take all necessary precautions and stagnate the information." Himmler had on his own accord ordered that the entire town be wiped out. One fine day, fifty or so armed guards marched into the town and rounded up the entire population. Each and every Jew was weeded out and pushed into the waiting trucks that left and never returned. No one except Himmler knew where they disappeared to.

Han on the other hand, was kept immensely busy. There was not a time when he could lay down defenses around Hitler as day by day; he grew powerful and prominent amongst the masses. Apart from that, Hitler sent him on reconnaissance missions to procure information on various ministers. Han keenly observed this mad hunger for power that stemmed within Adolf and consumed him. He hadn't forgotten the day when Adolf slain the family of four and that memory tainted Hitler's image in Han's head forever. Although utterly shaken by that incident, Han swore to take care of Hitler and protect him as long as he lived. This would be a mark of loyalty, a repayment in fact, for the extreme trust that Hitler had shown in him when he was a boy. Han had been handpicked by Hitler at a point in life when he was lost and broken, not knowing where he was born or where he would go next.

From that moment of dilemma to this day, Han stood commanding and protecting the leader of the world's greatest army. It was a tremendous journey and one that only a few knew of. Hitler and Himmler were now together, governing great forces that were growing rapidly. Han saw this as a great threat and tried to slow down Hitler on many occasions. He would argue; saying that the forces were turning into a huge monster that even Hitler wouldn't be able to eventually control. But he was merely a sniper whereas Himmler was a much greater and important politician. Han had a little respite from Eva Braun, Hitler's love interest. He had slowly but surely found love again in her. Eva saw things from Han's perspective and tried to talk to Hitler with regards to how Himmler was merely using the powers to his personal advantage. Hitler, power-drunk and afraid at the same time, turned a deaf ear to this.

Himmler now owned factories which manufactured medicines, arms and a host of other industrial sector related production units. These, he procured over the years and under guise. None were directly connected to him, yet he governed them all. Under pretense of development and expansion for the country, he played his biggest and most cruel ploy: the strategic evacuation of people that weren't productive to the society. Himmler ran experiments which had medicinal implications and directly used human subjects. His own firms were developing drugs for many diseases and he gathered human subjects from all over the war troubled lands. What started in the small towns with a few trucks now grew into the largest amassing of individuals in history. Train carriages moved back and forth into unnamed destinations. There were areas which did not exist on any map or records. They were born and bred in Himmler's mind and existed only due to that very thought. His experiments had gone out of hand as the number of prisoners and slaves grew. As the numbers grew, the space required to house them became as a grave problem to him. Hitler had shown no interest in Himmler's plan on these genetic experiments and this became a bigger issue for him. At this point, Himmler started communicating with overseas politicians. He contacted many people secretly under the guise of political talks and tried to push his projects so he could get the required land for his insane experiments.

After many failed attempts, Himmler finally established contact with a Russian warlord named Konstantin who agreed to run a concentration camp for him; in return for a terrible price. As far as his cruel experiments were concerned, Konstantin's camp was a gold mine for Heinrich Himmler, the Nazi Architect.

The Silver Ghosts

The night was calm and silvery. Han walked as nothing more than a shadow through the gardens of Fuehrer house. It was a guarded fortress as usual; but Han had dismissed most of the guards from duty tonight. The Fuehrer was away and Han had arrived early from his mission. He checked the time on his watch, 'any minute now' he thought. The moon shone brilliantly through the skies, it was out and up like a bright white lamp in the heavens.

Han's heart fluttered in anticipation as he stood in shadows of the tree covered lawn. An endless forest stretched from where he stood. His gaze was anxiously fixated on the entrance as he waited for the door knob to be turned and for it to herald the presence of an angel. He couldn't wait for the woman of his dreams to emerge. For years and years, Han secretly loved. He never had a family and never knew what it was to feel belonged. He never knew love and yet in all of these conditions he found it, he found a lady whom he dearly loved. Han never understood how it culminated to this and he thought that all of this would just pass one day. But yet he couldn't stop himself from loving her, it was as if they were meant to be.

Han heard the faint click of a lock. His heart picked pace out of fear and anticipation. He looked around in concern to check for guards or other prying eyes. Han had gone over the plan again and again in his mind. The guards, house help and cooks, everyone was inside and on the other side of the house. He looked at the windows to double check for any people looking down from there.

The wooden door opened up and a woman strolled out. Han craned his neck from the shadows to get a better view of her. She was covered in white from head to toe. 'Of all the days to wear white' he thought. She walked gracefully across the silver-bathed gardens. Han was hoping that she would hurry up and stop being so elegant. A faint smile crossed his face; he thought it was practically impossible for her to not be so. Ever so gracefully, she walked across the gardens with her white robes flowing behind her. Han scanned the area once again; everything looked quiet and in place as she walked through moonlit gardens like an angelic apparition. Finally she reached Han as he hurriedly held her hand and dragged her into the tree cover. The broken rays of moonlight filtered through trees and they walked deeper into the forest sanctuary. It was the most unlikely activity to be happening around the Fuehrer house.

Han and his lady walked through the thick foliage. They neared a dense area which overlooked a serene water body far below. Without another word, Han pulled her close. She gasped and looked at those intimidatingly profound green eyes and before she knew it, they kissed. Under the silver moonlight that bathed them through the forest cover surrounding the Fuehrer house, they passionately kissed. The air was chilly and Han pulled her closer, holding her tight and warm. She shivered at the touch. She wanted to ask questions, to make sure they were safe, to know what was happening but she melted instead. Those questions could wait; for the moment was immensely overwhelming and she loved him dearly.

Han and Eva Braun loved, looking like apparitions from the light that shone over them, their bodies slithered. Han slowly disrobed her, letting the fabric slide off her body. Eva shivered with the slight winds and bore into Han's eyes. Han's rough hands slide down her arms and cupped her tender breasts. A gasp escaped her mouth as her body reacted to his touch. She was nervous, what if someone was watching? Her white form tightened at that very thought. Han drew closer; his powerful arms shielding Eva as he gently pushed her on the forest ground. Eva felt the leaves and foliage rustle below her nude self. Han was breathing down her neck and she felt the warmth caress her aware breasts. Eva gasped and dug her hands into Han's back, holding him close as she felt him move over her. Eva loved how Han fiercely claimed her and yet; how very tenderly he could love her. A soft gasp escaped her lips as Han entered Eva, uniting with her under the silver skies. The entire forest range was quite but for their breathing and soft moans.

Far away in the cover of trees a small glint was visible as prying eyes keenly observed them. Looking at the two stand under surreal moonlight, he noticed that Eva was unnaturally white while Han was a tad browner. A smile broke over the face that held round rimmed spectacles as he looked at the silver ghost-like lovers.

Silver Bullets

Adolf stood staring at a map laid out on the wall. It was a dark rainy night and he was in a pensive mood as he paced the floor of an apparently massive room. Unflinching and unmoving, he stared at the huge canvas that was laid out in front of him. As usual, Wagner played softly in the background. Adolf's eyes traversed over the map, taking in the sights, eyeing one country after other before his gaze slowly fixed over Austria. His victory there had been great, ten long years had passed to that moment but it remained etched inside his memory till date.

Germany had triumphed over the years and succeeded in conquering many lands, some by deceit and others by brute force. Germania stood commanding on the map and Adolf's sight was now set on Russia, the vast and expansive lands were his answer to the needs of the growing war. He stood in front of the map thinking about how all of this would now finally end and how this dream would conclude.

The final battle against the powerful Russian warlord Stalin was well on its way. The pact between Germany and Russia had been dissolved and they were now at war. Too much was at stake, there were too many decisions to take and too many people were going to perish in this massive war. Both countries were infiltrating illegally but over the past few months that had changed. Hitler devised attack plans and had declared complete war. This would be the final call for Germania and all other countries as well. A war of this magnitude couldn't be fought single-handedly by any side. The German ministers were working day and night to procure strategic alliances from any country possible. To take down Russia would require mighty effort on their part. The industries were working overtime to produce war materials. Many civilians now saw hints that there was a planning deficiency and wanted the war to end but for Hitler, this was the final call. The war would now conclude only if they'd fought and defeated Russia.

For a moment Hitler closed his eyes, lost in thought and transported back to his serene spot on the cliff. Through the years he always did this. Any moment of emotional turmoil and he would find himself visiting the cliff. He looked tired and insignificant in front of this huge map. His eyes were sullen and exhausted but as he stood on the cliff like a small boy, in his mind he was alert and agile as ever. Every movement around him, any minute sound or rustle and his ears picked it up instantly. He felt mighty reverberations of thunder as he stood within his study and so did the small boy feel them all the way back to the cliff.

"My Fuehrer" a small whisper hung in the air. The fresh air suddenly vanished from around Adolf and in its place hung a damp and dark surrounding. Thunder continued to rumble somewhere in the distant environs. Cold blue eyes opened up and they were still staring into the map. They bore an intense emotion and were no longer a brilliant clear blue that they once used to be. "My Fuehrer" a louder and more urgent cry came from behind him. It was Han; he was drenched from head to toe and was standing at the door. Hitler merely nodded, indicating for Han to enter. Han closed the door behind him with a soft click and walked across the hall to take a seat.

Hitler continued his study of the map while Han uncomfortably looked around the dark room. Well laid out furniture of the finest quality wood, marble arched windows robed in crimson red drapes and a huge desk with a single high backed chair that bore the imperial eagle took up the room. The tapestry behind the chair was vast and vivid, covering almost every part of the entire wall. It was the richest and finest fabric sewn across with golden threads which made up the map of Germany. Adolf slowly turned and walked to his chair as he motioned Han to take a seat.

Han sat and looked at Hitler, he looked tired and weak. "What is the verdict Han?" Although he looked disturbed and weak, his voice was full of authority. "Guilty" replied Han. He placed a bag on his table and spoke, "tapes, documents, correspondences and reports. All of these point against Himmler" he said. "I trust you Han. I do not need these proofs from you" he said pointing at the case lying on the table. Han tried to speak further but Hitler cut him short. Adolf moved closer to Han, he had to take considerable effort to move the heavy chair closer to the table. Han noticed that he looked weaker by the minute.

Hitler's life since the past couple of years had been mired in sleepless nights. The Russian offensive consumed too much of his energy. He spent all his hours planning and directing forces. From the data provided to him, he drove battle squadrons to victory. He would stay up all day and night to speak to them over radio and only when there was a positive response from the war front, would he retire to bed. Hitler had let his hatred run deep down within him but Han was no longer in a position to judge. He moved around with a heavy heart and a deep-set fear about his love for Eva. In every sense of the word, he was being unfaithful to the man who gave him a life.

"I should have paid heed to your warnings. Himmler is now acting on his own accord" Hitler spoke after a bout of silence, breaking Han from his thoughts. "Is it true that he continued his experiments even though I forbade him to do so?" "Yes my Fuehrer. It is true" Han replied. "He is running experiments and killing thousands on recaptured lands because of which the credibility of him coming under question reduces greatly" he explained. Hitler nodded in acknowledgement. "What has come as a greater shock to me is that he is working with Konstantin, the Russian warlord who is running these camps for him. I have laid hands on detailed reports of the experiments going on in these camps" Han further explained. Hitler smiled and asked "Are you sure he has contacted the Russians?" "Yes my Fuehrer" replied Han. "What has the bastard promised in return?" Hitler asked Han as he looked at him with bloodshot eyes. "Nazi war strategies, codes, names, layouts, industry plans and…" Han drew a deep breath before he spoke again "You."

A maniac like laugh escaped Hitler as Han concluded. He sank back in his chair and laughed loudly. Locks of his neatly combed hair fell lose over his face. Han was troubled and waited for Hitler to calm down. "He has promised to deliver me?" Hitler banged both his fists on the table and spoke in anger. "That bastard will regret it!" Hitler spat as Han looked on. Hitler's eyes were turning red as his features contorted in fury. "Let Himmler be in this position" Hitler continued to talk vehemently. "How will that help?" Han asked.

Hitler rose from his chair with surprising agility. "We are at war with Russia right now. Our victories are small but sure. If they do not yield within a year, we will have used up all our resources. The entire nation is going to war, Han. If we do not join hands with the British forces soon, our chances at victory are bleak" Hitler explained. "The British army will never yield to us my Fuehrer" Han tried to reason with him. Hitler nodded at the statement. "You have learnt so much Han." Hitler smiled as he continued to talk. "I know, and that is why we must keep Himmler alive. He is currently in talks with the British forces too."

It was Han's turn to be surprised and he leapt out of his chair. "It cannot be. He is going to sell us out straight away" he retorted. "Yes, exactly my concern now that Himmler's involvement with the Russians is confirmed" Hitler said. Han was trying to figure out where this conversation was heading. "Himmler is talking to the British people and his claim is of a tall order. He hopes to directly talk to the British high command, namely the prime minister. Though we have no confirmatory evidence about that, it might be true. We do need their help and if Himmler succeeds, it will win us the battle no matter the cost" Hitler explained. Han was thoroughly confused by now.

"You Han, will from this day hunt down Konstantin. Find him, break him and kill him" Hitler spat. "Konstantin is a bigger threat to us. Take him out, till I assign more people to convince other governments to join hands with us." Hitler spoke as he paced restlessly. Han stood rapt in attention by the table as he grasped the orders. "Tailing him will not be easy Han. You will probably have to infiltrate enemy barriers, which is why I'd trust only you for the task. Leave my security concern to the others now. I want this man dead" ordered Hitler. Han was taken aback. "While this battle rages on, I cannot possible leave your side my Fuehrer" Han argued. The room fell silent as Hitler came to a halt by the window. "If only I could trust you Han" Hitler spoke in a mere whisper as he turned around and pulled open a drawer. He picked up a small black box and opened it for Han to see. There were two silver bullets in the box. "These bullets have the same metal that killed Geli" Hitler spoke and showed them to Han. "They are forged in Geli's blood. I found a craftsman who practices this rare art. This forging technique is old and forgotten. The great rulers would forge their swords in this manner" he said, holding the silver bullet up in ambient light. Han was thoroughly confused at what was happening. "Not many people know of this but when you die at the hands of your loved one, death becomes more tolerable and this is the closest I will ever get to Geli" said Hitler. Han didn't comprehend what Hitler was trying to convey. Hitler pocketed one bullet and slid the box across to Han. "Keep it, it will answer a lot of questions" said Hitler. Han pulled out the other bullet and studied it, still confused as to where this conversation was headed.

"You have two most important orders to carry out Han" Hitler spoke. Han stood away from the table, scared and confused. "Get behind Konstantin, learn all that you can and kill him" Hitler commanded. "This will leave Himmler baffled and he will have no choice but to stay true to us. Till such a point that you kill him, I have no option but to give Himmler a free hand" he said. Han was intently listening without moving a muscle. "My second and most important order to you is that you are relieved from my duty" he concluded.

Adolf settled in his high backed chair, "You Han, are the best man of this army; yet you betrayed my trust" he said. Han was shocked as he stood still. "Just as you stand here Han, so stood Himmler, he told me everything" in the slightest of whispers Hitler spoke. Han was dumbstruck. "She will stay with me and if we lose, she will die with me. For the loyalty that you have shown, I spare your life" Hitler concluded as he lifted a glass to drink from it. "Send me Konstantin's head and never see me again, Edmund" he said. Silence hung in the room as absolutely nothing moved or made noise. "Sorry, Han" Hitler concluded with a choked voice and looked away, a lone tear rolling down his cheek.

Han had no option but to leave. He stood there for a second, wanting to speak but eventually decided against it. He quietly opened the door and stepped out into the torrential rains, his mind blank, his love lost. There was no meeting Eva anymore. Somehow, this felt like the last he'd ever see of Hitler as well. He put his hands inside his pockets as he walked into the rains and felt the cold metal of the silver bullet.

Han's Hunt

L ife had come to a standstill for Han and Eva. There was no
turning back on their love and there was definitely no
moving forward. Hitler had dismissed Han from all duties
towards him. Hitler's security was now overlooked by
forces commanded by Himmler and with that, he got the final
leeway into Hitler's inner tier. The battle with Russia was well on
the way and hourly reports came in, giving detailed accounts of
war. Over the next few months and eventually a year, Hitler was
extremely busy. His base was constantly shifted to keep him safe
from enemy wrath. Many rebellions now cropped within Nazi
ranks as they were losing hope from Hitler; the Nazi party ran
unchecked.

All decisions were to be taken by the Fuehrer and he didn't
have the time or resource to overlook all of it. The Nazi hierarchy
was breaking apart; orders being relayed were not reaching the
required people and generals were manipulating orders to earn
maximum benefits for personal gain. Hitler was ordering to kill
people within his own ranks as and when they defied him. The
beacon of hope, the ultimate supreme legacy of the Nazis' was
now falling apart piece by piece. The world was joining hands
against them and their cruelty. Hitler too, was cracking under stress
as his health regularly failed him and Dr. Morell, his personal
medic was constantly on the move with the Wolf as he changed
base after base.

Han on the other hand was undercover like never before.
He was used to it because of Hitler's tactics to keep him hidden but

this time, things were different. He now lived off taverns, street side inns and forests. He was stripped of his privileges and government clearances. He was tailing Konstantin off records and there was no way to make use of the unlimited Nazi resources which he'd previously had access to. Hitler had played extremely well and Han had no option but to hunt down Konstantin. He couldn't single handedly reach Eva and there was no way to touch Hitler. In his hunt, Han united with General Felix who had been discharged from duty and was on the run just like him. Han and Felix met regularly at locations across the country. They were recruiting a small band of soldiers for themselves as they tried to move towards a common goal.

Han and Felix set up meetings with many undercover soldiers and spies. They were sitting at a local country tavern waiting to meet an extremely successful anti-Nazi. Today, Han was sitting by the window while General Felix sat at the desk in civilian clothes. A crisp knock on the door made them turn their heads. "Enter" said Han, his hand gripping the gun as usual. A shabby old man wearing robes entered the cramped room. Traugott closed the door behind him and pulled out his pipe "Do you mind?" he questioned Han. Han nodded a negative. "I would have anyways" Traugott muttered and pulled a chair to sit.

Han closed the window shut as the three of them sat and Traugott smoked. "So you are Han, the legendary shadow of Adolf Hitler?" he asked. Han eyed Traugott and nodded. "I am looking for Konstantin" he curtly replied. Traugott blew a long trail of smoke into the air as everyone waited for him to react. "He is very difficult to get" he replied. "I don't care" said Han. "I want him dead" he concluded and looked at Traugott. "Why?" said Traugott, who was intently studying the trail of smoke as he spoke again. "Why do you need him dead?"

Han looked at Felix, slightly frustrated with Traugott's weirdness. "Gentlemen let's cut this short. Han wants Konstantin, I want to save Germany, get out of this mess lest Hitler or Himmler kill me and Traugott wants Hitler dead too. Let's move into a common goal and finish this. The very walls of the Reich leak information today. We must help each other with this, that's the only way out. We need to trust in each other and set this situation straight" Felix concluded and silence fell over the small tavern room as they sat staring at each other.

"I will win in my quest anyways and I want Hitler and Himmler both dead" Traugott spoke through his smoke trails. "Afraid is the heart that has something to loose. I am blessed that way" Traugott spoke as he continued to study smoke trails that he left hanging in the small room. Both Han and Felix were waiting for Traugott to speak further. "I am ready to co-operate, no matter the cost. But I need to know *why* you are doing this." Traugott concluded and settled back as he looked at Han. Felix looked at Han and then towards Traugott. "While you gentlemen whether to trust each other or not, we need to have proper channels of communications" Felix spoke with authority. "I have a place in Berlin, its underground and can protect us. We can set up radio and other equipment to communicate efficiently. If we are getting to Hitler, there is no better place than Berlin" Traugott offered. "What's your story Han?" Traugott questioned yet again and eyed him suspiciously. "If I have to trust you I must know what you are doing this for. Very few people even know Konstantin. You are on his tail and want him dead. What is it? Treasure, information, Jews?" he asked.

"Eva Braun" said General Felix before Traugott could question further. Han merely looked out the window as the faint light hit his green eyes. Traugott raised his eyebrow in amusement and smiled. "Of all the women on this planet" he said. Deeply and heartily, he laughed. Felix tried to look away but the amusement on his face was evident. Traugott laughed even harder as he banged his fist on the small wooden table. Even Felix and Han chuckled along; they couldn't hold a straight face. They looked at each other and laughed at their lives as the sun steadily went down on them.

The trio of Traugott, Han and Felix set up a base at Berlin over the next few months. They smuggled radio equipment into an underground section at Traugott's house. A small set of people were being put together by General Felix, a radio operator and another German soldier who wished to see the Nazi downfall joined them. Traugott had a surprising amount of information about everything that went on in Nazi politics. He even had information from prison camps and was secretly helping a lot of people escape. General Felix was trying his best to set up a meeting between Han and Eva. Han was impatient, he knew that nothing could be done and Hitler would now treat Eva as he saw fit. He quietly pushed those thoughts away and focused on Konstantin. For Han too, killing Konstantin and Himmler was priority now. Himmler because he knew about him and Eva; and Konstantin because there was a chance that Hitler would let Eva live if Han delivered Konstantin's head to him.

Han hunted, he did so mercilessly. He got a list of the top warlords of Russia. Igor, Vlad, Mark were all connected to each other and had a hand in supporting Himmler. Most of them were usually seen reporting to Stalin but the one name that evaded Han was Konstantin. Traugott had put all his resources to use and was trying to get the exact location of Konstantin's whereabouts. The elusive Russian warlord operated from utmost secrecy and there were no official records of him reporting to the high command.

Han and Traugott hunted through records, individual information and drew maps that would eventually lead to the Minotaur's secret camp. After extensive work on procured maps and moths of gathering endless information, they drew out a massive area deep in a formidable forest range. It was most probably the place from where Konstantin operated. The camp area looked endless and huge on the map. "There is another problem Han. Rumor has it that Hitler is sending Eva to an undisclosed location soon" Traugott spoke to Han. Han's heart missed a beat in fear. He tried to keep his features straight and looked at Traugott who spoke "He might have already done that, given the threat to his life" he said.

Han drew a deep breath. "I have no idea Traugott, for now, all I can do is to hope and get Konstantin. Once I am back, I might be able to save her." Traugott nodded as Han concluded his statement. "I am trying to gather proof on that front and hope to get to it soon. I will not be able to openly communicate with you and only time will tell us what steps to take" Traugott concluded. Han nodded and sat there, looking at the map which was laid out in front of him. "There is this fierce new boy, they are naming it operation Valkyrie. With any luck, they might get Hitler. I hope he succeeds before you Han. Once Hitler falls, I'll use all that I have to help save Eva" Traugott offered his help as Han kept absorbing the places on the maps laid out in front of him.

With this, Han was thrust into the biggest and fiercest battle of his life. From the underground room at Traugott's he had acquired enough information about the Russian Warlord's whereabouts. Thus begun the fiery hunt of Han, who was no longer Hitler's shadow.

Spit Fire

Konstantin sat in his cabin, consumed by his thoughts. Too much was running through his mind as he sat smoking a cigar, watching the scientists work over the dead bodies. They had set up a refrigeration unit to keep temperatures under control and had also injected the bodies with something that Konstantin didn't know of. He understood parts of it though, that blood would remain thin and wouldn't coagulate. They had also found a way to keep the blood circulating through a dead body. A small device outside their bodies worked like a pump, or more accurately, like the human heart. It kept blood and chemical agents flowing through vital organs, thus ensuring they were healthy enough for further use. This was exactly how they kept their subjects in a state of induced life, making them viable for experiments.

All of this and much more came from the research that Himmler's team was conducting at his camp. No one else in the world was even close to cracking these problems yet and Konstantin's camp held answers to them and much more. The nuclear material procured from Germany was priceless too for their research and knowhow on the subject was amazingly far ahead. They had developed warfare material that could wipe out entire cities with single bomb drops. Their aviation technologies were unmatched and beyond time for anyone to make or even consider in their minds. They were very close to discovering technology that could effectively hide airplanes from enemy radars and their war machines were getting lighter, stronger and easy to maneuver at high speeds. The research was endless and Konstantin's team of Russian scientists worked in tandem with Himmler's team to make incredible breakthrough in many departments.

The radio suddenly crackled to life as Konstantin pulled himself out of his thoughts. He picked the receiver and turned the dial. "I trusted you Konstantin" Vlad barked over the radio. Konstantin had prepared for this all along. He spoke with precision: "The prisoners broke loose and attacked while I was in Berlin." "I do not buy this, how did you reach the camp in that case? Where is your aircraft?" Vlad accused Konstantin over the radio. "The prisoners could have never caused so much mayhem under your watch. I have reached the nearest safe house from your wretched camp. We were forced to land here unannounced and we heard the blasts." Vlad was plain angry with Konstantin. "I am using their radio and it might not be secure. You will ride out to meet me at the safe house or I will barge into your camp with brute force. Yes, I have the nation's resources at my disposal and I will use them to set you right." Vlad's threat hung in the air as Konstantin sat there with raging eyes, not knowing how to respond. "Riding out to you will be a difficult Vlad. Do not test my patience" Konstantin hollered over the radio. "You will do exactly as I say" spat Vlad. "I give you half an hour to sort out your mess and ride out to me at a safe spot in the forests. Carry details of all the material that you house and I can help you fix a deal. I hope the bodies are safe with you" Vlad gave his orders and waited for a reaction. "I will ride out to you, Vlad" Konstantin curtly concluded and sat back. He took a long puff from his cigar and exhaled slowly as the smoke hung around him.

The camp was relatively quiet now. In the past five years, Konstantin's camp hadn't been this deserted. Erik had effectively overlooked the entire evacuation process. Soldiers had been marched away to nearby safe houses and there was no stopping high command from interfering, now that Himmler had slipped up. Trucks and jeeps filled with supplies were moving through the forests to other safe houses as Konstantin didn't want interference from soldiers. A lot had already leaked; if any more information went out, it would spell disaster for him and his plan. The trucks that Konstantin had asked for were lined outside for his inspection. Erik wondered what this strange material was and why was it kept under so much security; as he anxiously waited for further orders.

'One trip to Berlin had cost him his entire camp' Konstantin wondered what to do next. 'Could he risk it again?' Han was important now. He would know if these bodies were actually Hitler's and his mistress for sure. Konstantin had chanced upon this information from Himmler as he tried hard to buy out Hitler's loyal shadow. The only way was to find Han's weakness; Eva Braun was the answer. 'Right under Adolf Hitler's nose, they fell in love' Konstantin thought as a smile broke over his face. 'Love was such a weakness' he thought, 'people spoke of love, honor and strength.' Konstantin knew better, there was no love and there was no honor. There was only strength and everything that weakened him had to be pruned away. 'There was only strength' he thought repeatedly.

Konstantin's feelings were heavy upon his mind as he planned and plotted his further moves. Everything until now had fallen into place; these were mere hindrances that he would have to pound to dust as usual. His mind was a terrible place for anyone to be, the thoughts that it brewed were beyond treacherous. Even he felt uneasy at times with things that he could come up with when he closed his eyes and took a deep breath. It was as if his brain was a snake and his thoughts, venom. The venom kept him alive as it seeped through his body, filling him with uncanny strength. "There is only strength" he told himself and the answer came to him instantly. Konstantin picked up the radio and turned the dial. "Identify yourself" a voice barked over the radio. "Konstantin" he said. The voice on the other end froze. "What is the reason for you to contact high command?" asked the voice. "Channels of communication are extremely busy." "Listen carefully now, I will not repeat" Konstantin spoke through the wafting smoke as he cut short the talk. "I have the dead bodies of Adolf Hitler and his mistress, Vlad tried to sell them off to me. The bodies which he sent to high command are fakes. He tried to bribe me but I love my country much more than my money. I wish to turn them in…" he spoke, and lingered on a little. There was silence on both ends of the radio as faint crackle buzzed. Konstantin was plotting his biggest move yet. He took in a few deep puffs from his cigar and waited for high command to react. In the smoke filled room, his eyes shone with pulsing venom. He smirked at himself, imagining the immense commotion that must be unfolding at high command.

The deal was set, Konstantin had turned Vlad in. He now had to reach him and finish the final deal with Vlad's buyers. He needed proper channels to strike deals with foreign buyers. Since Himmler and his buyers were history, Vlad now filled that gap. His security with high command would double once he turned in Vlad and slipped illegal activities under his name. Vlad had to be sacrificed along with his beloved camp and Konstantin made a mental note to finish off Mark, he was such a bothersome pest that needed to be squashed.

"Erik" Konstantin spoke as he strode out of his cabin. The plan was now cognizing in his mind and everything was falling into place. "Get ten soldiers to drive the trucks and have them parked a thousand meters from here. You will leave from the southern gate and take six trucks containing nuclear material. I will personally drive out in one of them for inspection as soon as I set these intruders straight" and as he gave out these orders, he also loaded his ammunition. Konstantin had it planned; the trucks would disappear underground into the Honeycomb mazes. Those routes would be locked for only he knew the exact workings of the junctions. Himmler or Hitler's capture would have given him unimaginable power but now he had to act resourcefully. Konstantin scanned for the last time, his beloved camp as it stood silent, dark and broken. Erik gathered the trucks to drive them out and left a last batch of soldiers to stand guard by the Minotaur.

From under the hatch, a pair of eyes watched Red army soldiers move about on the ground above. He silently closed the hatch and looked below at the waiting line of prisoners. "It's time to surface, fellows. Hold your steel and spit rage with your bellows" Traugott said as the prisoners nodded in reply. He had managed to move through the mazes and surprisingly all three teams had converged with many other prisoners joining them from various tunnels. Konstantin only knew about Han and the two Germans who fell into the maze. He didn't know of others who'd carefully assembled themselves below his camp. His junction re-orientation strategy had opened up pathways that led these teams to unite. The prisoners, with their scythes pointed out, were ready to spit fire at the Red army.

Pyres at Dawn

Theodor sat propped up against the tunnel junction. His clothes were drenched with blood and he sat dumbstruck at what Han narrated to him over the past twenty odd minutes. They had travelled all the way from Berlin to this labyrinth to save Han and procure documents but here he sat, a witness to the most audacious story ever heard.

On the other hand Albert had failed at reversing the junction and there was no way for him to get through. Han had left Theodor a hand gun and some meager ammunition so he could get through the tunnels. The shadow had departed to take down Konstantin, while Albert was going to surface above with a band of prisoners. Theodor safely tucked the diary in his shirt, strapped on the holsters and loaded some ammunition. He scrambled to his feet, took in a deep breath and focused on the one thing that he had to achieve now. The intimidating maze stood in front of him as he ran into it.

Fedor reached a junction and cursed Konstantin for reorienting them. But he was the last person to give up for he was a brilliant tracker. His mind continued to calculate the odds of where exactly the Germans had fallen and how far they could have travelled. All through his run, he noticed traces and markings; it was difficult to tell if it was the Germans or slaves who'd left those behind. Fedor was burning with rage and seemed possessed; he could take no chances this time. He could literally smell different people in the tunnels as he looked for clues. Fedor had a huge pack of dynamites which he strategically placed as he covered ground through the labyrinth.

Theodor was running at breakneck speed. 'It was time to leave and go back to Berlin' he thought to himself. 'It was time to return to Adelheid.' Just as he would get back to Adelheid, Han too would be back with Eva soon enough. He felt a surge of energy as the audacity of Han and Eva's situation moved him to believe in himself. A huge explosion rattled in the distance as he felt the heat wave surge forward but it didn't slow him down. He had to trust his instinct and so, he kept going. The sections were passing by in a blur as Theodor kept up his pace through the lowly lit tunnels.

A series of loud explosions rocked the Honeycomb Mazes. Konstantin was on ground level with his guards and ordered low intensity dynamites to be dropped into the open hatches. He knew that any moment from now, the Germans were bound to surface out into the open. Simultaneously and unannounced, the hatches flew open in the Russian camp. They burst out and landed on the camp grounds with resounding crashes. "It's them. Unleash hell on those bastards" ordered one of the soldiers. "I want the sniper alive" shouted Konstantin as he saw the soldiers open fire. A loud round of firing went about as they fired at the open hatches in vain. Suddenly, they ceased from firing in tandem with a loud roar from Konstantin for them to stop firing. He was furious; if they killed Han, it was all over. In a sudden motion, glass bottles flew out of the hatches and crashed on the camp floor. A pungent fluid oozed out of them as they broke open. Red army soldiers yet again opened fire and the resounding bullet clanks sparked a huge wave of fire around them.

Theodor kept up his tense pace as he ran; hopefully, he was getting closer to the opening that would lead him into forests. He heard another explosion behind him and fumbled from the reverberations as he kept up his sprint. He was sweating, with his breathing being extremely labored. Within the next moment a bullet ricocheted right behind him with a loud echo; and he ducked in panic. Dread built up within his mind and he chanced a glance over his shoulder. With fast long strides and an unmatched anger in his eyes, Fedor was on his tail.

The fury in the prisoner's war cry rang deep through the hearts of Red army soldiers. They clambered out from the hatches that were least guarded and their scythes seared through Red army flesh with deadly wrath. Traugott climbed out and for a moment, his gaze locked with that of Konstantin; who stood protected by a group of soldiers as the fight unfolded. "We'll fight it their way then" muttered Konstantin as he charged furiously at the slave army. His war cry was nightmarish and people made way as he charged forward like a rouge battering ram.

Fedor was close on Theodor's tail; as angry as hell. Without a second thought, Theodor pulled out his gun and blindly shot at him. Fedor easily dodged the attack and raced towards him. Theodor had limited ammunition and Han had instructed him to find more weapons at a shed outside; till then, he had to sustain on the meager resource. Fedor swiftly caught up with Theodor who was running with inhumane strength. One wrong move; and Theodor would collapse at Fedor's Mercy. There was a diversion coming ahead, Theodor took his chance and jumped into the tunnel leading towards his right. These sections were completely new and didn't look affected by the blasts, unlike the previous ones. Fedor rained bullets on him as Theodor jumped out from sight. They barely missed Theodor and the curvature of pipes proved to be a huge disadvantage. Bullets hit the walls and bounced off in fury, making it difficult to dodge them. The sound was extremely disorienting in the enclosed space. Theodor saw bright red sparks all around as he desperately ran into the diversion.

For each slave Konstantin came in contact with, he beat them to instant death. Each of his punches spelled fatality as his iron fists smashed through their frail skulls. Some of the prisoners were fighting amazingly well though. They fought in teams of two, the bulkier one smashed through Red army soldiers and the swifter one took out soldiers from a longer range. Konstantin was looking for their grey bearded leader as he searched through ranks of fighting prisoners. Traugott was engaged in a fierce hand-to-hand combat with Red army soldiers. His skill and agility were surprising as he cut through their defense, landing punches onto the soldiers with surprising strength and precision. They were taken aback by Traugott's fierce strength as they dodged and countered his blows.

Konstantin checked the time; he didn't have much time on his side, and he had to tackle Vlad too. He had to go assure him his share before contacting high command. An unwary slave smashed a bottle onto his head as he fought off other Red army soldiers. Konstantin fumed and grabbed the man's neck as his iron clasp cracked the slave's neck into two. He threw him away and sniffed the air, imitating a dog. His coat was off and with his shirt torn from the attack, he flexed his hands and roared into the cold morning "I smell you; Nazi bastards."

Far away in Igor's cabin, Han heard Konstantin's cry as he surfaced through the trap door. Konstantin knew these mazes well, and so did Han. Even though the orientation had changed, Han was able to surface out exactly where he wanted. He rummaged through the room, gathering rapidly, a host of weapons. He ripped open a cabinet and stood in silence at what he saw. His rifle had been kept in the cabinet. As Han pulled it out, he looked at it with a lover's gaze. It was an exquisitely crafted rifle which had served him well over the years. His journey into the Russian camp began right here; and from here, he would finish his mission. He rummaged through the General's personal cabinet and found bullets for his rifle; he loaded it and packed some extra ammunition. The satisfyingly familiar click of the rifle reacted to his touch. Han quietly sneaked out of the cabin and onto the battle grounds.

Albert ascended vertically along with an army of prisoners behind him. He had made sure Theodor was up and conscious before he departed, taking a different route. They were going to surface and head to the camps where the remaining slaves were held captive. If all the prisoners united, Konstantin wouldn't stand a chance to their strong uproar. One after other, they silently piled out of the hatch and onto forest grounds.

Fedor was gripped with a dreadful need to finish off the intruders. Theodor panted in exhaustion; a good number of his bullets had already been wasted on Fedor. Fedor, on the other hand, was possessed with a callous energy that made him unable to either slow down or give up. No matter where and how Theodor dodged, he was on his trail; shooting away relentlessly. A few bullets had already managed to scrape Theodor; it was only a matter of time before he made one wrong move and fell prey to the ruthless assault. He had yet again reached an intersection within the maze; the lights here were flickering and casting confusing shadows all around him.

He slowed down and ducked, dashing into one of them. When he reached the junction, he thought he saw someone move behind him as he braced himself to fight. If Fedor was around, this would have been very easy; he could take out anyone from where he was. The shadow moved and Theodor shot. The bullet ricocheted off the pipes, and in an instant, Fedor jumped from the opposite end; kicking Theodor in the chest. With panic struck eyes, Theodor rammed into cold metal. With no time to spare, he got up and ran ahead, shooting blindly behind him with the hope of slowing Fedor down. A few rounds fired and his hand guns were exhausted, he now faced the sad reality of spent ammunition . He encountered another intersection in the maze and took a turn, jumping over strewn debris. Fedor's footsteps were loud and clear but extremely confusing as echoes intensified through the mazes. Theodor couldn't figure out the exact source of firing as he took a turn and had an head-on collision. His vision blurred and he fell backwards, with his head hitting a cold hard metal pipe. There was no time to waste and he tried getting up. Fedor stood right in front of him; he had outdone Theodor as his fists clenched in an anticipated fight.

Traugott evaded the Russian soldiers and crashed through the locked door; instantly breaking into Konstantin's cabin. He knew Konstantin well enough to be sure that something of consequence would show up in his cabin. He looked around to see a room with strange controls. Traugott scanned the area and instantly located a bizarre refrigeration unit. He approached it, afraid to touch it, thinking of the possibility of it exploding or triggering off something. He moved closer to the two caskets that were connected to various pipes and picked up a piece of parchment that read "Mr. & Mrs. Hitler."

Han moved through shadows and reached the centrally placed light tower in the camp. He was going to fight it his way.

He was a sniper, not a foot soldier. He was a shadow, not the light. He drew a deep breath and let his lungs fill up with fresh air as it had been a while since he was out in the open. He silently scaled the light tower to get to his vantage point.

Traugott was petrified as he stared long and hard at Eva Braun's body. He was thinking of the consequences this would have on Han and this entire mission. Traugott was one of the selected few who knew Han's secret; this was disastrous news. Too much now depended on what he chose to do because Han's only motive was to get through this to be with Eva. Traugott broke down and knelt down by Eva's body. Tears escaped his eyes as he saw her sleep peacefully in the coffin. More than anything, Han wanted to be with her; yet here she lay, defeated as Mrs. Hitler. Traugott said a small prayer with his tear-filled eyes and covered the coffin. This was going to be difficult for him but he had to decide; for without Han they wouldn't be able to finish Konstantin. Traugott slowly turned towards the other coffin and looked at Hitler's body. Anger flared up inside him, rationality had to be suspended in this moment as he came to a salient decision.

The battle outside raged and amplified as a small glow emanated from Konstantin's cabin. Traugott walked out and charged into battle, a fire silently rising behind him. The flames swiftly spread and licked everything in its wake; as the pyres of Adolf and Eva Hitler lit up on Russian grounds.

General Felix

Theodor managed to get on his feet from the terrible crash and instantly turned around. Fedor was now only a gunshot away from killing him. "You possess information that I need, soldier" said Fedor. Theodor was surprised; Fedor seemed to be requesting was for information. Theodor's vision was back to normal and without a second thought, he lunged forward; thrusting Fedor into the wall of the tunnel.

Fedor crashed with a massive force but was not someone Theodor could take out single handedly. Fedor recoiled and punched Theodor in the stomach. "Wrong answer" he growled and kicked him squarely in the face. Theodor bent low, spitting out blood onto the tunnel floor. Fedor attacked and punched him on the head. Theodor fell flat as Fedor rained assaults on him. Theodor was no match for Fedor as he tried dodging the oncoming blows.

His fumbling hands found a broken pipe on the floor which he swiftly picked up and smashed on Fedor's head. Fedor screamed in pain and fell back momentarily. Theodor was already on his feet but before he could attack further, Fedor had pointed his gun straight at him. Theodor slowly raised his hands and stepped back as something under his foot clicked. Fedor looked down at the sound and a huge explosion rocked the tunnels. Theodor stepped on Fedor's dynamite trigger and they were both thrown off their feet from the unexpected explosion.

Theodor didn't wait to recover from the fall; he swiftly scrambled to his feet and began sprinting away. He now had no clue as to where he was headed, the chase had put him totally off track and now, he was totally disoriented. He heard footsteps echo behind him, Fedor was not going to give up on him so easily.

A crisp shot rang through the campsite as Han composed his breathing, almost bringing it to a halt before aiming again. The soldier's head split open and he lay dead at the tower post as another loud shot rang through the camp. The Red army soldiers were dropping dead one by one; as Han was back to what he did best. He noticed a fire raging in the camp as he scanned the Russian grounds through his scope.

Konstantin panicked at the sight of fire and rammed through ranks of prisoners to reach his cabin. "Get inside and get me those coffins, secure the dynamite trigger from my desk" he said before dismissing his personal guards to carry out their assigned tasks. Konstantin was raging with fury as everything was slipping away from his clutches. 'These wretched slaves had caused too much unwanted mayhem' he thought as he heard a loud, prominent gunshot. His thoughts stopped dead. 'It was a sniper rifle.'

Albert, along with his company of prisoners hid behind a tree as they observed a convoy of trucks passing through. The prisoners pooled around him; watching from behind the tree cover. "I need you to spread out" Albert spoke to his team. "We need to tackle these soldiers" he gave orders as his mind saw through their own defense. His plan was to arrange transport so they could effectively escape from the camp. Albert also planned to help the prisoners and slaves escape; it was the least he could do in honor of David's sacrifice.

Theodor was exhausted as Fedor mercilessly kept up in pursuit. He could now see a huge tunnel stretch far ahead of him without any openings or turnings. This was not a good sign; the lights were also flickering and dying out. Fedor was getting dangerously close with every passing step. A few meters ahead, Theodor could see nothing as the tunnels plunged into complete darkness. "There is nowhere left to run; soldier" Fedor growled. The classic fighter that he was, Theodor kicked the ground with his feet and launched into air. If the gate had not been bolted shut he would push it open; or die here for sure. Fedor's patience was broken, and he fired. Theodor was still in midair when he felt a whizzing sound in his ear. The bullet made contact with him, scrapping his arm; and the soldier screamed in agony before colliding against the gate.

The gate flew open on impact and Theodor crashed to the ground, screaming in pain as he slid on the wet soil. His brain was thinking and functioning in overdrive as he quickly got up on his feet and began running. Fedor was now walking calmly; relishing the moment; as he knew that Theodor would never get far enough on the open grounds. Theodor stumbled from his frantic attempt and fell into the muck as he turned around to face Fedor. He heard a snarl around him and saw a hound closing in on him. The ferocious beast had one eye and instantly recognized Theodor. "Easy mate, you'll have him soon" whispered Fedor. "Where is Han?" Fedor asked Theodor as he pressed the trigger.

Han's scope was fixed on Konstantin. He curled his finger as his ear picked up a familiar scream. A loud shot rang through the camp and Fedor screamed in pain. Theodor had triumphantly gotten the window he wanted and punched Fedor in his face. Han didn't have to think twice as he abandoned Konstantin and shot Fedor through the arm. The ferocious beast leaped onto Theodor and bit into his arm, opening up his wound once again. Theodor screamed in agony, he pulled out his knife and stuck it through the hound's throat.

Before Fedor could get up, Theodor had swiftly kicked him on the bullet wound. Fedor let out a barely audible scream before he recoiled, and instantly punched Theodor in the stomach. Fedor ran into Theodor and smashed him against a tree, easily overpowering him. Fedor and Theodor fought out on the Russian grounds; with Fedor gaining the gained upper hand. He punched Theodor on his wound, as the German screamed and fell. Before he could recover, Fedor lifted him up with inhumane strength and gave him a straight punch in the face. Theodor tried to dodge the blows but was getting slower with each move. Fedor, on the other hand, was extremely fast, even with his injury. Theodor's face met Fedor's knee and he spat blood as he fell to the floor with a loud thud. Theodor stumbled and his hand flinched against a metallic object in the soil. He picked up a gun from the muddy soil and whacked Fedor's face. Fedor was caught off guard and he stumbled backwards. Theodor flipped the gun and fired, a loud and precise shot ringing with utter clarity through the chaos. Fedor could not move an inch as a dark crimson patch formed over his tunic. Theodor was breathing heavily as he looked Fedor in the eye and slowly sunk his blade into Fedor's stomach.

Fedor's eyes held unimaginable angst; but Theodor simply gleamed with satisfaction. Ever so slowly he pulled out the blade and watched him collapse, face first, into the forest floor. Theodor wiped his knife clean on Fedor's tunic and looked at the gun that had been his salvation; it was a fine looking hand gun. He looked at the crafted handle 'As always, the dawn breaks the darkness' was inscribed on it. surprisingly; General Felix's gun still worked.

Surrender

Konstantin let out a blood curdling scream through the camp grounds. Here he was, standing in the middle of his burning cabin, yet unaffected by the flames that surrounded him. The bodies had been charred beyond any possible recognition and fires had spread uncontrollably. Traugott's army of slaves and prisoners had managed to push back the Red army forces very well. A soldier came running towards him and stood there, panting. He had a broken nose and was bleeding from several points due to his innumerable wounds. "Commander Vlad sends a message my lord. He demands that you meet him at the safe house immediately" he said. Anger surged through Konstantin's body as he took in a deep breath and closed his eyes.

Konstantin's remaining warriors broke out and opened fire at the prisoners as they unleashed their entire ammunition on the slave armies. Traugott ran swiftly, taking cover behind a truck along with a few prisoners, all of whom were shielding themselves from the fresh assault. Traugott had heard the gunshots too; he knew that Han was out.

Any confrontation with Han and this mission would fail miserably. His thoughts were laden with guilt but he knew what had to be done. "One of the Germans is out in the forests and is planning an assault on the trucks." A prisoner reported to Traugott as they took cover behind the truck. Traugott instantly knew what had to be done. He got onto the truck behind which they were hiding and gathered prisoners to ride along with him. "Let's find them" he said and turned the ignition. Konstantin had managed to pocket the dynamite triggers as he walked out of the fires and got onto a motorbike. His mind was calculating new possibilities now; equations were changing by the second and he had to maintain the status quo lest he fail miserably. Even if the bodies were now useless, Konstantin had the ultimate secret to keep Vlad engaged.

Theodor burst through a door leading to a shed at the far end of camp. Cautiously, he strode in and searched around for ammunition or anything that could help him go out and join the others. He was wondering as to who was leading these prisoners; they had surprisingly put up a rather successful fight and the commotion was tremendous. He peered through cracks to see more prisoners and slaves join in the battle. Something behind him suddenly moved and he swiftly turned his neck around to see what it was. Theodor slowly moved through the dark shed to see animals housed there, moving closer, he saw fine looking stallions tied to the stables.

Han's vantage point was well covered for anyone else to reach him but Konstantin being who he was, had been thinking in the same lines as Han. A loud rumble of an engine was audible as Konstantin burst through the flames and rode out into the open. Han's eyes were fixed on the Minotaur as he composed his breathing. He pressed the trigger and a massive crack filled the air. Konstantin swerved as a bullet seared past him and he sped into the tree cover. The ground below the light tower caved in and shifted under sudden strain.

Han quickly burst through the door to run out and jump from the falling tower. The tower shook and groaned under strain. Han was hurriedly running through the stairs, he half-ran, half jumped and clambered over the railings. He was thrown off his feet as the tower shifted onto one side and the overhead beams came crashing down. Struggling, he managed to avoid the impact and leaped into air, going down two floors as the tower began to sink into the ground. Konstantin slit the palm of his hand and a trail of blood dripped onto the floor. "By my blood you were born, by mine you shall die" he muttered under his breath and looked at his camp for the last time. His dynamite trigger lay spent and a massive wave of explosions rocked the camp. The trigger merely fired a heat grid raising temperatures through the concrete as the very earth now began to crack from strain; splitting open in several places. The pipes that made up the Honeycomb mazes lay exposed across the length of the camp. This was Konstantin's last stand to curb the intrusion as he brought his camp down on them. The dynamite laced concrete exploded with deadly force and his beloved camp began to cave in. "There is only strength" Konstantin muttered and rode away as the rumbles intensified around him.

Theodor burst open through the gates of the shed as it went up in flames. He quickly covered much ground as he burst forth on a stallion. He had always been a better farmer and now, he rode through the fires with extreme precision. He steered his horse and led himself straight into battle. The other animals were let loose and they ran aimlessly as explosions engulfed the Russian camp. Theodor charged and flung at Russian soldiers, he had hauled a bagful of hammers and farm tools onto his horse. He rode through angry fires, tossing the hammers with fatal precision. The hammers met their targets and enemy skulls split open at the lethal blows. He took them out effortlessly and the prisoners roared in acknowledgement as a new member joined their ranks and rode by. Theodor easily dodged fires and jumped the many cracks in the earth as he swiftly took out Red army troops.

Erik sat in the truck as they made way through the forests to reach safer grounds. "Drive to the safe house" he ordered the driver and out of nowhere, a huge log smashed through the windscreen of the front truck. The driver hit the brakes as the massive truck came to an abrupt halt. It skid from the sudden brake and another truck rammed into it. The entire convoy came to a standstill as they butted into each other and swerved out of control. A swift unannounced swoosh was heard through the air as a scythe sliced through the driver's neck. Erik panicked and jumped out in alarm "Get out, cover the trucks. It's an ambush" he said, hurriedly ordering the soldiers to fan out. Albert was coordinating the prisoner army and one after the other they unleashed wire traps; as per his expertise Albert figured their layouts and unleashed them onto the Red army. A slew of wooden barks flew and smashed through the trucks and soldier ranks. From behind the tree cover, the prisoner army unleashed their fuel-filled bottles onto the now confused Russian soldiers. They quickly opened fire in defense and this sparked a wave of fire. Erik panicked and shouted through the commotion, ordering them all to stop. Since the trucks were carrying volatile material; these fires were spreading very rapidly. Red army soldiers ran for cover from looming flames that were appearing from all directions. As they scattered, more prisoners joined the assault and ripped through their flesh with deadly fury. Albert came around the front truck and saw Erik desperately trying to command his soldiers.

He quickly opened the door and got in as Erik turned around at the sound. Albert swiftly kicked the opposite door and whacked Erik's face, and not having any time to react, the befuddled man fell with a thud to the forest floor. The prisoners needed no better invitation to rip as they lunged onto the unwary Russian. Albert started the ignition and looked through his side view mirror. He heard the Russian scream as the prisoners finished him along with remaining enemy soldiers. "Take the trucks and let's ride!" Albert ordered.

Theodor dashed through the camp and into the forest area. He nudged his stallion to move at a faster pace as he rode through the trees. A sudden roar filled the air and he glanced over his shoulder to a startling picture of Konstantin riding towards him. Theodor panicked and kicked his horse to move even faster. Konstantin sped menacingly towards Theodor and opened fire on him. Theodor ducked; and trying to avoid the assault, he changed his direction. Konstantin was extremely agile as he sped through the impossibly thick forest before closing in on Theodor. The stallion moved amazingly well through the trees and sped ahead as Theodor tried to keep low, dodging the rain of bullets. He glanced behind to check and in the next instant whacked his head onto a tree branch. Screaming, he fell to the ground as the stallion galloped ahead. Theodor instinctively dragged himself and tried to get up as he heard the heavy boom of an engine right next to his face. He turned, frozen in raw fear as he heard the strong footsteps, before he looked up to see the mighty Minotaur towering over him. The tired German stood there in surrender; Konstantin was pointing his gun straight at Theodor's heart.

Hitlers

Konstantin came to an abrupt halt where the small company of men waited. Throwing Theodor at Vlad's feet, he continued to make rapid strides towards them. "Secure the perimeter; there is a Nazi sniper on the loose!" he barked through the silence. Vlad stood there unaffected as Mark stepped out of a waiting jeep. Konstantin eyed Mark with hate-filled eyes. "You little pest" he muttered through clenched jaws.

Mark merely stood there, unaffected by the warlord's threat. With Vlad by his side, Konstantin wouldn't dare touch him; that much was true. Theodor's hands were tied as he lay helplessly on the forest floor, listening to the Russians converse. "Listen Vlad" Konstantin barked yet again as he took his eyes off Mark. Vlad held up his hand, indicating silence. "You tried to turn me in?" he asked. "Bloody high command" Konstantin spat. "I have the Amber room, I have nuclear material and I know for sure that Hitler is still alive" Konstantin spoke and then tossed a canister at Vlad. He caught it, observing it suspiciously. "Open it" Konstantin said . Vlad turned the top lid and a flash of yellow met his eyes as he stared at the most intricately carved gold he had ever seen. Konstantin moved closer to Vlad and spoke "Listen, the trucks contain treasures. I also have a definite know-how on Hitler." Vlad held up his hand; silencing him for the second time in a row. Konstantin was getting angrier by the second. "Who is this little maggot?" Vlad asked, pointing at Theodor. "He is one of the Blood Moon kin" said Konstantin as he stared at Theodor. "They have been causing too much trouble lately and that sniper is sure to come looking, so he is useful" Konstantin concluded and without any warning, kicked Theodor. He was caught unawares and flew a short distance on the forest floor. The Minotaur's boot hit him squarely in the face as Theodor spat blood and lay fazed on the ground. "Are you sure that sniper is on the loose?" Vlad questioned. "Yes, he will be here any moment from now. I know him too well" he replied. "Disperse" Vlad ordered. His guards obeyed and began spreading out in the forests. "Do not kill him yet" he said.

"Konstantin" Vlad continued, staring the warlord straight in the eyes. "High command has asked me to take control of your camp. You cannot turn me in; for I am your only ticket to freedom now. I have authorization to communicate with foreign buyers who will pay handsomely for this and I refuse to do any of it on your terms anymore. Mark here, can share his list of buyers too" he concluded pointing at Mark. Konstantin took in a deep, but ragged breath; he would certainly not give up easily. His efforts had secured victory for Russia and had gotten them this far, he wanted his share of money and freedom. "And do know this; Konstantin. Nothing is in your command anymore. Erik is waiting for me with the trucks. You do not command his loyalty" Mark spat. "First it was Viktor and now Erik; they are both my men" he concluded.

Konstantin was extremely agile for his bulk and Mark didn't know what hit him as Konstantin's punch threw him flying onto the forest floor. "Stop right there" fumed Vlad. He stalled Konstantin's next punch as Mark tried to get up from the sudden assault. "Walk away from him and explain what you know of Hitler?" Vlad tried to reason along as he pushed Konstantin away from Mark. "Hitler lives" Konstantin spoke as he heaved in anger. Vlad was shocked. "Explain how and where?" he asked, nudging the conversation further. Konstantin nodded in amusement, paused for a moment before continuing his interesting speech. "Yes, everyone wants to know where he is." "Tell me, we have very little time on our hands. The high command awaits my call" said Vlad. Konstantin smirked; he turned over in his mind, the decision to reveal his most prized secret. Vlad was losing patience as he spoke "They have ordered me to dispose you, brother" he said. "You don't have what it takes to kill me" Konstantin said with a sneer, standing an inch away from Vlad's face. The two brothers stood still, the very air around them stood quiet and lifeless. "Hear me out carefully, Vlad" Konstantin spoke in a whisper as he divulged.

Adolf Hitler sat on his high backed chair with the intimidating eagle towering over. Rain lashed on the windows and thunder rumbled in far-away skies as he sat alone, devastated and torn from within. Himmler, Han, Eva; they had all betrayed him. Everything he had built over the years was falling apart. Controls of the Reich were slipping from his hands, the Nazi party was now a monster that roamed untamed and out of control. People who didn't follow his orders were instantly disposed but right now, he needed Himmler alive; if only to win the support of neighboring countries.

And as far as Eva and Han were concerned, he couldn't kill them. Hitler loved Eva dearly, never as much nor as truly as he did Geli; but he loved her nonetheless. Han, on the other hand, was just like Edmund, a younger brother to Adolf. A crisp knock on the door brought him back to his senses as he picked up a glass and got up from his desk. He lazily mumbled "enter" as he took a few steps towards the open window. The secret door in Adolf's study opened up and a pair of boots made soft thuds on the carpet. A man and woman entered the Fuehrer's room. Hitler had put out the lights and only lightening threw blue luminance in the otherwise dark room. Hitler settled on a chair and drank from the glass. Dr. Morell had given him his dose of nerve relaxants a few hours back and he had dismissed all staff from around him.

Hitler shifted his gaze and saw his guests standing in front of him. The man and woman stood rapt in attention as Hitler gazed at them. In front of him stood Adolf Hitler and Eva Braun, similar to every last bit of detail on their bodies, the hair, moles, skin texture it all matched. Hitler got to his feet; dropping the glass on the carpet, it fell with a soft thud and liquid seeped into the fabric. He walked closer to his decoy and inspected the mirror like double that stood in front. He examined them up-close; standing a hair's breadth away from himself. From Hitler to Miss Braun, he looked and studied.

"You are the final part of a strategy that I now have in place to protect myself" Hitler spoke as he accusingly looked at the Eva Braun look-alike as if blaming her for betraying him. He handed out envelopes to them. Each one of the given envelopes contained a protocol to explain their exact movements in the coming months and days. A list of circumstances was laid out and how they were each to act if any of those situations arose. The decoys read the information intently. The letters had maps and vital instructions on the journey that each one of them would soon have to undertake. Over the past few months Adolf Hitler had secretly planned this, he knew that the noose was closing down on him rather fast. Hitler had only one option now and that was to trust no one.

He spoke in a small whisper "this is it" and burnt the sheet of paper in his hand. It went up in flames, the others followed suit and did the same. Their faces lit up in orange red light that emanated from the flames. With both Hitlers' showing the exact same mannerisms, it was absolutely impossible to tell the difference. Deep within this room was brewing the biggest and most potent conspiracy of the Nazi regime. The Eva Braun decoy sat elegantly as she watched the Hitlers putting to flames the final plan of their life. It was impossible to tell one apart from the other. They looked quite unnatural and frightening, because as though one wasn't enough, there now stood two Hitlers.

Eagle's Flight

Albert and his convoy were crashing through the forests trying to get far away from Red army areas. As he passed the route leading to the camp, he saw a huge fire raging over the mountain tops. The debris from explosions was flying high, scattering all over the place as he pushed the pedal harder to avoid obstructions from the explosions. One of the prisoners had informed him about a bearded man who was leading underground armies. Albert hoped that Traugott had lived and for a second, he thought about how they were doing up there. He asked the prisoners to keep on a look-out for Theodor because Albert had no idea where he was. Another loud explosion ripped through the air, jolting him back to his senses as he continued to drive through the rough terrain.

Han was tracking the bike trail as he rode through the forests. He had managed to jump out of the collapsing tower and was now on Konstantin's tail. He had to finish Konstantin before he departed from these lands; this was the only chance he held onto now. Out of nowhere, a tree bark splintered near him and he heard the familiar whoosh of bullets. He swiftly ducked and continued his frantic ride. Vlad's soldiers were well camouflaged and had spread out effectively in the nearby forests. Han sensed them and steered into thicker tree cover.

Traugott drove the truck at breakneck speed as they escaped random explosions and picked up several prisoners along the way. He still couldn't come to terms with Eva's death and numerous thoughts played on in his mind. He seemed disturbed and steered absentmindedly through the rough terrain. Out of nowhere, another convoy of trucks appeared and he nearly rammed into them. The prisoners instantly jumped out in an anticipated fight as Traugott came to an abrupt halt. Through the windshield, he noticed a familiar spectacled face; they had converged with Albert and his convoy.

Vlad had a smile on his face. "If what you say is true and if we can prove it, there is no need to go back to high command. We can strike a deal here and I'd make the necessary calls" he said. Konstantin was beaming from ear to ear. Even if it meant that he would have to split the loot, he was still way ahead in this. "Ask that maggot to call Erik and get the material here. My camp is finished" Konstantin spoke as he looked at Mark with hate-filled eyes and much venom. "Mark, make the call. We are victorious; thanks to the three of us; we are able to stand above everyone!" Vlad spoke as he patted Konstantin. "Well done brother, what about this filth now?" he asked pointing at Theodor. "Once our sniper arrives, we will dispose him" said Konstantin. Theodor was on the floor and seemed to have passed out. Konstantin looked at Mark as his expression suddenly changed. "Erik has been ambushed" Mark dropped the radio and stood dumbstruck.

Konstantin couldn't control his anger any further; he pulled out a gun from his holster and pushed Vlad back. He hollered and shot hard as the bullets tore through Mark. Konstantin yelled through the commotion "you hopeless maggot!" and fired. Theodor got the window he needed and ran into the forests. He heard the warlords yelling behind him as he frantically searched for an escape route. Konstantin instantly opened fire, trying to take him down. Theodor ducked and ran, before he took shelter behind boulders.

He suddenly heard a familiar neigh as the stallion dashed through. Theodor didn't have to think twice; in one swift move, he mounted the horse. "Get him" he heard; Konstantin shouted from far. Theodor desperately tried to undo his tied hands before he balanced himself on the stallion. A sudden roar of an engine was audible from his side as he glanced to see a jeep headed his way. He panicked and forced the horse to go faster, pushing him through a detour. Theodor went completely off the road and sped into thick trees. The jeep was close behind him but he expertly maneuvered the horse through dense tree cover and rode on with great agility. Horses weren't the usual forest animals but this one was well trained and agile; he turned at the slightest pressure and raced through the forest with impressive speed.

Han sped through the forests as two bikes tailed him. The Red army soldiers seemed to be leading him into a trap. They were driving him towards Vlad and Konstantin where they could corner him. Vlad had given clear orders to not kill Han; so they merely fired to put him off track. Han didn't want the hindrance and in a sudden move, he turned. The bike spun as he faced the soldiers and fired, these soldiers were no match for his bullets. The Russian swerved out of control and fell as the tailing bike crashed into it. Han instantly recovered and roared loudly into the forests.

Theodor was effectively dodging the jeep that tailed him. The forest range was covered with wire traps and he was trying his best to maneuver through them. Suddenly, the jeep's sound died down and Theodor thought for a moment that he'd lost them in the tree cover. He rode ahead, maintaining his speed for he didn't know if the jeep had gone off track or just detoured. For a second, a smile flickered over his features, he was finally going to outdo the Red army. He kicked the horse and kept up his frantic pace.

Dodging and turning, he went deeper into the dense forests; it was the best way to keep them off his back. The sudden roar was enormous as the air borne jeep hit the ground and crashed beside Theodor. He looked around in panic as the jeep rammed through trees and landed right next to him. The soldiers seemed resilient as they sped forward in their bid to take Theodor down. Theodor rapidly leaned on the horse and directed it to take an extremely sharp turn. He flung himself on one side of the horse, shifting his entire weight while the horse turned. The horse neighed, turned, buckled and pulled through magnificently while the jeep went crashing ahead. Theodor patted the horse and kept up his pace as the soldiers continued firing in his direction.

Theodor ducked blindly, not knowing where to take refuge. The driver instantly took a sharp turn and headed back for him. He seemed to be resilient as he maneuvered easily through the impossible terrain and caught up with Theodor in no time. Theodor was now riding parallel to the jeep and bullets were raining down on him brutally. Only the trees provided cover for him as they splintered and burst all around him. The horse panicked as bullets seared around them and Theodor began to lose control. In the next instance a stray bullet flew through the tree cover and hit the horse's hind leg. The horse violently twitched, nickered in pain and crashed to the floor. Theodor was thrown off the horse and went flying through the trees.

Han abandoned his bike as the forest grew extremely dense. He dodged his way and neared the safe area with his senses highly alert. The soldiers were opening fire from random spots as he moved nearer but nothing could stand in his way. Up ahead, he could see two huge figures in the distance, and Konstantin was certainly one of them. He kept to the tree cover as he expertly dodged and moved towards his kill.

A series of shots rang through the forests as Theodor ran, avoiding the line of fire. The jeep was close on his heels and they were firing away, trying to knock him down for good. The bullets whizzed past as Theodor ducked, avoided them blindly. He was skirting near the edge as he kept up his pace and sprinted forward. The jeep easily caught up with him and was following him from close proximity. The Russians' had their weapons out, ready to take Theodor down. They fired mirthlessly, the noose was closing in on Theodor and he now had no other option but to take the plunge. As he ran, he threw himself off the cliff, lurching with all his might and flying over the foliage. Not knowing where he would fall or land, he jumped and turned around midair to see the Russian soldier pointing his gun at him.

Mark was dead from the many bullets that mired his body. "Konstantin; you fool!" Vlad barked. "We need him. If Erik falls we have nothing left to strike a deal!" he hollered, wondering why Konstantin would act so foolishly. Konstantin was frustrated and tried to radio Erik about his location. The radio simply crackled and there was no response. Konstantin loaded his ammunition and settled onto the bike. "I will have to get back to the trucks, one of them is parked on the outer periphery of the camp" he said before kicking the bike to life. "Stop right there brother" Vlad threatened, holding a gun to Konstantin's head.

On the far away horizon, the sun was rising as the rays travelled through ether and reached earth. On the topmost peak of a mountain an eagle was stirring to life as the sun hit its eye. The eagle came out from its nest, gently spreading its powerful wings before jumping off the cliff. Golden yellow rays were filtering through trees as Han closed in on his kill. 'Eva' his mind whispered but he simply pushed away the agony. Slowly the chaos around him died, all he could now hear was the sound of nature and the slight wind picking up, pushing him towards his goal as Han charged forward like a predator. The tree barks around him were bursting and splintering as bullets made contact with them but none of it seemed to bother him. He was getting too close for comfort and the soldiers were gaining in on him.

The Minotaur sensed Han's presence as Vlad held a gun to his head. "You are my only ticket to freedom brother" he said, pressing the cold metal against Konstantin's temple. The Minotaur's agility was incredible as he swiftly spun and slipped a blade into his brother's heart. Vlad's flesh ripped and his eyes held shock as the blade sunk in. "There is only strength" Konstantin muttered.

Han lurched with inhumane strength; in one swift jump he made contact with the wall of sacks that demarcated the camp territory. He thrust his foot on them, jumping higher and arched into an impressive flight. His finger curled around the familiar metal and his eyes locked on his kill. Not even the bustle roaring up beneath him could stop him. Han pressed the trigger as he hung in air for the minutest of a second and began his descend from the jump. A loud and crisp shot rang through the morning air.

Konstantin fired back at Han in a swift unexpected move as Han's bullet seared through Konstantin's shoulder joint. He screamed in pain and fell to the ground as his joint splintered from the bullet. Vlad's soldiers panicked and unleashed fire. For an intense moment; Han and Konstantin locked eyes, holding limitless hatred for each other. Han was descending as he felt the bullets impale his body. Soldiers were shouting in dismay and anger, Konstantin was cowering in pain as Han's bullet had fractured his shoulder. "Don't kill him" he roared through the commotion. Han felt the impact as he crashed to the ground and slid down the slope. The bullets had pierced him at innumerable places throughout his body as his rifle fell away from him, faithful and spent.

Warm sunlight filtered through trees and hit Han's eyes. He felt pain but did not bother to acknowledge it. He took a long breath and looked up; though his vision was blurred he could see massive trees tower above him and a heavenly glow of the morning sun filter through them. He heard a faint and far away screech of an eagle as it flew above, a true master of the skies.

Berlin Year Zero

Theodor was crashing through the steep valley. He smashed against trees and boulders as shooting pain erupted through his arm. His bullet wound was open; it was bleeding profusely once again. The massive plummet strained his injury as he tried to break his fall. Theodor tried to get up on his feet and stabilize himself but his efforts were in vain, he stumbled and crashed to the floor cowering in immense pain.

Distant voices were audible around him but he couldn't make them out…were they Red Army soldiers, or were they prisoners? The sudden pain was blinding him and he seemed to be losing focus. He suddenly felt a tug at his arm as someone lifted him off the ground. Theodor thought he recognized the voice as he tried to clear his mind to listen.

Cold water splashed onto his face as he screamed and tried to breathe through the cold. Theodor looked around to see himself at the base of the valley, he had literally fallen down the entire length of the mountain. A soldier was dragging him towards a waiting truck as he registered the friendly voice. Theodor mustered courage and ran through the chaos as many hands helped him; something told him that he must trust the guiding voice. He saw a waiting convoy of trucks through his blurred vision. A hand pushed him into the truck and he turned around to see one of the prisoners helping him climb up. The familiar voice suddenly disappeared from his range.

Theodor collapsed into the truck as he heard gun shots around him and the back door close shut. Everything around him was suddenly dark as he twitched in pain. Streaks of light seeped in through slits in the truck walls as he heard bullets ricochet off the metal body of the truck. He slowly dragged himself up, sat against the side and felt a sudden jolt as the truck began to move. He was breathing heavily and tried to steady himself as the truck moved through winding roads, making their way downhill.

Through a gap in the sides, Theodor looked outside. His vision was blurred but he tried to make sense of the surrounding. Far away in the mountain top, thick black smoke wafted through the air. Mild fires were burning around them as the truck sped through rough terrain. He thought about Han, hoping that he would have killed Konstantin. The few prisoners that he saw outside were surely from the camp; that he could tell from their uniform. He was wondering if he made it to safety. Theodor collapsed as the truck turned around and the camp disappeared from sight. He thought about all that had happened; while in his thoughts exhaustion overpowered him as he fell unconscious from excess blood loss.

Many hours later, he woke up with a start. His head was heavy and it hurt terribly. Usually after such trauma, he would wake up to see Ralf but this time, he heard new voices around him. He tried to move but experienced extreme discomfort and the blinding pain erupted once again through his arm. He glanced up to see himself dressed in prisoner clothes and being led away on a stretcher. He was trying to recollect what happened and where was he being led to, but his mind remained fogged with pain. He suddenly realized that the diary was supposed to be tucked in his shirt. "Oh no!" he muttered, as he tried to get up and ask questions from the people who were carrying him, to no avail. His world was spinning and he couldn't push himself up and as he gave up and fell back, his eyes closed shut.

Walking into Berlin now looked like walking into the very gates of hell. Everything around was austere and dead. With the proclamation of Hitler's death, raiding armies plundered without fear. Piles of dead bodies were being burnt at alternate junctions; civilians were hunted down and taken as prisoners. Berlin was a void, a blank slate now. Red army flags fluttered with pride throughout the broken city and soldiers marched through each and every street. The greatest war witnessed by mankind was drawing to an end as General Helmuth declared surrender and awaited his fate. A band of prisoners was carrying injured people through the crowds.

A section of the city hospital still remained standing and the injured were taken there for treatment. Many prisoners broke out from hiding and sought help as there were no Nazis' to fear now. Theodor was unconscious and breathing laboriously as others carrying him neared the hospital building. He was three days late from the mentioned date of meeting on the letter. He still had the letter from Adelheid. It was faded, crumpled and torn; but the pieces were safely tucked in his shirt pocket. He slept, drenched in blood and exhausted as the unknown group of soldiers led him into what remained of the hospital.

The Wolf Stands Alone

A villa stood magnificently over sprawling green acres. On faraway and inaccessible lands stood this glorious house, away from people and any possible social interaction. It belonged to a wealthy old industrialist who owned the biggest arms manufacturing unit in the world.

More than fifteen long years had passed since the terrible war that had brought death and misery to millions, the world over. The industrialist had accumulated wealth through that very war; and as it brought desolation to millions, it brought riches to him. Evidently enough, his villa adorned finest pieces from history and was exquisitely done up. A lone car steadily moved towards the huge gates of the villa. The gates opened to a wide spread landscaped garden and then onto a driveway.

This house seldom had visitors but it seemed to be a busy day as the maids and butlers moved about in a hustle. All visitors needed prior appointments and had to be scanned through various security tiers to enter. A doctor and his assistant alighted from the car as the butler greeted them. A security guard came forward to lead them through the usual security protocol but the butler intervened. "Time is of the essence, Master is unwell" he softly spoke. The doctor nodded as he and his assistant skipped the security procedure to follow through with the butler. Two guards with ready guns followed them into the room. The door opened as the doctor strode in along with his assistant. The industrialist, an old man in his seventies; had been unwell for a very long time. His wife sat by his bed as he barely drew breath, she seemed distant and disengaged. The doctor looked at the industrialist who lay on the bed with his eyes shut. The wife slightly turned at the noise but seemed lost. "The doctor is away, I will be here to treat him today" said the bearded doctor. The butler nodded and explained to the wife that he had spoken to their family doctor, who was currently down with a bout of food poisoning. "He has sent forth his trusted friend madam" the butler assured the wife. She hardly cared and continued to stare out the window. The doctor slowly studied the patient while his assistant stood with the briefcase open for use. He moved his hand over a number of small vials, drew clear liquid into a syringe and asked his assistant to draw blood from the patient. The industrialist seemed unaffected from the pricks and continued sleeping. The doctor then administered an injection to the patient and waited.

He slowly looked at the butler and hung his head, about to deliver some bad news. "I am sorry, nothing much can be done" said the doctor. "We can shift him to the hospital and keep him breathing on support but there is no telling if and when he will wake up from this slumber. We have drawn blood to conduct some tests" the doctor explained. "There will be no need for that" said the wife. She spoke with tear laden eyes and looked into the endless horizon. "Nerve relaxants have been administered madam and it should keep his pain at bay" the doctor concluded. He looked at the wife waiting for some acknowledgement; there was an uncomfortable silence as everyone waited for her to react. "Very well then madam, I will request your leave. I have left my hospital duties and rushed here in emergency" he said.

The lady remained quiet as the butler came forward to break the uncomfortable silence. "I will inform her, I am sorry she is a little taken aback" he told the doctor. "I can completely understand" he replied. His assistant had packed up and they were ready to leave when the butler stopped them abruptly. "Tell me the truth, how much time does he have?" he asked in a concerned whisper. The doctor looked up and replied "About twenty five minutes." The assistant's grip on his suitcase tightened as the butler stared back at the doctor, surprised at such a precise time estimate. A girl entered the room; she was probably in her early teens and had striking green eyes. The doctor looked at her and nodded as he gathered his bag and left hurriedly with his assistant. The industrialist continued sleeping, taking slow, ragged puffs of air into his lungs as his eyes rolled rapidly under his eyelids. The butler walked them to the door and thanked them. The doctor looked at the house one last time and he and his assistant settled into their waiting car.

Little Adolf stood in the outdoors, watching vast mountains spread ahead of him. The leaves rustled as they were swept by powerful stray winds and he felt a new emotion grip his senses. A painting lay discarded by a nearby rock. It was a riot of colors, somehow imbibing his deepest thoughts, emotions and wishes. Splash after splash of color overlapped on the canvas. Everything around him looked surreal and well defined. The cliff's edge stretched ahead and ended into a steep dive, a dive that would lead him to water.

As always, Adolf hesitated to take the plunge. The mysterious blue veil of liquid that he feared was calling out to him, in deep but certain whispers. It stirred up emotions within his heart; he felt a chill run down his spine as the forces around him took on a course of their own. He felt new fears, new emotions flooding his thoughts but somehow it felt different. He knew that he could control his fears, every thought that crossed his mind was crystal clear and every emotion he felt was pure. Everything that ever happened to him in life was now connecting. One event to another, it all stood in front of him like a gossamer web. Adolf gently closed his eyes and thought about the cold blue water below him, thought about how he was never able to take the plunge into its enigmatic icy depths.

He felt a strange power surge through his body, a power that pushed fear at bay and without notice Adolf broke into a sprint. His feet moved with inhumane strength as the clarity of his thoughts pervaded his entire soul. He was gripped by an emotion that he hadn't known to exist within him, he could only feel the water and its cold silence waiting for him.

Hitler silently strode the last few feet and locked the door behind him with a faint click. His feet moved silently over the soft carpet as he moved around the room in a state of trance. His mind now existed on the cliff's edge while his body moved like an apparition. He sat on the couch and removed a phial from his pocket. His breathing was calm and composed as he took in sights of the room. Eva Hitler sat next to him; she too had a phial placed in front of her. Hitler gently retrieved his Whalter hand gun from its pouch. Longingly he looked at it; it was the same gun that Geli had used to take her life; it was loaded with the blood forged silver bullet. He looked at the table where his mother's photograph was placed and stared at it longingly. After what seemed like an eternity, he turned away and gently closed his eyes.

Meanwhile, far away from all the chaos, Adolf Hitler and Eva Braun were being escorted to a waiting U boat. They climbed down the narrow ladder and were ushered into a small dingy compartment. This was the best they could arrange for Adolf Hitler and Eva Braun in the given circumstances, as their supplies were stocked for a long journey. It was impossible to tell if they would survive but the team that was to travel with them was proficient enough and only they knew their travel locations. Adolf Hitler looked tense as he sat next to Eva Braun in a cramped space within the compartment. The soldiers gave them a final salute and walked out shutting the door and plunging them into darkness. Eva Braun felt cramped and suffocated as Adolf Hitler merely closed his eyes and took a deep breath, his time here was over and he had to move on. Deep within his mind; he was running on the cliff, getting ever so closer to the water.

The Hitler sitting in the room gently placed a cyanide pill in his mouth and looked at his handgun with fire in his eyes. What had to be done was clearly printed on his mind. He placed the gun on the temple of his head, now, it was just a bite and finger movement away for him to know what lay beyond the blue veil.

Adolf reached the edge of the cliff as his feet left the ground with a massive thrust. The world around him began to distort as he jumped and felt the air inflate his lungs in a sudden gust. In a splendid arc, he rose into the skies. His hair ruffled as the wind weaved through it and for a moment he remained suspended in eternity. The pit of his stomach did a sudden flip as he began to give in to the fall. It was now just the waiting water below as everything else fell quiet. He saw someone standing at the water's edge; she was standing there calmly and serenely. A mild laughter emanated from her, it was of the same character and intensity as the one which he'd heard and tried to follow through the forest for all these years. Adolf felt the laughter permeate his mind and soul as he continued his fall into the waiting icy blue coldness.

The pressure change in the cabin was massive as the U boat propellers churned underwater. Adolf Hitler's body adapted to the sudden pressure change as he uncomfortably shifted in the cramped space. The U boat was heading many leagues under water and a looming feeling hovered over Adolf Hitler now. His mind was going blank; the silence here was killing him. He tried to calm down as he focused his thoughts.

Hitler bit into the phial containing cyanide and pressed the trigger. A shot echoed through the small confined room. The liquid cyanide spread into his mouth and travelled down his throat. The hand gun fell onto the carpet with a subdued thud and he slouched into the sofa as a crimson trail of blood pooled around him. Eva Hitler lay next to him; dressed as her usual elegant self; even in death.

Adolf felt the powerful impact of cold water and was submerged in its blue depths. His eyes opened to the eerie world around him. It felt cold and strange to his senses as he swam and resurfaced. The wind was unnaturally cold against his damp skin. His gaze instantly darted towards the girl standing on the water's edge. He looked at her and felt bizarre warmth spread throughout his body. She was emanating a warm glow like the spring sun would. From the edge, she smiled at Adolf. Her mouth was bleeding profusely and she had a bullet wound on her chest but seemed unaffected by it. Adolf smiled back at her and laughed softly as warm blood surrounded him. They both continued laughing and looking at each other. Adolf knew this was something strange and different, he knew he had finally defeated his fear and crossed the barrier. He looked around as everything began to fade. Slowly, the girl too faded away and he was left alone. The deep red stain remained in the clear blue water around him as he gently fell back into it. The skies were a brilliant blue as they reflected through his eyes. The cliff too disappeared from sight; everything now seemed surreal, the picture was of a vast, untouched ground.

Adolf smiled, after many years he smiled. A huge burden lifted off his chest and the wolf was by himself.

To Freedom

The industrialist's body stopped twitching as he drew his last breath. The butler gently patted Eva and stood beside her in silence. He noticed a strange case that the doctor had forgotten behind in the room. "What is that?" she asked. "I think the doctor left it behind, madam" the butler replied as he bent forward to inspect it. "Check if there is an address and have it returned" she spoke, now holding the little girl's hand. As she stared at the body, a silent tear escaped her eyes. Hitler was her last known connection to Han and now he had also passed into a dreamless death. "Madam this is something bizarre!" the butler exclaimed. He held out an exquisitely crafted rifle in his hands. It was blood stained and old but the engravings stood out magnificently on the weapon. Eva's heart froze in shock and her eyes widened in disbelief as she stared at the rifle. She couldn't control herself as tears trickled down her cheeks, "Get me that doctor" she yelled. Get me that doctor anyhow" she wept as she snatched the rifle from the butler's hand. The butler nodded and ran away to alert the guards. Eva touched the rifle with quivering hands. It was Han's rifle and probably stained with his blood. Tears were freely escaping her eyes as she fell to the floor clutching Han's rifle; she caressed the weapon as if it were alive.

How she longed for his touch, longed to look into those green eyes, even if it was just once more before death would consume her into the void. "Han" she cried in a whisper and held onto the only artifact that belonged to him, the only testimony to his life. She hugged her daughter tightly as she cried. The little girl was clearly confused but nonetheless kept quiet and hugged her mother back. 'After all these years' she thought. Eva had no clue of where Han was, if he was alive or not. There was never a word from him or anyone else. She cried uncontrollably at the overwhelming swell of emotion.

Traugott pulled away his fake beard and asked the driver to speed up. The vintage car picked up speed and cruised on open country roads. Traugott's assistant sat beside him, none of them spoke as the old man rolled down his window and looked out to the open lands. The landscape was brilliant; the skies were nice and blue, the wind weaved through his hair as he finally felt some beauty return to his world. After many years, he appreciated the gentle air that caressed his face. He seemed old and tired as he took in a slow deep breath. Traugott couldn't contain his emotions anymore and he cried, the old man wept as he looked at the vast landscape around him.

This was the end of the road for him in more than one way. Everyone he knew in his life was dead. His family fell to his brother's wrath. He had never forgiven himself, not once, for writing that letter to Hitler, the letter that explained his blood relation to him. Himmler had mixed up the address and his son's family went missing since the day Himmler laid eyes on them. Traugott hadn't been able to manage a good night rest for all these years, he couldn't never forgave himself and all he thought of was retribution. Twenty five long years had passed since Hitler pulled the trigger and wiped out his family. Traugott cried uncontrollably and far away, he saw his grandchildren playing in the fields. His purpose was fulfilled, Blood Moon finally succeeded in its motive. He sat there, looking at a dream. He handed a small box to his assistant. "Keep it, it is your burden now" he whispered. The car slowed down and the assistant nodded, ready to get off. "Where will you be driving to now?" he asked, stepping out of the door. Traugott took a while to answer as the silence lingered on for a moment. "To freedom" he replied. Traugott's eyes were filled with tears as he whispered "thank you Theodor Bachmeier." Theodor nodded back; grinned broadly as the car stuttered to life and cruised into the horizon.

The Fuehrer's Blood

W arm yellow rays filtered down to the ground as parched leaves rustled softly, being carried by the mild wind. Theodor Bachmeier walked through the boulevard, old and frail, he took each step carefully. With his walking stick firmly held in one hand and a box in the other, he slowly made his way through the park. The veins on his hand were green and showing through his aged skin as he gripped tightly onto the box.

His bullet injury had never fully healed and his arm still remained stiff from the same. Theodor reached a small pond, the water was still and mirror-like as he slowly and with great difficulty sat on the soft grass. He gently touched the blades with his fingers, they felt wet from moisture. The area around the small pond was deserted, apart from a few kids who played and laughed merrily. He looked to see if anyone was around and observing him. It didn't seem like it. With shaky frail hands, he pulled out a battered diary from his inner pocket and held it in his hands. More than fifty long years had passed since that fateful day when Ralf put him on the aircraft that took them across Berlin and into the Russian camp. Fifty long years had passed since he stumbled upon this black diary. 'Han' he whispered, letting out a sigh. His existence would remain an enigma for years to come, such an ambiguous personality and yet capable of loving so fiercely.

That journey had certainly changed something within him ; it now looked like a distant dream to Theodor for time had healed his wounds. All these years Theodor had never heard from Albert. The day they parted ways from the camp, they had to keep their mission to themselves and they succeeded in doing so. They had both carried out General Felix's orders to save Germania. Traugott too had extensively tried to trace Albert throughout the years; but to no effect. Albert had personally carried Theodor into the hospital and then vanished for good. Many controversies cropped up over the years but he never heard Albert's name which seemed to be a good sign. Also, the night Adolf & Eva disappeared from Berlin was the last anyone ever saw them. No one heard about them or had any hints whatsoever regarding their existence or whereabouts. One fine morning, Theodor had an unexpected visitor and they had one last mission to carry out. Theodor always knew that this would haunt him till he completely laid it to rest. He and Traugott set out yet again and yet, through all of this, Albert remained untraceable.

However, on a recent pleasant morning Theodor had received a letter stating Albert's death. The old man had peacefully traversed into the ether and had asked his son to write to Theodor. He gathered courage and made the long journey to attend Albert's funeral. As he sat there watching Albert sleep peacefully in his casket, a fine looking man appeared and introduced himself as Albert's son. He sat beside Theodor and handed him a box. "It was specifically mentioned in his will that this be passed on to you Mr. Bachmeier" he said.

Theodor was surprised that Albert had remembered him after all these years and mentioned him in his will too. He looked at the box and then at Albert's son. "If I may?" Theodor questioned him. "Go ahead sir, the contents belong to you" He gestured and replied politely. Theodor opened the box and pulled out a pair of extremely old leather boots. They were torn and cracked with a faint emboss of the Imperial eagle on its side. Theodor widened his eyes in surprise, wondering why Albert passed on these boots to him. They had the Nazi insignia on them; just the act of owning such material was now forbidden. He put them back in the box and sat there watching Albert sleep. "This is a great honor" Theodor spoke as he abruptly turned to look at Albert's son with tear laden eyes.

Albert's son nodded in reply, not sure what else he would say if he ever got used boots as an inheritance. "You both fought side by side during the war I believe?" asked the young man. Theodor looked at him for a long moment and nodded back in reply. After a long silence, he finally spoke "we survived where others did not and the pain of that far supersedes the glee of victory. Your father was a brave soldier" Theodor concluded, gave a mock salute, and smiled at the young man.

Theodor had left the funeral and wanted some time by himself; he got this by sitting by the pond. He carefully opened the diary; the pages had gone yellow and extremely frail. Theodor had left Berlin without this diary and never bothered to think about it again. The ink had faded from its pages to a great extent, though Hitler's signature stood out disturbingly sharp and bold. Over the years, this diary had provided Traugott with enough information to put the pieces together and track down Hitler. He gently let the diary slip from his hands and into the water with a small plop. He watched as water soaked the diary and it slowly began to sink.

Within a few minutes it had sank all the way down to the bottom, its pages withering away in water and ink; leaving the pages in smoky blue trails. The surface of the water was calm once again as if nothing had happened. It engulfed the diary in all its elemental form and would degrade it till it became a part of the very earth. Theodor picked up the box and removed the boots from it. 'These didn't look like the boots that German soldiers wore back then' he thought. The insignia on it was different and didn't seem to be like the shoes he had worn as a member of the army.

Theodor looked at them wondering why Albert would pass on such an artifact to him. He was inspecting them and to his surprise, a small compartment slid out from underneath it. Theodor's heart picked up pace as he pulled out the compartment to notice a silver bullet lodged safely within it. 'These belonged to Han' he thought. Realization dawned upon him as he kept the shoes aside and looked at the bullet. It felt light as he moved his hand over it to find an abnormal protrusion. As if presenting itself to Theodor, a small portion of the bullet came lose. This was too much for an old man to digest as his heart began palpitating. A small vial of crimson red liquid fell into his hands from within the bullet and a parchment slipped out, falling into Theodor's lap. The liquid was viscous but flowed smoothly within the vial which was sealed from both ends. Theodor tried recollecting events from the diary that would help him understand this dilemma. Easily enough, he remembered the conversation that Hitler had with Han. Hitler had mentioned that this would answer a lot of questions for him. This was blood and he was sure it wasn't just anybody's blood. Han had cleverly passed it on, for he knew Albert had better chances of leaving the camp alive. Also, Albert would be better poised to present this to the world when the time was right.

Theodor got up on his feet and the small parchment fell into the water before he could notice it. Here stood Theodor, more than fifty years later holding on to Adolf Hitler's blood. He too had drawn blood from Hitler's veins years ago. What was he to do with it? The answer came quickly to his mind; he removed another vial from his coat and crushed them with all the force his old hands could muster. With a small crunch, they cracked and thick liquid dispensed from it. It fell into the clear water surface, spreading in deep dark droplets. Whenever it came in contact with the water it spread, looking dangerous and demanding. Theodor stood at the water's edge looking at the droplets disappear, now, the book was gone; as well, the blood was gone.

"Let's go" a gentle voice called from behind him. Theodor quickly pocketed the silver bullet and looked at the water body yet again, it was calm and clear as if nothing had happened. He picked up his walking stick and the boots as he turned to face the little girl who stood there waiting for him. He gently took her hand as she smiled and hugged her grandfather. Theodor gently hugged her and they playfully walked away into the calm boulevard.

The small parchment was slowly being soaked by the water and over its folds, a small text was remarkably visible. In neat blue ink was probably the last message left by Han. It read: "The Fuehrer's blood"

"Blood Moon remains the most successful anti-Nazi group till date. Their ability to be discreet led to their success."

"Traugott was single handedly responsible for funding numerous groups that plotted to take down Hitler. He later emptied his entire fortune for the rehabilitation of victims from various camps. He also helped soldiers and others who suffered from the war; after which he disappeared to his much sought after freedom."

"Heinrich Himmler was supplied a cyanide pill by Traugott's aid who made sure he committed suicide while in custody of the British forces."

"Konstantin and his secret camp remain one of the best kept Russian secrets of World War II. It was completely destroyed with the explosions and was never traced back to him."

"Eva Braun fostered kids but no one is sure of their father. She died in the same house as Hitler. Han's rifle adorned the walls of Hitler's mansion till Eva died, after which it was never seen again."

END

About the Author

While writing "The Fuehrer's Blood" countless WW II stories came to the fore. It must have taken a herculean number of sacrifices to put an end to the reign of the Nazis'. One can only remain in awe; maintaining a strong stance of respect and high regard for the innumerable lives that were laid down for the freedom of mankind.

"The Fuehrer's Blood" goes down a road seldom traversed. It has taken a substantial amount of research and work on the author's part to brave this road. The author, Shreyans Zaveri, credits his varied storytelling skills to a relentless curiosity and a burning desire to challenge the superficial truth.

His spark for fiction evolved with every new subject that he learned. He holds a Bachelor's degree in Science and a double Master's in Philosophy & Visual Effects. A visual effects & video artist by profession, Shreyans sees a story in everything that he does. From the photographs that he clicks to the movies he makes and the novels he authors, there is always a story waiting to be told.

"The Fuehrer's Blood" is Shreyans Zaveri's first literary fiction novel. The author is currently working on his second novel titled "Aarya" and hopes to continue writing compelling stories.

You can connect and know more about the author at www.thefuehrersblood.com